UNWRITTEN RULES

GRAHAM DONNELLY

The Book Guild Ltd

First published in Great Britain in 2020 by
The Book Guild Ltd
9 Priory Business Park
Wistow Road, Kibworth
Leicestershire, LE8 0RX
Freephone: 0800 999 2982
www.bookguild.co.uk
Email: info@bookguild.co.uk
Twitter: @bookguild

Typeset in 12pt Adobe Jenson Pro

Printed and bound by CPI Group (UK) Ltd, Croydon, CR0 4YY

ISBN 978 1913208 202

British Library Cataloguing in Publication Data.
A catalogue record for this book is available from the British Library.

For Carolyn
and for all those who have given me encouragement

Are not there little chapters in everybody's life, that seem to be nothing, and yet affect all the rest of the history?

– William Makepeace Thackeray, Vanity Fair

"I WILL KILL MYSELF," SHE SAID.

Anthony surreptitiously felt behind him to make sure the emergency button was within reach. "Please don't talk like that," he replied.

"I will kill myself," she repeated. "It is too much to ask me to leave within a week. I couldn't go on."

Anthony raised his eyes from her case file and looked at her again. A second appraisal confirmed his first impression that she could easily be a model or a film actress, her physical beauty complemented by a natural elegance and well-groomed appearance. He calculated the threat of suicide was almost certainly an idle threat, a bluff; surely this woman had so much to live for? But it was still disconcerting. He looked for a clue in her expression, but there was none. She sat in her chair, watching him, waiting for him to say something, her face a mask of impassivity.

He had told her twice that he could do nothing to change the situation. She had come to the UK on a three-month visitor's visa and this had been extended to six months, but she had not gone home when the visa expired. Now she had been told to leave the country in the next seven days in accordance with the regulations. He had dealt with this sort of case hundreds of times. There were strict controls on people who had entered the UK on a visa, such as this woman from Iran, so there was nothing he could do to change the situation. But her silence, coupled with her beauty, was intimidating.

Eventually he asked, "Why exactly do you need more time?"

"I have to pack all my belongings and arrange accommodation at home. Also I have to transfer my money to go back to Iran and the system takes a long time. It is very difficult for me." She spoke calmly in near-perfect, slightly stilted English and he found her accent attractive.

Anthony nodded and assessed the situation for a few moments. There were times when he could bend the rules a little and grant an extension without anyone querying the decision, but this was not one of them.

"I can't change the order to leave, but the position is not as serious as you think. Although you've been told you must leave within a week, nothing will happen for at least two weeks before a check is made that you've left. Then it will be another couple of weeks before the police are sent round to your last known address, so you have probably at least four weeks before you must leave. If you're still here after that, you will be in trouble."

The woman's face lit up into a smile. "You are allowing me four more weeks before I must leave?"

"No, I can't do that. I'm telling you that you have perhaps four weeks before the order to leave will be carried out. That gives you the time to do what is necessary to sort out your affairs before you return home."

"Thank you, sir, you are very kind," she said. "I will go by then, I promise, thank you." She stood up as Anthony rose from his chair and walked towards the door.

"Please make sure that you do," said Anthony, controlling the urge to smile and adopting a stern expression as he held the door open for her.

He watched her walk down the corridor, then noted on the file that he'd advised her that the deadline for her departure could not be deferred and must be adhered to.

It was a humid August, and he found the conditions in the windowless, stuffy room almost unbearable. He left the door open and waited for a few minutes before sending for the next client, in the meantime taking off his jacket and fanning himself with a file. He took a Senior Service from its packet then put it away again; it was too hot to smoke. Unlike most public offices, August was not a quiet month for the Enquiry Office as there were plenty of tourists who came in with queries or problems at this time of the year. For the staff, there was little opportunity to take some air and cool down, except in the lunch break.

Anthony was only in the Enquiry Office to cover for people on leave and, although it made a change from his regular duties, he didn't really enjoy it very much. As an Executive Officer, he would have one of two jobs. In the first role, he would be on the reception desk, dealing with queries and sending people to the right person for a straightforward issue. Sometimes, with embarrassment, he would have to tell people they had been queuing in the wrong place and that they had to go to the Aliens Registration Office or their embassy or some other department. Alternatively, he would be seeing people in private to deal with a major problem or emergency, as with the woman he had just seen. The reception desk he found repetitive and usually uninteresting, while the people with problems were often agitated or upset because they had allowed the situation to become critical and little could be done for them; hence the need for a panic button. Despite his lack of enthusiasm for the Enquiry Office, he'd been asked more than once if he would like to have a permanent posting there. Yet, though he had to admit it sometimes gave him a buzz working under the pressure of the place, he always turned the offer down.

He sat back in his chair and tried to work out why the woman had been reluctant to go home. After all, she seemed quite well off and he would have thought the Shah's regime favoured people of her class.

His reverie was interrupted by a knock on the door as the file arrived for his next interview. It was brought in by one of the Clerical Officers, Sue Brand, who had recently joined the Enquiry Office.

"This is one for you, Anthony," she said. "Some irregularity with his papers."

Anthony looked pained. He'd had to correct people more times than he could remember. "Anthony is pronounced AN-TON-Y; the 'h' is not sounded, like the 'h' in Thomas isn't sounded."

"Sorry," said Sue, smiling sheepishly. She placed the file on his desk and went to leave but stopped at the door. "What did you do for that Iranian lady? She seemed quite happy when she left here."

Sue was now grinning, and Anthony wasn't sure if there was an innuendo in the comment. He treated it at face value.

"I just calmed her down a bit; she was in a state. She's got things in perspective now, I think." He stood up and put his jacket back on. "Right, give me a couple of minutes to look through the file and then send him in."

The rest of the day – indeed, the rest of that week – passed without incident.

The following week was his last in the Enquiry Office for the time being and he expected, and got, more of the same.

He was looking forward to returning to the more soporific atmosphere of his own office, but on Tuesday the day was brightened up by the appearance of a young lady from Spain and her British interpreter.

Isabella Mendez was aged nineteen and had arrived as an au pair to learn English, ostensibly living as part of a welcoming family. However, for some middle-class households, no longer able to afford servants but desperate for domestic help, an au pair was the perfect solution; a source of cheap labour disguised as a philanthropic gesture to broaden the educational and cultural horizons of a young person from abroad. This had been one such case, with Isabella treated as an underpaid servant, half-nanny and half-skivvy, not even allowed to take her meals with the family. Talking to other Spanish au pairs in England, she had found a more congenial household, one whose current au pair had been very happy with the arrangement but was now returning to Spain to begin her career. Isabella's English was still rudimentary and to assist matters she had brought along an interpreter who introduced herself as Carrie Burdine, a friend of the family Isabella now wanted to au pair with.

The case was fairly straightforward and presented no difficulties for Anthony. What made the interview interesting for him was the striking attractiveness of Miss Burdine, a young woman of about twenty-five. He was also impressed by her fluency in Spanish as she translated almost instantaneously both the questions of Isabella and the responses and explanations given by Anthony. Every word she delivered in what he could only describe as a mellifluous voice. She had also had the foresight to bring a letter from the new au pair family stating that they would be delighted to take on Isabella and giving a brief outline of how the arrangement would work. This was purely a matter of courtesy, as there were no regulations governing the au pair system. Anyone over the age of eighteen with a mother tongue other than English could apply to become an au pair and any household could engage them as such.

Anthony read through the letter and placed it on the file, making a note to record the change of au pair domicile. Then he filled in the empty spaces on one of his stock of template letters, giving Isabella approval for the change of arrangements, and signed it.

"There, that's all done. You will just need to record your change of address with the Aliens Registration Office, but you can do that by post if you don't want to go there in person."

Isabella looked at her companion who nodded encouragingly. "Thank you very much, Mr..." She stopped as she found his signature on the letter indecipherable.

"Fernard, Anthony Fernard; I am glad we could sort it out." He shook hands with both of them.

"Thanks for all your help," added Miss Burdine as they turned to go, and she gave him a smile that, for today at least, made working in this busy, stuffy atmosphere tolerable.

The next week, Anthony was back in the large room he shared as an office with a dozen other staff. His return was acknowledged by his own section members with brief hellos and smiles and a cheerful enquiry from the section's Clerical Officer, Freddie Pilling, as to how things were in the 'Complaints Office'.

Anthony sat at his green-topped wooden desk and looked at the three trays: 'out' and 'pending' trays both empty and the 'in' tray full of green cardboard files. Anything marked 'Urgent' or 'Immediate' would have been dealt with by his colleagues during his two weeks away, but everything else had been allowed to pile up. Most of the cases were contained in single files, but there were two multiple files tied together with white tape, white having long ago replaced the red of the bureaucratic cliché. He glanced through the files and put them back in the tray. Anthony's principal function was dealing with visa applications and related matters from those countries whose citizens needed a visa even to visit the UK and whose surname began with C. This resulted in a large proportion of his casework coming from China, both the People's Republic on the mainland and Nationalist China on the island of Taiwan, but also many from Eastern Europe, apart from Russia, which had its own designated section.

He wasn't ready to tackle his workload yet. Instead, he leaned back in his chair and put his hands behind his head, avoiding the reproachful expression of Daphne Raynott, his section head. He reflected, as he often did, that he had never wished to be in the Immigration and Nationality Department at all. When he had joined the Civil Service, he had chosen as his first preference the Home Office, hoping to be involved in constitutional matters where his A-level in British Constitution would be of use. If not, he would also have been interested in the criminal area or state security, but he had been posted here and here he had worked since 1954; eight long years.

The problem was that he had never known what to do with himself after he left his grammar school in North London. His first two years had been decided for him when he was called up for National Service and he had spent his time unenthusiastically, but not sullenly, in the Royal Army Service Corps. The best part had been a tour in Germany, where he learned a bit of German and a bit more about German girls and beer. Afterwards, he had tried banking and then insurance, but neither had really grabbed his imagination as a potential career. He had investigated several options across industry and commerce but either they didn't want him, or he was not sure about them. The difficulty was not finding something that he was attracted to or cared about but actually getting a job in one of these areas.

He had even attended a rather odd event in a house in Eaton Place for a company recruiting representatives to sell encyclopaedias to American military personnel in Germany. He didn't particularly want to be a salesman, but he was drawn to the idea mainly because he spoke a little German and felt he knew something about the forces in Germany. Also, rather bizarrely in retrospect, he fancied trying it because it was totally different from his previous work experience and alien to his natural inclination. The irrationality of this second motive soon came home to him as he sat in a circle of about a dozen people listening to a presentation by the recruitment manager, a smooth-talking, very self-confident man in a sharp suit and sunglasses, to whom he took an instant dislike due to his rather supercilious tone.

He very quickly realised he had neither the temperament nor the ethical disposition for the hard sell and his mind soon wandered from the speaker to his fellow listeners: a mixture of keen young men, cynical professional salesmen and a couple of idealists actually interested in the education of their potential customers. He spent much of the time wondering why it was that, if the criteria for appointment stressed the importance of being aged under thirty, the one woman in the group, who sat opposite him, seemed so far over that age that he doubted if she was under forty. After outlining the job and what was expected of the successful candidates, the recruiter conducted a question and answer session. He then told them which of the group he thought would wish to take the matter further. He correctly forecast that Anthony would not be interested.

While working for an insurance company, Anthony had met his future wife Ruth at a party. When things became serious between them, he realised that, if he was intending to get married, his days of experimenting with different occupations would soon be over. So he had been drawn to the Civil Service for a career. It meant a job for life, a notable attraction to one of a generation which had grown up under the shadow of the 1930s Great Depression. There was also a non-contributory pension and the chance to do something that was important to people's lives. His future father-in-law, like most fathers dubious of the calibre of his daughter's choice, was instrumental in convincing Anthony that this would be a good career move. On the negative side, Anthony could see his career mapped out before him: probably a promotion to Higher Executive Officer, possibly another one to Senior Executive Officer and that was likely to be it; retirement at sixty with a pension and a minor gong like an MBE. None of this was terrible, but it meant finally accepting that all the day-dreamt ambitions of what he once might have been were finally cast into the incinerator, along with the first five pages of an unwritten novel, the business cards of the start-up market research business with an old school chum and the rejection letters from exploration bodies, adventurous entrepreneurs and pretty much everything he'd ever wanted to do.

When joining the Home Office in a division he wouldn't have chosen, he was attracted, as well as surprised, by the responsibility and power that was given to even relatively junior and inexperienced civil servants. He was almost immediately granted the authority to decide the fate of people who had applied to come to this country to live. Of course, civil servants were not free to do as they wished, since there were clear rules and guidelines by which they must operate. But there was room for discretion and when a situation was not clear-cut, they could tip the balance one way or the other by the decision or recommendation they made.

Anthony looked at the files in his in tray again. They were a varied lot but most of them were similar to previous cases he had dealt with. They included a number which he had already seen but which had been almanacked in the file repository for two weeks while he waited for further information, usually in response to his enquiries.

The first one concerned a Polish woman applying to join her husband in Britain. Like every similar case of this type, the woman had not seen her husband for over twenty years. He had escaped from Poland when it was invaded by the Germans and the Russians in 1939 and, after service in the Polish army under British command during the war, had settled in Britain. Finally, after many years of trying, his wife had obtained a costly exit visa from Poland and was now able to join her husband, who had become a naturalised British citizen. The file's papers contained a translated copy of the wedding certificate and a letter of support from the husband, so granting her residence was automatic. Anthony looked at her passport photograph. It was of a middle-aged woman who had spent ten times as long apart from her husband as they had been together. In cases like this, he could not but admire the couple's constancy to each other. He wrote a note on the file to grant permanent residence and sent it over to George, his Clerical Assistant, to do the rest.

The other cases were less poignant and not all of them were so straightforward. Next up was a large file of two outer covers tied together. It was the case of a stateless person of Russian origin who had lived in Britain off and on but had now lived here as a businessman for four years continuously and was requesting permanent residence prior to seeking naturalisation. Anthony looked at the photograph of the man in the travel document. He seemed quite distinguished and may well have been a Russian aristocrat, as he claimed in his unauthenticated documents, but then almost every stateless person of Russian origin he came across claimed to have aristocratic forebears. In any case, that was all over now; the main thing was he fulfilled the criteria for permanent residence and Anthony had no problem granting his request. He wrote his approval on the file and sent it to George.

So, he continued working methodically, but not too swiftly, on the cases in front of him. He had learned through past experience that, sooner or later, an empty in tray meant he would be asked to help out another officer who had a backlog. At first, he hadn't minded and had seen the request as a compliment to his own efficiency. But, after a while, he began to ask himself why it was that he never had a backlog while others were often taking the opportunity to unload onto him their most dire and complicated cases. Nowadays, he never had an empty in tray.

He looked at his watch and it was half-past ten. Taking his towel and soap, both stamped 'E II R,' he took a gentle stroll to the gentlemen's lavatory and washroom, stopping to talk along the way to one of his colleagues. By the time he was back at his desk, he could hear the tea trolley approaching and he produced his mug from the same drawer in which he kept his towel. Over coffee and a Chelsea bun he made a first stab at the cryptic crossword in his newspaper but was interrupted by Freddie Pilling looming over him, holding his own mug of coffee in both hands.

"How was it the last couple of weeks; busy, I suppose?" said Freddie, in his slight West Country burr.

Anthony looked up, only half-engaged with the question; he was trying to work out a three-word anagram for 'latest whitener.' "Er, not too bad, Freddie."

"Any interesting cases?"

Anthony smiled. Freddie had been in the Home Office for over forty years and had worked in most of its departments, so it was unlikely that Anthony could tell him anything he hadn't heard before. But Freddie had retained his enthusiasm for the job, so much so that he'd stayed on ten years after the official retirement age, even though this had meant dropping a grade. Anthony told him about one or two vaguely interesting cases. He didn't mention the suicide-threatening Iranian woman.

The morning wore on and Anthony continued to work at his steady pace, despite the arrival of several new cases into his in tray. At twelve-thirty he went to lunch. Despite the subsidised meals, he rarely ate in the staff restaurant. He'd joined the department at the same time as an intake group seven or eight years younger than him and he had not made friendships of any substance from this group or with anyone else. In any case, he preferred to go out at lunchtime. So he usually lunched alone at a very reasonable Italian restaurant in Red Lion Street, serving both English and Italian dishes. On a typical day, he would have an Italian main course with an English dessert for less than five shillings, and then take a walk. With his office located on High Holborn, he could walk in different directions as far as Whitehall, the Embankment, St Paul's or Bloomsbury. Occasionally he met friends for lunch and they would go to somewhere a little more expensive.

Today he felt like a change from his regular lunch venue and decided to go to a large restaurant in Bloomsbury which catered for office workers and usually promised a quick turnaround of diners. This would leave him the opportunity for a good walk, especially as it wasn't a hot day.

The restaurant had a large, bland dining room in a symmetrical layout with all tables set for four people. Because of its lack of smaller tables, a solo diner like Anthony would always have to share with one or more strangers. Nobody minded because the customers maintained an unspoken etiquette of polite indifference which avoided any awkwardness. Interaction between the enforced fellow diners was rare, with most having a book or newspaper to avoid the necessity for direct eye contact or staring silently into space.

Anthony looked around the nearly full restaurant and saw a table with one free seat and walked briskly toward it. As he approached, his gaze ignored the two middle-aged women in animated conversation and alighted on the young woman with dark hair whom he thought he recognised. She was reading a book and was either waiting to be served or between courses.

"Excuse me, is this seat taken?" he asked.

The two middle-aged women looked round and shook their heads before continuing their conversation.

Anthony had actually addressed his question to the young woman and she looked up. "No," she said and smiled briefly before returning to her book. But then she looked up at him a second time. "Hello again," she said.

Anthony smiled. "I thought I knew you from somewhere."

"I'm Carrie Burdine; I came to the Home Office with Isabella Mendez and you arranged things for her move to a new family."

Anthony was aware that their two table companions had stopped talking and were interested in this chance meeting. "Ah yes, of course," he said, "the au pair young lady."

"I *am* sorry, I don't remember your name."

"Anthony Fernard."

"Anthony with or without an aitch?"

"With."

At that moment a waitress arrived, laid a ham salad in front of Carrie and produced a pad to take his order. "I'll have the ham salad too," he said. "With a round of bread and butter, please."

The waitress went off and the two women returned to their own conversation. After a slight hesitation, Carrie began eating her salad.

"This is quite a coincidence," said Anthony. "I don't think I've ever had a chance meeting with somebody I'd met previously at the Enquiry Office. Do you work around here?"

"Yes, near Russell Square. I suppose this is where one of us should say 'Do you come here often?'"

Anthony smiled. "Actually, I don't. I just eat here for a change or if I'm in a bit of a hurry; they turn the sittings round quite quickly."

"Are you in a hurry today?"

"Not particularly. I thought I might take a walk after lunch. What about you?"

She raised her eyebrows. "Are you inviting me out for a walk? You don't hang about, do you?"

The two women looked over at Anthony and waited for his reply.

Anthony laughed. "I meant..."

Carrie grinned and cut him off. "I know what you meant, just teasing. I do different things at lunchtime. In the summer, I often bring a sandwich and sit in the gardens, Red Lion Square or Bloomsbury Square usually, but I wasn't very organised this morning."

They were silent for a couple of minutes. Carrie was eating and Anthony was trying to think of something worth saying.

Carrie raised her eyes from her lunch. "Thanks again for dealing with Isabella's case so quickly. She was worried it would take a long time to sort out."

"It was nothing, perfectly straightforward. Is she with her new family yet?"

"Yes, I think she's very happy there. It was horrible for her before. She cooked all their meals but then had to eat alone in the kitchen. Now she's treated as part of the family."

"That's how it should be," said Anthony, sitting back as the waitress slammed his lunch in front of him.

His lunch had arrived just as Carrie finished hers. She refused the offer of a dessert from the waitress and looked at her watch. "I would like a coffee though, please," she said.

"Would you make that two, please?" added Anthony.

The two women took the opportunity to ask for their bill and within a couple of minutes they had paid it and left. There was a gap of several minutes before anyone took their place.

"You must be always very busy, working in the Enquiry Office," said Carrie.

"It is nearly always busy, but it's not my regular job. I was just covering for holidays; usually I'm deskbound, handling visa applications and that kind of thing from people overseas."

Carrie sipped her coffee. "It must be interesting; lots of variety?"

Anthony smiled. "It's like any job really; six months learning the ropes, six months enjoying being good at it, then six months becoming bored as the repeated pattern of the work sets in."

Carrie laughed and asked him a couple of general questions about his work, but then two new diners arrived and Anthony felt he ought to change the subject.

"That's an interesting stamp," he said, indicating the envelope which Carrie was using as a bookmark.

She removed it from the book and looked at it. "Airmail from Andorra," she said. "Are you interested in stamps; a stamp collector?"

"I used to be when I was a boy, like most boys, I suppose. It provided lots of opportunities in the never-ending game of swapping things with each other. I was very lucky; I lived near a nice old chap who was an avid collector of British Empire issues and he would give me any stamps surplus to requirements. Every now and again he'd show me through one of his albums while his wife sat knitting and brought in tea and cakes. Needless to say, once I became a teenager, I lost interest and the poor old boy never saw his protégé again. I've still got my old albums – nostalgia, I suppose – but I don't do a lot now; you have to specialise at some point and then it can get expensive."

Carrie smiled. "But your eyes are still drawn to an attractive stamp."

Still more to an attractive woman, thought Anthony. He nodded. "Well, as much as I do anything these days, I collect airmail stamps; I think there's a certain sense of adventure or romance about them and I like some of the designs very much. Also, fewer countries issue them these days, so it's not impossible to keep up with new issues; not that I do it myself."

"You're the first adult I've called a 'stamp collector' who didn't correct me and say 'philatelist.'"

Anthony laughed. "Perhaps they take it too seriously. Do you know what the word 'philatelist' actually means?"

"Mm, lover of... No, I don't know the word 'ateleia' or whatever it comes from."

"Literally it means 'lover of tax paid' or something like that. I understand where they got it from, but I think it's a bit precious to be worried about what you're called when it's only a hobby, especially if the title you prefer is even less lyrical than 'stamp collector.'"

Her slight smile gave a silent gesture of affirmation. "So, would you like this stamp?" she asked, placing the envelope in front of him.

"I wouldn't wish to put you to any trouble."

"It's no trouble," she said, tearing the envelope carefully around the stamp.

"Thanks," said Anthony.

"I really must be going," said Carrie, placing the envelope back in her book, without worrying about its original function. "We get dozens of airmail stamps at work. I could let you have them if you like; they only get thrown away."

"Well, if you don't mind."

"I'll have a rake round and see what I can find. I'll post them to you if you like. I could send them airmail." She raised her eyebrows.

Anthony laughed as he rose from his seat. "Sorting out some stamps would be very kind of you." He hesitated. "I hope you don't think I'm being pushy, but I'd rather thank you personally for putting yourself out like this. Perhaps we could meet up again when you've got the stamps together?"

She smiled. "That would be nice; just give me a couple of weeks to see what I can find?"

"Great, how about after work at the Kardomah Café in Southampton Row two weeks today, say five-thirty?"

"OK, see you then." They shook hands then, with a final smile, she walked quickly off to pay her bill.

Anthony wanted to leave too but decided to wait for a few minutes so that she didn't think he was a bit of a limpet. He hadn't even noticed the two people who had sat down at their table, a couple of young men engrossed in talking about the football matches they'd attended on Saturday. After a suitable time had elapsed, he paid his own bill and, lunch having been rather longer than he'd expected, he abandoned his planned walk and took a leisurely stroll back to the office.

The afternoon proceeded much as the morning had done. The first case he looked at was that of a Yugoslav who had come to Britain on a visitor's visa but had now started working in his brother's business and wanted to alter his status accordingly. This was not an uncommon tactic to avoid the requirement to apply for a work permit before coming to the UK. It was usually accompanied by a letter from the employer saying that local labour was unavailable. Despite the fact that Anthony didn't like being presented with a *fait accompli,* he was in a good mood this afternoon and he chose not to make further enquiries; he allowed the application.

Then there was a visa application for a chicken-sexer from South Korea. For some reason he'd never quite understood, Korean poultry workers could detect the gender of a baby chick much earlier in its life than anybody else. So there was a regular demand for their services in intensive poultry farming where early gender classification was essential. He had no hesitation in granting a visa for employment.

So the day meandered on, until eventually the clock showed five-fifteen and Anthony joined those of his colleagues heading for the exit. His commute to and from work was on the Central line to Woodford and as his office was between the two, he alternated between walking to Holborn and Chancery Lane stations. Today he chose the longer walk to Chancery Lane, past the Meteorological Office with its radio studio, the Russian Shop and the Pearl headquarters among its buildings more worthy of a glance. The train was packed, but he was able to get a seat at Leytonstone and he half-heartedly looked at the newspaper crossword while he reflected on the charms of Carrie Burdine. From the station, there was a walk of ten minutes or so to his road with its grass-verged pavement and long rows of 1930s mock-Tudor semis. He looked ruefully at his aging Hillman Minx as he walked past it on the drive; it needed a service and a new tyre. He pressed the tyre with his thumb to check its pressure.

He put his key in the lock and as he opened the door, he was greeted by the younger of his two sons running in the hall. "Hello, Daddy."

"Hello, Jonathan," said Anthony. "What have you been up to today?"

"I played in the garden and helped Mummy make some cakes," Jonathan said and skipped out of the hall, through the kitchen and into the garden again, ignoring his mother's command to wash his hands and sit at the table.

"Hello, Tony, good day?" said Ruth, coming out of the kitchen, taking off her apron and giving Anthony a peck on the lips.

"Just the usual, had to catch up on the backlog left for me while I was in the Enquiry Office."

"It does seem a bit mean, leaving it to you. It's not as if you were on holiday; you were still at work."

Anthony shrugged. "It's just the way it is. I can cope."

Ruth smiled. "You're in a good mood, did you have lunch?"

"I had a salad."

"Really, a salad? That's not like you," she laughed. "You can have one of the cakes to tide you over, but avoid the ones with pink icing; Jonathan's fingers played more than their fair share in those. We've got shepherd's pie tonight."

She went back into the kitchen and called out to her sons, "Boys, will you come in and wash for dinner *now*?"

If asked, Anthony would always have replied that he was happily married, not that anyone ever did ask him. After eight years of marriage, he and Ruth had settled into a comfortable, predictable life together. Neither of them had any all-consuming interests. Those interests they did have they pursued separately, except for some socialising with their married couple friends and spending time with their children, whom they both adored. Anthony had just last week introduced his elder son to one of his old hobbies, presenting him with his first stamp album, a bumper pack of stamps and a box of stamp hinges. He looked forward to the time when he could encourage both his sons to share his interests and perhaps be a support in whatever activities or careers they sought to pursue. As a general rule, he was of the opinion that fatherhood became both more interesting and more accountable as children advanced towards maturity.

Anthony's secure and steadily rising salary was sufficient to give his family a comfortable standard of living, as he was not extravagant and Ruth managed her household budget well, though there was never much slack. But although money was often a bit tight, Ruth's father was generous to his daughter, so Ruth could always find a way if they encountered a large, unexpected bill. They were always able to afford an annual two-week family holiday, usually in Devon, though they'd also been to Broadstairs and Worthing. They had been vaguely contemplating a trip to the continent but thought they ought to wait until the children were a little older. In any case, Anthony was worried about the reliability of his six-year-old car. He doubted if he could be sure of getting to the air ferry at Southend, let alone touring round France.

With no insurmountable money worries and an amicable relationship, their marriage cruised along well enough, but Anthony was not sure he was in love with Ruth anymore. He certainly loved her, and even liked her too, but the passion seemed to have largely gone for him and, unless Ruth was suppressing her deepest emotions and not revealing any disappointments to him, it had probably faded for her too. No matter, it was the way of the world for most people and life trundled on. What was important was that there were regular high spots in their life together and only the occasional low one.

It was the middle of September when Anthony left work and took a slow walk to the Kardomah for his meeting with Carrie. A car radio was blaring out Frank Ifield's yodelling of '*I Remember You*' and from a café came Pat Boon singing '*Speedy Gonzales*'. He marvelled at the interminability of their popularity and couldn't remember the last time he had bought a single; he thought it was probably a '78'.

He was looking forward to seeing Carrie again, but he wasn't exactly counting the hours that day. This was sure to be just a one-off meeting, a pleasant distraction, and then he would resume the humdrum pattern of his life. He arrived a little before the appointed time and found a table for two in the fashionably unfussy café with its bare tables and pine panelling. It wasn't very busy, and a waitress soon came over to take his order. Anthony told her he was waiting for someone and would order when they arrived. He got out his newspaper and turned to the sports pages to pass the time while he waited. There was a big article about Brian Kilby winning the marathon for Great Britain the previous day at the European Athletics Championships which aroused his interest. After that, he glanced down reports of the rest of the weekend's sport, then noticed that the time was just after five-thirty. He set to work on the crossword and the next time he looked at his watch, it was nearly five-forty; he wondered if Carrie had been delayed. As the clock in the café showed a quarter to six, he thought perhaps it had all just been a mere whim on her part and she wouldn't show up. He sought to soften his disappointment by telling himself it probably hadn't been a good idea anyway to see her again. As the waitress was now looking at him a little suspiciously, he thought he might as well have a coffee anyway. He had just placed the order when he saw a flustered-looking Carrie rushing towards the door.

"I'm so sorry I am late," she said, sitting down at the table. Although the weather had turned cooler, she was still fighting the onset of autumn and was dressed in a red-flowered white summer dress with a cardigan to ward off the cool breeze.

"That's quite all right, I'm in no hurry," said Anthony, his mood instantly lifting. "What would you like?"

"Oh, just a coffee please. I hope you haven't been waiting too long. We had a job that just had to go off tonight and there were one or two hitches. Anyway, I hope this'll be worth the hanging around for you." She produced from her bag a bulging foolscap envelope and handed it over to Anthony.

He ordered Carrie's coffee then looked inside the envelope to find the remains of at least forty envelopes reduced of their bulk so that just the stamps with their surrounding area survived. Even a quick check showed that they included stamps from the USA, Italy, France and the French colonies in Africa and the Pacific, and some more from Andorra.

"You've gone to so much trouble; it's very kind of you. Do you get a lot of mail from abroad?"

"Yes, I work for a translation agency."

"Oh, but I'm a bit puzzled why you would get so much correspondence for translation from abroad."

"It's not as odd as you might think. Obviously every country has translation companies like ours but sometimes the idioms and ways of saying things get missed when they are translated into English by a local translator, so they send it to us. For example, yesterday I looked at a document from France in which *vagabondage* had been translated as vagrancy. It *can* mean that but not in the context of that document; 'roving' was a better choice. The same thing happens in reverse, so we sometimes send documents abroad for cross-checking, especially when there are technical terms or medical terms. What sort of business do you think a French *bonneterie* is?"

"It sounds like a hat maker."

"Yes, but it's actually hosiery and knitwear. So we have to be careful when the words are similar but have very different meanings, otherwise you get absolute howlers. Tell French doctors you feel debilitated and they may well assume you are mad and phone for the men in white coats."

Anthony laughed, but he thought the work sounded pretty boring. "So that's what your job consists of, translating documents and letters?"

"That's the main part of it, though I also act as an interpreter sometimes."

Anthony nodded. "Like you did for Isabella. I was very impressed when you translated as she spoke. What sort of interpreting work would you do normally?"

"Oh, all sorts of things: police interviews, people with documentation problems, business meetings, conferences. It can be quite interesting."

Anthony nodded. "It sounds it. Only in Spanish or do you speak any other languages just as well?"

"Well, I suppose I would count myself as fluent in Spanish, French and German, but I can manage Italian, Portuguese and Dutch pretty well too."

Anthony whistled his admiration. "That's incredible. How did you do it? I'm absolutely hopeless, just the usual schoolboy French, the odd bit of German and that's about it."

Carrie shrugged. "You're still better than most. I've just always been good at languages, like some people are naturally gifted at mental arithmetic or can play the piano by ear. In my case, it's nothing to do with being clever or working hard or anything; I just pick languages up easily and it's never a chore to learn another one. I'd like to try one of the Asian languages, perhaps Japanese."

"You've definitely got a gift. What about Eastern European languages?"

"I haven't really tried but guess I could pick up Romanian fairly easily. The Slav languages would be more of a challenge, but I should give Russian a go; it would be quite useful." She paused for a moment. "Do you think there will be a war?" she asked.

Her tone was curious rather than concerned, but Anthony was still taken aback by the question. "*A war?* Why do you ask?"

"Well, the Americans and the Russians seem to be getting more and more aggressive in the way they are standing up to each other."

Anthony relaxed. "What, over this Cuban business?" He shook his head. "No, I don't suppose it'll amount to much, just a war of words."

"You don't think Gromyko's threat should be taken seriously then?"

"No, I'm sure it's just the usual cold war sabre-rattling. He's got to say something to stand up for his ally, otherwise he'll be accused of weakness. I've got a friend who works in the Ministry of Defence and when I spoke to him recently, he seemed to be of much the same opinion. Both sides do it and then find a way to climb down." What he didn't say was that when they had talked about it, his friend had been a little more guarded in his assessment of the situation.

Carrie sipped her coffee. "The newspapers seem quite bothered, but I suppose they always exaggerate things."

"Of course, the newspapers are having a field day, but we are at the end of their silly season. They are looking for something to liven up the news."

Carrie shrugged. "Well, I suppose you're right; Cuba would be a poor excuse for wiping out half the planet. It's reassuring to get the perspective of someone who works in 'Whitehall'."

Anthony smiled. "I'm afraid I don't know much really; just reporting what I've heard. Still, if past practice is anything to go by, they will find a way to avoid things escalating." He checked the time. "I'm sorry, but I really must be going." He looked at the bill and left enough money for a generous tip.

"Me too, thanks for the coffee."

They rose from their seats. "Which way do you go?" asked Anthony.

"Holborn, for the Piccadilly line. I go to Barons Court."

"Holborn's where I'm going, so we could walk together if you like?"

"Yes, OK."

As they walked along, Anthony said to Carrie, "You know, those stamps you have given me are not that common and they are quite high denominations, so they are probably worth something if you took them to a dealer. I'd very much like to thank you properly for the trouble you've taken; perhaps I could give you some payment based on their value?"

Carrie laughed. "No, honestly, it was no trouble and I don't want anything for them."

"Then will you let me take you out to lunch as a thank you?"

"There really is no need, but if you would like me to go to lunch with you, I'd be pleased to."

"Oh good, perhaps one day next week?"

Carrie thought for a moment. "All right, how about Wednesday?"

"Wednesday would be fine. Do you know that little French restaurant just off Kingsway, the one with the maroon canopy?"

Carrie nodded. "Yes, about what time?"

"Oh, would twelve-thirty be a good time?"

"Twelve-thirty it is. I'll try to be punctual this time." She winked at him.

They arrived at Holborn station and showed their season tickets before going down the first escalator.

"Well, this is me," said Anthony, indicating the Central line eastbound platform.

Carrie held out her hand. "I'll see you next week."

"I shall look forward to it," said Anthony, as they shook hands. The noise and rush of air as a train swept from the tunnel into the station ended their conversation abruptly and, with a smile, they went their separate ways.

When Anthony arrived home, it was well after seven and the boys had already had their meal and were getting ready for bed. "You're late this evening," said Ruth, without the usual preliminary greeting.

"Yes, sorry. I met somebody who gets a lot of post from overseas and they sorted out some stamps for me. By the time I had collected them, it was later than I thought it would be."

"You could have rung," she said and turned on her heels to get his meal from the oven.

Anthony walked into the dining room and emptied out the envelope onto a teak side table. Like most of the furniture in the house, it was modern and pleasing to his eye; not like the heavy, dark-stained, sometimes over-embellished furniture he'd grown up with. His father-in-law had been very generous with his wedding present so that it was almost a dowry. In consequence, all the main rooms had been furnished when they moved in with new good quality pieces from Heal's, Gordon Russell, Gomme and others. Anthony had once or twice regretted that, though they had added a few items of furniture during the course of their marriage, they had somehow missed out on the challenge and ultimate achievement of building a home from scratch. But that was in the early days of the marriage; since then, having often had to deal with a tight domestic budget, he'd grown out of the view that there was nobility in economic struggle.

While he was looking through the stamps, his elder son came in.

"Hello, Dad," he said. "Stamps! Where did you get those from?"

"Somebody who works near where I work gave them to me."

"Is he a stamp collector as well?"

"No, somebody who works at a place that gets foreign stamps on letters sometimes."

"They're really good and lots of them have planes on," said Laurence, rifling through them and admiring a French stamp with a Caravelle airliner in a contrasting colour to the border, "This is a great one."

"Yes, they're all airmail stamps so that means they're used especially for parcels and letters delivered by aeroplane."

"Can we do some stamps tonight Daddy? You could show me where to put the stamps you gave me 'cos I don't know some of the countries."

"After I have had my dinner and if your mother says it's OK." He winked at the boy and patted him on the back, shepherding him out of the room. He listened and could hear Laurence asking his mother if he could spend a few minutes with his stamp album and the response came in that catch-all phrase "We'll see," from Ruth.

"I'm sorry I didn't ring, Ruth," he said when she came in bearing his dinner on a plate held in oven gloves.

"That's all right; I just like to know so that the dinner won't be spoiled. Mind the plate; it's very hot."

He sat and ate his dinner, a rather dried Barnsley chop, in silence while Ruth and the children carried on with their evening rituals. He began reflecting, as he had done for much of the time on the tube, about his meeting with Carrie. He had enjoyed it and was glad that he was going to see her again. But he was also wary about the potential consequences of his sudden, unplanned offer to Carrie of another meeting.

He knew himself well enough to be aware that he had what some would call an 'eye for the ladies'. This well-developed interest in women did not take the form of heavy-handed flirtation, suggestive remarks or unwelcome attention, let alone taking physical liberties or groping. Rather, he had a tendency, very occasionally, to meet a woman, take some interest in her and then, without warning, to become infatuated. The pattern was always the same. He would come across a person at work, or perhaps in a social context and, after getting to know her superficially, he would find himself, almost out the blue, besotted by her. The infatuation would be pursued often only in his dreams and through fantasising, unless he summoned up the courage to test whether his feelings would be reciprocated. When he was single, this had presented no problems, since he could always show interest in the woman in question and she could say 'yes' or 'no'. A 'no' always put paid to his interest while a 'yes' led the relationship to take its natural course until the infatuation eventually subsided.

What had caused him some misgivings was that, despite his becoming more circumspect about such relationships since he married, this cycle of minor, sometimes unrequited, dalliances had not come to an end but persisted with three more women. The first time it happened was a year after he married, when he became interested in a young woman who was a secretary to one of the senior officers in the department. He made absolutely no impact on her whatsoever and her patent lack of interest in him soon led the hurricane of infatuation to blow itself out. The second case was Karen, a new barmaid at his local pub. She seemed quite friendly, but the complications of arranging meetings, other than in the pub, proved too great a stumbling block.

Only on the third occasion did the situation develop. This was Denise, a married woman who was an Executive Officer in one of the other sections in his division at the Home Office. She was very pretty, with long, dark hair and a nice figure, and she reminded him of Claire Bloom. He became interested in her after they went on a one-day course together and he went so far as frequenting the staff canteen regularly to make her acquaintance. Once they sat together at lunch and both were so equally dismayed by the particular menu that day that they practically invited each other out to try somewhere else to eat. Denise seemed just as keen as Anthony on meeting again, so they did go out a couple more times before Anthony lost interest. This is how his infatuations always ended. They would deflate as rapidly as they had erupted, and he would sometimes wonder what had made him attracted to the woman in the first place. So the rapid process of disengagement from the imagined or actual entanglement would follow and he would tell himself that he was now too old for such teenage fantasies. In the case of Denise, things had not got very far, but she was always rather frosty towards him after he twice made an excuse when she invited him to go out with her again.

This rise and fall of unfulfilled passion was so similar in each case that Anthony was even able to trace the evolution of a relationship with a degree of detachment, rather like Dr Jekyll watching himself in the mirror as he turned into Mr Hyde and later back again. So far this weakness of his had never led to a serious situation and no harm had been done, nor had there been any repercussions, at least as far as he was aware. In any event, he felt that perhaps now he was over this rather immature and slightly ludicrous pattern of behaviour. After all, there had been no fantasy build-up or shilly-shallying around with Carrie. He had got straight to the point and asked her out for a purely social engagement. Obviously he had changed and he had changed for the better.

Having resolved his internal concerns about his growing interest in Carrie, he was pleased to turn his attention to more simple pursuits. True to his word and with the permission of Ruth, he spent half an hour with Laurence, helping him to identify the stamps of countries whose own spelling of their name was nothing like that shown in the album. Then they went through the airmail stamps and selected the duplicates, which Laurence was very pleased to have.

"Can I soak them off the envelopes now?" he asked.

"Tomorrow," said Anthony. "Off you go to bed and I'll be up to say 'goodnight.'"

He put the stamp albums away in the bureau and went upstairs to his two sons. First he went to Jonathan's room to read a story from one of the less horrific collections of fairy tales on his little bookshelf. When ten minutes later, he went to Lawrence's room, he discovered his elder son looking at a few of the stamps he hadn't yet found a home for.

"Where's 'Bayern', Dad?" he asked, showing his father a stamp with the head of an elderly, bearded man on it.

"It's in Germany, but it used to issue its own stamps once; we stick it on the page called 'German States.'" He flicked through the album and showed Laurence the page, which had a picture of a Bavarian stamp by its title. "Bavaria is the English name for 'Bayern', Laurence. Now put the album away and settle down." He kissed his son on the forehead. "Goodnight, Laurence."

"Goodnight, Dad."

Anthony went downstairs to the living room. Ruth was sewing a button on one of Laurence's shirts while half-watching the television.

"It's good of you to spend time with Laurence after you've been at work all day."

"But?"

Ruth smiled. "I think the stamps are not a good idea just before he goes to bed; it gets his mind racing. He's probably looking at them now with a torch under the bedclothes."

Anthony laughed. "You did it, I did it and our parents knew we did it. It's being naughty but staying within the unwritten rules."

"Well, you can see to him if he says he can't sleep." Ruth bit through the cotton thread and put the shirt down. "I'll make some coffee."

ANTHONY FOUND HIMSELF LOOKING AT HIS WATCH every ten minutes as the time crept towards his lunch appointment with Carrie. He surprised himself with his impatience and a definite longing to see her again. Finally, it was time for a quick trip to the washroom and a spruce up, then a five-minute walk to the restaurant. He took the alley to cut off the corner of Holborn and Kingsway, not because he was in a hurry but because he liked alleys and lanes where the pedestrian could escape from the ubiquitous car.

This shortcut took him past a few shops and especially the outsize men's outfitters. He stopped to look at the suited rotund dummies smiling benignly from their pedestals and a pair of brown size 34 shoes in pride of place in the window. Anthony stared closely at the shoes for a moment, trying to work out if they were a genuine size 34 and welcoming the distraction from his rising sense of anticipation. He looked at his watch yet again and slowed his walk to make sure he wasn't too early in case Carrie was delayed; he hated loitering outside shops or restaurants. When he arrived at the restaurant, he passed the time by casting an eye over the menu in the window; he had booked a table so there was no need to worry about finding one.

At exactly half-past twelve, Carrie came round the corner. It was a dull day and she was carrying a dainty maroon umbrella and wearing a dark jacket over her cream blouse. She gave a little wave and Anthony waved back, musing that she was even more attractive than he'd thought her the last time they'd met. They greeted each other with a smile and the usual pleasantries, then Anthony opened the chrome-handled glass door for Carrie. Most of the white-clothed tables were empty and they were offered one in the window, but Anthony chose a more discreet one, away from prying eyes, a little further back in the restaurant. The head waiter held the seat back for Carrie and made a token gesture with Anthony's chair before presenting each of them with a menu.

"I've never been here before," said Carrie, taking off her jacket. "I like it; the decor's not too heavy."

A waiter came over. "May I get you something to drink?" he asked.

Anthony looked at Carrie. "A tomato juice, please," she said.

"I'll have a Scotch on the rocks, please," said Anthony.

"It's very nice, but do you think this is the sort of place that can get us through lunch in an hour?" asked Carrie.

"Hmm," Anthony nodded. "I know what you mean. Are they strict about punctuality where you work?"

"Well, not exactly, but I can't just swan in and out as I please." She noticed Anthony's disappointed expression and smiled. "It's all right, I took only a half hour yesterday so that I can take an extra half hour today; if we don't run out of things to say, that is."

Anthony smiled. He had organised things so that he would not be missed if he was out of the office for more than the regulation hour. They glanced at the menus, but Anthony found himself staring at Carrie rather than the card in front of him; the nearly black hair, the almond eyes, the elegant nose and shapely full lips. *My God, you're beautiful,* he thought.

Carrie looked up. "Have you chosen yet?"

Anthony hastily returned to the menu. They were just about ready to order when the waiter returned.

"I suppose menus in French or Italian present few challenges to you," said Anthony.

"Sometimes the terminology and the vocabulary are a bit different to what I usually work with, but I don't often have too much trouble. You know where I live," said Carrie, changing the subject. "What about you?"

"Woodford Green in Essex."

"Is that where you were born?"

"No, I was born in Palmers Green. I moved to Woodford when..."

"When you got married?"

Anthony felt a little uncomfortable. "Yes," he said.

"What would your wife say about you going out to lunch with another woman?" Carrie smiled, with her eyebrows slightly raised.

Anthony was more flustered. "I don't think she would mind, as this is not exactly a date."

"Isn't it? That's a shame," she replied, without a flicker of a smile.

Anthony was momentarily tongue-tied, unable either to respond or to change the subject. His mind was locked into the thought that in two sentences Carrie had raised the issue of his marriage and then seemed to say it made no difference. Rescue arrived in the form of their starters.

"Mm, these Dublin Bay prawns are lovely," said Carrie, ignoring Anthony's lengthy silence. "Do you have any children?" she asked, suspending her fork with a speared prawn in mid-air.

"Two boys, one aged seven and the other four-and-a-half."

"So one's at school at least?"

"Yes, the younger one starts soon. How about you, I take it you are not married?"

Carrie smiled. "Why do you say that?"

Anthony's composure, which was just getting back to normal, was jolted again. "You aren't wearing a ring, so I assumed."

"One mustn't assume," she said reproachingly, but adding with a smile, "You're right, of course; I'm just an old spinster."

"I am sure that someone as beautiful as you would've had many opportunities to marry," he said, immediately thinking how crass that sounded.

Carrie took the fulsome praise in her stride. She smiled. "Not that many, but thanks for the compliment anyway."

Anthony took that to mean that she had been offered marriage but refused and he sipped his wine, pondering her likely reasons.

This time his long silence seemed to provoke Carrie into responding to his unanswered question. "Actually, I have had a couple of offers of marriage. The first I didn't even consider but the second I took seriously. In the end, I didn't think I was ready and wasn't sure I could stay the course."

They fell silent and resumed eating, both retreating to their own thoughts. Anthony called the waiter over and ordered two more glasses of wine then resumed the conversation on a lighter note. They talked about their families, both having their parents still living and both having a younger brother. Carrie didn't ask about Ruth.

"That's enough of our families; let's talk about you," said Carrie. She focused her eyes on him and leaned forward conspiratorially. "Apart from stamp collecting, what else interests you outside work and family?"

Before Anthony could respond, their main courses arrived and Anthony, given a moment to reflect on the question, made only a passing reference to his hobbies and sporting interests. Thinking she might be more interested in serious pursuits, he concentrated on his love of history, especially the Wars of the Roses. Carrie asked him who his favourite king of that period was, and his answer of Henry V soon led onto a discussion about the Shakespearian play of that name.

"I think Henry V is my favourite Shakespeare historical play and it's hard not to like the king; Shakespeare saw to that," said Carrie. "I saw Richard Burton as Henry in 1955 at the Old Vic and loved his performance. I guess I prefer self-torturing heroes and Burton does self-torture very well."

"Do you go to the theatre much?"

"Yes, I absolutely love it! Not just Shakespeare; Chekhov, Rattigan, Miller, Williams, Ibsen, especially Chekhov. I go whenever I can, cheaper seats mostly. In the gallery you're among the real theatre fanatics."

Anthony smiled, admiring her enthusiasm. "With your love of theatre, you haven't been tempted to get involved in it in some way yourself?"

"Now you've guessed my secret; I'm a keen member of my local dramatic society."

Anthony laughed. "Why a secret?"

"Well, you know, enthusiastic amateurs with frustrated thespian ambitions and a desperate need for applause."

"Is that how you would describe yourself?"

Carrie smiled. "Probably."

"I did a bit of acting at school and quite enjoyed it, but what always put me off was having to learn all those lines."

"Now that's one thing I've had no problem with. I've always been able to remember poems and things. It's just luck, really, but I've never forgotten my lines on stage; I suppose I must have a photographic memory or something. Do you like poetry?"

Anthony grimaced a little. "Some; nothing too demanding, I must admit. There are odd bits from school that I recall when someone else starts them off, but I'm hopeless at remembering poetry. I'm not really a very cultured person, I'm afraid."

She tutted. "Why do you say that?"

"Well, you know, some people quote from the classics, rattle off a poem, understand modern serious music and are into the latest trends in art. I usually find myself floundering a bit if I go off the beaten track."

"Don't be silly, being cultured is not about learning things by rote or having esoteric knowledge. Too often being cultured is thought of as understanding things that nobody else knows, but I think to be cultured is to have a true understanding of those things that everybody knows."

Anthony smiled. He doubted he came in either category but liked listening to Carrie expound her views.

They decided to pass on dessert and talked about Carrie's amateur dramatics group while they had their coffee. "What's your next production going to be?" asked Anthony.

"We're doing an adaptation of *The Secret Garden*. It doesn't require any young men, thank goodness, as we're rather short of those at the moment. Our last play, *The Importance of Being Earnest*, had fairly elderly leading men." She chuckled when she mentioned it.

"When will that be on?"

"Oh, not till the end of October. You're welcome to come and see us if you like."

Anthony grunted affirmatively but doubted their relationship would last that long.

Carrie asked, "How did you get on with those stamps?"

"Ah! The stamps," said Anthony. "Well, they were all very interesting and my elder son was pleased because he got the duplicates for his own album."

"I can trawl the archives next time, in case there are some more of interest in there."

Anthony shook his head. "No, really, please don't go to any more trouble."

"I liked doing it, so we'll see."

"Out of curiosity, is Carrie actually your name or is it an abbreviation for something else?"

Carrie screwed up her face a little. "I was dreading you asking that question," she said. "Everyone does and then I have to explain."

"Oh, I'm sorry I raised it, but I just thought it might be short for Caroline or something like that."

"I wish it were. My parents couldn't decide what name to give me; I think they were expecting a boy. So after I was born, the days dragged on and then the weeks and they still couldn't agree on a name, and the deadline for registering the birth was fast approaching. Then my father remembered that I'd been born on Sunday morning when the church bells were ringing and he came up with the name '*Carillon*', which means a peal of bells in French. In a moment of madness or desperation my mother went along with it, so that's how I got the name. You can understand why I use Carrie."

"I think Carillon's a great name and certainly unusual."

Carrie snorted. "Unusual isn't the same as good."

"Your surname is unusual too; I haven't come across it before."

"Yes, it's a Huguenot name, according to my father, and I think that encouraged him to go for a French name like Carillon. But," she added in a mock menacing voice, "you make sure you stick to 'Carrie'. Your surname is quite unusual too. Where does that come from?"

"I don't really know. It *is* rare, though. My father has no brothers and his father had one brother who had four daughters; so the future of our line is down to my two sons, unless my bachelor brother gets his act together. I don't know any other Fernards apart from my own family and as my father is ex-directory, I'm the only one in the London telephone directory."

"Easy to find if someone needs to get hold of you," said Carrie.

They had finished their coffee and Anthony, looking at his watch, realised it was nearly two o'clock. "I really ought to be going," he said and beckoned a waiter over for the bill.

"I think we should go Dutch on this," said Carrie, taking her purse out of her bag.

"Thank you, but no, it's fine; it was my idea."

Carrie hesitated and then concurred and put her purse away. "Next time, it's my turn."

They walked out of the restaurant and Carrie pulled her jacket round her. At the top of Kingsway, they stopped at the corner. She held out her hand and said, "I've had a lovely time, thank you very much."

Anthony had begun lunch expecting that this would be a one-off, but from the encouraging comments she'd made, he was as sure as he could be that she wanted it to go on. Now she'd said 'next time'. "I enjoyed it very much too," he said. "Let's do it again soon."

"Yes," said Carrie. She gave him her business card then smiled and turned to cross the road.

Anthony watched her begin her walk up Southampton Row, then went back to his office. He was very late and realised that his section head, Daphne, would have seen him go to lunch before twelve-thirty and still be absent from his desk when she returned from her own break at two o'clock.

He resorted to his emergency procedure to be used in this situation and went first to the file repository. When he walked into his office, he appeared deeply engrossed in the file of someone he had never dealt with and was unlikely to do so in the future. He smiled at Daphne as he resumed his seat and continued with his examination of the file.

Daphne Raynott had been in the Home Office all her working life, starting as a Clerical Officer and then being promoted twice to where she was now. Quite short, with glasses and dark hair and not unattractive, she usually wore a twin set with pearls. She was always very precise and neat, both in her appearance and the methodical way she went about her work, which she did with a pleasant manner and, so far as Anthony knew, very competently. Their work generally only interacted when Anthony referred a case to her because he felt he needed the confirmation of a senior officer to ratify his judgement. They had worked together for seven years but had never had a conversation on any subject other than work and he knew nothing whatever about her life outside the office, except that he assumed she was unmarried, as she used the title 'Miss'. However, he liked having her as a boss and much preferred her to his last two (male) bosses in the financial sector: one an inadequate neurotic constantly in a flap about things and the other a supercilious autocrat with a bullying streak. He always deferred to her experience and expertise and called her Miss Raynott in front of the other staff.

He had yet to receive any comment from her as to his occasional lapses in punctuality and today was no exception. He sat at his desk deep in thought and had to be asked for a file twice by a messenger before he responded; it was not a productive afternoon, so far as work was concerned.

However, that afternoon Anthony laid down some rules for his relationship with Carrie that he was determined to follow. First, it would be a friendship and any fantasising about anything deeper would remain merely flights of fancy. Second, it would be a platonic relationship, possibly with some minor physical contact but certainly not sexual. Third, he would see her not too often so that she did not believe the relationship would become more serious, whatever her hopes.

At first, he held fast to these rules; the occasional friendly lunch date with no hint of anything serious and all quite platonic. Things developed at his pace and he controlled the situation, Carrie assisting in this by acquiescing in whatever he chose to do in their relationship.

As time passed, however, the gap between his intentions and his desires grew ever wider. Each mark in the sand beyond which he would not go would be washed away by the tide of his own passion and his consequent actions. He took every opportunity he could to spend time with her and only the rule against a sexual relationship remained inviolate.

Later that month on their fourth date, he broke new ground with Carrie by suggesting they go out for the day together. They both took a day off work and spent it at Hampton Court. It was one of those days which began rather mistily but later settled down into soft sunshine and showers.

After assuring the reluctant Carrie that they would not get lost, they went into the maze and did get lost. Much to his own chagrin, he was forced to follow the sound of voices outside the maze to locate a way to the exit while Carrie traipsed along behind him. Fortunately, Carrie was gentle in her teasing and said she found the episode hilarious. The rest of the day went without a hitch as they enjoyed the last of the summer walking round the grounds and the areas of the palace open to the public, getting to know each other better than they ever could over a hurried lunch.

When they parted company on the way home, Anthony went to kiss Carrie on the cheek, but she turned her face to his and they kissed briefly on the lips.

"Thank you for a lovely day; shall we meet again next week?" she asked.

Anthony stared at her for a few moments. He was still trying to recover from the effect of the kiss, which seemed to have sent a shock wave through his body. He couldn't quite believe that he had felt such an acute physical reaction to something that was in essence so trivial, and it wasn't as if he'd never kissed anyone before. "Er... how about Thursday?" he said finally. "I could meet you after work and we could do something."

"I'd like that."

V

A FEW DAYS AFTER HIS TRIP TO HAMPTON COURT, Anthony met up with Ronnie Benson, one of his oldest friends and the one he had quoted to Carrie to reassure her that a war over Cuba was unlikely. They had maintained regular contact ever since they were at school together and these days had lunch together about once a month. They usually met at a grand bustling dining room with quiet tables for two or four on the first floor of a large pub near Covent Garden.

Ronnie had gone straight into the Civil Service after leaving school and had worked ever since at the Ministry of Defence. In the early days of his career he had been fairly open about what he did; telling the odd story about logistics in the Army and defence contracts he'd worked on. But then he was transferred, and he became more reticent about what he did, mentioning only that it had something to do with strategic planning. He'd already been promoted and in addition now had the courtesy title of Captain for use in his dealings with military personnel. He had also acquired a certain gravitas that Anthony could only marvel at, remembering that at school he'd been given the nickname 'Fudge' from his lack of application to almost anything.

From a scruffy persona at school, Ronnie had developed a well-groomed look and bordered on being something of the Edwardian dandy with his gold watch chain (without watch attached) in his double-breasted waistcoat. He always carried an umbrella, perfectly rolled and almost never opened. If, in an emergency, he had to open the umbrella, he would later have it professionally rolled so that it was restored to its previous pristine condition. On one occasion, somebody had taken his umbrella while he was at lunch in a restaurant and now his umbrella had printed on the panels: "This umbrella may be stolen; please check with the owner at WHI 2380." His umbrella had since been unfurled a few times but never taken from where he'd left it.

They spent most of the lunch discussing the ongoing stand-off between the United States and the Soviet Union over the location of Soviet missiles in Cuba. Ronnie sounded less blasé about things than Anthony had expected and hinted that his own department had growing concerns about the way things were developing.

"You see," said Ronnie, leaning back in his chair with the front legs slightly off the ground, "the problem is that both sides think they are in the right. The Russians think that Cuba is a parallel with Turkey. So, the Americans have got missiles in their NATO ally Turkey and would protect Turkey if the Russians invaded it. In the same way, the Russians would wish to protect their ally Cuba and can't see why they shouldn't install defence capabilities in Cuba so to do. On the other hand, the Americans cling to their beloved Monroe Doctrine, which says basically that the United States will not allow any new imperialism by European powers on the American continent or its offshore islands. The present US administration interprets that to include a satellite state of Russia. They also have an almost psychotic hatred and fear of a communist Castro regime a few miles off the US coast; the spirit of McCarthyism is not dead yet. Thus there are principles at stake here."

"Aren't there always?"

"Not at all," said Ronnie, warming to his discourse and sticking his thumbs in his waistcoat pockets. "Sometimes one side has principles and the other is trying it on, like us in China during the Opium Wars or Israel invading Egypt during the Suez crisis. Of course, often the side trying it on still wins, as when Hitler marched into the Rhineland or the Russians put down the Hungarian uprising."

"Or the Americans in the war against Spain when they took over Cuba."

Ronnie nodded and placed his elbows on the table, his chin resting on his clasped hands. "Precisely, quite ironic isn't it? Anyway, that's the problem. It's not just posturing; they are both pretty serious."

"But surely..."

"Exactly, since when have the great powers allowed principles to get in the way of *real politik*. I'm sure they'll find a way out of it, though not all the precedents are good; the First World War, for example." He ran his hand through his slightly faded auburn hair. "Changing the subject, I bumped into Malcolm Vinton the other day. Do you remember him?"

Anthony thought for a minute. "Plumpish bloke with curly blond hair and glasses?"

"Yes, that's the one; he hasn't changed much."

"I remember he was in our class, but I didn't know him very well; I haven't seen him since we left school."

"Nor me, he was a bit of a loner at school. Went on to Reading and read Government and now he works in the Foreign Office. We met at a NATO conference last week. I got the impression that he's a bit of a sad case. He's spent a lot of time abroad, naturally, but he has few friends here now. I don't suppose he had many to start with."

"Is he married?"

"No, and no prospect of that at the moment; he doesn't appear to have any lady friends."

"Perhaps he's not interested in women?"

Ronnie rubbed his chin. "Oh! What, you mean he might prefer boys? I never thought of that. I suppose he might."

Anthony shrugged. "I meant that it's possible he's not interested in an intimate relationship with anyone."

Ronnie shook his head. "Oh, right. I really have no idea. I'd only got as far as thinking he might like a bit of sociable company from time to time. I did think about asking him if he would like to go out for a drink or something, but you know how it is. It's out of the question for me at the moment; I'm completely tied up with things connected to this bloody business in Cuba."

Anthony muttered his concurrence. "Is he in the phone book?"

"No, he's ex-directory, but I have his direct line at work." He took out his pocket diary. "It's Whitehall 4236. That'd be very good of you to get in touch and I am sure he would appreciate it." Ronnie looked relieved.

Anthony made a note of the number in his own pocket diary. "Well, I'll try to, but I can't promise."

"No, of course not, just if you get a chance."

Ever since Carrie had mentioned the play *The Importance of Being Earnest* the idea had been coalescing in Anthony's mind that he might be able to invent his own variation on 'Bunbury', the fictitious friend of Algernon in that play. He didn't actually phone Malcolm Vinton, but that evening he told Ruth about his lunch with Ronnie and that he felt he ought to get in touch with Malcolm as he needed cheering up.

"Is he unwell?" asked Ruth.

"Not exactly; he's lonely and a bit down in the dumps and, as we're old friends from school, I thought I ought to look him up."

"Good idea; we should keep up with old friends. I don't recall you mentioning him before."

"You know how it is; we gradually lose contact with school friends. Ronnie's the only one I keep up with now."

"What about Jim Stanton; you meet him for lunch too?"

"Yes, but we know each other from when we went to a youth club together, not school."

"Right, anyhow it's good to keep up with old friends. I only see Marjorie and Libby of my friends from school and none of the people I used to work with, oh, except Janice. There's nothing like marriage to kill off your friendships."

Anthony smiled. "How was the car today?"

"Well, it started eventually, but I think the rattle's worse. We really ought to get the service done before the bad weather sets in."

"I will when I can. I haven't got the money at the moment."

"You know my father would be happy to help."

The volume of Anthony's voice rose a little. "We can't keep running to your father every time we have a problem. I'll sort it out."

"I could pay the bill," proffered Ruth, sounding almost apologetic.

"Where would you get the money from? Ultimately it would have come from your parents. It's demeaning; I will sort it out before the end of the month."

Ruth nodded with a look of resignation and went back to her book.

Malcolm was put to use almost immediately as an opportunity for Anthony to see Carrie without having to think of an excuse. So when they went to the pictures to see *Term of Trial* a few days later, Malcolm made the first of his appearances in Anthony's diary. The date was, for him, quite notable because it was the first time they really kissed and held hands. It was also the first time that Anthony had been to a suburban cinema where the audience had applauded the film at the end. Afterwards they went for a drink in a bar and then Anthony took a tube home. Walking from the station, he analysed their relationship for the umpteenth time and thought that it was now about right; pleasurable but not too intimate and therefore not guilt-inducing.

When he got home, it was about ten o'clock and most of the lights in the house were off. He went up to the bedroom where Ruth was reading in bed. "You're in bed early," he said.

Ruth looked up from her book. "Nothing on the television. Is your friend all right?"

"Not too bad; I'll keep in touch now we've met up again. Would you like a drink of anything?"

"Yes, please, a cup of warm milk. I don't feel very tired tonight so it might help me to sleep."

Anthony went downstairs and had a nightcap of Scotch and soda before warming some milk for both of them. Propped up in bed they drank their milk and read their current novels: *The Spy Who Loved Me* by Ian Fleming for Anthony and *The Pumpkin Eater* by Penelope Mortimer for Ruth. After she finished her milk, Ruth turned off her light. "I'm still not tired, but I can't be bothered to read any more. Read me a bit of your book."

He read a few more pages of his book out loud then asked her, "Are you sleepy yet?"

"Not really. It doesn't sound very much like a James Bond book."

"He hasn't actually appeared yet and I'm over halfway through it. It's quite racy, though."

"So I gathered," said Ruth.

Anthony turned off his light and lay down with his body facing Ruth's back. He felt a growing desire to make love and he put his left hand up her nightdress and placed it on one of her full breasts. Their sex life had declined steadily over recent years and it had probably been a month since the last time. Ruth neither resisted nor encouraged him as his hand explored her body, but she opened her legs as his hand reached her pubic hair and she put her hand inside his pyjama trousers. Soon they were making love the way they had got accustomed to and even perfected over the years as Anthony had learned to slow down a bit and Ruth become more proficient at reaching a climax.

Afterwards Ruth said, as she usually said, "We should do this more often." Anthony agreed, as he always did but then they would not find the time again for several weeks. Anthony lay on his back. He had only thought once, or maybe twice, of Carrie as he had lain on top of his wife.

Over the next week or so Anthony saw Carrie twice. They had lunch at his regular Italian restaurant on Monday. Then on Thursday they went to the theatre, courtesy of another supposed visit by Anthony to Malcolm, to see the RSC production of *The Devils* at the Aldwych. It was the first time that Anthony had been to the serious theatre for a few years and he was looking forward to it, as the play was based on a book by one of his favourite authors, Aldous Huxley. They were slightly perturbed by the sight of a group of demonstrators protesting against the staging of the play, but there was no attempt to prevent them going into the theatre.

Afterwards they had a drink at the Waldorf.

"What did you think of it?" asked Anthony.

"I thought the acting was great, Dorothy Tutin especially. The play's set in strange times, isn't it? It's no longer medieval but hardly modern if they are still burning people at the stake and persecuting heretics. You can't help but feel that the educated and informed elite know that witchcraft and demonic possession are just superstition, but they still use the medieval rationale when it suits them. The powers that be just wanted to get rid of the difficult priest any way they could."

"They also knew that it would play well with the mob. I'm glad I saw it, but it *is* a very weird story and it's certainly stirred up a lot of people, what with protests outside and demands for a ban. Still, there's nothing like a protest to get people queuing up to see something. At least they won't protest about your next production. It's coming up soon, isn't it?" said Anthony.

"Yes, a couple of weeks. Will you come? I don't mind if you bring your wife."

"It'll certainly be a bit different to the play we just saw. I wouldn't take children to see *The Devils*."

"Nor would I, but they are not at totally different ends of the theatrical spectrum."

Anthony laughed. "How do you mean?"

"Well, the tendency to portray people with a physical deformity as being unpleasant, like the Mother Superior or Colin in *The Secret Garden*. There's an element of hysteria too, both Colin with an illness that is not real and the nuns getting into a frenzy. Then there is the outsider disturbing a repressed and isolated community and causing upheaval. Of course, in *The Secret Garden* the consequence is liberation and renewal while in the *Devils* it's repression and destruction."

Anthony held up his hand. "Yes, I'm convinced. But I am surprised it's been so successful these days with the fashion for 'angry young men' plays and 'kitchen sink drama'. Perhaps it's the sensationalism of the story."

"I think it's the universal theme of the little man falling foul of the elites because he threatens their authority or position. A story which appeals to people in any age, even if the context seems so alien to us."

Anthony nodded. "Aren't there supposed to be only seven main plots in fiction?"

"Yes, something like that." She paused for a moment. "Will you come to my play? I'll understand if you can't."

"Of course. When's it on?"

"Thursday the 25th to Saturday the 27th October."

"I'll come on the 26th."

Anthony didn't care about seeing the play, but Carrie looked very pleased with his answer and he liked her to be happy.

After their drinks he offered to take her home, but she refused, saying she had to get home by herself most days, so it was silly to waste his time. They walked together to Holborn station and kissed for several minutes on the almost empty platform until the distant rumble heralded the arrival of the next train.

V

The following week, conversation in the office seemed to gravitate towards the issues surrounding the Cuban crisis. Every day brought with it more revelations about the stand-off between the superpowers or fresh rumours and speculation. Ever since August, the Soviet Union had been denying claims by the Americans that there were Soviet missile sites in Cuba, but on 15th October an American U-2 aircraft flying over Cuba confirmed their existence.

After that, there was always someone with a story from unrevealed sources claiming inside knowledge about planned US air strikes or threats by either side. The temperature wasn't exactly cooled by the latest in a series of nuclear tests by the United States; a hydrogen bomb on 18th October, followed by another nuclear test two days later. Anthony tried to maintain a healthy scepticism about the escalation of the crisis but there were always plenty of others only too willing to play the part of Cassandra or Jeremiah. Fortunately, he was able to ring Ronnie at home and obtain a more balanced view, though Ronnie, less ebullient than usual, admitted that he was not privy to the highest-level secret and sensitive information coming through the department.

Naturally, Ruth was troubled by the turn of events and very worried for the children, and Anthony had to use his most blasé manner to reassure her there was little to worry about. He wasn't sure how Carrie felt about things, as he didn't see her that week. There was so much going on at the office and he'd slipped behind on his casework.

A strange atmosphere greeted Anthony when he came into work on the morning of 23rd October. Like everyone else, he had heard on the radio the main points of President Kennedy's address to the American people concerning the crisis. Though hardly surprising in the circumstances, Kennedy's naval blockade of Cuba and stated willingness to retaliate against any attack on the United States or its allies revealed how close to a crisis things were, especially as Soviet ships continued to steam towards Cuba.

From his demeanour Freddie Pilling seemed to have thoroughly enjoyed the dramas of the previous week. He had ridden the waves of apprehension and fear in the office with tales of previous brinkmanship he had encountered or been told about during his time in the department. As he regularly pointed out, he'd worked under every Home Secretary since Winston Churchill in 1911, apart from the four years he'd served in the First World War, and he'd seen many crises come and go. Freddie always claimed to be 'in on the know', as he called it, but it was not always easy to check his stories since, by their nature, they were only occasionally publicly reported. However, he did have a reliable reputation for titbits of gossip, and it was from Freddie that his colleagues knew that Lady Dorothy Macmillan, the wife of the Prime Minister, had reputedly had an affair for over thirty years with the Conservative politician Robert Boothby. They also knew through him of rumours that a number of prominent people could become embarrassed or even compromised because of their connections with the so-called Cliveden set. This was bound to have future repercussions. Freddie was a master of the 'astonishing but true' variety of story so everything he said about the current crisis was given some credence by his colleagues.

As Anthony entered the room that morning, Freddie was holding court and relating what he had been told by his friends in the wider Home Office. Apparently, Harold Macmillan had refused to mobilise Civil Defence volunteers for fear of causing panic, but there were exercises taking place to ensure the readiness of regional government institutions in the event of a war.

"We're definitely on the brink," said Freddie. "Neither side seems to be able to find a way to back down without losing face and that makes the situation very dangerous. I don't want to alarm anyone," he continued, his expression resolute with just the hint of a smile, "but I think it would be wise to take at least the most basic precautions. I have been stocking up my cellar with tinned food and bottled water and other essentials. I also have breathing apparatus and oxygen canisters. Of course, it may all come to nothing, but it would be foolish to ignore the possibilities."

His colleagues seemed less than inspired by his speech, most returning downcast to their seats. One of the Executive Officers in his own section, Patricia Lovell, looked absolutely desolate and quietly cried into her handkerchief. Patricia was a young woman of about twenty who had been in post for just over a year and in this section for only a few months. Like many of the young women in the department, she wore fairly bland clothes and a nondescript hairstyle to work. Anthony thought her quite pretty but in danger of not making the most of her best years. She was very quiet and conscientious about her work, and this was the first time he had ever seen her show an emotional response to anything.

Sitting opposite her, the third Executive Officer in the section, Rosemary Pitman, tried to console her.

"Don't worry, Pat, the people in charge aren't mad. You watch, in a month from now life will be going on just the same and all this will be forgotten," she said, patting Patricia's arm.

When these and her other soothing words had little impression, she rose to her feet and marched over to Freddie's desk.

"You ought to be ashamed of yourself," she said, glowering at him, her pale complexion now imbued with a bright red hue. "How dare you frighten people for no purpose other than your own self-importance? It's all right for you, you've only got another few years either way, but to be unable to see a future when you are twenty is too cruel."

Everybody in the room was watching in silence, though there had been a few intakes of breath when Rosemary made an oblique reference to Freddie's age.

Freddie himself sat open-mouthed during this tirade but was unrepentant when he replied. He spoke slowly and quietly. "I was merely letting people know what is going on. I did say that it will probably come to nothing, but it's up to everyone to make their own mind up as to what they do about it."

Rosemary wasn't quite finished. "Just keep your warnings to yourself or arrange meetings outside work if you want to issue dire prophecies or stir things up. Haven't you got any work to do?" She made a sharp about turn and walked back to her desk.

Daphne Raynott was aghast by this flare-up of ill will between two of her staff; she couldn't remember such a thing happening in the section before. She quickly sought to restore order. "I think we all have work to do and should get back to it," she said and oversaw things as one head after another turned back to the case at hand.

Anthony smiled at Rosemary, nodding his appreciation, and she winked back at him. He thought it admirable that she could speak out so eloquently on the subject when her own views were perhaps not quite as philanthropic as those she had just espoused. Rosemary was a few years younger than Anthony and was married to a civil servant at the Board of Trade. She dressed older than her years, with her red hair pinned up and her scarf tucked in her blouse, itself tucked into her cord or woollen skirt. Her clothes were nearly always in the colours that are supposed to flatter her hair colouring, greens and browns and so on. She never wore any make-up, at least to work, and her style might best be described as clean, tidy and sensible. Anthony had worked with her for five years and he knew her well enough to see past her cultivated image of the kind of schoolmistress he remembered from his childhood.

Rosemary's overriding passion was palaeontology and she spent all her holidays with her husband on trips to Lyme Regis, Dob's Linn, Bembridge Maris and similar places on the hunt for plesiosaurs, ammonites, graptolites or ostracods. She was interested in history, not by century but by eon, or at the very least by epochs. Objectively, as she had more than once told Anthony, she regarded humanity's tenure of the earth as a temporary interlude between eras when no self-conscious life roamed the planet. So in the scheme of things, as she saw it, a nuclear holocaust was no worse than any other calamity that might lead to the extinction of our species. However, she did feel considerable sympathy for Patricia and others who might not see matters as clearly as she.

Anthony opened his Home Office directory and turned to the Civil Defence section. There were all the regional government office listings and named directors, together with details of the Civil Defence structure. Many of his colleagues in the Home Office would have been allocated roles in a Britain ravaged by nuclear war and consequently have a place reserved in one of the bunkers scattered throughout the UK. He was not one of them, as the need for immigration controls on a post-apocalyptic island to which there were no flights and few sailings might well be regarded as superfluous. Any border controls needed would be taken over by what remained of the armed services. The fact that all the people listed in the registry would probably survive to govern a totally destroyed Britain after his own demise gave him no comfort whatsoever. He threw the directory into his bottom drawer.

He had been due to have lunch with Ronnie later in the day and wondered if Ronnie would be tied up or even still in London. He asked the switchboard for an outside line and rang him. Ronnie sounded his usual cheerful and relaxed self. He said there was nothing going on that couldn't spare him for an hour and would be glad to see Tony at their usual lunch venue.

Anthony arrived a couple of minutes early, but Ronnie was already there, sitting on a red leather banquette and halfway through a pint of beer. He looked up from his newspaper and took off his glasses when he saw Anthony. They shook hands warmly.

Neither was very hungry, and they had a mainly liquid lunch with just a starter from the menu. They went through the motions of talking briefly about other things before being drawn inevitably to the Cuban crisis.

"It is a very tricky situation," said Ronnie. "Macmillan and de Gaulle are, shall we say, giving Kennedy restraining support, but the hawks in the US would've bombed Cuba already if they'd had their way. They don't seem to realise that being quick on the draw was all very well in the Wild West but not much use if your rival still has four minutes to shoot a 1.6 megaton hydrogen bomb after you pull the trigger. I know I keep saying that we must assume everyone will see sense, but at the moment it's all rather dicey. It's the old story that events can have a momentum all of their own and no one at the present time appears to have the will to stop them. What makes matters worse in the age of nuclear weapons is that the military on both sides are leaning towards a pre-emptive strike in case they are too flattened to retaliate if the other side attacks first."

"The Americans wouldn't act without our approval, surely?" said Anthony.

Ronnie looked at him quizzically. "Does a boxer look for approval from his seconds before he lands an uppercut? The best we can hope for is that Kennedy tells Macmillan what he will do in advance of doing it. Trouble is, that might not be enough notice to get Lady Dorothy out of harm's way, let alone the rest of us."

Anthony fell silent for a while, then he finished off another Scotch on the rocks and signalled to the waiter for a further round. "One of my colleagues, Freddie Pilling, told me that Civil Defence capabilities aren't being mobilised for fear of panic."

Ronnie nodded. "Probably a wise move; what could they do anyway with a full-scale nuclear attack? What could they have done in Nagasaki?"

"Freddie was talking about stocking up the cellar and that kind of thing."

"Waste of time, all this sleeping under the stairs and facing away from the blast nonsense. If the two big boys cock it up, the Russians will hit us first, and London and all the major cities will be toast. Somewhere like the Hebrides will be your best chance, but then it depends how much nuclear dust is flying about. Take your pick; a quick death in London or a slow one in Lewis. I've made my choice."

"What about Jane and the children?"

"I can't leave London and Jane won't leave without me. The children will stay with Jane; I can't get her to change her mind. I've got a ticket for a bunker, but I doubt I'd use it if the time came."

After finishing lunch with one more drink, Anthony walked slowly back to his office. He was already twenty minutes late but wasn't in the least bothered about it. Compared to what was imminently facing humanity, a concern about punctuality was barely more important than deciding what tie to wear in the morning. He wished he could share Ronnie's attitude of cheerful resignation. Walking into the foyer, he showed his pass to the doorkeeper on duty.

"There's a letter for you here, Mr Fernard; I hope I don't have to remind you about private mail?"

"Thanks, Bill; sorry, I've no idea what this is about." He took a letter addressed to him and marked PRIVATE & CONFIDENTIAL. Without reading it, he went up to his office.

"I'm sorry I'm late back," he said to Daphne Raynott. "I had lunch with a friend from the Ministry of Defence and he was updating me on the Cuban situation, without going into security matters of course."

"Anything I should know?" asked Daphne casually, as if it didn't really matter to her.

Anthony was aware that all ears in the office were now trained on him. "Not much to add to the reports we get in the papers. All he'd say is that negotiations are ongoing and that he thinks that common sense will prevail. There's no real news."

Anthony went to his seat, noticing that neither Rosemary nor Patricia were at their desks, and opened the envelope with a ruler. It contained a handwritten letter:

Dear Mr Fernard,

I am writing to thank you personally for your kind consent to allow my younger brother to stay in England. It means so much to my family to be reunited at last.

I do hope you will not be offended when I ask you to accept the enclosed small gift in grateful thanks for your generosity of spirit.

Yours sincerely,

Wicus Cavalir (Lt. Col. Retd.)

Inside the envelope was a cheque for £100 drawn on Martins Bank in the account of WS Cavalir Esq. Anthony stared at the cheque for a minute and then put the envelope in his top drawer. In his mind he revisited that course on security during the first weeks of his service. Much of it had been spent emphasising the need to be on one's guard against the methods by which foreign agents sought to recruit British officials into their espionage web. Principally these were socialising, bribery, blackmail and entrapment. Could this be an attempt at entrapment of some kind?

He recalled the Cavalir case which had appeared on his desk about a month ago. He remembered it well, because he had thought at the time what an appropriate name for a former Polish cavalry officer Cavalir was. It was a familiar story; as a young captain, Cavalir had escaped from Poland in 1939 after the invasion of his country by Germany and then the Soviet Union. After a long trek across Europe, he joined the Free Polish forces attached to the British army and had served with distinction in Italy. His wife had joined him in Britain some years ago and last month his younger brother, who was in poor health, had sought a visa to join him in Britain. Anthony was not absolutely sure that this was a valid application and knew he should make a recommendation to

Daphne and let her decide. But he had felt sorry for the man, who had no other family. Unmarried and with no dependants, he would not later be applying for an extended family to join him. Anthony thought that, despite custom and practice, the man should be allowed to come to Britain. He had therefore taken the decision to grant the visa.

Anthony stared at the letter, searching for clues. Was this an enticement? Given his background, was Cavalir likely to be an agent for the Russians or anybody else? In any case, Anthony was required to report an offer of money or any other gift to his superiors and the security services would be able to follow this up. So how would this ploy be of benefit to Cavalir if he was up to no good?

He couldn't make up his mind what to do. He opened the drawer a little and looked at the envelope. *If only I knew,* he thought. His internal debate was interrupted by the sound of laughter as Rosemary and Patricia burst into the office. Rosemary's face was slightly flushed, while Patricia's was positively rubicund. Arm in arm, they meandered across the floor and lurched into their chairs, giggling as they did so.

All ten of the other people in the room stared in silence for a few seconds and then the gaze of nine of them shifted slowly in the direction of Daphne Raynott.

Daphne watched as Rosemary cleared her throat, shook her head and began to look through one of her files. Meanwhile, Patricia, after giggling again for a moment or two, placed her arms on her desk and rested her head on them.

"Could I have a word, Rosemary?" said Daphne.

Rosemary rose gingerly to her feet and walked slowly in a stately fashion to Daphne's desk, slumping in the chair beside it.

Daphne spoke quietly, but those of her colleagues in the immediate vicinity could make out the gist of what she was saying. She was pronouncing a judgement rather than having a conversation.

"What do you mean by coming back from lunch, not only late, but in an inebriated state? I would speak to Patricia too, but she is in no condition for me to do so at the moment. I hold you partly responsible for her condition as the more senior member of staff and the instigator of this unacceptable behaviour."

It was true that Rosemary had suggested, in Daphne's hearing, that she and Patricia go out for lunch 'for a change'.

"I was just trying to cheer her up. She was very upset by all this missile business and I thought a drink or two would help her put things in perspective." Rosemary's speech was slightly slurred and a little slow, but she was perfectly intelligible.

"Well, perhaps a drink or two under the circumstances, but Patricia looks as if she has had rather more than that."

Both of them glanced in the direction of the prone form of Patricia, from which emanated a rudimentary snoring sound.

"We didn't have that much; it's just that we couldn't face anything to eat and Patricia isn't used to alcohol. I'm sure we'll both be fine after a cup of tea and something to eat. I'm sorry, Miss Raynott."

Daphne nodded and her tone softened. "Well, I'll let it pass just this once, but I won't be able to be so lenient if it happens again."

"Thank you, Miss Raynott," said the rapidly sobering Rosemary.

While this mild disciplinary procedure was taking place, Anthony opened the desk drawer and looked at the cheque again. He could do a lot with a £100: sort the car out, perhaps pay off the HP on the new carpet, manage his more demanding social life. He convinced himself this wasn't an attempt at entrapment. Perhaps he had exceeded his power of discretion a little, but he hadn't actually broken any written rules, so how could he be blackmailed? Of course, he should surrender any gifts he received to the Staff Office for their consideration, but it was just a thank you. He doubted that anyone would declare a free lunch or a bottle of whisky, and this was not that different. He stared and stared at the cheque while Daphne and Rosemary's conversation faded from his consciousness.

Sod it, he thought. He looked at the clock; the banks were still open. He put the cheque in his pocket and walked past Rosemary and Daphne, still deep in conversation, out of the office and down the stairs out into High Holborn. By the time he was in the street, he was not so sure about his original idea to pay the cheque into his current account. He thought it might be less likely to be scrutinised if it went into his savings account. He didn't have his savings account book with him, but the cashier in the bank updated the ledger and gave him a receipt to keep with his book. Then Anthony went back to work. His brief absence was barely noticed.

When Anthony got home that evening he waited until the children had gone to bed, then told Ruth about the Cuban Missile Crisis and how potentially serious the situation had become.

"In all probability, things will calm down; I can't believe that either the Americans or the Russians are that stupid. But I think it would be a good idea if you and the children left London for a few days to avoid getting caught up in any exercises or drills or that kind of thing."

Ruth frowned. "Do you really think we should leave London? I'll have to rearrange a couple of things."

"I know I'm being ultra-cautious, but Laurence is on half-term, so why not take a few days off and go and stay with your parents, just until things settle down?"

"What about you?"

Anthony said the first thing that came into his head. "I'll be fine. If there is a test or an alert while I'm working, I'm sure to be given a place in one of the staff quarters in London." He smiled and nodded encouragingly.

So Ruth telephoned her friends to change the planned day out with the children, then rang her parents and arranged to go down to Rottingdean in Sussex the following morning. Due to the unreliability of the car, she decided to go by train. The whole family travelled to London together and when they got to Holborn, Anthony put them in a taxi to Victoria. Ruth's father would meet them at Brighton station.

"You *will* be all right?" said Ruth as she kissed him.

"Don't worry. If I'm not at home when you call, I shall probably be held up or working late. Nothing will happen and I'll see you in a couple of days."

VI

Carrie had sent Anthony a couple of complimentary tickets for *The Secret Garden,* which was performed in the theatre of a secondary school in Earl's Court. He attended, as he'd promised he would, and before the performance left a note for her at the makeshift stage door, saying that he would wait for her there after the show was over.

Anthony took his seat in an auditorium that also doubled as a gym. The hard chairs were distributed over the wooden floor, which was painted with the lines of netball and badminton courts. There was no proper rake and visibility could have been better, but Anthony's height enabled him to see comfortably over the row in front of him. Despite the fact that the windows had been open for some hours, the theatre still bore the residue of the stale, slightly damp smells from its previous activities during the day. He didn't care. This may not be the Theatre Royal Haymarket, but he wouldn't care if it was a Nissen hut in a graveyard to see Carrie on the stage.

Carrie had a leading role as Martha the maid, and when she came on stage she looked first in Anthony's direction. Anthony couldn't take his eyes off her while she was on stage and he indulged the freedom to stare at her for as long as he wished without her becoming self-conscious. The accent she adopted for the part did nothing to affect the clarity of her voice and her sweet tone was not lost in the greater projection she employed. Anthony clapped as loudly as he could at the end, not just because he wanted to support Carrie, but also because he had loved her performance.

Afterwards, he hung around in the foyer for ten minutes then went round to the side door, temporarily labelled 'stage door'. After a little while she appeared, her eyes searching for him. Then she smiled and gave a little wave.

"Sorry to keep you waiting, I got caught up in a conversation with the stage manager. Did you enjoy it?" Carrie asked.

He hugged her. "Yes, it was great and you were wonderful." She had no make-up on and he thought he'd never seen her look so young.

She smiled and squeezed his hand. "I'm glad you could make it. We usually go for a quick drink after the show; you'll come, won't you?"

"Yes, I'd like to very much."

"The pub is just down the street; it isn't far. Most of the others will be there already." She took his hand as they walked.

"It was very well done," said Anthony. "So professional, but all that work for just three evenings and a matinée."

"We all enjoy it," she said. "Personally, the short run suits me; I wouldn't want to do it every evening for weeks. It's getting chilly, isn't it?" She took his arm and pressed herself closer to him as the cool of the evening began to penetrate her coat.

The large Victorian pub was stuffy and crowded, and Carrie led Anthony through the crush into a corner of the saloon bar where a dozen people, some he recognised from the stage, were already ensconced.

"Carrie, hello!" one of them, a middle-aged man dressed in a sports jacket and colourful cravat, called out. "Well done, my love, lines perfectly delivered as usual. It couldn't have been better. What are you having?"

"Thanks, Ralph, but that's because everyone else was spot on too. I'll have a Bacardi and Coke, please. This is a friend of mine, Anthony Fernard. Anthony, this is Ralph, our director."

"Pleased to meet you, Anthony," said Ralph, extending a hand. "What can I get you?"

"Hello," said Anthony. "That's very kind of you, I'd like a..." he looked at the beer pumps at the bar, "pint of Courage, please."

"Did you like the show?" asked Ralph, lighting a cigarette and placing it in a short, ivory cigarette holder.

"Yes, I did. The whole production was excellent; congratulations on a really enjoyable evening."

Ralph beamed. "Well, thank you very much, nice of you to say so. The cast and crew all worked very hard. Wasn't Carrie absolutely splendid?"

Anthony nodded. "I thought she was wonderful."

"He's as smitten as I am, Carrie, I'll have to watch him," said Ralph, waving a pound note at the barmaid.

Carrie smiled at Anthony. "Let me introduce you to the others," she said and gestured towards the people in their group. She reeled off half a dozen names, all of which Anthony instantly forgot, half of them actors from the play and the others she introduced as 'backstage on this occasion'.

One of them, a tall, handsome woman of about fifty who had played Mrs Medlock, smiled and offered her hand. "So you're Anthony, how nice to meet you. Carrie said you would be coming tonight. You're something to do with the Home Office, I believe." She spoke with that cultivated accent perfected by British actresses of the 1950s.

"Yes, that's right."

The woman took a packet of Du Maurier from her handbag and raised the lid for him to take one.

"Thank you," said Anthony. "Very appropriate for the theatre," he added, as he raised his lighter to her cigarette.

She smiled. "Thanks," she said, taking a light and blowing her smoke into the air while holding her cigarette aloft, away from them both. "Have you worked there very long?"

"About eight years."

"I have a friend who works at the Home Office; something to do with children. Her name is Blanche Foster, I don't suppose you know her?"

"No, I'm in the Immigration Department so I wouldn't have come across her. What do you do?"

"I'm the secretary to one of the directors at ICI. I worked there before I had the children and they let me come back when I wanted to; what I lack in youth I make up for in experience." She smiled, but then her expression became serious. "Bit of a worry about this Cuba business. I know it's not your department, but I hope you can reassure us that we won't all be blown to kingdom come."

Here we go again; everyone wants my reassurance, he thought. He nodded. "I hope so too. I'm sure it's just a bit of posturing and good sense will prevail; I think we can be confident that there's nothing to worry about." He was beginning to think that people were casting him in the role of Julian of Norwich, going round saying 'All shall be well, and all shall be well and all manner of thing shall be well'.

"If he's wrong, we won't have much time to fret about it, Helen," said a man about Anthony's age, squeezing past Ralph to join their conversation. Carrie had introduced this man to Anthony as having something to do with the scenery.

"Four-minute warning," said Helen. "Doesn't give you a lot of time to do anything. What would you do, Rod?"

"Four minutes, just about time for a fag and a very big drink," he said. "What about you, Helen?"

"Hmm, depends where you are when it happens. Not many options if you find yourself alone in a lift. If I was at home, there wouldn't even be enough time for a bath. I suppose I'd sit at my dressing table and make myself up to look as good as I could for my final bow."

This little game had attracted the interest of other members of their group. A man with thinning fair hair, whom Anthony had last seen wearing a dark wig and acting the part of Archibald Craven, said, "I'd grab hold of the first available girl, and you know what."

"The first available girl who is willing, I hope," said Helen.

"And what would you do for the other three minutes and fifty seconds, Les?" asked Carrie, which made even Les laugh.

"Your turn, Carrie," said Ralph.

"Mm, it gets harder when all the obvious options are gone. I think I'd do something illegal, as I'd never have to worry about being caught and it wouldn't matter anyway. Perhaps I'd do a smash and grab at a jeweller's and wait to be vaporised wearing a diamond tiara."

"What about you, Ralph?" asked Helen.

Ralph laughed. "Well, quite easy for me, really. I'd feed the cat so that he was busy when it happened and then, with a minute to go, I'd climb up onto the roof and face the direction it would come from and wait to be obliterated and become pan-cosmic. That's always been my ambition for the end; be like that chap in Hiroshima whose shadow is still on the step of the bank even though he was blown to nothing by that first atomic hit. So much better than ending up drooling in an old people's home or dying slowly of some bloody awful condition."

"I'll drink to that," said Helen, raising her glass to him.

Nobody laughed or came up with any more ideas. After a pause, the conversation turned to other subjects, chiefly connected with the theatre production or their plans for the weekend.

By their light-hearted enthusiasm for the 'four-minute game', Anthony surmised that most of them didn't really believe it was going to happen. Maybe some of them were covering their fear well with the sort of dark humour of the Blitz; after all, they were all quite good at acting. Perhaps that was what he was doing too. He bought a round for those standing around him and had an interesting and informative conversation with Rod about producing and setting up stage scenery. Before long, the bell was rung for drinking-up time and the pub began to empty. Some of the theatre group had already gone and Carrie motioned to Anthony that she would like to go.

"Anthony's got a long journey home, so we'd better be off. See you all tomorrow."

With the sound of farewells in their ears, Anthony and Carrie walked from the loud, humid atmosphere of the pub into a clear, quiet night.

Carrie took his arm and said, "It's too cold for a walk, but I'd like to have you to myself for a bit before you go. Perhaps I could come on the tube with you for a few stops?"

"Why don't I go to Barons Court with you?"

"How will you get home? The trains don't run very late."

"There's a train to Chingford at about one o'clock that stops at Wood Street. I can get a taxi to Liverpool Street if necessary, then from Wood Street I can thumb a lift or walk; it's only a mile and a half or so."

Carrie looked sceptical. "But won't your wife wonder where you are?"

"She's staying in Sussex at the moment."

Carrie's expression was transformed from concern to open-mouthed elation, but just for a moment. Then it changed to one of concern. "You sent your family away because it's safer out of London, didn't you? You think we *are* in danger."

Anthony put his arm round her waist. "If I'm honest, I really don't know. Part of me believes the politicians are in control of the situation, but we never know until after the event. I thought I should do something for my children. It probably isn't necessary and in any case I'm not sure that it'll make any difference."

"Why didn't *you* go?"

"You know why. Come on, let me take you home."

They walked to the station and caught a Piccadilly line train almost immediately. It was busy and they stood in the walkway between the rows of seats, one hand on a hanging strap and the other holding onto each other.

When they came out of the station, it took just a couple of minutes to walk to Carrie's flat, one floor of a large four-storey terraced house. Carrie unlocked her door and opened it onto the main room.

"Sorry about the mess," she said as she turned on the light. "I didn't expect you would be coming back here." She swiftly scooped up her breakfast things from the oval dining table and put them on the drainer in the small kitchen off the sitting room.

It was the first time that Anthony had been in the flat. "You have a nice place here," he said.

"It works for me," Carrie said, disappearing into the bedroom for a moment.

Anthony took in his surroundings. This room was perhaps fourteen feet by twelve with sofas, a coffee table and a television near a bay window, while the dining table and chairs were located near the kitchen. The furniture was modern G Plan and the walls, decorated in a soft green and blue wallpaper of irregular shapes, were hung with copies of theatre posters by Toulouse-Lautrec, a reproduction Utrillo and a poster from *Twelfth Night* at the Aldwych. *Dorothy Tutin again,* thought Anthony, looking at the poster and remembering her from *The Devils*. Apart from the kitchen, there were two other doors.

Carrie emerged from the bedroom, leaving the door ajar. "The bathroom is through that door if you want it," she said, pointing to the only closed door, while she busied herself tidying up newspapers and books that were on the dining table. Then she walked over to the tiled fireplace and offered a match to the gas fire in the hearth. With a cough, the fire burst into life.

"Would you like some coffee? I'll put the kettle on. Make yourself at home." She walked out to the kitchen, dragging her scarf off her neck and undoing her dark blue coat.

Anthony took off his overcoat and threw it on a chair, then sat down and looked at the headlines of the newspaper on the coffee table. They were inevitably about the crisis over Cuba and he felt too saturated by it even to scan them.

Carrie came back into the sitting room, sat next to him and entwined her arms with his. "I can't believe I've got you to myself this evening," she said and pulled him towards her.

They kissed for longer and more passionately than they had ever done before; he held her tight and felt her breathing quicken. After a while, they broke away from each other and she went back into the kitchen to make the coffee.

She returned after a few minutes with two cups of coffee and some shortbread biscuits.

"You must be starving," she said and quickly consumed one of the biscuits. "Would you like me to get you something to eat?"

"I had something before I left for the theatre. A biscuit will be fine."

Carrie stood up and went over to her pale blue Dansette record player and put on a Nat King Cole album. The flat was warming up now, and he took off his jacket and put his arm round Carrie as she placed her head on his shoulder.

"You were so good tonight," he said. "Everything was good; it was a classy production. But I thought you were great."

"Thank you," she said, "it meant a lot to me that you came to see it and I'm so glad you liked it. You have made me very happy. Are you sure there is nothing else you want?" She looked at him with her head slightly to one side and that glimmer of a smile that he had grown fond of.

"Nothing, just you."

"I want you too," she said quietly, and she undid his tie and started to undo his shirt buttons.

They were kissing more intensely now, and her hand was wandering over his chest, adeptly slipping inside his shirt.

This is not supposed to be happening; it's not what you said you would do, thought Anthony. *Desire Carrie, but make love to Ruth; that's what you said.* But his body was disagreeing with him and the way they were sitting, he knew that Carrie might be aware of that too.

Sure enough, Carrie was encouraged by the effectiveness of her manual dexterity to undo his belt.

Anthony found his own hand seemingly determined to seek out her waist and then move upwards, and he contemplated calling a halt to it, thinking again of his promise to himself.

Then Carrie said, "Let's go somewhere a bit more comfortable," and Anthony embraced the luxury of acquiescence as she took him by the hand into the bedroom.

They sat on the double bed and resumed their embrace, soon falling back on the sheets. It was more comfortable lying on the bed, but after a minute or so Carrie said, "I had better take my dress off, I mustn't get it too creased, you know," and she winked at him.

She unzipped her dress and took off her stockings and suspender belt before placing them on the chair. She left her slip and other underwear on and came back to the bed. Her arms felt delightfully cool and smooth as he held them while she stood over him, and then she pushed him back on the bed with a laugh and lay next to him.

As he ran his hands over her shoulders and arms, Anthony had a feeling of déjà-vu, as he remembered lying like this with Ruth just before their wedding. They had not consummated their relationship before the marriage, preferring to wait, as was customary, or at least the supposed custom at the time they were wed. However, they had got pretty close to it as the wedding neared and they had spent many afternoons like this, partly undressed, in each other's arms. Anthony was being nostalgic about the early days of a physical relationship and he was basking in the glow of excitement and anticipation of a new love. He was not even thinking about the next step at this moment; he could be content if this was as far as things went.

Actually, it was Carrie who was making the running physically and Anthony was pleased to be led rather than to take the lead as it gave him a kind of exoneration. After they had been lying there for some time kissing and cuddling, Carrie said, "You do find me physically desirable, don't you?"

Anthony was surprised and he pulled back from her so that he could look into her eyes. "Of course I do, I think you are beautiful. I've never known a woman I thought so beautiful or desirable."

"It's just that you said you wanted me, but you haven't shown it very much since we came into the bedroom."

Anthony looked at her earnestly. "I do want you, but I didn't wish to take advantage of you or make you feel you had to do something you'd rather not."

Carrie pulled him to her. "You are silly. I'd always tell you if I wanted you to stop." As a sign of encouragement, she took his hand and placed it on her breast and their petting became more intense as they gradually discarded their clothes.

Seeing her naked for the first time, Anthony thought how much she was like he'd imagined her to be: the slender, long limbs which he already knew; but also the slightly sloping shoulders and smooth neck and chest; the shapely, but not voluptuous figure he'd sketched in his mind. She was perfect.

They explored each other with their hands and mouths, and Anthony was able to think of nothing but the present for the first time for days.

"Come into me," said Carrie, lying over him and guiding him towards her.

"I shouldn't, what if...?"

"I don't care, not now," she said. "This might be the only time."

He could feel the heat of her and knew she was right. Everything else was pointless.

Afterwards, they lay in the bed with the covers over them. Carrie looked at her watch. "It's half-past twelve, I don't think you'll get that train now. You'll have to stay!" she said, exultantly.

Anthony smiled. "It's what I hoped would happen." He felt stupidly happy and, as she cuddled up to him, he broke another of his self-imposed rules and blurted out, "I love you."

"I know," she kissed him. "Let's have a drink to celebrate."

"Celebrate what?"

"Everything about us." She jumped out of bed and shivered but didn't bother to put anything on.

She came back a few minutes later with a bottle of gin and another of tonic, with a couple of glasses. "The tonic's probably flat, but it'll do and I'm afraid I've got no lemons or ice." She poured them both a drink and they chinked glasses and drank to each other.

The following morning, Anthony awoke alone in the bed. He looked over at the clock. It was half-past eight. He went to leap out of the bed, late for work, then remembered it was Saturday. He lay on his back and rubbed his eyes. He could hear noises, domestic noises, from somewhere beyond this room: a kettle whistling, toast popping, crockery banging as it was moved around. His eyes scanned the room for his clothes and he spotted his underpants on the floor. As his hand reached out for them Carrie came into the room, wearing a tartan dressing gown with a cord tie.

"Don't get dressed yet," she said. "I'll bring you breakfast in bed; but don't get excited, it's only tea and toast." She beamed at him. "Did you sleep well?"

"Like a log."

"Me too. Sit up."

She walked over to the bed and put her pillow behind his head, then kissed him and stood back. "I like the hair on your chest, nice pattern and perfectly symmetrical. It's darker than the hair on your head, nearly black." She nodded as if pleased with her analysis and went back to the kitchen.

A few minutes later, she returned with a tray on which were two mugs of tea, some buttered toast, marmalade, a bowl of sugar and a knife. She placed the tray on the bed and sat diagonally to Anthony while they had breakfast.

"What are your plans today?" she asked him.

"I hadn't really thought about it. I guess I'll have to go home and keep in touch with events. Ruth may be trying to phone me too. What about you?"

"What I'd *like* to do is to stay here with you, but I know you've got to go. In any case, I have a matinée this afternoon and the performance tonight."

"What time's the matinée?"

"Three."

"We don't have to rush too much then," he said, taking a piece of triangular cut toast and spreading marmalade on it.

Carrie smiled. "We have time enough," she said. "I listened to the news; nobody has backed down yet. It's very scary, isn't it?"

"Yes, it is, there's no point in denying it. Fortunately, most people don't seem too frightened by events; they have faith in their leaders to find a solution. In a way, they're right; there's no point in worrying about something that's beyond our ability to do anything about. It's like when we get in a car; there's always the possibility that we'll be killed in a crash, but we choose to assume it'll be all right."

"But sometimes it isn't all right."

He nodded. "That's why we have to live in the present. Carpe diem and all that," he said.

They finished their breakfast and Carrie took the plates, put them on the tray and placed the tray on her bedside cabinet. Then she took off her dressing gown, revealing her nakedness. She stood still for a moment and then climbed into the bed.

At about ten-thirty, Carrie got up again and went to the bathroom. Anthony lay still, listening to the water filling the bath and almost drowning out Carrie whistling a tune he didn't recognise.

She came back a few minutes later. "If you'd like a bath, you can go first, but save the water for me. I'll make some coffee."

Anthony felt oddly flattered by her gesture of granting him the intimacy of sharing her bathwater first and a few minutes later he was lying in a three-quarter length cream bath, his head against the rim and his knees sticking out of the water.

Later they had coffee and a piece of walnut and coffee cake together, which he thought another surprisingly intimate moment, before he made his way home.

She walked with him to the station. "You'll let me know if anything happens and you have to leave London or something like that won't you? Just let me know that you're all right."

"I'll be fine, so don't give it a thought. This time next week we'll all be laughing at ourselves for taking things too seriously."

They kissed, affectionately rather than passionately, as they parted. She clung to him for a moment before letting him go.

When he entered the station, Anthony saw a number of people heading for the District line and inviting others to join them for a sit-in at Whitehall. He was about to go towards the Piccadilly line platforms but on impulse he joined those going to Westminster. On arrival at the station, they poured out and walked, almost marched, to Whitehall. He hung at the back, behind the main body of the crowd; not quite part of it.

There, surrounded by the grand government buildings of Britain's imperial past and watched over by the Cenotaph and the statues of field marshals and generals, the marchers sat down. They joined rows of silent men and women, mostly young but of all ages, sitting down, being removed by police and then queuing to sit down again. Anthony guessed from their college scarves and studied, serious looks that many were university students, but there were others: older men in suits, some wearing clerical collars; women in scarves or hats and topcoats, some young ones dressed in the all-black style of Juliette Gréco; even a few men in donkey jackets or leather bomber jackets. Some had CND banners or placards opposed to war, but most did not; their own presence spoke for itself.

Anthony stood on the pavement and watched them for some time, admiring their quiet dignity and silently wishing them well. None resisted the police, who, for the most part, seemed in good humour and benevolent in the way they went about their job. He was not tempted to join them, as ultimately it was only a gesture; they could not change events in Whitehall because the politicians and civil servants watching from the windows had no power to change events. The decisions were being made elsewhere.

After ten minutes or so, feeling there was nothing more he could or wanted to do, he returned to the tube station. He took the train as far as Tower Bridge, where he got off and stared for a moment at the Tower of London, with its crowds of tourists being shepherded around by the Yeoman Warders, before heading for Aldgate High Street. As he passed the old Hoop and Grapes pub with its slightly wonky door, his mind went back to the Tower. *A Norman fortress and the pub which survived the Great Fire of London; all those years here and neither of them would have a chance if the worst happened,* he thought. Then he pushed on up Houndsditch, past the Houndsditch Warehouse, which was doing its usual busy trade, and on to Liverpool Street and the Central line for home.

Anthony looked round the busy station concourse at the mass of people pre-occupied with the destination boards and timetables or waiting patiently, sometimes impatiently, for their train. He suspected that a casual visitor who'd been away from civilisation for a week would be surprised to learn that we were in the middle of an existential crisis. Indeed, an existentialist would be proud of their behaviour; aware of the absurdity of their situation but nonetheless continuing to give it meaning by their actions. If further confirmation of this was needed it awaited him at Woodford station. Once again, there were crowds, smaller this time. These were Leyton Orient supporters, cheerfully enjoying to the full their first-ever season in the top flight of English football as they boarded the train for Leyton and a day of destiny with a home match against the mighty Tottenham Hotspur.

When he arrived home, he chatted for a few minutes with his next-door neighbour who was cutting back the roses in his front garden. They talked of the weather and tidying up the garden for the winter. It was just like any other day in late October.

He opened the front door, bent down to pick up the newspaper and post, and went to telephone Ruth at her parents'. It was answered almost immediately by the instantly recognisable upbeat voice of his father-in-law.

"Hello, Alec, it's Tony."

"Hello, Tony, glad you called. How are you? I expect you must be very busy. Ruth tried to phone you a couple of times last night, but you weren't in."

"Yes, I've just come back from Whitehall. Things are hectic at the moment."

"They must be; your department would be at the centre of things if the worst happened. I know you can't tell me too much, but I hope tensions are calming down a bit."

"No news is good news at the moment; things will be resolved this weekend, I'm sure."

"That's good to hear," said Alec. "I'll get Ruth."

A couple of minutes later Ruth came to the telephone. "Hello, Tony, everything OK?"

"I'm all right. I guess the boys are enjoying their little holiday. How are you?"

"Worried about you, principally. Where were you last night?"

"I was working late and stayed up in London. I've been in Whitehall today; it's all rather high-pressured."

"Why are *you* having to do so much, surely you're not senior enough to be involved in making any big planning decisions?"

Anthony laughed. "You're right about that, but it's all hands to the pump at the moment in case emergency procedures have to be put into effect."

Ruth snorted and sounded sceptical. "Well, you can't work all hours; you need *some* rest."

"I have this afternoon off and I won't be going in tomorrow."

"Is it as bad as you thought?"

"It's difficult, but I think we'll be all right. They'll sort it out this weekend."

"No chance of you coming down here today?"

Anthony thought the suggestion over for a moment. "I like the idea of it, but I really think I should stay here. Just in case I'm required."

"Well, make sure you get some rest today and look after yourself," said Ruth.

"You too, and don't worry. Kiss the boys for me."

When he put the phone down, Anthony thought again about joining his family and at first couldn't answer the question, *Why don't I want to go?* But then he realised. If he went to Sussex, it might be that he would be with his family when they were destroyed, but if he stayed here, he would always have the hope that they made it, even if he didn't.

These morose thoughts were given more substance by developments later that day. Listening to the radio, Anthony learned that evening that, while Kennedy and his advisors were discussing the crisis, a U-2 aircraft was shot down over Cuba and the pilot of the spy plane was killed. Sitting in the silent house, he heard himself speak out loud as he tried to calculate how the Americans would react. It was difficult to avoid the conclusion that, if they made a military response, it might be impossible to stop a process of retaliation and counter-retaliation. He now kept the radio tuned to the Home Service and left it on all the time. Every so often he would listen avidly to the news bulletins as they came through. He also watched the news on the television and read again through the newspapers he had bought at the station. Disheartened by repetitive updates of the current situation, he thought for the first time that a nuclear war between the superpowers was a probability. If he went to bed, would he be woken by the four-minute warning or not wake up at all? With all the complications of his personal life and uncertainty as to how he would sort it out, the thought of not waking up the next morning seemed, for a moment, but just for a moment, not such a terrible possibility.

To fill his time, and hopefully his mind, he got out his stamp album for airmail issues and went through the mechanisms of his neglected hobby: soaking the stamps off their envelopes and drying them on blotting paper, checking them for watermarks and other features against the catalogue, using stamp hinges to stick them in the album. He drank a few glasses of Scotch from the bottle he'd bought last Christmas and seldom touched since.

Despite not wanting sleep, he eventually relented and went to bed at about midnight, retuning the radio to the World Service. Much to his surprise, he went straight off while listening to the radio and when he woke in the morning, the BBC was still broadcasting the regular programmes. He listened for a few minutes about the economic issues facing rubber plantations in Malaya and then got up. He pulled back the curtains on a bright morning and instinctively felt positive about the day. The lack of news meant that the superpowers were still talking and there was therefore hope, even if they were staring at each other across a bottomless pit.

His optimism was justified as, over the course of the day, the news bulletins revealed that the crisis had so much evaporated that it was pretty well over. The BBC reported that the Soviet Union had backed down and that Khrushchev had agreed to remove the Soviet missiles in Cuba in return for a pledge that the United States would not invade Cuba.

Thank God for Khrushchev, thought Anthony. Listening to those commenting on the turn of events, he found the smug satisfaction with which some of them greeted the outcome distastefully triumphant; one side had backed down so the other side must have won. The senseless chatter of people wise after the event finally drove him to get up and he went down to the kitchen feeling rather hungry, in fact very hungry when he realised he hadn't eaten anything much the previous day. He soon rustled up a breakfast of bacon, egg, tomatoes and fried bread with a mug of tea, all of which he consumed with gusto.

About half-past ten the phone rang; it was Ruth.

"What a relief," she said. "I suppose you knew last night."

"No, I heard about it from the news programmes, the same as you."

"I didn't sleep a wink. Anyway, you were right, they did see sense. Weird isn't it; one minute the world's coming to an end and the next everything is pretty well back to normal? We'll be getting a train soon; I don't see any point staying down here now and Laurence has school tomorrow. I'll get a taxi at Victoria; can you meet me at the station?"

"Of course, I can come to London if you like."

"There's no need, it's only one suitcase and I can manage that. See you later."

"What shall we do about food? I know; we'll have lunch out as a treat."

"Are you sure, I thought you said money was a bit tight this month?"

"I think we can push the boat out a little; we've got something to celebrate after all."

"Yes. Well, I certainly don't fancy having to cook so that would be lovely. I'll call you when I get to Victoria to give you an idea when to expect us. See you soon, bye."

"Bye," said Anthony.

He had barely replaced the receiver when he picked it up again and phoned Carrie.

She answered on the fifth ring, sounding a bit sleepy. "Hello, Empress 6120?"

"It's Tony, how are you?"

"Oh, hello, Tony, not too bad, I've just got up."

"Sorry, would you like me to call back later?"

"No, it's all right; I'm glad you called. As it was our final performance last night we had a party afterwards; I drank too much and didn't get to bed until two-thirty. I had the falling bed and spinning room combination, but I'm OK now, just a monster of a headache. How are you?"

"I'm all right, thanks, I slept well and ate a hearty breakfast."

"Like the condemned man? Is there any news? Obviously we're all still here."

"Yes, they seem to have sorted it out."

"You were right when you said they would. I didn't think too much about it after you left yesterday morning. I suppose I'm an optimist, or perhaps I was in too good a mood to worry about the end of the world."

"How did the performances go yesterday?"

"Really well, thank you. Both a sell out and we all had a great time."

"I'll let you get some rest and get rid of the bad head. It was great on Friday night; I mean after the show."

"Yes, for me too; will I see you this coming week?"
"I hope so, I'll give you a ring."
"OK, see you soon," and she put the phone down.

VII

The atmosphere at work the next morning was back to its usual placid state after the excitement of the previous week. Following the scenes on Tuesday with Freddie holding forth and the subsequent drinking session of Rosemary and Patricia, Daphne and the other section head jointly forbade any further discussion of the political situation in the working day. A strange, heavy silence had fallen on the room ever since.

As it happened, it had been what people wanted. Everything to be said had been said, the various potential scenarios had been thrashed out several times and the worries had been explored ad nauseam. It was just a case of waiting for the drama to play out and, as much as possible, carrying on with life as normal.

So, on this last Monday morning in October there was a sense of calm and tranquillity at work. Most people were just grateful that the worst had not happened, aware that the final decisive step had been a walk away from the brink. Apart from expressing a wish that such a situation should not be allowed to occur again, they were happy to drop the subject. No one could be bothered to discuss in detail the fact that the two sides had made an agreement to stand down, any more than one would wish to discuss at length the fact that a car crash had been avoided or a broken ankle had turned out to be a strain. The only exception was Freddie Pilling, who was willing to explain how he thought the crisis had been averted to anyone who wanted to listen. No one did.

While not wishing to discuss the end of the crisis in the office, Anthony would have liked to follow up his conversations on the subject with Ronnie Benson to find out exactly what had happened to defuse the situation. He was therefore pleased when his old friend invited him to what he termed a 'debriefing/un-post-apocalyptic lunch' at Rules restaurant. He thought he probably couldn't afford it, but if this outcome of history wasn't worth marking with something special what would be? So he accepted and asked Daphne for an extended lunch hour which he would make up for at the end of the day. She graciously granted the request and that Thursday they took a table in a quiet corner of the restaurant. Over a lunch of potted shrimps and roast rib of beef, Ronnie updated Anthony on the way the crisis had played out.

"Well," said Anthony, "it hardly seems just over a week since we last met and certainly less than a week since everybody feared the worst. It feels more like a month, in fact sometimes I think I dreamt the whole thing."

"It was real, all right," said Ronnie, "and it was a bloody close-run thing as well, to paraphrase Wellington."

"Thank God that Khrushchev backed down. Had it been up to the Americans, who knows what would have happened?"

"Kennedy backed down as well."

"Did he?" exclaimed Anthony.

"Yes, although that won't come out for a while. Kennedy's not a fool; he knew that any attack on Cuba would not be able to prevent some Russian missiles in Cuba being launched at the United States. Once attacks and counter-attacks started, it would end badly, to say the least. When the U-2 was shot down and he was being urged to retaliate, he said something to the effect that he wasn't worried about stage one of retaliation, but what would stages four or five be like? And there would be no one left to see what happened in stage six."

"Still, by the looks of it, Kennedy was able to keep his own military in check and his blockade of Cuba did the trick. He seems to have got what he wanted peacefully without having to give up anything. I don't quite see how he backed down."

"That's because the whole story hasn't come out yet. As part of the deal, he's agreed to withdraw the American missiles from Turkey in due course. You could argue that the Russians won. Before the missiles were installed in Cuba, the Russians had no strategic missiles on America's borders, but the Americans had missiles in Turkey. After the deal is fully implemented, in about six months or so, the Russians are back where they started in Cuba, but they will have got rid of the missiles aimed at them in Turkey."

"I see what you mean. We never get the full story until a long time after the event," said Anthony, shaking his head and drinking some more of the fine wine Ronnie had ordered with the beef.

Ronnie smiled. "We don't need the full story, because the big story is that we're all still here. With hindsight, it seems obvious that we would find a way out of it, but it didn't seem that straightforward at the time. There were some very sweaty palms at some of the meetings I went to, none more than mine." He signalled to the waiter and pointed to their empty jug of water.

"It must have been quite something to be part of all this, even if Britain was only on the sidelines."

"Well, we were on the sidelines as far as negotiations went, but we were *fully* involved in the planning for a war. The V bombers were on standby and were not far from taking up their strategic deployment positions. We would have been involved in delivering the carnage as well as copping it."

"I don't suppose anyone will receive public appreciation for what you did in the department, but I hope it helps with your career prospects, perhaps promotion or something."

"It's nice of you to say so, but I didn't do much as an individual. Anyway, however useful I was won't count for much. You know as well as I do what it's like being in the Executive Class; we're there to implement the policies but not to make them. We're the prison governors, colonial administrators, tax officers, etc.; those who deal with actual cases and clear up the mess of half-baked, ill-thought-out initiatives. We won't be asked for our views on policy and if we offer them, they'll probably be ignored. In the rare cases where they do adopt our suggestions, our superiors will then take the credit themselves."

Anthony laughed. "It must be frustrating for you; I never get near enough to serious policy-making to be bothered by it."

"I probably sound bitter, but I don't mind really, it's the system or the structure or whatever; it's just the way it is."

Anthony had heard these grumbles from Ronnie before but never delivered with quite as much feeling.

"It's a pity, though, Ronnie. Why didn't you ever go for the Administrative Class, take the exams and become one of them? We had a chap in my department who did just that."

Ronnie smiled. "I did think about it several times, but I don't know; I'm a bit too long in the tooth to start as a junior again. I think I'm happier being a big fish in a small stream with the occasional foray over the rapids, like I had this past week. Talking about people in the Administrative Class, did you ever give Malcolm a ring?"

Anthony shook his head. "No, I haven't got round to it yet, with all that's been going on. I'll try to get in touch this week."

"That's good of you, thanks, Tony. Perhaps all three of us could get together sometime. How's the family?"

"Fine, thanks, looking forward to next week."

"Next week? Ah, yes, mine too. Look, I've got to go. I'll get this."

"Ronnie, I couldn't possibly."

"No really, I did pick up some unusually generous expenses over the last couple of weeks. You can get it next time."

VIII

November began very well for Anthony. With his gift from Cavalir, which he thought of as a windfall, he was able to book his car in for a long-overdue service and buy a new tyre. He also paid one or two outstanding bills and bought a large box of Brock's fireworks to celebrate Guy Fawkes Night. In the cause of enterprise, he helped Laurence to make a guy so that his son could seek to raise a few extra shillings to buy sparklers and bangers for the big night the following Monday.

Ruth had not been too surprised that Anthony had found the money to pay for the car to be serviced. She put it down to his salary coming through. But the extravagance of a quite expensive box of fireworks coupled with his lack of hesitation in taking them all to a nice restaurant for lunch the previous Sunday did worry her a little, because Anthony was not usually careless with money. She didn't say anything until Guy Fawkes Night.

This was just the second time they had celebrated Bonfire Night as a family, Jonathan only being old enough to fully enjoy it at last year's more modest celebration. The boys were very excited about it and had been looking forward to it impatiently for a couple of weeks. Laurence had raised about 2/6 from standing outside the house with his guy or walking up to the station with his friends. He'd bought some penny and tuppenny bangers from the local newsagent as well as a couple of packets of sparklers. Both he and Jonathan were wearing Guy Fawkes masks and were marching around the kitchen, chanting, "Remember, remember, the fifth of November, gunpowder, treason and plot."

Actually, that was what Laurence was chanting. Jonathan's version ended 'gunpowder, reason and plop' as Laurence was quick to remark, with a giggle.

"Shush now boys," said Ruth. "Be careful of the hot plates. We'll be starting soon; come on, let's put your coats on."

"Help me take the fireworks out to the garden," said Anthony, once the boys were dressed for the outside.

The boys carried the smaller fireworks ceremoniously out to the garden while Anthony carried the large box and a couple of other special fireworks he'd bought.

"What does that mean, Dad: 'gunpowder, treason and plot'?" asked Laurence as Anthony sorted out the fireworks on a dry plastic sheet.

"You know what gunpowder is, don't you?"

"Yes, it's the stuff they sprinkle on the ground then set fire to and it burns along the line until it blows up the dynamite."

"Right, so the gunpowder is a kind of explosive and on the fifth of November about 350 years ago, some bad men wanted to blow up the king and all the people who worked with him, using gunpowder. A plot is a secret plan to do something bad and treason is a plot against the king. So, there you are: 'gunpowder, treason and plot.'"

"Did they kill the king?"

"No, somebody found the gunpowder and saved the day."

"Like in the cowboy films when somebody kicks earth on the gunpowder and puts the flame out before it blows up the dynamite?"

"Yes, like that. Now, let's put this firework up." Anthony walked over to a pear tree halfway down the garden and nailed a Catherine wheel to the trunk.

"Why did you put that firework on the tree, Daddy?" asked Jonathan.

"When we set light to it, the firework should spin round and it works better like that because it's more fun to watch."

Anthony looked at the other fireworks and assembled the rest of his equipment: matches and the fuse from the box, gloves for the boys, milk bottles for the rockets, an old Christmas tree holder packed with earth for the large Roman Candle, and the 'bazooka'. Finally, he set up a makeshift ramp for the aeroplane firework.

Ruth had made some sausage rolls and mince pies and had put some smallish potatoes in foil under the bonfire to see if they were a success later. She had also bought toffee apples as a treat. She carried them out into the garden with hot cocoa for the boys and coffee for herself and Anthony.

"I've put a little Scotch in the coffee," she whispered as she passed a cup to Anthony. "It's a grim night."

Anthony looked up at the sky. There wasn't a star to be seen and, though not raining, the air felt damp and was doing its best to drizzle. Anthony took a bite from a sausage roll and a gulp of the fortified coffee. "Right, let's start," he said and set light to the paper at the bottom of the bonfire, on which was perched Laurence's guy, resplendent in an old blue pullover of Anthony's and a pair of Laurence's cast-off pyjamas.

The boys cheered as Anthony lit a couple of rockets, which burst into coloured stars as they reached their apogee. Then, as his father had done when Anthony was a boy, he set light to three bangers, one after another, holding each in his hand for a couple of seconds so they went bang when he threw them in the air. With the cheers of the boys and the alarms of Ruth ringing in his ears, Anthony now set light to the Catherine wheel and, as usual, had to prod it with a stick to make the spinning start.

"Your turn now, boys," said Anthony, producing two 'golden shower', hand-held fireworks.

Ruth put their gloves on, and the two boys stood still for the first time that evening as they watched, open-mouthed and arms outstretched, the fireworks produce a steady stream of light into the glowing sky around them.

On the evening went with a Mount Etna, more rockets, the Roman Candle, pumping mortar-like small explosions into the air and then the giant fireworks like cannon shells, which propelled bangs and showers of coloured lights into the sky above them. This mock artillery barrage was punctuated by interludes when the boys played with sparklers, waving them round to make patterns and competing to see whose sparkler lasted longest. The most exciting moment came when the aeroplane firework, resplendent with its RAF markings, took off correctly but then turned and dived straight for Ruth before veering off to hit a tree while Ruth screamed and ran, and Anthony and the boys collapsed with laughter.

In the afterglow of the evening, as the boys ate their toffee apples and prodded around in the burnt-out shells of the fireworks, Ruth and Anthony relaxed with another laced coffee. The potatoes had been abandoned; two being still raw and the others charcoal black.

"It was very good, Tony," Ruth said. "Even if I was dive-bombed by that mad firework; you didn't do anything to make it go like that, did you?"

Anthony laughed and shook his head. "No, of course not."

She smiled. "I know what you're like." Then she lowered her voice. "Tony, those fireworks must have cost a packet. Could you afford it, what with the car and everything else?"

"They weren't that much, and anyway, it's only once a year."

"You didn't have to borrow money to get the car fixed?" she whispered.

"No, it's all right. I had more money left over last month than I expected, that's all it was. Don't be a worryguts."

"Sorry, it was a lovely little party and the children so enjoyed it."

"So did I… didn't you?"

Ruth nodded and squeezed his arm.

November was also the month Anthony instituted a notional regular weekly get-together with his old friend Malcolm, so that he could guarantee at least one evening a week with Carrie. Although it was a purely self-serving decision, he'd come to the conclusion that he ought to see Malcolm at least now and again if only to salve his conscience and give his alibis more substance. So the day after the bonfire party he rang Malcolm on his direct line.

"Vinton," a voice answered almost immediately.

"Hello, Malcolm, it's Anthony Fernard; I don't know if you remember me?"

There was a slight pause. "Fernard? Of course, we were at school together; it must be at least fifteen years. How are you?" His voice was deeper than Anthony had expected and sounded confident, if a little circumspect.

"I'm well, thanks, glad you remember me."

"Well, the unusual surname helps; I might have struggled more if you had said Wilson or Carter. After all this time, how did you know where I was?"

"I meet Ronnie Benson regularly for lunch and we were talking about old school friends when your named cropped up. Ronnie said he'd bumped into you at a conference and we both thought it would be nice to renew our acquaintance with you, so he gave me your number."

"You beat him to it," said Malcolm. "I'm sorry, but I don't remember us mixing that much at school. I'm rather flattered you thought it worth going to the trouble to make contact again."

Anthony felt a twinge of remorse for his subterfuge and he wondered if he could maintain a friendship based on false pretences. For now, he kept going. "Actually, I have for some time wanted to look up some old school friends and you're as good a person to start with as any."

There was another pause. "What did you have in mind?"

"Well, I thought perhaps we could meet up for lunch or a drink sometime."

"Right, yes, I think that would be rather nice. Let me have a look at my diary. How about next week, before the Christmas socialising gets into full swing?"

They discussed the possibilities and eventually agreed to meet for a drink at the King Lud. Malcolm was taking a train from Holborn Viaduct that evening to have dinner with his mother in Sevenoaks, so that would suit him well.

Anthony arrived at about five-thirty and almost at once spotted Malcolm leaning at the bar and sipping a nearly full glass of beer. As Ronnie had said, he was instantly recognisable and hardly different to when he had last seen him sixteen years ago, just a bit heavier and with a little less of the fair curly hair. He greeted Anthony with a tentative smile but a firm handshake.

"Hello Anthony, you haven't changed a bit, how are you? What would you like?"

"Hello, Malcolm, nice to see you again; you haven't changed either. I'll have a pint of bitter, please. I haven't been in here for ages; I remember coming in here with my father donkeys' years ago. It was very popular with journalists then."

"Still is," said the man behind the bar as he poured Anthony's drink.

They took their drinks over to a table and sat down in seats near the window, the hubbub of Ludgate Circus droning, humming and occasionally screeching in the background.

The conversation was easy, much to Anthony's relief. Naturally, they began with their old school and shared recollections of idiosyncratic teachers, amusing anecdotes of their schoolmates, as well as fond and not so fond memories of their school days.

"Actually, I hated school," said Anthony. "I couldn't wait to leave."

"Why was that?" asked Malcolm.

"Hard to say why exactly. It wasn't the teachers; I quite liked most of them and even the bullies and windbags were tolerable for as much as I had to put up with them. I suppose it was the petty rules and the ethos of the place that we not only had to accept but were assumed to buy into. I coped with it all at eleven, but by the end I found it stifling. What about you?"

Malcolm looked slightly apologetic. "Well, I liked the school and I didn't even think about the rules, they were at worst just a mild irritant for me. I was lonely sometimes, though, I don't make friends easily and I was cast as a bit of a loner whether I wanted to be or not. I did get quite a bit of minor bullying in the lower school."

Anthony frowned. "I'm sorry to hear that. I hope I was never responsible?"

Malcolm smiled and shook his head. "No, I always thought you were a bit of a rogue, getting into scrapes and all that, but never nasty, certainly not a bully. I think I admired you and wished I could be more like you, though I was pleased I didn't get the cane with the regularity that you did. Anyway, all that bullying stuff is in the past now and who knows, it might have made me stand up for myself more later on."

"Do you have many friends from school now?"

"No," Malcolm laughed. "I didn't have many to start with."

"Then you went to Reading, Ronnie told me."

"Yes, I read Government with a foreign language option, so I typecast myself for the FO I guess."

"Administrative Grade presumably?"

"Yes."

"Where have you served overseas?"

"Lebanon, Denmark and Uruguay so far."

"I suppose you'll be First Secretary somewhere for your next overseas posting?"

"Not necessarily. Anyway I've just taken up a new post, so I shan't be moving for a bit."

"What job is that, if you don't mind me asking?"

"Don't see why not; you've signed the Official Secrets Act as well. I'm in the Eastern European division at the moment – I suppose I'll get a posting to a Warsaw Pact country next time."

They talked a bit about careers, what they did outside work and their families. Anthony could see why Ronnie had thought Malcolm was lonely. His family was small; his father had died some years ago and his only sibling, a sister, had emigrated to Rhodesia so his mother and a spinster aunt were his only close family in Britain. His interests – the opera, watercolour painting and astronomy – could be convivial but were often solitary pursuits. But Anthony found him easy company and got on with him well enough. He was no longer the gauche, tongue-tied loner of their schooldays, even if his quiet, introverted personality had remained intact.

Anthony bought a second round and conversation turned to current affairs and the state of the world, but after another half an hour or so, Malcolm said he would have to be going soon; his mother didn't like to eat too late.

"It was good of you to make contact again after all these years, Anthony, I've enjoyed this get-together. I wish I'd known you better at school." He took a pocket book from his jacket and scribbled out a telephone number. "Here's my home number if you want to keep in touch."

"Yes, we must do it again some time," said Anthony as they rose to say their goodbyes.

Anthony travelled home feeling he had done a good deed and when Ruth asked how Malcolm was, he was able to answer truthfully.

"He was in pretty good spirits and going down to Sevenoaks to see his mother."

"I'm glad you are getting to know him better. I've always said you should see more of your old friends; I try to keep up with mine."

He was thankful that Ruth had taken this view, because he wanted to spend as much time with Carrie as he possibly could and the existence of Malcolm was the means to this. Of course he felt guilty about Ruth in a way he hadn't done when he'd had previous infatuations with women, but at the moment there was nothing he could do about it.

Carrie was the most exciting woman he had ever known, both as a social companion and in their physical relationship, where she displayed an imagination and expertise that he, with his limited previous experience, had thought beyond the capacity of a respectable, professional woman. It was this apparent contradiction that led Anthony to be at first curious, then bothered, about Carrie's past relationships.

One early evening late in November, they were lying naked on her bed with the covers pushed away. With all the heating appliances on, the temperature in the flat was very warm and they were both hot and sweaty from their love-making, physical contact now reduced to the holding of hands.

"You weren't inexperienced sexually when we met, were you?" he asked.

She was silent for a moment. "No, but why do you ask?"

"It's not important, really, but I was puzzled as to how you could be so good in bed unless you'd had quite a lot of experience before you knew me."

"How do you know it wasn't just beginner's luck?" she retorted. "I thought it was only prospective wives who have to answer as to their past sex lives. Surely the one advantage of being a mistress is that you don't."

"I am not trying to pry. It's just that..."

"It's just that you are looking for an excuse to be jealous or judgemental or something. I don't think you have anything to complain about." She raised herself up and looked at him, her head leaning on the bed's headboard. Her voice was calm. "Why do all men want to know what a woman did before they met her? Didn't Oscar Wilde say, 'Men always want to be a woman's first love. That is their clumsy vanity.'?"

"I'm sorry, I shouldn't have asked," he replied.

"Don't worry about me, I'm a woman of no importance," she said, pulling her pillow up behind her head.

Anthony was annoyed with himself. He should have found a better way, if there were a better way, of broaching the subject. She was quite right; he didn't have anything to complain about. After all, compared to the satisfactory, if rather unimaginative, sex life he had with Ruth, his physical relationship with Carrie surpassed anything he had dreamed about. Why couldn't he leave well alone?

They were silent and Carrie slowly slid down in the bed, pulling up the covers until her body disappeared.

She sighed. "I'm twenty-five; you didn't expect me to be a virgin did you?"

"No, of course not." His own benchmark view, which he kept to himself, was that any normal woman would probably have lost her virginity by twenty-one.

"Look, if you must know, I have had one real lover before you; anything else was brief and rare. He was that soldier I told you about. I met him about five years ago and I was in love with him. He was older and quite experienced, and I was happy to try different things with him. The great thing was I didn't have to pretend I wasn't enjoying it. You know what it's like; most women are frightened to say they like it in case they are thought of as a tart or something."

"Were you happy together?"

"Yes, we were, but I told you what happened; I didn't feel ready to make a commitment and we drifted apart."

"What happened to him?"

"I don't know; I purposely tried not to find out. That was three years ago so, as long as he's all right, he's probably got someone else now."

"You weren't interested in anyone else afterwards?"

"I went out a few times with other men, but I wasn't that bothered about them until I met you. Now of course I am a double tart for liking sex and sleeping with a married man." She smiled.

Anthony held her hand. "I want you to be happy, just as you make me happy. I'm sorry to sound jealous or ungrateful."

Carrie threw back the covers and embraced him. "I do love you, you know," she said. "I love making love, but only to you. And I *am* happy.

No, make me mistress to the man I love;
If there be yet another name more free,
More fond than mistress, make me that to thee!"

IX

For Anthony, the good month of November was followed by the equally good month of December. The £100 from Colonel Cavalir had been almost the equivalent of another month's salary after tax and he was disposing of it prudently to make life just a bit more comfortable: better fireworks on Guy Fawkes Night, treats for Ruth and the children, and dates with Carrie.

One lunchtime, he walked along to Gamages and went to the top floor, which had one of the finest toy departments in Britain. It was crowned by an enormous model railway layout, which was constantly in action and even had a lighting system to imitate day and night to add to the spectacle for the watching crowds of young and not so young boys. Anthony spent some time admiring the scene and his nostalgic pleasure convinced him that he should buy a 'grown-up' train set for Laurence. He could help Laurence to set it up and run it until he was old enough to manage it himself. So he bought a mainline passenger train set with a Princess Victoria locomotive and added a station set and a diesel shunting engine. His other purchase was a cowboy outfit and cap pistol with accessories for Jonathan. When he arrived home with the presents, Ruth was surprised but also very impressed by his initiative, as she usually bore the brunt of Christmas present buying.

By December, his relationship with Carrie had settled into what he considered to be a happy equilibrium. They had lunch together two or three days each week, spent an evening together at least one day a week and had the occasional dates on days off from work or at the weekend when Ruth was otherwise busy. Their sex life was excellent, although less frequently exercised than both wished for. Perhaps best of all, Carrie made no demands on him, either about the time he spent with her or where the relationship was going. Such guilty feelings as he had experienced early on in their affair had gently subsided, with just the occasional flare-up. Objectively, he was aware that he would be described by others as a philanderer or womaniser or worse, but he pardoned himself from the severest of judgements as he loved Carrie and, so far as he was concerned, this mitigated his behaviour.

Anthony also saw Malcolm again in December. Following their ice-breaking meeting at the King Lud, Anthony thought it would be good to see him again over the festive season. Another meeting would give a bit more substance to their supposed friendship. In addition, Malcolm might need cheering up a bit, Christmas being a notoriously difficult time for people with a despondent nature and living alone.

They met for lunch at the Cheshire Cheese and Malcolm seemed much more relaxed than at their first meeting. He was warm when greeting Anthony and made a joke about Dr Johnson while they were making their way to the dining room.

"I'm glad you suggested lunch," he said, as they sat at a table with cushioned, high backed settles. "I enjoyed our last get-together very much."

"Me too," said Anthony, erring a little on the enthusiastic side. "What have you been doing with yourself since our last meeting?"

"Not much," said Malcolm. "Work is winding down for what is a fairly quiet month for diplomatic initiatives; lots of social events, of course, embassy receptions and so forth."

"Do you go to many?"

"Not too many; I spend most of the time in idle chatter and trying to get away from total bores. I have little or no small talk, so I usually end up asking people about themselves and fortunately that seems to be, for most people, their favourite subject. They drone on while I keep nodding. The most interesting thing about these receptions is a kind of slow dance."

"Dance? How do you mean?"

Malcolm smiled. "It's a kind of strange, unconscious ritual. I only became aware of it when, at one particular reception, I was absolutely certain I'd been standing on pretty much the same spot for an hour, whereas I had actually walked backwards halfway round the room. Now I notice it happens all the time, and it's always the British, Australians, Scandinavians etc. going backwards. It must be something to do with people from a North European culture preferring more space or distance from the other person in a conversation than those from Latin countries, whether from southern Europe or South America. In a conversation between, say, a Swede and a Portuguese, the Swede will always be trying to open a bigger gap between them while the Portuguese will be trying to close it. So during the course of a reception with lots of Italian or Spanish people, I spend my time going backwards to keep my comfortable distance, while an Italian or a Spaniard spends his time going forwards to keep his. Nobody is aware they are doing it at the time because it happens so slowly, but gradually, we all move round the room. I don't suppose for one minute that I'm the only person to have noticed it."

Anthony laughed. "I'd like to see that happening myself. Still, you must meet some interesting people at these events."

"Of course, you get different perspectives talking to people from other cultures and political systems. I have met quite a few senior people from other countries at these events, though they're usually guarded in what they say about anything sensitive."

"How do you get on with colleagues in the department? Is it a convivial sort of place to work?"

"Yes, it's OK; I get on all right with most people. Though I don't have many I'd call friends."

"Oh?"

"The department is very much an old boy network. If your school is not in *the* book and you didn't go to the right university, you're never going to be at the top table, either socially or professionally. It's nothing personal, but you don't quite fit in: the people you don't know, the interests you can't share, the in-jokes and silly banter that you're purposely excluded from, etc. Like anyone does, as we would probably, they mix with people that are most like them and with whom they'll feel comfortable. Naturally, they also tend to appoint people who are like themselves." He shrugged.

Anthony shook his head. "But you got in; it's not a closed shop. They might think you're stand-offish if you don't try to fit in and that could hold you back more than your background. I understand the system favours those with connections; it does everywhere. But do you really believe that good connections count more, even when a person's useless?"

Malcolm nodded. "Yes. I do, perhaps especially when a person's useless. I don't mean to sound resentful. I know it's partly my own fault if I don't get on; perhaps I should try more. The trouble is that if you're an outsider you have to work so hard to break down the unseen barriers. I am absolutely convinced that connections are what really matter when a person is not much good at the job. Of course, if you are good at what you do *and* have connections, you'll generally rise to the top but with a system based on 'who you know', the inadequates are never weeded out. Some of these types have stunted personalities, but they are not forced to see what life is like outside their protective cocoon. If they make stupid or ill-informed decisions, the group closes ranks and covers things up. They would see it as a defeat to ask people outside their own group to sort out a problem. They are more likely to launch into their puerile banter to cover up their own inadequacies and make someone else feel uncomfortable, or even take the blame for them. The culture enables the well-connected hopeless cases to survive and even thrive until they cause a disaster; look at Guy Burgess, for God's sake."

Anthony was pleasantly surprised. It was the first time he'd seen Malcolm really animated and obviously caring about something. He nodded his approval. "Well, of course I know what you mean and Ronnie has said something similar. I guess that you probably have enough of those types at work without mixing with them socially, but what about the department in general? You could always socialise with people in other roles or in lower grades if you don't feel comfortable with those you work with."

"You know what I'm like. I'm not as bad as I used to be, but I'm still shy and I always tend to go quiet in social situations. So I'm not much good at making friends and people can't usually be bothered to persevere with me; I'm not the easiest person to get to know."

"Oh, why do you say that?"

Malcolm smiled. "I don't like talking about myself and I don't try hard enough."

"Well, you're talking about yourself to me. As you said before, perhaps you don't really care that much. You might be the sort of person who is happiest in their own company; I can understand that."

Malcolm screwed his face into a dubious expression. "I've tried to take that view of things, but I don't know if it's really true for me. The fact is I tend to be lacking in self-confidence in a social context and I always assume people will find me boring. I think that people pick that up and it becomes a self-fulfilling prophecy."

"Malcolm, you mustn't be so negative about yourself. How do you get on with women? I suppose you're shy with them too?"

"Worse, I'm not exactly a catch."

Anthony regarded Malcolm critically. He was no Sean Connery or Steve McQueen and he was a bit overweight and balding with a rather dour expression, but...

"Don't underestimate yourself, Malcolm. You've got a lot going for you: a good job with prospects and a more dashing image than the Home Office or the Ministry of Housing. You're thirty-four and at a peak age for the largest pool of women; not too old for those in their early twenties and then the right age for those up to forty or whatever your cut-off point is. There must be hundreds of women in the immediate vicinity that would consider you a good catch if you just put yourself out there. Go to some clubs and nightspots and see what happens." He added, as an afterthought, "Best to avoid clip joints and those with hostesses, obviously."

"I'll give it some thought, Anthony," said Malcolm, not looking very convinced.

"Call me Tony, my other friends do."

Anthony thought back to that conversation he'd had with Ronnie about Malcolm's interest, or lack of it, in women and felt that Malcolm's responses just now had not clarified the situation one way or the other. Had he been a woman, or a different kind of man, Anthony might have taken on Malcolm as a project and tried to find a match for him, but like most men, this was not something Anthony saw as being within his remit. He would encourage and give advice, but he did not see it as his role to engineer a situation for anybody other than himself.

So the conversation settled into safer territory for both of them and they talked about their plans for Christmas. These were essentially to follow arrangements instigated by others. Anthony would have Christmas dinner at home and then visit his parents in the evening, going to Ruth's family on Boxing Day. Malcolm was to spend Christmas with his mother and aunt in Sevenoaks.

They wished each other well for the Christmas period and Anthony said he would see Malcolm sometime in the New Year. Despite wishing Malcolm well, however, he wasn't sure if he had the mental stamina to sustain a friendship with someone who seemed so hopelessly defeatist about himself. It might prove hard going.

Work at this time continued to be undemanding, if at times dull, as the visitor numbers fell off, apart from those on shopping expeditions or visiting family. However, it promised to be livened up to some extent by the staff Christmas party. Not that Anthony was particularly looking forward to it; there was always an air of slight discomfort about these parties and the ever-present risk of something embarrassing, not to say toe-curling, happening.

Arrangements for Christmas were left to individual sections. As the room he worked in was such a large one, the staff of these two sections had agreed, as in past years, to invite another two sections based in small rooms to join them. This made their party a larger gathering of about twenty-four people. There was a whip round among all the intending participants, and younger members of staff did most of the organising, buying drinks and snacks and a few decorations.

The party was held in the week before Christmas, starting at about three o'clock. The young Clerical Assistant for one of the visiting sections brought along his record player and a substantial number of LPs and singles, thoughtfully with some belonging to his parents as well as his own, and he acted as DJ for the session. So the party was accompanied by background music as diverse as Glenn Miller, Ella Fitzgerald, Buddy Holly, Shirley Bassey, Billy Fury and The Beatles. People served themselves drinks and nibbles and, as they all knew each other well enough, the party was soon going along with a swing.

There were only two rather awkward moments and they could hardly have been more different. At around half-past four the Assistant Secretary for the Division, Henry Dawlish, made a courtesy call on the party as he was doing the rounds. He was given a drink and was soon working the room quite successfully. He was a quietly spoken man in his mid-fifties with the demeanour of a university don. Anthony had had cause to go to see him over a particular case no more than four times in the eight years he'd been in the department and had always found him approachable and helpful. Everyone was very polite and spoke only when spoken to, except for Patricia Lovell who, fortified by a couple of large gin and tonics, ambushed the unprepared Assistant Secretary by bringing up one of her cases with him.

"May I just say that I was very disappointed that someone I had recommended on perfectly good grounds to work here was turned down for a visa."

Dawlish looked slightly bewildered. "I don't follow you."

"That very talented Czech lady who applied for a visa to work with one of our most prestigious orchestras; she had been offered the job as a viola player."

Dawlish nodded slowly. "I see. Yes, I remember the case now."

The case had been supported by Daphne, but she had passed it to her superior, a Senior Executive Officer, for ratification. He had rejected the application but had referred it himself to Dawlish to be the arbiter and Dawlish had also rejected the application. If Dawlish had not agreed with the Senior Executive Officer, he would have referred up to the next level and so on. Anthony had once had a case which went right up to the Permanent Under-Secretary of State who, rather pleasingly, had agreed with his original recommendation.

Dawlish was patient with Patricia. "It is important not to get too personally involved with such matters; every case is assessed on its merits. This was a very difficult decision and that was why it was referred to me. I assure you, I considered it very carefully but felt unable to grant the application."

"Had she been Rudolf Nureyev or somebody else famous, I bet she would have been granted the visa then," said Patricia, throwing her head back and sighing with some force.

The music continued in the background and several conversations were still taking place, but among those around these two the chatter had been replaced by an apprehensive silence.

Dawlish turned to Freddie Pilling. "So you are still with us, Freddie; not thinking about retiring anytime soon, I hope?"

One of the young men took Patricia's hand and coaxed her into dancing to Chubby Checker's 'Let's Twist Again' and the party atmosphere was resumed.

Once the dancing had got going, several couples joined in and the party's tempo went up a notch. Seeing there was a market for dance numbers, the DJ put on 'Let's Dance' by Chris Montez and then 'The Loco-motion' by Little Eva. It was when he put on 'Moon River', sung by Danny Williams, that the second awkward moment occurred.

Recognising it was a waltz, a Clerical Assistant from one of the visiting sections, Andrew Horton, decided to ask Daphne Raynott for a dance. Horton was about the same age as Daphne and dressed quite smartly but in a slightly crumpled way. When he asked Daphne for a dance, she rejected the offer politely. This rejection seemed to galvanise Horton into being more assertive and, with a quick 'Come on, Daphne', he grabbed her hand, put his arm round her waist and attempted to glide out into the small throng of dancers. Unfortunately, Daphne remained resolutely where she stood, her feet glued to the floor. In consequence, Horton's glide became something of a lurch and Daphne toppled over rigidly, like a statue, bringing Horton down with her as they landed in a heap on the floor.

This time there was no other distraction or a quick thinker to divert attention. There was total silence and gawping shock as the entire room watched the prostrate couple slowly disengage themselves from each other and get back on their feet, the group's squirming only heightened by Daphne's refusal of a helping hand from her quixotic suitor.

Then everyone began talking, saying anything and nothing to their neighbour, in an attempt to restore normality while Horton lit a cigarette and brushed himself down. Daphne left the office with her towel and E II R soap, not to return for some considerable time.

Anthony was reminded once again why he disliked Christmas work parties. These embarrassing moments were amusing in the telling afterwards, but at the time they were so often excruciating. As often happens, this one served to evaporate the high spirits that had been developing and the party took on a more subdued tone. After a few minutes, he excused himself to go early and, after buying a decent bottle of claret from Findlaters, took a tube to Barons Court to spend the evening with Carrie.

He had offered to take her out to dinner for their personal 'Christmas Party', but she had insisted on cooking him a meal so that they might escape the strained jollity of West End restaurants and public houses in the run up to Christmas.

When he arrived, Carrie was wearing her new, black Kiki Byrne dress and had laid her small dining table with candles, festive napkins and crackers. They embraced and kissed before she opened a half bottle of champagne and they toasted each other with a glass.

"Before or after dinner?" she asked, sipping her champagne.

"You choose," he said.

She smiled. "After, or we'll probably never get round to eating."

She went out to the kitchen to prepare their dinner of salmon paté, Steak Diane and a lemon tart. "Only one course of which I shall actually cook," she admitted.

"What will you do at Christmas?" asked Anthony, as they sat down to the first course.

"Usual family stuff on Christmas Day and then I have been invited to a lunchtime party on Boxing Day. It's a regular thing that some old friends have been doing for years and we shall all go to it. I look forward to that. Then in the early evening I shall head back home; I have work on Thursday."

"You did tell me, I know, but I forget; where do your parents live?"

"Near Saffron Walden; not too bad a journey. I suppose you'll be playing 'Happy Families'?"

Anthony nodded. "Yes, we have to fit both sides in. Boxing Day is a bit of a slog, but at least I don't have to be back for work next day."

"I shall miss you over Christmas. Silly, really, it's only a day like any other."

"We can have lunch together on Friday, still Christmas, twelve days and all that."

"Just as long as you don't buy me four calling birds."

The ingredients were already prepared and cooking the Steak Diane didn't take long. It was served with the wine Anthony had brought. "You know, this is the first time I've tasted your cooking," he said. "It's very good."

Carrie looked pleased. "I haven't exactly done anything difficult, but thank you, I'm glad it's OK."

As the courses proceeded, they ate more quickly and chatted less. After the lemon tart, Carrie picked up her glass of wine and stood up. "Let's have coffee later," she said and took Anthony by the hand into the bedroom.

When, an hour and a quarter later, they did eventually have a cup of coffee, Carrie went over to a cupboard and returned with a package wrapped in crepe paper and ribbon. "Happy Christmas, Tony," she said.

Anthony opened the package and inside the box was a very handsome silver Dunhill cigarette lighter. "It's great," he said, as it fired first time, justifying Anthony's faith in it. He lit a cigarette from this first flame.

"Nothing too personal, for obvious reasons; I'm pleased you like it."

Anthony took out the small card that came with the present; she had written inside 'For in my mind, of all mankind I love but you alone, Carrie.'

"Ah, that's lovely, Carrie," he said and kissed her. "I don't know that quotation."

"It's from 'The Nut-Brown Maid'. I wish it had been me," she smiled. "Now that *is* personal, but you don't have to keep it."

Anthony walked over to his overcoat and produced a package of his own, wrapped in gold paper. "Happy Christmas to you too, darling."

Carrie unwrapped the present to reveal a long jewellery box. When opened, it contained a pendant necklace with a small diamond at its centre. "It's lovely," she said, but then she noticed the name of the retailer. "I don't want you to spend this sort of money on me."

"Our first Christmas, I wanted to give you something special."

"Yes, but it's too much."

Anthony thought it was the sort of thing Ruth might say. "I had a little bit of a windfall last month, I won't bore you with the details, but it gave me a little extra for the luxuries of life."

Carrie embraced him. "Thank you very much, it's lovely; you have such good taste."

"I just thought it would look good on you. I'm pleased you think so too."

They sat on the sofa and Anthony put the necklace round her neck, not having too much trouble with the fiddly clasp. Then they kissed and his arm went inside her dressing gown and felt her warm flesh.

"I really ought to go," he said, releasing his hold and sitting up.

"Spoilsport," she said and got up to look at her necklace in the mirror. "Yes, you must get going. I don't suppose I shall see you before Christmas?"

"No, Monday will be hectic."

"Friday it is then," she said, helping him on with his jacket and coat and giving him one more hug before sending him out into the cold night.

X

CHRISTMAS FOLLOWED THE USUAL PATTERN FOR Anthony. After a morning spent opening presents and setting up new games and toys for the boys, the four of them sat down to Christmas lunch with a good bottle of wine at about half-past one. After lunch, they played games as a foursome and then the children were allowed to watch television while Anthony helped Ruth clear away.

Then it was off to Anthony's parents for a light tea and a small family party which went on till about midnight. Anthony got on well with both his parents, the result of a happy, if slightly staid, childhood. His father had worked in the accounts department of the local gas board for all his working life and now, at sixty-three, was counting down the days to retirement, a gold watch and a decent pension. He was a man of the upmost probity and good manners: kind to his children, loving and effusive in his praise for his wife in everything she did for him, loyal to his employer and his friends, scrupulously honest in his dealings with others. He was totally lacking in ambition, had a sense of humour limited to excruciating puns and, when confronted with a choice, always chose that which offered the greatest degree of past practice and the least opportunity for risk. Conservative in all things, his temperament led him always to lean towards 'Safety First', the slogan of his favourite Prime Minister, Stanley Baldwin. Anthony loved his father but thought him dull.

Anthony's mother did not appear to find her husband dull, as she never seemed in the least unhappy with her marriage. Despite having been a schoolteacher with presumably a gift for communication, she was by nature taciturn and Anthony could not recall ever having had a serious conversation with her. She had undoubtedly been a good mother and had played with him and his brother a lot when they were children, rather more than their father had. It was usually she who would bend the rules of parental discipline and give way to her sons' demands for greater freedom and self-reliance when they were growing up. Having been a wife and mother, then a carer for her own mother, she had now happily settled into the role of grandmother, and would have seen Laurence and Jonathan much more often than she did if offered the opportunity. She also missed seeing her younger son, Robert, who rarely came down from his home in Huddersfield, though he made the effort each Christmas.

Robert was three years younger than Anthony, similar in looks but an inch shorter and with straighter, light-brown hair. He had inherited his father's talent for meticulous, accurate analytical work, though he had applied this to quantity surveying and latterly project planning rather than accountancy. Early in his career, he had moved to the north of England to work for a large civil engineering company and was rising steadily up through the management structure. He was by nature more outgoing than his father and he appeared to enjoy a diverse and busy social life as an eligible bachelor. Anthony welcomed his presence at the party as a support to him in seeking a lighter, more convivial atmosphere.

Unlike previous years, Robert had not arrived alone. He was accompanied by a friend, a young American man in his mid-twenties named Brett whom Robert had got to know through a civil engineering project involving both their companies. As Robert had explained, it wasn't worth Brett going home to Santa Fe for a couple of days and he had no family ties in England. So he had jumped at the chance to enjoy a traditional English Christmas.

The prospect of an interloper to the traditional family get-together had been received by Anthony's father with some perturbation initially, especially as he'd never met Brett before. However, he had become reconciled to things not being exactly the same as usual, especially as his wife impressed upon him that it was an opportunity to show an American how 'it should be done'.

Brett was an amiable young man with one of those semi-crew cut hairstyles that were common in the United States but rarely seen in Britain. He was taller than both the Fernard brothers, revealed a muscular physique when he removed his jacket, and had a light tan, which Anthony thought remarkable for someone who'd spent December in England. He was very polite and friendly with an infectious laugh. By the time Anthony and Ruth arrived, he had already won the approval of Mr and Mrs Fernard with his witty conversation, gracious, vaguely Southern charm and old-fashioned manners.

After introductions and a brief chat about the weather drawing in, they all sat down to a tea of smoked salmon, cottage cheese and cucumber sandwiches. Immediately afterwards, Brett showed his gratitude to his hosts by presenting a magnum of champagne, chocolates and marrons glacés for them, a box of chocolate liqueurs for Ruth, a fifty-cigarette gift box for Anthony and cap guns for the boys.

Brett's generosity and winning ways ensured that the evening began well with champagne all round and much light-hearted chatter. The boys were allowed to go off and play 'cowboys' for a while, which Anthony thought appropriate since the mere mention of Santa Fe conjured up an image of pioneering settlers heading west to the new territories of New Mexico and California. Then over drinks and chocolates, the family settled down for their customary Christmas evening of card games: 'Crib', Rummy and Canasta. Robert and Brett endeavoured to get them all involved in a session of charades, but that was a step too far for the older Fernards, so the latter part of the evening was spent in conversation with music in the background. It didn't matter to Anthony, as Brett and Robert kept them entertained with amusing anecdotes of their work sites and Anthony was spared playing his usual role of keeping the conversation above the level of dreary. In fact, the presence of Brett seemed to galvanise Robert into being more relaxed and entertaining than usual. He even danced with both his mother and Ruth as the evening wore on.

At about eleven-thirty, with Jonathan asleep on a sofa and Laurence nodding off on an armchair, Ruth suggested they ought to go home.

"The boys are so tired, perhaps you could stay tonight," said Anthony's mother, in another break with past practice.

All heads looked to Anthony's father and he nodded in confirmation.

"That's very kind of you," said Ruth, "but where would you put us all; you only have four bedrooms?"

"We could share a room," said Robert, looking at Brett, who nodded and smiled.

"We wouldn't dream of putting you out," said Anthony. "In any case, we have to make an early start in the morning to go to Sussex."

Robert shrugged and Brett smiled again.

So the boys were wrapped up in their coats and the goodbyes were said in whispers as Anthony and Ruth thanked everybody for a lovely day and crept out to the car.

Ruth, who had abstained from alcohol after a couple of glasses of champagne several hours ago, drove and in less than half an hour they had covered the route round the deserted North Circular to Waterworks Corner and on to Woodford.

"That was the best Christmas evening we've ever spent at your parents," said Ruth, glancing in the rear mirror to check the boys were asleep.

"Yes, Brett's a nice chap, isn't he?" said Anthony. "Livened up Mum and Dad; they seemed to enjoy it a lot too."

"Yes, and Robert was happy tonight."

Anthony thought to say something else but decided not to. Instead he reflected on how he always looked forward much more to Boxing Day with Ruth's parents than Christmas evening at his parents' home. This year would be no different, but the race to be the more pleasurable was likely to be much closer than usual.

It began snowing at Rottingdean on Boxing Day. The snow came too late for those betting on a 'White Christmas' but what it lacked in punctuality it made up for in abundance. The anticyclone which brought it seemed to get stuck in its position over southern England and it snowed for much of the next twenty-four hours.

The weather forecast had indicated some snow so Anthony and Ruth, despite the optimism of the previous night, debated at some length whether to travel to Sussex. Ruth was more worried about the journey home than the less cautious Anthony. He took the view that the weather forecast was usually wrong and that even if it did snow, it was unlikely to be that heavy. Eventually, the disappointment that was sure to follow for Ruth's parents and for the boys, rather than Anthony's optimism, swung Ruth round to risking it.

In the evening, as the snow became quite heavy and the television news reported more to come, a larger forum, now including Ruth's parents, decided that it would be too risky to attempt the journey home. With five bedrooms, it was hardly a challenge to find accommodation for them all in Ruth's parents' house, and mother and daughter went upstairs to prepare the beds. Meanwhile, their husbands kept the children amused by playing the horse racing game '*Escalado*' which Ruth's father had given to Jonathan for Christmas. While both boys loved the game, Jonathan in particular was very pleased, because he could compete equally with Laurence. He was required only to turn a handle rather than navigate the rules and reading of cards which most of the board games at home involved and were sometimes beyond him. The game contained another feature called betting, which neither he nor his brother understood, but which his father and grandfather seemed to derive much amusement from doing before each race.

Despite the worsening weather, Anthony had agreed to stay the night with some reluctance. As a civil servant, he received a 'privilege day' at Christmas which meant an extra day off on the day after Boxing Day. He had been looking forward to this third day of the holiday as one he could spend with the boys at home, setting up Laurence's new model railway, playing games, going for a walk if the weather was fine and so on. There was also the mild inconvenience of not having his own pyjamas, shaving things, etc. On the other hand, he would not miss the drive back that evening, since he would be free of the need to be sensible about drinking before a long drive. Instead, he could relax and enjoy dipping into his father-in-law's extensive range of malt whiskies and vintage ports as the evening moved into its post-children phase.

"I hope you've not been introducing these children to the murky world of gambling, Alec," said his wife, as she came into the drawing room just as he was placing a dual forecast wager with Anthony.

"No, strictly for the adults," said Alec.

"Well, don't let it get too serious," counselled Monica.

"I'm only down £80," said Anthony.

Ruth raised her hand to her mouth.

Monica gave her husband a withering look. "Alec! That's far too much; playing for a few coppers is one thing but..."

Alec laughed. "Don't panic, Monica," he said. "We're only playing with Monopoly money." He waved a red £500 note at her and then stuck his hands in his beige cardigan with its leather football buttons.

Monica smiled with relief. "Honestly, you two are more trouble than the boys."

"One more race while you have your milk, then it's up to bed for you two," said Ruth, placing the glasses of milk a safe distance from the racetrack. "There'll be plenty of time for games tomorrow."

"Right, boys," said Alec, pushing his glasses up his nose and rubbing his hands together. "Let's make this last race a good one. Three, two, one; we're off!"

The latter part of the evening followed the pattern Anthony had anticipated. With the children in bed, the grown-ups could play their own games of charades and gin rummy. They'd had a substantial lunch in expectation of a drive home so the change in plans did not lead to a need for more cooking for Monica. They had an informal buffet of cold turkey and ham, cheeses and salad and, after a glass or two of wine, Anthony and Alec attacked the port and whisky accompanied by a cigar. Anthony didn't really like cigars but deferred to Alec's generous wishes and he restricted himself to one glass of port due to its potential backlash the next morning. Monica was more abstemious with a solitary glass of sherry, but Ruth polished off the rest of a bottle of Sancerre and couldn't resist a couple of gin and tonics as the games got under way.

The evening was interspersed by occasional looks out of the windows at the steadily falling snow. After the games, the foursome sat talking for a while with a nightcap then, at about half-past eleven, Ruth polished off her drink, looked at Anthony and said, "I think I'll go up now." She kissed her parents goodnight and looked once more out the window before going upstairs. That acted as a signal for everyone else to think about retiring and a few minutes later, Anthony followed her up to her old bedroom, which was now, thankfully, furnished with a double bed.

Having cleaned his teeth with a brand-new gifted toothbrush and had a quick wash, Anthony climbed naked into the bed, his body immediately retreating into a foetal position. "God, it's freezing, isn't it?"

"The heating was on, it's just a very cold night," replied Ruth, buried under the blankets.

"Not reading tonight?"

"A bit too squiffy. I think I drank more than I'm used to. Luckily, I don't feel sick or anything, just a bit gone."

Anthony was slowly exploring the nether regions of the bed with his feet in what he felt was an Arctic expedition without the proper equipment.

After a minute or two, Ruth turned round and cuddled him, bringing her legs up to form a lap for his bottom. "We made the right decision to stay the night. Mm, you feel so warm to me, how lovely. We might have to stay in bed for a week." Her hands began rubbing his back and then they moved between his legs, stroking rhythmically and encouragingly.

"You're not too drunk for this," said Anthony.

"Nor are you, I do believe."

Anthony endured perhaps five seconds of hesitancy as his love for Carrie flashed through his mind, then he was happy to concede to his wife's conjugal rights.

The next morning, the boys couldn't wait to get out into the snow, which was several inches thick outside the back door and still falling on and off. By the time their grandmother, the first adult to do so, had come downstairs, Laurence had already served them both a breakfast of milk and cereal, so they were dressed and sitting by the kitchen door.

Monica rebuffed their initial pleas to be allowed out. "You've had nothing warm yet. I'll make a cup of tea and after that you can go and play."

Much later, Anthony came down, leaving Ruth apparently comatose in the bed. His head was not feeling at its best, but after a cup of tea and a bacon sandwich, he felt strong enough to borrow a pair of Alec's wellingtons and join his sons for a game of snowballs. He retired hurt when a particularly hard one caught him in the mouth. After a recuperative cup of coffee, he shovelled the snow as the boys constructed a very large snowman, so large that he had to place the head on top. They decorated it with an old beret and scarf from Monica, a truncated old clay pipe Alec always had in stock, a carrot from the kitchen and pieces of coal from the shed.

The snow continued on and off for much of the day, and Alec and Anthony abandoned their attempt to clear the long drive. The snow was several inches deep already and Anthony wondered if it was even worth attempting to get the car into action. However, he was loathe to accept defeat by not going to work on the following day. He had never missed a day's work because of the weather since he'd joined the Home Office, despite trudging through snow several times. He would be sorry to give up and lose his record now. There was also the matter of his lunch appointment with Carrie.

After much oscillation between the options of attempting to make the journey home or staying put, Anthony decided to take up Monica's suggestion of staying another night. He would take the car to Brighton station and go to work by rail, finally making the journey home to Woodford the next day. The children were delighted, Ruth was pleased and Anthony satisfied that it was the sensible thing to do. They gave the car and the roads a test run by driving into the village and getting a few provisions. The snowfall had eased and everywhere there was that still, sound-dampening, white landscape, decorated by trees elegantly clothed in snow drapes and icicled tinsel. The pristine state of the snow was only occasionally pockmarked by the heavy steps of human footwear, the lighter touch of small animals and the dainty patterns of birds. Its dazzling whiteness was besmirched only when it was adjacent to the roads where a greyish tinge mixed with salt and gravel lowered the tone. The pavements were largely clear in the village, as socially conscious householders and shopkeepers had cleared the areas outside their property into mounds along the pavement edge.

After a make-do lunch and a dinner produced by Monica from items in the larder, the children, exhausted by their all-day miniature Winter Olympics, were in bed unusually early. However, a more sober evening than the previous one followed, as the joviality of Christmas began to run out of steam. Once again, Anthony declined the offer of a loan of pyjamas and instead took a hot water bottle up with him to act as a vanguard for the conquest of the ice-sheets on the bed. As on the previous night, Ruth was pleased by his lack of attire and the intimacy it engendered.

The following day, a slow, steady drive to the station was followed by a punctuated journey to Victoria and then two stops on the Circle line before the Piccadilly line to Holborn. The Underground and the streets seemed noticeably quieter than usual but everybody in his office had managed to get in. None of his colleagues had come as far as Anthony, but he was glad not to have been the only one absent. Snow was naturally enough the main source of conversation, especially with Rosemary, who was sporting a large bump on her forehead, the result of coming off a sledge in a park the previous day.

When he went for lunch with Carrie at his regular Italian haunt, she was already waiting for him. She jumped up as she saw him and gave him a lengthy hug.

"I'm so pleased to see you," she said. "I thought you might be trapped in Rottingdean."

"We were yesterday. I left the car in Brighton and came in by train. I'm going to try to go back to Woodford tomorrow. How about you; did you have any trouble getting back into London on Boxing Day?"

"Not really, it wasn't too bad when we were at the lunchtime party and I took a train early in the afternoon before the weather really closed in. I was supposed to be having a drink with a couple of girlfriends but we called it off because of the weather. I spent Boxing Night in bed with a book and glass of mulled wine." She laughed. "Did you have a good Christmas?"

"Yes, I did actually. Christmas evening was much more fun than usual. Robert brought an American friend for Christmas and he was the life and soul of the party. Then we went to Rottingdean for what turned out to be a long stay. Fortunately, my in-laws are easy to get on with, especially as we spent two days with them, three if you count today. So, yes, it was good, and the children loved it all. What about you?"

Carrie nodded. "Yes, it was fine; same as always."

"Have you got plans for New Year?"

"I suppose there's no chance?"

"I'm sorry, I don't see how I can."

She smiled. "No, of course not."

"No harm in asking. What will you do on New Year's Eve?"

"I've been invited to a party at Ralph's, you know from the amateur dramatics group." Her expression brightened. "It's sure to be quite a laugh; he's going to put on a mock pantomime or some similar sort of entertainment."

"Sounds great. Are you working on New Year's Day?"

"Yes, I don't want to waste a day's holiday when I shall probably feel crapulent anyway."

Anthony laughed. "I know what you mean, but we could have the hair of the dog together if you like?"

"Yes, OK."

"Is anything the matter? You seem a bit subdued."

"Just jaded post-Christmas; nothing to worry about."

Anthony didn't pursue the subject further and the lunch was a quiet affair, with conversation mostly limited to small talk and the odd anecdote from the news or their respective Christmas experiences, most of which were contributed by Anthony.

"Well, I mustn't be late," said Carrie, after they had eaten. "There are a couple of people still away, so I've got to mind the shop." She pulled on her coat and scarf and a woollen hat in which Anthony thought she looked younger and rather cute.

"I'll walk with you a while, I'm all right for time."

"No, it's fine, I have to pop into Boots for some ladies' things. I'll see you on Tuesday."

The reverse journey back to Rottingdean was even quieter than the journey into London, as some organisations had let their staff go early because of the weather. When he arrived at his temporary residence, Anthony learned from Alec that more heavy snow was predicted at some point the next day. In a moment of horror, he visualised being trapped in Rottingdean for the foreseeable future. Despite his desire to go home, he realised that it was impracticable, let alone risky, to try to make the journey that night. Instead, after an early night, they left first thing in the morning to try to outrun the snow as it headed north from the English Channel. The plan worked and the family arrived back in Woodford in the late morning after a steady drive in often tricky conditions. They were relieved that they had decided to leave the heating on while they were away.

The snow did come again and again as the coldest winter for eighty years settled on the country. The winter wonderland of the first few days became permanent and therefore less interesting; later it ceased to be worthy of note and finally became a tiresome cliché. The piles of snow at the side of the pavements were no longer a novelty but a permanent feature of life in towns as well as the country. For two months, the temperature was rarely above freezing, but it didn't snow all the time and many days were quite sunny. It's just that the snow that fell didn't go away. While for those with responsibilities in life the weather remained a looming presence in the background of their daily lives, for Anthony's sons and their peers it was only rarely inconvenient. Schoolchildren throughout the country escaped grazed knees and torn clothes as the playgrounds at school and the hard landscaping of their gardens and parks were under a permanent sheet of white. For over two months, they could dive in goal, slide on their knees and do all manner of stunts while coming off less damaged than they would normally have been.

For adults, with higher fuel bills, regular problems with transport and the cancellation of many activities, especially professional football, the winter was less of a delight. It seemed the snow would be there forever.

XI

NEW YEAR'S EVE WAS A QUIET AFFAIR FOR Anthony and Ruth. Even had they wanted to, they would have struggled to find a babysitter to enable them to go out. However, the thought of work for Anthony the next day coupled with the inhospitable weather were enough to limit their celebrations to seeing the New Year in with the television. They watched *The White Heather Club* on the BBC with lots of kilts and traditional Scottish music against a background of wobbly stage sets and familiar figures from the world of Scottish entertainment clearly enjoying real alcoholic drinks. This annual celebration of Hogmanay by the BBC gave the impression that the New Year was a peculiarly traditional Scottish festival of which the Irish, Welsh and English were mere observers, especially as only in Scotland was 1st January a bank holiday. They listened to Big Ben chime at midnight, drank to the New Year and were in bed well before twelve-thirty.

The next morning, Anthony sat on the tube going into London surrounded by a vision of quiet discomfort as many of his fellow passengers were ruing their over-enthusiastic embrace of the celebrations associated with the coming of

Janus. He had told Ruth that he would be seeing Malcolm that evening to cheer him up a little, as Malcolm was prone to depressive thoughts over the festive season. Ruth nodded, as New Year's Day was much like any other day and she didn't mind if her husband was out.

Anthony phoned Carrie at work and asked her if she would like to go out to lunch or meet after work.

"I am feeling a bit fragile at the moment and can't really talk," she said quietly. "Can we meet later?"

"Yes, this evening."

"That'd be great."

They met on the westbound Piccadilly line platform at Holborn station. The train was fairly quiet and they both got a seat and held hands quietly; it was too noisy to talk. Then they went to a restaurant near her flat and had a light meal with the 'hair of the dog' in the form of a bottle of white wine.

"Gosh, I'm feeling so much better now," said Carrie. "When you phoned this morning, I had a terrific headache and couldn't have eaten a thing. This afternoon, the cloud began to lift and now I feel quite good. I'm really enjoying this; I think I'll have a pudding too."

Anthony smiled. He liked women to enjoy their food rather than pick at it. "I take it the party went well?"

"Yes, too well, I'm afraid. You know what it's like; you start off with a punch bowl with fruit and a sweetish concoction which you think is almost a soft drink and it turns out to be deadly, and by the time you realise it you've already had a few real drinks and it's too late. I saw Rod, you remember Rod from the get-together after *The Secret Garden*? Well, I saw Rod standing outside in the freezing cold trying to sober up and one of the girls just flaked out and was left for dead on a chaise longue in the dining room."

Anthony smiled as similar memories from his own past flashed through his mind. "How was the pantomime?"

Carrie laughed. "I'm glad I was sober enough to watch it as it was quite a hoot. The story was a spoof on *Puss in Boots* with lots of innuendo and downright filth. Ralph was in his element."

"Did you have a part in it?"

"No, I think it might have been a bit hazardous to be at the mercy of Ralph's humour. I was more than happy to be a member of the audience."

"That's a shame; I think you'd have looked good as the principal boy in tights."

"Smacking my thighs and all that stuff? The principal boy was a boy this time, one of Ralph's protégés, if you know what I mean."

Anthony grinned. "So what time did you get home?"

"I think it was just after three." She shook her head at the thought of it.

They left the restaurant in freezing rain and walked as briskly as they could to Carrie's flat. The flat was only relatively warmer than the street and Carrie lit the gas fire immediately. "God, it's cold, isn't it?" she said and put the kettle on while Anthony, still in his wet overcoat, warmed his hands by the fire.

While the kettle was boiling, Carrie went into the bedroom for a minute or so. "I've got a surprise for you later," she said, as she went back to the kitchen.

Anthony took off his coat with reluctance and lit a cigarette with the lighter Carrie had given him. Then he resumed his position, keeping watch over the gas fire until Carrie returned with two mugs of coffee.

Carrie went to a cabinet and returned with a medium-size envelope. "I've got this for you," she said.

"What is it?"

"It was very quiet last week, so I took the opportunity to search the archives and I found some more airmail stamps. There aren't too many, but they look quite interesting."

"Thanks, but you shouldn't have gone to so much trouble."

"It was fun really, going through the old documents from before the war and so on. I didn't realise our firm had actually done some work for one of the German ministries in the 1930s. Anyway, I liked doing it for you."

Anthony opened the envelope and saw there were thirty or forty stamps from various countries, including German ones from the Nazi era. "They're great, but I hope you won't get into trouble, taking envelopes from the archives."

Carrie shook her head. "It's not a problem, they were not required; the documents are safe in the files. In any case, I've worked there three years and I've never known anyone go through the archives. One day they'll all be thrown out when more room is needed."

"Did you make any New Year's resolutions?" asked Anthony, sitting back in his chair and holding his mug of coffee in both hands.

"*Make* any? I have already *kept* one."

"Oh, what's that?"

"You'll see. What about you?"

Anthony smiled. "I can't keep them, so I never make them."

"That's a bit defeatist."

Anthony shrugged. "You haven't told me what other ones you've made. How else will I know whether you managed to keep them?"

"Let me see: first, not to feel as bad next New Year's Day as I did this one; second, learn a bit of Russian and third, have more sex. The first I can't break until the last day of the year, the second I'll let you know and the third I'm going to start today." She finished her coffee and jumped up, kicking off her shoes. "Give me five minutes and then I'll be waiting for you," and she walked over to the bathroom on her way to the bedroom.

A slow consumer of hot drinks, Anthony still had at least half his coffee left and he resisted the impulse to drink it all in one go. Instead, he took off his jacket, tie and shoes and took his time drinking the strong, sweet coffee while he finished his cigarette. When he gauged about five minutes had passed, he went into the cold bedroom.

Carrie was under the covers with just her head protruding. "Hurry up. Take all your clothes off quickly and get under the covers."

"What's it like in there? Have you warmed up my side?"

"You'll see, hurry up!"

Anthony felt the cold air enveloping him as he abandoned each item of clothing. Finally he scrambled into bed with the expectation of a swimmer about to dive into the North Sea in January.

"It's warm!" he shouted.

Carrie laughed and rolled over on top of him. "It's an electric blanket; isn't it wonderful? I bought it yesterday."

"Are they definitely safe?" asked Anthony, feeling slightly vulnerable again.

"Of course, as long as you don't wet the bed. Mind you, I wouldn't go to sleep with it on, just in case. It was the New Year's resolution that I've already kept." She ran her hand through the hair on his chest and began kissing him.

"Do you think we ought to turn off the blanket though?"

Carrie laughed. "You think we might have a power surge or blow a fuse?" She leaned out of the bed to switch it off and quickly resumed her previous position. "I hope *you* have a power surge," she said, running her hands over him.

"You're the only blanket *I* need," said Anthony, holding her tight to him. "God, it's so good with you," he said as he ran his hands over her body. "I don't just mean this, I mean everything."

"I know, it's the same for me. Perhaps it's because we never have enough of each other, but who cares?"

Without remembering having been asleep, Anthony found himself awake. He moved slightly away from Carrie's arms into a cold part of the bed and looked at his watch. The luminous hands showed eleven-thirty and he sat up with a start. As he looked for his clothes, he felt Carrie's hand reach out for him.

"I wish you didn't have to go," she said, holding his arm.

"I must hurry, it's late."

"What time is it?"

"Half-past eleven. We must have been asleep for a couple of hours."

"You haven't time to get home. What if you're too late for the Central line? You can't be out in this cold weather."

Anthony was dressing quickly, with a purpose, but his mind was calculating the odds. The last Central line tube for Woodford would be at Liverpool Street just after midnight; even if he got a train in five minutes it would be too late to catch that last train at Holborn. He would have to get a night bus or taxi to Liverpool Street and then get the Chingford train just after one. It would be a mile and a half walk from Wood Street. His will began to wilt, and he stopped looking for his tie.

"May I use your phone?"

"Of course," said Carrie. She had sat up now and pulled the covers over her shoulders.

Anthony phoned his home and Ruth answered immediately.

"Oh, Tony, I was beginning to get worried about you. Where are you?"

"Still in London. I'm afraid we got talking about things and I completely lost track of the time till now. I could try to get home but I'm not sure I'll get the connections."

"It's very cold. Could you stay there?"

"Yes, there's room."

"Well, stay in town tonight and I'll see you tomorrow."

"Everything all right at your end?"

"Yes, we're all fine; very cold though."

"Sorry about this, I made a mess up."

"At least you phoned. Goodnight, sleep well."

"Goodnight, hope you sleep well too."

Anthony felt vaguely uneasy as he walked back into the bedroom, undressed and climbed into the bed.

"I know you would have preferred to go home, but it's an ill wind and all that; I am happy to have you all night," said Carrie, sliding down under the covers.

"I didn't want to go home, but I felt I ought to try, I don't know why."

"Was your wife good about it?"

"Yes."

"You're so cold already," she said and rubbed his arms vigorously as if he were about to become hypothermic. Then she kissed him passionately and cuddled up to him.

The next morning, the flat was very cold, and Anthony realised how much he had got used to the heating he had in his own home, even if it was only night storage radiators. This reminded him of his childhood when, as he was growing up in his parents' house, the bedrooms were not heated. When, in winter, the weather was very cold, his mother would light a fire in his bedroom in the evening, but every morning he would dash downstairs to the kitchen or sometimes the living room to sit in front of the fire while having breakfast before dressing.

Carrie was most efficient at getting a breakfast of boiled eggs and toast while he washed and dressed for work. The biggest challenge to his preparation for the office was a shave. He had to use one of Carrie's 'lady's razors' to achieve a sore, not very smooth face. He made a New Year's resolution to keep a razor and shaving soap at her flat.

They travelled into work together and parted company at the top of the escalator. As he came out of the station, Anthony looked at his reflection in a shop window. He was pleased that he had worn a white shirt the previous day as people at work might not notice that he was wearing exactly the same clothes again. To add to the subterfuge, he popped into the outsize men's shop to buy a new tie, almost the only item the shop had which was not too big for him. He did enquire about a shirt, but the smallest collar size available was seventeen and a half.

XII

When he arrived home that evening, everything was very much as usual with the boys rushing out to greet him and Ruth busy in the kitchen. He made a point of going to the kitchen as soon as he got in to apologise again for his absence the previous evening.

"I suppose it's just one of those things, Tony, but it's not like you to lose track of the time. You must have been having a very deep conversation with Malcolm," said Ruth, as she carried on getting the evening meal.

This was one of those rare moments when Anthony's love for Carrie could not anaesthetise the discomfort he felt about betraying Ruth. "Yes, he was having one of his bad days, you know what it's like," he said rather limply.

Ruth ignored his invitation to agree with him. "I think you ought to let me have his number so that I can ring him if I don't know what's happened to you, especially with this bad weather."

A stream of potential nightmares ran through Anthony's head at the suggestion that Ruth might ring Malcolm. He thought he detected a slightly cold atmosphere in the room and there was no way of knowing if that was really the case or whether it was just paranoia on his part. But the phone number presented a problem.

"Malcolm's number is ex-directory; I don't even have it myself. I always ring him at the office," said Anthony, this lie seeming to him even more lame than the last.

Ruth didn't answer but carried on with her jobs.

Anthony resisted the temptation to plough on, to seek Ruth's acquiescence of his excuse. Instead he changed the subject. "Thanks for suggesting I stay over; it would have been difficult to get home."

"It was the only sensible thing to do. Where did you get that tie? I don't remember you having it before."

"I bought it this morning. Do you like it?"

"Yes, it's very nice. What made you do that?"

"I didn't want to turn up with exactly the same clothes on as I wore yesterday."

"Couldn't Malcolm have lent you a tie – and a shirt for that matter?"

Anthony hesitated. "Yes, but I would be too small for Malcolm's shirts and I didn't think about changing the tie until I got off the tube." He looked closely at Ruth to see if he could get any clues to her thoughts, but her expression betrayed nothing.

"Go and spend some time with the boys; they missed you yesterday," said Ruth.

Anthony was happy to terminate the interrogation and did as he was told by joining his sons in a couple of games of Ludo, while asking them about their day at school.

"What's an atomic bomb, Dad?" asked Laurence, as they finished the first game and set the counters for the second.

"It's a very big bomb. How did you hear about it?"

"It was too cold to go into the playground today and at playtime Miss Dacey let us play marbles in the classroom.

Martin French had this great big marble and he sent everything flying with it and won easily and he said it was his atomic bomb."

"There you are, just as I said, it's a very big bomb."

Laurence nodded. "Your turn to start, Jonathan."

Later, while Ruth was putting the boys to bed, Anthony looked at the stamps Carrie had given him. There were French ones again, the German stamps of the 1930s featuring Zeppelins and the ubiquitous swastika of that period, and various other issues from Italy, Spain and elsewhere. He was sad that so many countries had stopped issuing airmail stamps. He assumed that the familiarity of flying and the growing use of aeroplanes to carry mail had rendered the special stamps for airmail unnecessary and anachronistic. Some of the stamps looked as if they might be quite unusual, if not exactly rare. He checked them in the catalogue and saw that several had a catalogue price of over £10, so that he could get £3 or perhaps £4 for each at a dealer's; another windfall to boost his financial position. He put the stamps in the bureau to deal with another day.

With the children bathed and tucked up in bed, Anthony and Ruth settled down for the evening. Ruth was knitting a new jumper for Jonathan with a reindeer decoration at the bottom and Anthony always wondered at her ability to knit without much having to look at what she was doing. They were watching *Z-Cars* and Anthony was looking forward to *Sportsview* and highlights of the Ashes Test in Melbourne.

Ruth put down her knitting. "Oh, I forgot, we did get some post today after all. It came ever so late, after half-past eight. The postman said deliveries are up the creek because of the snow. I'll get it."

She came back with two letters addressed to Anthony. The first was a bank statement which Anthony gave a cursory glance. The second was handwritten and underlined at the top of the envelope were the words 'Private and Confidential'. He had a vague idea that he recognised the handwriting but opened the letter casually, as the importance of the contents rarely matched the stern notification on the front. Then he gave an involuntary gasp.

"Is something the matter?" asked Ruth.

"Er, no, just a surprise. It's a letter from someone I had some dealings with through work and they would usually write to Princeton House."

"How did they get our address?"

"I'm the only P Fernard in the London telephone directory."

"Not a problem, is it?"

"No, nothing to worry about. Would you like a cup of coffee?"

"I'll get it," said Ruth, putting her knitting down again.

"No, you sit down, I'll get it for a change."

Anthony put the letter in his pocket and went out to the kitchen. While he waited for the kettle to boil, he took the letter out and read it again. After the initial shock when he'd opened it, he'd realised that, pushed to one corner in his mind by what else was going on in his life, he'd been half-expecting this. He read the letter for a third time; this time slowly, trying to analyse its meaning and consider its ramifications.

Dear Mr Fernard,

May I begin by offering you my very best wishes for all happiness and prosperity in 1963.

You were kind enough to agree to my brother joining my wife and me in this country recently, an act of generosity for which I was pleased to show my appreciation. I wonder if I might prevail on your kindness once more by asking you to facilitate the entry visa for another person whom I believe to be a deserving case.

Mr Boguslaw Cieslak is a highly qualified chemical engineer and he has been offered the chance to work for a short period at one of the British firms in his industry. This would be a great opportunity for him and I'm sure the company will benefit a good deal from his expertise.

My reason for approaching you on his behalf is that he is my wife's cousin and I am able to vouch for his integrity and suitability. I should be most obliged if you could see your way clear to granting him a visa to work in Britain for a few months.

I shall be eternally grateful for your assistance in this matter.

Yours sincerely,
Wicus Cavalir (Lt. Col. Retd.)

The kettle boiled, but Anthony didn't notice for some time. He was still reading the letter over and over again while a strange feeling gnawed away at his innards, a feeling he hadn't experienced since he was placed on a charge during his national service and before that when he was disciplined at grammar school, which he was frequently.

Finally he saw the steam rising around him and he put the letter back in his pocket while he made the coffee. He took the cups in on a tray with some chocolate digestives and set them on the table between their two armchairs.

"Thanks very much, Tony," said Ruth as she took a sip of her coffee. "Ugh, no sugar!" she exclaimed, grimacing.

"Sorry," said Anthony, rising to get the sugar bowl.

When he returned, Ruth ran through what he'd missed on the television and he nodded, though he hadn't heard a word. Nor did he hear anything of what happened in the programme after that.

When the programme ended Ruth got up. "I think I'll give my mother a call and leave you to the sports for now."

"Give her my love," said Anthony.

He did watch *Sportsview*: the interview with Donald Campbell and another with the newly appointed England football manager, Alf Ramsey; then the coverage of the fourth day's play in the Second Test between Australia and England. But afterwards, he could barely remember anything of it; not even Brian Booth's fine century or Freddie Truman's five wicket haul. The television was a series of moving images with a faint soundtrack which could not break through his fixation on the contents of the letter. He had noted that the address was a PO box in Leeds and there was no telephone number. The name of the person seeking a visa had a surname beginning with C, so Cavalir knew how the Home Office worked. He also knew where Anthony lived.

His thoughts were interrupted by Ruth returning to say that she was going to take a bath and would return later to make a night-time drink.

He smiled at her weakly and returned to his thoughts. He desperately wanted to believe that Cavalir was an ordinary Polish émigré; a pillar of the expatriate Polish community and a fiercely anti-communist supporter of the Polish government in exile. But the more he went over the sequence of events, the shakier his belief became. He was moving reluctantly to the view that he may have been the victim of an entrapment of some kind. There was only one way to find out. He went into the dining room and took a scrap pad from the bureau. After three or four attempts at the wording of a letter, he took some plain writing paper from the bureau and wrote to Colonel Cavalir.

Dear Colonel Cavalir,

Thank you for your letter dated 31st December concerning a visa request for Mr Boguslaw Cieslak.

As I am sure you are aware, all such applications must go through the formal channels of the Home Office and not privately to a member of the Civil Service, so I am unable to comment in any way on this matter. If Mr Cieslak does apply for a visa, his case will be dealt with strictly on its merits, but there can be no guarantee that his application will be granted.

Yours sincerely,

Anthony Fernard

He placed the letter in an envelope and put a stamp on it, ready to be posted the next morning and then tried to put the whole business out of his mind.

He'd barely put the envelope in his overcoat pocket when Ruth came down in her dressing gown. "Did you enjoy the cricket? On the radio they sounded confident that England will win tomorrow."

"Yes, it was good," said Anthony.

Ruth went out to get a cup of cocoa for herself and tea for Anthony and when she returned, they sat and drank in silence.

"Are you all right?" asked Ruth. "You seem a little distant."

"Sorry, just puzzling over why that chap wrote to me here."

"Perhaps he didn't understand the right way of going about things. Well, don't be too long, the bed was cold without you last night." She took the cups out to the kitchen and locked the front door as she made her way up to bed.

When he went to bed, he provided the warmth that Ruth demanded as she cuddled up to him and fell asleep. But nothing he tried, mentally compiling alphabetical lists of this and that, thinking of prime numbers between one hundred and a thousand or even the clichéd counting of sheep, enabled him to drift into sleep. Eventually he gave up and went down to the very cold living room for a cigarette and a glass of Scotch. He read the letter again and then went through the known facts for the hundredth time, asking why he had received the letter. It was always the same answer: the one he dreaded.

His brain finally gave up working on his problems and surrendered to sleep. He woke with a stiff neck and a left arm which had gone to sleep under his body. The clock on the mantelpiece showed twenty-past six. He stood up rather stiffly and waited for the pain as his dead arm came back to life. Then he went slowly upstairs to go to the bathroom and prepare for the day. He spent the next ten minutes swearing at himself in the mirror as he washed and shaved, cutting himself twice in the process. He hardly touched his breakfast but rushed off to work. His sterile self-recrimination had given way to the impetus to do something.

On the way to the station he posted the letter to Colonel Cavalir and as soon as he'd checked the file, he telephoned the enquiries section of B4, the Home Office Naturalisation Division.

"Hello, it's Anthony Fernard from B2. I have a query about a Polish resident here and I wondered if he had acquired British nationality."

"What's the name?"

"Wicus Cavalir, born 23rd March 1903 in a village near Kowel."

"Just a minute, I'll go through the register." The man was gone for a few minutes.

"Hello, Fernard? There was an application made for naturalisation in 1956, but it was terminated."

"Why was that?"

"He died while the application was being processed."

Anthony held back an expletive and took a deep breath. "I see, thanks for checking it out for me." He put the phone down and noticed the sweat on the handset.

He rose from his desk and, taking his towel and soap, went to the men's washroom. Fortunately, there was no one else there and he could stand still with his head in his hands for a few minutes while the clammy, slightly shaky sensation began to subside. He looked at his pasty face in the mirror. "Well now you know," he said. Then he washed his face, straightened his tie and walked around the building for a few minutes until he felt relatively normal and could face going back to his desk.

In the days that followed, he felt like a man in the condemned cell waiting for the governor's call to tell him his plea for clemency had been denied. He went through the motions at work and at home as best he could but cancelled his social engagements, including his pre-arranged lunch appointments and even an evening session with Carrie. He felt quite unable to engage in any meaningful conversation and told people he was under the weather. Almost as a relief, the anticipated reply to his letter soon came. After a miserable weekend in which he seemed completely distant and incommunicable to all those he lived with, there was a telephone call on Monday evening half an hour after he arrived home.

"Buckhurst 3869."

"Mr Fernard?"

"Speaking."

"Good evening, this is Colonel Cavalir here." The voice sounded pleasant, with precise pronunciation and only the slightest of accents.

Anthony caught his breath, unable to respond for a second or two. The telephone was in the hall and he closed the kitchen door. "I don't know who you are but Colonel Cavalir died some years ago." He could feel his heart pounding and sweat was surfacing on his forehead.

The person on the other end of the phone laughed. "I am very much alive, I assure you. Thank you for your letter, Mr Fernard, but..."

Anthony interrupted him. "My reply was perfectly clear; any applications for visas must be done through the proper channels." He struggled to speak quietly, even though he was conscious that Ruth was only a few feet away.

"I don't think you understand," said the voice calmly. "As far as I am concerned, these are the proper channels."

"Don't be ridiculous," said Anthony.

"I think we should meet to discuss the matter raised in my letter."

"Are you mad? How many times must I tell you?" Anthony said, conscious his voice was rising but unable to lower it. "I have nothing else to say on the matter, on the telephone or face to face." He hoped he sounded more assertive than he felt. He wanted to put the phone down but didn't.

Cavalir began sparring with him. "I think you would be wise to spare me a few moments of your time. Or perhaps you would rather I spoke to your wife?"

"What do you mean?" Anthony cupped his hand defensively over the mouthpiece. "This is no concern of my wife," he rasped in a stage whisper.

"No, but I believe that Miss Carillon Burdine would be of concern to her."

Anthony had received the punch to the solar plexus his guard was unable to prevent. The uppercut followed swiftly.

"There is also the matter of the cheque, which I am sure would be of interest to your employer."

Anthony knew his situation was hopeless and he threw in the towel. "Where and when do you suggest we meet?" he asked quietly.

"There is a telephone box on the corner of Hatton Garden and High Holborn. Wait there at five-twenty-five tomorrow evening and I will ring you to tell you where the meeting will take place. Please don't do anything brave or foolish; it will serve no purpose and you will not avoid the consequences. I look forward to seeing you, goodbye."

Anthony replaced the phone. He felt sick and wanted to be on his own, somewhere quiet where he could think. But the kitchen door flew open and Ruth appeared carrying some plates of food.

"Who was that? It sounded like you were having a row. You look very pale. Are you all right?"

"Erm, nothing important and certainly not a row."

He looked in the mirror and he did look awful. "I feel a bit seedy, that's all. It was Chris Lowell from the bridge club; he wanted to know if I was interested in playing next week."

"Gosh, you haven't played bridge for ages."

"No, but they are a couple short for the annual competition. I said I was a bit rusty, but I'd think about it."

"Dinner's ready," said Ruth, bustling past him.

Anthony did his best to eat the beef casserole Ruth had placed before him and explained his failure to finish on the seedy feeling expressed earlier. After passing on the dessert, he sought distraction in games with the children until it was time for them to get ready for bed. Then he sat in the living room mulling over his options while Ruth took the boys upstairs. He tried to be analytical about his choices. First, he could go to his superiors at the Home Office. He would face disciplinary action at the very least for accepting a payment and Cavalir, or whoever he was, would probably tell Ruth about his affair with

Carrie. Second, he could tell Ruth everything and hope she would forgive him and stand by him while he went through the investigation into his conduct and the disciplinary process afterwards. Third, he could do nothing and see if Cavalir carried out his threat. Fourth, he could meet Cavalir and hope to avoid getting into anything more serious than perhaps one more favour. After all, the case Cavalir had raised might be one he could legitimately sanction.

"The boys are ready for stories!" called out Ruth.

Number four, thought Anthony. "Coming!" he called and went upstairs to read another chapter of *The Wind in the Willows.*

The next afternoon he made his way along High Holborn. He walked past the dark pink neo-gothic Prudential building and glanced over at Staple Inn Chambers, the Tudor shop frontage of which always reminded him of the tobacco smoked by his grandfather. He finally arrived at the telephone box just after five-twenty. His worst fears were realised when he could see from a distance that someone was in the box; a man in an overcoat and trilby hat. He arrived at the box and waited, making himself visible to the man inside, and watched. The man held the handset to his ear but seemed not to be saying very much. He turned away when he saw Anthony looking at him. Anthony checked his watch and saw it was five-twenty-four and still the man had not finished his call. He could feel the panic rising within him and thought about banging on the door to say that he had an emergency. Then, at five-twenty-five the man replaced the receiver and opened the door, holding it for Anthony to go in. He stood in the box, not sure what to do, but within ten seconds the phone rang.

"Hello," said Anthony.

"This is Cavalir. Are you alone?"

"Yes, of course."

"Walk down Hatton Garden on the left-hand side of the street. Turn left into Greville Street, right into Leather Lane and left into Dorrington Street. Wait by the first door on the left." He hung up.

Anthony followed his instructions and pulled his coat collar up against the biting wind as he walked along Hatton Garden. He looked behind him once and noticed that the man who had been in the telephone box before him was now about twenty yards behind him. He had the strange feeling of being in a John Le Carré novel or a film like *The Third Man*. *This is just like it would be in a spy film,* he thought, *but are situations like this art imitating life or the other way round? How many people wear trilbies these days, but the man following me is wearing one, just like a spy in a film.* He turned into Dorrington Street and stopped at the first door. It was closed and there was no sign of life. He waited, trying to appear inconspicuous, while the man who had been following him stopped at the end of the road and kept his gaze on Leather Lane. The man lit a cigarette. *Just like the man in the advert for Strand cigarettes,* thought Anthony.

After about a minute, a young man came out of a side alley and walked over to him. He was dressed smartly but innocuously like a typical office worker, perhaps a bank clerk or an insurance broker. "Come with me," he said, the accent not that of a typical office worker in Holborn.

Anthony accompanied him back down the alley to a grimy building which had that not unpleasant smell typical of a metal workshop; the regular beat of machinery could be heard on the ground floor. A side door led to a steep flight of stairs. Anthony followed the man up these stairs and then onwards up flight after increasingly decrepit flight to the fourth and top floor and then into a room about ten feet square, lit by a solitary, unopened, dormer window. The room was empty save for a desk and four wooden chairs with oiled-leather black seats. The walls were covered in a flaking distemper of indiscriminate colour and the whole impression was one of dilapidation. Yet the room was clean and the desk had been polished. The man who had led him up the stairs sat on one of the chairs by the door.

Seated behind the desk and dressed in a well-cut, black three-piece suit, light blue shirt and grey tie, was a man of about fifty-five. His black hair, greying at the temples, was swept back with a parting just off-centre and his aquiline features were creased into a broad smile.

"Welcome, Mr Fernard, I am Cavalir," he said, standing up and signalling with his hand to a tall, well-fed man standing behind him. "I'm sure you will not object to my associate, Mr Brown, checking that you are not carrying any kind of communication device."

Anthony recognised in Cavalir the voice of the man who had telephoned him on Monday. He shook his head and raised his arms outstretched.

The man referred to as Mr Brown frisked Anthony thoroughly and nodded to his colleague behind the desk.

"Do sit down, Mr Fernard. I apologise for all this cloak and dagger behaviour, but we have to be sure that you have not succumbed to the temptation to alert the authorities. I also regret that this is a rather insalubrious meeting room, but we shall only be using it this once so there was no point in redecorating it."

He looked as if he were about to laugh but merely smiled again and looked at Anthony but when there was no response he continued, "Have you had a chance to reflect on the little request I made of you?"

"Have I any choice?"

"There is always a choice; it's the consequence of choice that sometimes presents the difficulties."

"The thing is Mr Cavalir, do I call you Cavalir?"

"It's as good a name as any."

Anthony thought Cavalir sounded rather smug but didn't feel in a position to make anything of it. "I would like to know what I'm being used for; what will this man do when he comes to Britain?" he asked.

"He will work in a chemical company and learn some things that will be of use to industries in my country."

"Your country being?"

"Why, Poland, of course."

"So you are asking me to facilitate some sort of industrial espionage activity?"

Cavalir smiled. "That makes it sound very dramatic. Let's just say that we would like to learn a little of the company's expertise in a number of industrial applications."

"To what purpose?"

"Merely to help improve our own products and processes with the help of an added ingredient or a little adjustment to the way we do things."

"The problem is that even if I do agree to what you ask, I may not have it in my power to deliver the outcome you expect."

"But in principle you are willing to?"

Anthony thought briefly about his options in a quick re-run of his sleepless hours spent tossing and turning the previous night. But still he couldn't see any that didn't involve him losing some control of his own life. "As long as it is for commercial and not state intelligence, I guess I am prepared to help you. But what if I don't deal with the case or get overruled?"

"You must use the means at your disposal to ensure that doesn't happen."

"And if I can't?"

"Let's not consider that possibility. You will, of course, be financially rewarded for your efforts."

"And that will be it, once I've done this for you?" He looked at the three men for reassurance.

The other two remained statuesque in their impassivity, staring straight ahead, but Cavalir responded in a positive tone. "There may be other occasions, not often, but once in a while we might make a similar request. It will not be onerous."

"How will you contact me in the future? I'd rather you didn't telephone or write to me at home, or at work for that matter."

"We have various options, but your home address is the least difficult or suspicious one, as long as you don't give the authorities any reason to believe you are involved in nefarious activities. But don't worry; it will be in a form that would not make your wife suspicious. I think it best she knows nothing of this. There will be a payment in appreciation, as I indicated. It will be left for you in cash at this address and I will send you a postcard when it is due." He handed Anthony the business card of a newsagent in Leytonstone, with the notation 'Collect under the name C Phillipson'.

Anthony nodded. "What if I need to get in touch with you?"

Cavalir gave him the business card of a person named 'Joseph Sikora' with the telephone number of an office services company. "You can leave a message for me, in the name of Mr Sikora, at this number."

Anthony put the card in his wallet. "You think of everything," he said.

"I will take that as a compliment. My colleagues think I'm too careful, but it's always the detail that lets everyone down."

"When will this visa application come through?" Anthony asked.

"In the next few weeks; you still have the details we sent you?"

"Yes."

"Make sure you burn the papers we sent you once this matter is completed, for your security as much as ours. Do you have any other questions?"

Anthony racked his brains for anything they hadn't covered, but nothing came to mind. "No, I don't think so."

They stood up and shook hands, something which Anthony felt uncomfortable doing but thought unavoidable.

"Thank you for co-operating with us, Mr Fernard. We will not demand more of you than is reasonable and we will endeavour to reward you properly for your assistance," said Cavalir, as Anthony turned to go.

He was taken out of the office the way he'd come in and escorted to the end of the road by the nondescript man who'd brought him there. He then walked back along Hatton Garden to Chancery Lane station to take a tube home.

He was experiencing mixed emotions. On the one hand, he was annoyed and disappointed with himself for falling for an obvious entrapment and now he was at the beck and call of Cavalir and his cronies. On the other hand, he was relieved that he was probably going to be a very small cog in Cavalir's wheel; after all he was not privy to any information that Cavalir could not easily get himself. He would just be someone they could call on for small favours from time to time and he would be paid for his effort. He was reluctant to admit to himself that he was also a little excited by his involvement in the murky glamour of the world of espionage – a kind of reflected ingloriousness. What he found most difficult was that there was no one with whom he could share this news nor the worries and feelings which accompanied it: not Ruth, not Carrie, none of his friends, nobody; it was a secret between him and his inner self.

XIII

Every day at work Anthony waited for the arrival of a file marked 'Boguslaw Cieslak'. At times, the apprehension of its pending arrival and what he would do if it went astray somehow seemed to take over all his thoughts and most of his energy. He found himself examining all his cases from Poland more carefully for anything suspicious. He avoided seeing both Ronnie and Malcolm in case he let slip what was constantly on his mind and he was listless company for Ruth and the boys. Even with Carrie he felt distracted and weary when they went out; only in bed did he seem able to forget his preoccupations and show a degree of enthusiasm. Carrie could hardly fail to notice his change in demeanour, but he passed it off by saying that there were a lot of difficult cases at work and that he had not been sleeping well. The latter excuse was certainly valid.

Finally, on 23rd January it arrived; the newly opened green file headed with a C reference number and the name 'CIESLAK, Boguslaw'. Inside was a passport stamped with a Polish exit visa, completed application forms for a visa and a work permit and a letter of support from a specialist chemical company in Yorkshire. Anthony opened the passport and looked at the black and white photograph of a twenty-nine-year-old described as having blue eyes and dark brown hair. He looked pleasant enough and not in any way sinister. The forms were filled in impeccably and the letter of support waxed lyrical about Cieslak's expertise in his field and how he'd be able to make an important contribution to the company's development of groundbreaking products for the British and overseas markets. Everything pointed to a suitable application for a visa, except that Cieslak was a citizen of one of the European communist countries and therefore subject to stricter criteria than almost anywhere else. He looked at the letter of support again and wondered whether it was authentic or merely a fake furnished by the Polish authorities, or even whether the man was going to work for the company at all. In other circumstances he might have troubled to contact the company for confirmation of their offer, but there was no question of that now.

Anthony had rehearsed this moment in his head many times. The normal procedure was that he would recommend action and then pass it to Daphne Raynott for confirmation. If he authorised it himself this would be bound to raise eyebrows with George, his Clerical Assistant, who would wonder why he had not followed the normal procedure, even if he didn't say anything to Anthony. Knowing that Daphne would be most unlikely to authorise the visa without referring it to her superior, he realised he would have to authorise the visa and then do the clerical operations normally performed by George. The question remained as to whether he should forge Daphne's signature, though not to do so would only complicate matters. Once the visa was authorised the file would go into the archives and hopefully never re-appear as a live case. Certainly, if he counter-signed it for Daphne, the file would look as if correct procedure had been followed and have the additional advantage of diverting attention for the decision towards Daphne, should anyone ever review the case.

He checked in his out tray that there was a file with an instruction counter-signed by Daphne then put this file back in his pending tray. That done, he went back to his other work until lunchtime. At five-past one he was the only person in the office except for two people in the other section. All of his own team had either just gone to lunch or had yet to return from their break.

He took the file with Daphne's signature in it and turned the file upside down. Then he took a piece of scrap paper and copied Daphne's upside-down signature onto it. This was a trick he'd picked up when he was the letter forger for his class at school. When copying a parent's signature for a note excusing absenteeism or seeking exemption from games, he'd found that when the signature was upside down, he was less likely to let his own writing style creep in; he was, in effect, drawing not writing. Having practised it twice and happy with the results, he put the file back in his out tray and turned to the Cieslak file. He wrote his recommendation that the application be granted in black ink, changed his pen to a blue one and ticked his recommendation in the style of Daphne before turning the file upside down and adding Daphne's 'signature'. He had just turned the file back the right way when Patricia Lovell came into the room with her soap and towel. While she was fiddling with her purse and checking her make-up, he walked casually over to George's desk and did the necessary stamp in the passport. The file then went into his out tray for the post room and subsequent filing in the registry.

It's as easy as that, thought Anthony. When it came down to it, he was just doing his ordinary job with a twist. It was possible that someone at the chemicals firm was in on the subterfuge but even if not, what was the worst that would happen? Cieslak would probably contribute something to the firm's intellectual capital and help them develop some products. Then he would take the information he gained back to Poland, or perhaps the Soviet Union. If they did copy the British company's products, the Eastern European producers would not be selling them in the same market. Anyway, the Japanese copied European products all the time and then improved them and sold them back to Europe. The only thing that could trouble him would be if the products could be used in chemical weapons, but he thought that was extremely unlikely. Anyway, he had other things on his mind; the fourteenth of February was on the horizon.

Anthony and Ruth had sent each other a Valentine's card when they were engaged, but they hadn't bothered once they were married since, after all, their love had been consummated. However, they marked the date most years with a little gift or a meal out. They always spent the evening together. So this year presented something of a dilemma as he thought Carrie would also wish to spend the evening with him. It was moments like this that made him wish he could claim to be working late at the office.

The week before the due date he broached the subject with Ruth as they settled down in the living room for the evening.

"How would you feel about me seeing Malcolm next Thursday, as usual?"

Ruth was looking through the *Radio Times* to see what was on the television. "You don't usually ask my opinion," she said, raising her eyes with a slightly puzzled expression.

"It's Valentine's Day."

"Oh, of course; I forgot. Well, I don't know, we usually spend the evening together. Couldn't you make it another evening with Malcolm? I suppose it shouldn't matter." She smiled.

"You're right," he said; it was the pleasant smile that did it. "I'll make it another day."

At work the next day, he rang Carrie to tell her that he couldn't spend Thursday evening with her and they agreed to meet for lunch instead. They went to the French restaurant off Kingsway where they'd first had lunch and where they'd gone about once a week ever since. Anthony arrived at the restaurant with twelve red roses and a Valentine's card. Carrie was already there, reading a book. He stared at her in repose while the waiter took his overcoat and he thought she looked radiant. Her face broke into a broad smile as she looked up and saw him.

"Thank you, they're lovely," she said, taking the flowers. "I'll have some questions about these when I get back to the office; and a card too." It was a traditional-looking card, the cover having a heart in violet material with a lace border in the centre and a ribbon down the side. She opened it and read 'All my love – your most ardent admirer'. She took his hand and held it tight. Then she opened her handbag and passed him a card with a small wrapped package.

The card was a plain cream card with the words 'I love you' on the front. He opened it and inside Carrie had written in her fine hand:

'I have spread my dreams under your feet;
Tread softly because you tread on my dreams.'

Anthony read it twice and could feel a tear in his eye. He took the package and opened it to reveal a heart; it was in gold foil and Anthony supposed it contained a confection of some sort. "Thank you," he said. "It's lovely."

"You don't have to keep the card," said Carrie.

"I've got the desk at work, so I'll keep it. You know, I am sorry about tonight."

Carrie nodded and looked sad for a moment. Then she smiled. "I knew the score when I got into this. Anyway, it's only a day like any other, made into something big by the florists and the card shops. Really, don't worry about it. The main thing is we got to see each other."

Their exchange of tributes over, they didn't dwell on their relationship but enjoyed a happy lunch, talking about nothing but meaning everything. They didn't have too much time, so they skipped the starter and shared a chateaubriand, as a treat, with a bottle of St Estephe. They finished the wine off with some cheese and then asked for some coffee.

The waiter brought over two glasses of Grand Marnier with the coffee. "Compliments of the house," he said. "I hope you enjoy the rest of your day."

"That was nice of him, perhaps it's because we're regulars now," he said to Carrie as they raised their glasses to each other.

Carrie smiled. "Whatever the reason, it's a very nice gesture."

They left the restaurant and walked back along Kingsway. "I wish we could be alone together," said Anthony.

"Me too," she replied.

They turned right up Remnant Street and walked through Lincoln's Inn Fields. As it had been for weeks, the weather was still bitterly cold in the wind and the odd piles of dirtying snow hung on resolutely. Nonetheless, the netball court was still occupied by two teams of young women, their bare legs various shades of white, pink and light mauve. They were watched by an appreciative audience of men of all ages, wrapped up in their symbolic, as well as practical, overcoats. Anthony smiled knowingly and Carrie nodded with a raised eyebrow before they found an empty bench away from the hubbub.

They sat down and put their arms round each other and kissed.

Carrie opened the middle button of her coat. "Put your hands inside my coat," she said. "I want to feel your hand against me. I'll keep you warm."

Anthony did as he was asked, taking off his gloves and putting his hands inside her coat and against the warmth of her jumper, one hand round her back and the other on her breast. They kissed, murmured words of love and held each other like that for some minutes ignoring, not even aware of, anyone else who might be around. Then, simultaneously, they knew it was time to go. Anthony withdrew his hands and put on his gloves and Carrie did up her coat. Then they walked gloved hand in gloved hand up Gate Street and back onto Kingsway.

"I shall miss you tonight," said Anthony.

Carrie nodded. "I know, I shall miss you very much too, but it's been lovely today. Thanks for the roses and the card; I shall treasure them."

They kissed once more briefly and went back to work. As he had promised, Anthony hid the card at the back of his drawer and opened up the gold foil heart which revealed, when opened, some small violet creams and a card expressing her love.

When he arrived home that evening, Ruth was in the kitchen in her apron, but he noticed that she was wearing a dress and a necklace and had had her hair done.

"Hello," he said. "You look really pretty."

She gave a smile of quiet delight. "Thanks, we're not eating with the children tonight. I've got something special."

Anthony produced from behind his back a large box of chocolates, which he had bought from a specialist shop before he left Holborn.

"Gosh, that's a treat," said Ruth, admiring the tastefully understated box and expensive silk ribbon.

Anthony smiled and went upstairs to look in on the boys who were playing with Laurence's train set. He was both surprised and pleased by the speed with which Laurence had been able to take pretty much complete management of the system. He just watched them play, only becoming involved on the rare occasion his advice was sought. His days as station master were over; he'd been kicked upstairs to regional manager. When the boys were called down to eat, he went to the sitting room and read the newspaper.

With the children in bed, Ruth returned to the kitchen and cooked a second evening meal, this time of entrecôte steak with duchess potatoes, preceded by crab paté. Anthony was not very hungry but was determined to do her efforts justice and only faltered a little in the face of a dessert of pineapple upside-down cake.

He'd meant what he'd said earlier; Ruth did look really attractive in her dark green cocktail dress and her new hairstyle. He appreciated all the trouble she'd gone to.

"I hope the wine's all right," said Ruth. "I got it at the off-licence."

"It's very good," said Anthony, sipping at the 1959 Haut-Médoc. "Let me pay for that, it couldn't have been cheap."

"No, don't worry about it; I'm pleased I made a good choice."

After dinner Anthony offered to wash up but Ruth would have none of it. She soon cleared away and then joined Anthony, bringing with her the still one-third full bottle of wine and the glasses. She poured them both a drink and sat down in an armchair.

"This dress is getting a bit tight," she said, wriggling and pulling it in one or two places. "It must have shrunk or I'm getting fat; I don't think it's shrunk."

Anthony laughed. "Nonsense, you've got a lovely figure. You look great."

"Mm," she said, "I'll take your word for it. Is there anything good on the television?"

Anthony looked for the TV listings in the newspaper. "Well, we've missed *The White Heather Club,* thank God. *Steptoe and Son* is just starting and then there's a film on BBC, *A Dog for Father Fritz,* followed by *Amateur Boxing.* ITV has a Western and then *Hancock,* followed by the news and *This Week.* I suppose the news programmes will be all about Harold Wilson taking over as Labour leader. Take your choice."

"Let's watch *Steptoe* for now."

Anthony put the television on and they watched an episode called 'Is That Your Horse Outside?' which contained its usual mixture of comedy and pathos.

"Poor old Harold; always comes off worse," said Ruth, finishing her glass of wine. "Back in a minute," she added as she rose from her chair.

Anthony toyed with the idea of watching *Hancock* for old times' sake, but the problem was he just didn't find him as funny as he used to. So he left the BBC on and looked at the synopsis of the film with the unpromising title. That was enough to make him go for *Hancock* anyway.

After several minutes Ruth returned. She had taken off her clothes and make-up and was now wearing only a diaphanous one-layer négligée. "That's better," she said. "I was feeling really uncomfortable." She settled back in her chair and started watching the TV while breaking open the box of chocolates Anthony had given her. "These are lovely," she said, taking a second chocolate and offering the box to Anthony.

Anthony's interest in the programme, already tepid, was further distracted by Ruth's choice of apparel. He couldn't recall her adopting this attire for the sitting room since the earliest days of their marriage.

"Will you be warm enough?" he asked. "The storage heaters will soon be cooling down." He posed this rather vacuous question purely so that he could regard his wife without appearing to stare at her. He thought she looked magnificent, a little bit overweight she might say, but she carried it well, he might reply.

"I'm all right. I was feeling a bit hot actually. Do you want anything else to drink?"

"No thanks, not at the moment," he said, reluctantly looking back at the television.

They continued watching the television, both rather half-heartedly, for a few more minutes until Ruth said, "This isn't one of his best, is it? Fancy an early night?" She turned to him, smiling in anticipation of his response.

He thought she seemed pleased that he was looking at her. Given the thoughts going through his head, Anthony was not surprised to find himself, not merely acquiescing, but positively leaping at the idea. "Yes, I think we should," he said and followed his wife, turning off the lights as he went.

Ruth told him to come straight to bed, leaving his teeth and anything else till later and Anthony didn't object; he wanted to spoil the moment no more than she did. A part of him tried to think of Carrie, if only to experience a token pang of guilt but it wouldn't happen. Delightful though it was, his relationship with her seemed at times to belong to an entirely different life. He found it much easier at this moment to concentrate on this naked woman lying expectantly on the bed.

He hadn't heard anything more from Cavalir for nearly a month. Then, the Wednesday after Valentine's Day, a postcard arrived in an envelope stating that his book was ready for collection at the newsagent's in Leytonstone. On the way home from work he stopped off at Leytonstone station and went to collect his reward. There was nothing remarkable about the shop. The name on the frontage read 'J Grainger, Newsagent and Tobacconist' and the front window was dressed with an enticing display of cigarettes, courtesy of a window dresser from the Imperial Tobacco Company. Affixed to the side of the window were cards advertising various services, including a large one which stated 'Poste Restante Service – Apply Within'. Underneath the window, wire frames held newspaper headline posters from the *Star*, *News* and *Standard*.

Anthony hesitated a little. He had a feeling, not exactly of foreboding, but certainly of being exposed, as he reflected he was about to collect a package in a false name from the agent of a foreign country for controversial services rendered. He looked furtively both ways up the street then went into the shop. It was empty apart from a young fair-headed woman, dressed in a pale blue dustcoat, leaning on the counter and flicking through the pages of a magazine. She closed the magazine, a copy of *Boyfriend*, when she saw Anthony come in.

"Yes, please," she said.

"Hello, I believe you have a package for me, Mr C Phillipson?"

The woman smiled and went into a back room, returning a couple of moments later with a thick envelope and a receipt book. "Would you sign for it please, Mr Phillipson," she said.

Anthony signed for the package in a signature he'd practised a few times and put it in his overcoat inside pocket. The young woman thanked him, smiled again and then returned to her *Boyfriend*.

He came out of the shop even more warily than he'd gone in it and once more glanced both ways before he set off back to the tube station, turning off into a side road briefly and relieved that no one followed him. As far as he could tell, he was in the clear.

When he arrived home, he greeted his family cursorily and went straight upstairs to the bathroom. He opened the envelope to find £150 in used £5 notes and stared at the head of Britannia looking at him questioningly, or perhaps reproachfully, thirty times.

Whenever he had considered blackmail hypothetically, he had always been convinced that he would never succumb to it. He would have refused to co-operate and face the consequences. Yet, when he'd been confronted with the reality of it, he'd yielded to Cavalir's demands almost immediately. He had done everything asked of him purely because he was being blackmailed. He wondered whether taking money made it worse but, in a strange way, he felt better about it; he preferred to think of himself as a mercenary rather than a blackmail victim. He did not try to justify to himself what he'd done or pretend that in the scheme of things it wasn't really important. He knew full well that his actions were impossible to defend, but the simple truth was that he could live with himself.

Ruth called out, "Tony, dinner's ready."

"Coming," he said and went into the bedroom. He divided the money into smaller amounts of about £30 and then put these individual sums in his shoe boxes. The last £30 he put into his wallet. He hung his jacket in the wardrobe and put on a pullover before going down.

XIV

Life went back to normal. As Anthony had hoped, he heard nothing from Cavalir in the following weeks and the whole episode faded to the point that he rarely even thought about it. Perhaps it would be a one-off after all. Indeed, sometimes he had to remind himself that it'd really happened and wasn't some kind of fantasy. He used some of this latest money he'd received to book the family holiday in Devon at a superior hotel to their usual standard, reciprocating Ronnie's gift of lunch at Rules and taking Carrie to dinner at the Café Royal, to make up for any disappointment over Valentine's Day. The rest was kept in his shoeboxes to be used to lubricate the financial workings of his home and social life, but sparingly so as not to arouse suspicion.

As the end of winter approached at last and the snow finally disappeared, Anthony's appetite for socialising grew with the milder, if wetter, weather. Having used Malcolm as his 'Bunbury' for so long, he tended to think he saw him more often than he did, but in fact he hadn't seen him since before Christmas and thought it was time he got in touch. Early in March, he was on the verge of calling him when he got a call from Malcolm himself. He was helping to host a drinks reception for some of the diplomatic corps and other dignitaries at Lancaster House the following week and he invited Anthony along. This promised to be a new experience for Anthony and he was pleased to accept. He welcomed the opportunity to look round the building and observe the rites and rituals of diplomatic entertaining, including the slow dance round the room described by Malcolm.

Just to see inside the late Georgian masterpiece that was Lancaster House made going to the reception worthwhile, but he really enjoyed the whole experience. He seized the chance to look round the grand rooms, with their exquisitely ornate decoration and took a walk up the grand staircase. He was introduced to the Minister of State at the Foreign Office, exchanged the odd word or two with various guests and had quite a long chat with the wife of an ambassador who assumed he worked at the Foreign Office. As she was a rather attractive woman, he was in no particular rush to correct her misunderstanding nor to terminate their conversation. So he used his own frequent dealings with the Foreign Office, slightly exaggerated and full of narrator's licence, to serve up some anecdotes about Russian stateless émigrés and asylum seekers from various parts of the Middle East which she seemed to find of interest.

Anthony didn't get much opportunity to talk to Malcolm during the reception, but afterwards Malcolm asked him to stay behind for a final drink or two. "To use up some of the half-empties," as he put it.

They stood by one of the drinks tables and served themselves with what was still on offer. "Thanks for coming, Tony. I hope you enjoyed it."

"Yes, I enjoyed it a lot: looking round the building, seeing some of these characters up close and the occasional bit of chatter, all of it was interesting. So thanks very much for asking me along."

"Well thank *you* for showing up. You were a great help circulating the room and mixing with the other guests. It appears you were quite a hit with that lady you were speaking to for some time. She was full of smiles and compliments after your little tête-à-tête."

"She's rather attractive, isn't she? She's the wife of the Norwegian ambassador. Her English is perfect, but then of course it so often is with the Scandinavians. That's the sort of woman *you* should be chatting up at this kind of event."

"I don't think it would go down too well if I formed a liaison with the wife of the ambassador of one of our closest allies," said Malcolm, smiling.

"Perhaps not that lady, but certainly someone like that who's currently unattached."

Malcolm looked sceptical and changed the subject. "Talking about potentially inappropriate relationships, I suppose you've seen the hints in the newspapers concerning Profumo?"

Anthony nodded. "Yes, I've seen it, but I don't know much about it, at least not in any detail. I was first aware of the rumours in vague terms over a year ago when one of my colleagues mentioned it. I'd forgotten all about it until the press started making noises. I'm not a great one for gossip, otherwise I would've asked Ronnie."

"Yes, it's his department. I agree with you about gossip, but there's more to it this time. There's a Labour MP, Colonel Wigg, who's a bit of a ferret when it comes to security issues. He stirred things up because of the possibility of a security leak, something to do with Russian intelligence. I suppose it will all come out, it usually does."

Malcolm's last comment seemed too close for comfort and Anthony suddenly felt a bit queasy. He gave no response to Malcolm.

"Are you all right, Tony? You look very pale."

Anthony regained his composure. "Yes thanks. Just felt a little faint for a moment. It's rather warm in here." He took out a handkerchief and wiped his brow.

Malcolm was very solicitous. He looked round and brought over a chair for Anthony. Then he poured him a glass of water and watched as Anthony drank some of it. "Perhaps I'd better get you a taxi or something."

Anthony raised his hand. "No, I'm feeling much better now, please don't fuss over me. Sorry, I interrupted your flow; you were talking about Profumo."

"Oh, it's not important, just tittle-tattle at the moment."

"No really, I am curious about this whole Profumo business. I would like to hear about it."

Reassured by the colour returning to Anthony's cheeks, Malcolm told him what he knew. "Well, I got to hear about it because the section I work in deals with Soviet matters and we were kept informed as there is a Russian connection to people known to John Profumo. Apparently he had some kind of social relationship, possibly an affair, with this model Christine Keeler, not knowing that she was also involved with the Russian naval attaché. He in turn had links with Russian intelligence. They were all part of this social scene centred on Cliveden and including some rather dodgy characters as well as members of the upper classes. This led to conspiracy theorists coming up with the idea that Profumo had become a security risk since Christine Keeler could be passing on information acquired from him to her Russian lover. I don't believe anything of the sort actually; just because you sleep with someone doesn't mean you tell them everything you know about anything, let alone state secrets. Trouble is Keeler is very young and a bit of a loose cannon, not very discreet I'm afraid. Profumo should have been more careful in his choice of a bit on the side. Instead he seems to have been rather reckless.

"Now the powers that be are jumpy because of all the recent spy scandals, what with the Portland spy ring, George Blake and John Vassall. When you think of all the damage that a junior civil servant like Vassall did, imagine what could happen if a senior government minister became a security risk."

Anthony shook his head. He thought how it would shock Malcolm if he told him about his own activities but stifled the idea. He lit a Senior Service. "What do you think will happen now regarding Profumo?"

"Well, he still has the Prime Minister's support. After what happened to Galbraith, Macmillan is holding his ground; he's not keen to let another minister be forced out of office by hearsay or gossip. We shall have to wait until everything comes out in the open." Malcolm hesitated for a moment before continuing. "Incidentally, I think there's another tricky situation bubbling under."

"What's that?" asked Anthony, suddenly feeling slightly hot under the collar again.

"Apparently there's also another well-founded rumour that Kim Philby, who worked for MI6 on and off but also had links with Burgess and McLean, has vanished and perhaps defected. Luckily, the press haven't got wind of this yet but what a mess; it all makes it look as if our security service is a colander."

Anthony tutted. "It doesn't look very good, does it?"

Malcolm shook his head. "I know I don't need to say this, but I'd be grateful if you didn't let any of this go outside these walls at the moment. It's all very delicate."

"No, of course not, thanks for sharing a confidence with me. Well, I ought to be going; we must get together over lunch or something soon."

"Yes, I'd like that. Are you sure you're all right now? I could walk with you to the station if you like?"

"No need, Malcolm, I'm perfectly fine now. You will remember what I said about using these occasions to meet or at least practising to meet suitable women. '*Faint heart never won fair lady*,'" said Anthony as he shook hands.

"I know, '*Nothing venture, nothing win. Blood is thick but water's thin*', especially in my case. God, I still remember that song from our school musical. What with my mother and now you worrying about my love life." He laughed. "Hope to see you soon."

As he made his way to Green Park station Anthony was pleased that Malcolm seemed in good spirits. He was glad he'd got to know him again and was actually warming to him. He wasn't nearly as drippy as he remembered him at school.

On the other hand, Anthony was rather annoyed with himself for the little turn he'd had at Lancaster House. He was well aware that he could hardly allow himself to show his nervousness every time someone mentioned security leaks or espionage. He thought he would probably get more relaxed about it as time went on, but he determined to ensure this was so by being more open about such things. From now on, he would be prepared to take the initiative in conversations about security issues if the situation should arise. The more he reflected on his conversation with Malcolm, however, the more he realised how petty his own transgression in public duty was. He had not been directly involved in any security breach at all; just the grant of a visa application which might well have been approved if he'd followed correct practice.

He'd told Ruth that the reception might go on late and that he would stay with Malcolm. Instead, he'd arranged to see Carrie and he set off for Barons Court in an optimistic frame of mind.

It was about ten o'clock when he arrived at her flat and Carrie opened the door almost immediately. She still had her make-up on but was dressed only in her tartan dressing gown and slippers. She put her arms round his neck and kissed him.

"Did you have a nice time?" she asked, taking his hand and leading him over to the sofa.

"Yes. It was really good; I met some interesting people, even spoke to one of the Foreign Office ministers, Lord Dundee."

Carrie nodded, suitably impressed. "How's Malcolm?" she asked.

"He seems well enough and I thought he was quite cheerful."

"That's good. Although I've never met him, I've got a soft spot for Malcolm as he's been such a help to us, even if he doesn't know it. I hope he wouldn't hate us if he knew. Did you have something to eat?"

"Yes, there were canapés and other little snacks. I made sure I got my fair share."

"Would you like a drink?"

"Yes please. Actually I'd love a cup of coffee, perhaps with a brandy?"

"Then that's what you shall have."

She got up and went to the kitchen to get coffee and brandy for both of them. Anthony lit a cigarette and mulled over his conversation with Malcolm and his nervousness about his relationship with Cavalir and his cronies. He looked up at Carrie when she came in with the drinks and, as she smiled at him, he was almost overwhelmed by the urge to tell her about Cavalir. But he overcame the impulse and concentrated his thoughts on her. They hadn't seen each other for nearly a week because she'd had a couple of days off and both had been otherwise engaged at lunchtimes.

"Have you had a busy week?" he asked.

"Yes, we've started rehearsals for *The Circle*. You're probably bored with hearing about that. I also had a big surprise on Sunday; Eddie got in touch."

"Eddie?"

"Yes, Edmund Trafford, the soldier I told you about; my first serious boyfriend."

"Oh, really?"

"Yes, he rang my parents. They got to know him quite well when we went out together, so they were happy to pass on my number. I hadn't seen him for four years."

"What's he doing these days?"

"Still in the army; he's a major now, attached to the Sultan of Oman's forces. He's over here on leave."

Anthony was slightly troubled, a feeling he was trying hard to quell. "I wonder why he rang you again after all that time."

"He just wanted to know how I was and what I was getting up to."

Anthony knew the answer to his next question but asked it anyway. "Did you see him?"

"Yes. As you know, I'd already booked Monday and Tuesday as holidays so when he rang me, we arranged to meet for lunch on Tuesday. We had such a lot to talk about that we spent the afternoon together. It was very nice to see him again."

"Is he married?"

"No, not yet, he said he still hadn't completely got over me." She smiled, her thoughts elsewhere for a moment.

"Perhaps he was hoping to reignite an old flame."

Carrie looked at him with that slight smile which he normally loved so much, but this time it slightly irritated him. "I do believe you're a little bit jealous. It doesn't matter what his intentions were; it's what I think that counts and I have no desire whatever to rekindle my relationship with him. I was just glad to see how he is and to put a line under him and me on a good note."

"But you did spend the afternoon with him."

She laughed. "Not the way I would spend it with you. We went to the Tate Gallery and looked at some of my favourite pictures I hadn't seen for a while. It was just an enjoyable afternoon. How many times do you spend the afternoon, evening and night with another woman and I never say a word, let alone ask any questions?"

Anthony knew she was right and wondered how he had the nerve. He looked at her sheepishly. "Sorry, Carrie, I was being puerile. You have to remember that we men mature emotionally at half the rate of women, so you are well ahead of me."

She grinned and sat closer to him on the sofa. "I shan't be seeing him again, so don't have any more silly thoughts. You don't know how much I've been looking forward to another night together with you."

Once again, Anthony had to repress a desire to tell Carrie about his involvement with Cavalir and where it had led, but Carrie was already taking his mind off it by pulling him up off the sofa and taking him to the bedroom.

The following week, early on Friday morning, he received a call from Ronnie.

"Hello, Ronnie, how are you?"

"Fine, thanks. You know we talked about the funny goings on with Profumo and the Cliveden set? Did you hear that Wigg raised the issue of rumours of a relationship between Christine Keeler and a minister in the House yesterday?"

"Yes, I did."

"Well, Baron Profumo is going to make a statement in the House this morning. I shall be there, and you might like to hear it too; things are hotting up."

Anthony smiled at the reference to John Profumo's membership, through his father, of the now technically defunct Italian aristocracy. It was a title that Profumo never used himself. "Yes, I *would* be interested."

"Well, get down there early. Once the news gets round the galleries will be packed. I'll see you there, bye."

As a civil servant Anthony was permitted, with the approval of his line manager, to take time out of the office to attend Parliament, especially if there was an issue being raised which was of particular interest or relevance to him. He hadn't been to the House of Commons for a long time and Daphne Raynott raised no objection to his taking an hour or so out to go down to Westminster. Anthony set off straight away, but by the time he had got to the House, the Civil Service gallery was pretty full. He just managed to squeeze in and turned to acknowledge Ronnie who was in the row behind him.

After prayers there was a brief, polite interchange between front bench spokesmen concerning a change to the business of the House the following Tuesday. Then John Profumo rose to make his personal statement.

By this time the House was surprisingly crowded for a Friday; usually many of the MPs would already have left for their constituencies. The tension of the occasion was belied by the languid posture of those occupying the front benches, two or three with their feet up on the dispatch box table, following accepted custom. Elsewhere on the green leather benches, others were lolling about with their hands in their pockets or reading messages they'd been given.

As Profumo rose to speak, there was a marked change in the atmosphere of the House as distraction and ennui gave way to anticipation. There was an abrupt halt of all conversation and some members sat more upright. There were smiles, perhaps smirks, on the opposition benches and one or two Conservative members appeared apprehensive. Profumo spoke calmly in his plummy, slightly high voice as he delivered his 365-word statement. He referred to the allegations made by George Wigg, Richard Crossman and Barbara Castle the previous day concerning the relationship of a minister, possibly himself, with Christine Keeler and he insisted that his connection with Keeler was quite innocent. He pointed out that he had seen her a few times but always in the company of others, either at Cliveden or at the flat of a Mr Steven Ward. He concluded with the words, "Miss Keeler and I were on friendly terms. There was no impropriety whatsoever in my acquaintanceship with Miss Keeler. Mr Speaker, I have made this personal statement because of what was said in the House last evening by the three hon. Members, and which, of course, was protected by Privilege. I shall not hesitate to issue writs for libel and slander if scandalous allegations are made or repeated outside the House."

Profumo sat down to a silent House of Commons. Anthony looked over at George Wigg who sat motionless and expressionless for a few seconds before leaving his seat. The gallery began to empty and Anthony looked round for Ronnie; he was talking quietly to a couple of colleagues who left after a minute or so. Ronnie came over to join Anthony and they walked in silence down the stairs and out of the Palace of Westminster.

As soon as they had reached St Margaret's Street, Anthony felt he'd observed silent propriety long enough. He looked over at Ronnie and asked, "What did you make of that? Nobody seemed to react to the statement very much."

Ronnie nodded, pulling his coat collar up in the chilling north-easterly wind. "Well, it was a personal statement. It's a convention of the House, an unwritten rule, that such statements are made on the honour of the member and they are expected to adhere to a high degree of truthfulness. So they are never challenged or questioned."

"But the statement was not truthful."

"I know," said Ronnie, "and so do many of the MPs on both sides. The fact that there was virtually no response from Conservative members is more telling. We shall see how this pans out but he won't get away with it in the long run. I gather Profumo has an appointment at the races at Sandown this afternoon. Perhaps he wants to ride his luck today."

A few days later Anthony learned, to his dismay, that he was being transferred to a different section, though still within the same department. Turnover of staff was not very high, but there was a regular pattern of staff moving on and being replaced by less experienced newcomers; in an era of full employment young people had plenty of options elsewhere. In addition, there was movement between the Immigration Service at the ports and the office-based department, and some movement within departments of the Home Office. The other section in Anthony's room had just lost its most senior Executive Officer due to her being promoted. As this left that section short of experienced staff, Anthony was asked to take her post, a request he couldn't reasonably refuse. He was disappointed, both because he had felt comfortable where he was and also as it could further complicate his relationship with Cavalir. Nonetheless, at the end of March he moved to his predecessor's old desk and took over responsibility for the letters A, Q, U and X. He was meticulous in ensuring that he left nothing in his old desk but nearly left behind Carrie's Valentine's card, which had become caught between the back of the drawer and the desk carcass. He was replaced in his old section by a new Executive Officer from the Training Section, for whom he'd left no outstanding cases at all.

As soon as he knew he was moving positions, Anthony was presented with a dilemma. Did he inform Cavalir that he was no longer in charge of C, in case Cavalir wished to use him again to process applications or did he leave things as they were until the issue cropped up? To do the former would imply a greater acquiescence and deeper commitment to the role he was performing for Cavalir. To take the latter option might cause irritation to Cavalir, with unpredictable results.

He hadn't made his mind up what to do before the move and he still hadn't when he arrived home that evening.

Ruth greeted him in the hall. "Hello," she said, looking up from cleaning the telephone as he walked through the door. "How did the first day in the new job go?"

"Same as the last day in the old job," he replied and smiled. "A slightly different range of nationalities, with more Vietnamese and so on; still lots of Chinese though."

"People all right? I suppose you know them already?"

"Yes, my new boss is Frank Hodgkin. I think I've mentioned him to you before."

"Is he the one who was in the RAF and served in Iraq?"

"Yes, he used to be an Immigration Officer, so he knows the ins and outs of the Immigration Service from all angles. He's on the ball but seems pretty flexible, so I can't see any problems working for him. The other two EOs are young, and the CO and CA are women who have been there a long time. So, it's all fine; there was no real disruption to my working day at all moving from one section to the other."

While talking to Ruth, he had finally made up his mind that he *would* tell Cavalir that his role had changed and the letter C was no longer under his remit. He was aware that this would result in his being proactive in his dealings with Cavalir and inevitably have the effect of further cementing their involvement. But he could only shrug and mutter to himself the next line of that song he and Malcolm had quoted to each other from their school play: '*In for a penny, in for a pound*'.

Despite his reservations, which refused to go away, he duly wrote to Cavalir via 'Mr Sikora' at the office service company, explaining that his move to a different section would need to be taken into account should his services be required in the future. Two days later an envelope arrived in the post with the enclosed postcard bearing the message, "Stanislaus Cukier application already in system. Imperative you process it."

Fortunately the post was not late that day and he left for work early in the hope of finding out whether the application had arrived yet. The system was quite straightforward; when correspondence arrived, it would be applied to any existing file for that person and then taken from the registry to the appropriate officer. If there was no existing correspondence concerning the person, a new file would be set up and then this would go to the relevant officer for their attention. He went first to the registry to see if there was a file for Stanislaus Cukier; there was no file for this person yet, nor was his name recorded in the register. So Anthony would have to wait for the file to appear in the office.

When his replacement as the officer responsible for the letter 'C' arrived, he made a point of going over for a chat. This was Leonard Hilson, a young man of eighteen or nineteen who, fresh from his A-levels, had joined the Training Section in January and had just completed his three-month training period.

"How's it going?" said Anthony.

"Not too bad. I dealt mostly with non-visa applications in training so I'm a bit new to some of this." He looked fairly relaxed but keen, a slight smile on his boyish face. He felt an acne mark on his neck as he waited for the older man to lead the conversation.

"Well, if I can be of any help, just let me know," said Anthony. "If you see my signature in the file, I'm sure to know something of the case."

Leonard nodded and smiled. "Thanks, I will."

The first batch of files for the day came into the office half an hour later. Anthony wandered down to Leonard's desk and flicked through them, apparently carelessly, while he was talking to Leonard but looking for the name Cukier. It wasn't there. He wondered how often he could search Leonard's pending files without attracting attention. After all, nobody ever did this; going through a colleague's files without being asked. He considered the possibility of trying to get to the files before they came into the office, but that would mean waylaying a messenger and asking to look through the files or going into the registry to search there. Both ideas were ludicrously impracticable.

So he had to stick with Plan A. Each morning he arrived early and made sure he was always in the office when the first batch of files was brought in, after the morning post. He noticed that Leonard worked methodically, giving his attention to each file in the order he received it. So he took a chance that Leonard would probably not look at a new batch until after the arrival of the morning tea trolley or perhaps only after lunch. It was at lunchtime, and again when the tea trolley arrived twice each day, that Anthony had the opportunity to glance at Leonard's files while he and most of the other staff were out of the office.

For three days he kept up this intermittent vigil at Leonard's in tray, standing by Leonard's desk while he engaged Freddie or Rosemary in conversation, asking Leonard how he was getting on or having a brief word with Daphne, and always looking as best he could at the files on Leonard's desk. Then, on the fourth morning, when the messenger came in with files, he was on his way to the washroom and he stopped to talk to Freddie about nothing in particular. There, on the top of the pile was a new, pristine file headed with the name Stanislaus Cukier. Leonard probably wouldn't look at the file until later. However, a cursory glance at his in tray and Leonard would know it was there and he might possibly remember the name and later on wonder what had happened to it. Fortunately, at that moment, Leonard was going through a case with Daphne. Anthony leaned on the pile of files as Freddie talked to him and, with a certain amount of effort and a strange elbow movement, he manufactured a small avalanche and the top three files toppled onto Leonard's desk. Neither Leonard nor Daphne, deep in conversation, noticed. Rosemary and Patricia looked up and then back to their work. Anthony replaced the files with the Cukier file now third from the top. A couple of minutes later he left the office but, instead of going to the washroom, he went to the registry. Here he took out the file of a case he'd recently dealt with and brought it back with him to the office. Leonard was now seated at his desk, working on a file from his pending tray. Anthony waited.

Ten minutes or so later the tea trolley arrived outside the office and all the staff rose, took their cups and went out to queue up for refreshments. Anthony hung back until there were only two other people in the room, then he took his dummy file as far as Leonard's desk, laid this file on top of the in tray, made sure the other two were not watching and then reached into the pile for the Cukier file, slipped it under the file he'd been carrying and returned to his desk. Then it happened, and he never could quite understand how. He dropped the Cukier file by the desk of the Clerical Assistant in his own section, Coral Jones. The file was facing her and she bent down to pick it up as Anthony scrambled to retrieve it. There was a moment when both were holding it until Anthony asserted his proprietorial rights.

"It's all right, Coral, I've got it, thanks," he said.

"That's a C surname," said Coral. "You're not still doing your old job as well, are you?"

Anthony was fighting it, but he was still reddening and hoped Coral would assume he was flustered more than anything else. He laughed; a strange laugh he'd never had before. "No, Coral, I'm not that keen. It's a case I remembered was similar to the one I've got here, so I'm just reminding myself what we did last time." He hoped she hadn't noticed that the front of the file had not a single signature or date on it; no action had ever been taken.

Coral laughed too and turned back to her desk, taking out her cup and going off to the tea trolley.

He put the files at the bottom of his in tray and then went off to get a cup of tea. He could hear the pulse in his head while his heart seemed on the point of giving out.

He was standing behind Coral in the queue and he asked her about her holiday plans for the year; anything to get her mind off that file. She was a great traveller and was soon regaling him with her plans for the summer; he didn't hear a word.

After that, it was relatively easy to complete the operation. He waited until everyone had left the office for the day before processing the visa application. It was the first time ever he'd been the last to leave the office at the end of the day and there were one or two questioning looks from his colleagues as they departed. Finally, Frank Hodgkin, his new boss, closed his files and locked a confidential file in his top drawer before walking over slowly to the coat stand.

"Everything all right, Tony?" he asked, as he put on his coat.

"Yes thanks, I'm meeting a friend later, so I thought I'd make good use of the time by catching up on some reading.

I'm not so familiar with the sort of cases I'm picking up from Indo-China."

Frank gave a smile of encouragement and bid him goodnight with a slight air of apology.

With everyone gone, he opened the Cukier file. It contained an application on behalf of Professor Stanislaus Cukier of the Jagiellonian University in Krakow, to be granted a visa to work at an epidemiological research laboratory near Warwick. From the correspondence there was no doubt that this man was an expert in his field and could contribute to research studies in the UK. Presumably he would be limited as to security clearance if his work brought him into contact with potentially sensitive areas, but this was not for him to worry about. He granted the visa using his own signature, countersigned it by copying Daphne's signature upside down and completed the procedures that would normally be done by George. He kept the Cukier file at the bottom of his in tray overnight and the next morning he put it in his out tray, confident the messenger would not even notice, let alone care, that a file seemed to be in the wrong out tray.

Sitting back in his chair, the operation complete, Anthony tried but felt no compunction about what he had just done. He had no idea what this person was up to and he chose not to care. He would accept without hesitation the next package waiting for him at the newsagent's in Leytonstone. It did not even momentarily trouble him that he was having lunch with Ronnie later that week when the subject of espionage and security leaks was bound to come up.

Two days later Anthony and Ronnie met at their usual place and, for once, Anthony was the first to arrive. To his surprise, Ronnie was accompanied by Malcolm.

"Hello, Malcolm, this is a pleasant surprise," said Anthony, rising to his feet.

"Malcolm rang me this morning about a ministry matter and I thought it would be nice to have him along; it's about time the three of us had lunch together," said Ronnie. "We've certainly got lots to talk about." He glanced round the room.

It was a pleasant lunch. The three of them talked about work only fleetingly and ignored security issues which, for the time being at least, had dropped down the agenda, much to the relief of Anthony, whose own security issues were more than enough for him to be getting on with. Instead the conversation tended towards current affairs and items of particular interest to them such as the future of the economy. General de Gaulle having vetoed the British application to join the European Economic Community, they spent some time debating the options for an alternative economic strategy. They also talked about the Beeching Report on the future of the railways, published a few days before. Being a supporter, and regular user of the railways, Malcolm was aghast at the possibility of the report's proposals being fully implemented.

"Can you imagine," he said, "if we are left with just the main lines? Everyone will be forced onto the roads."

"Can't stop progress, Malcolm," said Ronnie, with a teasing smile on his face. He knew that Malcolm didn't drive.

"Well, they did get rid of the branch lines in Ireland," said Anthony.

Malcolm harrumphed. "The roads will never cope. Half the houses in England have nowhere to put a car, so they'll be parked in the roads. That means the actual space for the extra cars to drive on will get smaller and smaller."

"They probably won't implement all of Beeching, it will be a compromise. You'll still be able to get to Sevenoaks, Malcolm," observed Anthony.

Malcolm laughed. "You'll be sorry when you get into your car and won't be able to get out of the drive to join the traffic jam outside your house."

The conversation moved onto sport and the possibilities for the end of the football season and the arrival of the West Indies for the summer Test series and then ranged over other areas of common interest. Anthony enjoyed the exchange of views, the witty insights and the gentle teasing, and he was glad that Malcolm had joined their circle. It had done Malcolm good; he seemed happier and more relaxed but also he and Ronnie had benefitted from renewing their contact with someone who he felt was a good man. Anthony did have a spasm of concern that these two friends might not consider him much of a good man if they knew his secrets. But he consoled himself with the fact that he did not know theirs either.

XV

As he had expected, another postcard arrived at the end of April to tell him that a new book was available for collection. He once again got off the tube at Leytonstone to collect his package for Mr C Phillipson from Grainger's newsagent.

The same young woman was behind the counter and Anthony hung back as she served one customer with an evening newspaper and twenty Woodbines then another who couldn't make up his mind which box of chocolates to have. When he approached the counter the woman smiled. "Hello, Mr Phillipson isn't it?"

"That's right, you have a good memory," said Anthony. He hadn't really looked at her before; last time he'd been nervous and concerned only with getting the envelope and being on his way. Now he knew the ropes he was more relaxed and regarded her properly. She was young, no more than twenty-one, and pretty in a slightly loud way with bright lipstick and eyeshadow. She wasn't wearing the dustcoat this time but was dressed in a straight dark skirt and tight pink sweater which showed off her figure.

She smiled. "I don't remember everyone. I'll get your envelope."

She disappeared in the back room and returned, as on the last occasion, with the envelope and a receipt for signature. "What's the C stand for?" she asked as she put the package down, displaying bright red fingernails which matched her lipstick.

Anthony nearly replied 'Charles' as it was the first name that came into his head, but he hesitated and tried to come up with something more interesting. "It's 'Craig,'" he said, after a pause.

"Oh, like Craig Douglas," she said. "I was sixteen when 'Only Sixteen' was number one."

"I don't have to guess your age now, then," said Anthony.

He was about to say more when another customer came in. Anthony hadn't got his package yet, but the young woman didn't rush to finish serving him. She just looked at him with a smile then served this new customer with a *Star* and a two-ounce tin of Boar's Head tobacco. As that customer left, she said to Anthony, "Sorry to keep you waiting."

"That's all right," he said, signing the receipt. "Do you have many people who use this letter-holding service?" he asked, as he handed her the receipt book.

As she took the book back her hand brushed his. "Quite a lot. I wouldn't know the number. Some of them are regulars who use us all the time because they're often away or out on business, but there are a few who come in once in a while, like you."

They were interrupted again by two new customers and Anthony didn't leave; it seemed as if they had unfinished business.

The young woman served the newcomers then smiled at him again. "Is there anything else I can do for you?" she asked.

"Yes, I'll have twenty Senior Service, please, and one of those pound boxes of Dairy Box."

She turned round and took the packet of Senior Service from an open cabinet divided into more than thirty long, narrow compartments, each wide enough to accommodate packets of ten or twenty cigarettes. Then she got his Dairy Box from behind the other counter and gave it to him in a white paper bag.

"Thanks, er, sorry I don't know your name."

"Why would you?" she said with a quizzical look. "It's Shirley."

"Well, thanks, Shirley. I'll see you again."

"I hope so," she replied, gazing at him for a second or two before turning to unwrap a carton of Craven 'A' corked tip cigarettes and filling up one of the narrow compartments.

Anthony walked out of the shop and back to the tube station. He thought that Shirley might have been a candidate for one of his flights of fancy in the old days, or given her apparent interest in him, perhaps something more tangible. He knew that he might never have cause to go to the shop again and even if he did, he probably wouldn't be interested in her, she wasn't really his type, but it was nice to have the attention.

When he arrived home, he went upstairs to change and put the money, £150 in fivers and one-pound notes, in his shoe boxes. He was pleased to see that he still had fifty pounds of the previous payment left; he was pacing things well. It wasn't that he thought there was a serious chance that his petty infringements of the immigration code were likely to attract official interest, but he was mindful of how the Portland Spy Ring had come to the attention of the authorities. They had become aware of the lavish spending on generous hospitality, new cars and a house by Harry Houghton, a corrupted civil servant whose income could scarcely sustain such a lifestyle. Anthony was not going to throw his money around. Of course, it was easier to stay relatively parsimonious when neither Ruth nor Carrie made demands on him for material things, but he was never tempted to spend money freely purely to bolster his ego, as Houghton had done.

Ruth called upstairs to remind him that he was taking Jonathan to Cubs that evening and he thought what a busy life he now had. The following week he'd arranged to go to see Carrie in *The Circle*, though without much enthusiasm. It had been difficult to fit it in and he didn't feel like going to the theatre at the moment, even to see Carrie.

As usual, Malcolm unwittingly acted as the reason for his staying up in town for the evening and he was thus able to attend the same stale-smelling school gymnasium-cum-theatre where Carrie's company were performing. As the weather was warmer than the last time, the atmosphere was even riper, and he wondered if it could permeate his clothes.

The production was, as before, excellent. Carrie inevitably played Elizabeth and was both entertaining and enticingly beautiful in her 1920s dresses. Much as he wanted to be, however, he was not quite so enraptured by the experience as the last time he'd watched her in a play. He put it down to the fact that he was tired, and his mind was always drifting on to other things. They met up briefly after the final curtain and he lavishly praised her performance but said he couldn't stay for a drink in case he missed his connections.

Carrie looked at her watch and nodded. "Oh, what a shame, but I know it's awkward. If we go to the pub it'll be time to leave as soon as we get there."

"Let's have lunch tomorrow at the usual place."

"OK," she said, and they embraced briefly before he headed off to the tube station.

The next day, he and Carrie met at their regular Italian restaurant. It was a sunny day and Carrie was wearing sunglasses. He thought she looked pale and tired. She was drinking a tomato juice or perhaps a 'Bloody Mary'.

"How are you?" he asked as they kissed when he arrived.

"Hungover," she said. "We had drinks at the pub after the performance and I think I had one too many."

Anthony shook his head. "You are silly; you knew you had work the next day."

She nodded. "I know, but I missed you."

"You got home all right?"

"Yes, I wasn't drunk; just mixed my drinks a bit too much."

"Work must be hard today."

"I didn't go to work. I called in sick then came here half an hour ago to meet you."

Anthony's jaw dropped. "I hope nobody from work sees you."

"It'll be all right. I don't want anything to eat; why don't you come home with me?"

"Carrie, I can't. I'll be missed if I don't go back. Frank Hodgkin, my new boss, is less accommodating than Daphne."

"Have you tried him out for discipline yet?"

"No."

"Well, how do you know?" She smiled in that knowing way of hers and sipped her drink.

Anthony shook his head. "I don't see how I can."

"Spoilsport; you're losing your sense of recklessness. That's a shame."

Anthony wasn't in the least tempted to show he could be reckless, but he was aware that he had neglected Carrie lately with everything else that was going on.

"Give me a minute," he said, "and order something to eat for both of us." He nodded towards the waitress who had come over to take their order as he got up from the table.

Carrie smiled, obviously pleased, and quickly chose a couple of pasta dishes and two glasses of Montepulciano d'Abruzzo.

Anthony walked over to the newspaper rack, took the barely creased *Times* and turned to the Parliamentary report page, looking for the order of business for today. Then he went to the bar and asked to use the telephone.

He telephoned the office and spoke to Frank Hodgkin.

"Hello, Frank; it's Tony Fernard."

"Hello, Tony, everything all right?"

"Yes, thanks. As you know, I've been following with interest the Radcliffe Report on the Vassall case. We've talked about it a couple of times?"

"Yes, I read the Prime Minister's statement this morning. It certainly raises a number of unanswered questions."

"Exactly. Well, the Lords are addressing the subject this afternoon at a quarter to three. I'd very much like to hear what Lord Dilhorne has to say and some of the debate, if you could spare me this afternoon."

"Yes, don't see why not. You're fairly up to date with your caseload, aren't you?"

"Yes, the pending tray was almost empty when I went to lunch."

"OK, that'll be fine. I'll be interested to hear what you made of it tomorrow morning."

"Oh, that's great, thanks, Frank. See you tomorrow,"

He put the phone down and rejoined Carrie. "That's done. Did you order?"

"Yes, I hope you're happy with cannelloni?"

Anthony smiled. "Yep, that's fine."

They were soon served their food and, despite her previous statement about lack of appetite, Carrie ate well and even had a dessert. Then they surreptitiously made their way to Russell

Square tube station to avoid the risk of bumping into Frank Hodgkin or one of Carrie's colleagues near Holborn. Anthony was getting used to being on the lookout for people he might know, but it was a skill he could have done without needing to use today. Carrie, on the other hand, seemed oblivious to what was going on around her as she chattered on about the play she was acting in and how she was looking forward to tonight's performance now that she was spending the afternoon with him. Then he saw the Assistant Secretary of his division, Henry Dawlish. He was on the other side of the road, swinging his umbrella as he walked, a bowler hat and scarf high on his neck keeping off the worst of the cold.

Anthony gasped. "Quick, get in here," he said, pushing Carrie towards the nearest shop door.

"What's happened?" asked Carrie.

"Just get inside," said Anthony in a loud whisper.

The couple, arm in arm, burst into the shop with such force that the bell affixed to the door rattled with a frenzy which attracted the attention of everyone else in the shop. The assistant behind the counter looked startled and another assistant stopped in the middle of serving a customer to see what had caused the commotion.

"What's the matter?" asked Carrie.

"I'll tell you later."

"Can I help you, madam?" asked the shop assistant.

Anthony realised they were in a lingerie shop, which added to his embarrassment.

"Yes," said Carrie, walking over to the counter, "I'd like a bra in ivory or pale cream, size 34C."

Anthony hung back from the counter while Carrie chose a bra, not quite sure where to look and aware of being studied by the clientele and staff, an exclusively female group. The discomfort continued while Carrie went into the changing room to try the bra on. Eventually, she completed her purchase and they left the shop and continued their walk.

"What was that all about?" she asked, looking up at him with a frown.

"What?"

"You pushing me in the shop like that?"

"Oh, I saw my divisional boss coming along the street."

Carrie laughed. "What did it matter? You might be out for a walk after lunch with a colleague or something. You are silly."

"It's not funny. He would think it odd me walking away from the office at well after two, especially as I'm supposed to be going to the House of Lords."

She giggled. "Well, I thought it was funny when we almost broke the door down entering the shop."

Anthony smiled wanly. "I hope you didn't have to buy something you didn't need because of it."

"No, I'd been meaning to go to that shop to get a new bra in this colour." She showed him the bag and opened the top so he could see it.

Soon they were on a train to Barons Court.

The flat was very untidy and the kitchen had a couple of days' washing up stacked in the sink. On the dining table was a wine glass with a dried red stain in the bottom.

"Sorry the place is a mess," said Carrie, throwing her jacket on a chair. "I've been so busy with the play and work." She went into the kitchen.

"Shall I help you wash up?" asked Anthony.

"No, I'll clear up later, I didn't ask you here to do housework," she said, coming out of the kitchen with a bottle of white wine and two glasses. "Here," she said, handing him the bottle and a corkscrew while she pulled off her sweater and unzipped her skirt.

"Are you sure you want another drink?" asked Anthony.

Carrie smiled. "Don't be a puritan, I feel much better now."

Uneasily he pulled the cork from the bottle of Sancerre while she took off her stockings and suspender belt and came to sit next to him on the sofa.

He poured them both a glass of wine. "Is everything all right?" he asked.

"How do you mean?"

"I don't know; you don't seem quite your usual self. I can't put a finger on it."

She took a gulp of the wine. "That's good, coming from you after that outbreak of paranoia on Red Lion Walk." She shook her head. "I'm fine. I just missed you last night and I want to have now the night we couldn't have yesterday."

She kissed him and then she took off her underwear and began to undress him. Anthony looked down at her lovely body and forgot his concerns while she embarked on a sexual tour de force, using all of the techniques she knew he wanted, as they made love on the sofa. It was marvellous but also frantic, certainly from her but perhaps from him too.

Afterwards, they had another glass of wine while they lay together on the sofa.

"Are you on stage tonight?" asked Anthony, stroking her arm.

"Yes, why?"

"Well, I just thought you won't want to drink too much before you go on."

She wasn't defensive, as he'd feared she might be. "Don't worry. This is my last before curtain up."

"What time do you have to be at the theatre?" he asked, looking at his watch, which showed half-past three.

"Oh, I aim to be there at about five-thirty."

Anthony relaxed. "I'll stay with you until it's time," he said.

They both began to feel cold and Carrie got up and ran a bath while Anthony, despite her protestations, washed up and cleared away in the kitchen before getting in the bath with her.

Then, after a cup of tea and a couple of stale biscuits, they went off to the theatre. They were early and Anthony sat with Carrie in the makeshift dressing room while she put on her make-up. He had to leave when the rest of the cast arrived and there was the matter of undressing and dressing by the female performers. Carrie went with him as far as the stage door.

"Thanks for spending the afternoon with me," she said. "It's been lovely."

"I was glad to."

"You know you pump up my tyres and charge my battery. What will you do this evening?"

"I have to mug up on the House of Lords review of the Vassall tribunal, in case I get asked about it tomorrow by Frank."

She kissed him, not worried about her make-up. "I love you."

"Me too," he said. "Break a leg."

He walked to the station feeling ill at ease. Perhaps it was the sense that the edge had gone off of things: the slight drop in enthusiasm to see Carrie on the stage, the greater willingness to do things other than to see her, the feeling of irritability that sometimes being with her engendered in him. Perhaps it was the interest he'd shown in Shirley when he hadn't expected to or the fact that relations with Ruth seemed to be going well. Whatever it was, Anthony was slowly coming round to the conclusion that a nagging suspicion he'd had for some time but tried to ignore was true. Something was going wrong in his relationship with Carrie.

Much as he tried, he just didn't feel quite the same about her anymore. He had fought against recognising the fact, partly because he didn't want it to be true and partly because he didn't want to hurt Carrie. It's not that he didn't love her anymore, but that love was no longer an all-consuming passion and it was fading. While a marriage can accommodate such a cooling of ardour, he wasn't sure that he could maintain indefinitely an illicit liaison with all its lies and difficulties and planning, if the desire was draining away. Sadly, he was forced to come to the conclusion that he hadn't really changed as a person after all; Carrie was just the latest in a long run of these short-lived passionate relationships and he loathed himself for it.

The pattern beginning to be repeated here was always the same. It would begin with a slight fall in enthusiasm to be with the object of his love. Then the effect on him of her mannerisms and style of speech would become the complete opposite to what it was before. So teasing became irritating instead of amusing, the laugh shrill instead of lyrical, the positive smile a smug grin or smirk, jokes no longer witty but banal, the convivial chatter now mindless prattle, and the adjusting of his hair or tie ceasing to be a sign of affection and rather a mark of correction. Finally, even the physical attraction would wane as the most striking attributes faded to mundane and the less common feature which added charm, such as a dimple, mole or snaggletooth, became merely odd. These changes in attitude to the woman in question, like raindrops, were almost imperceptible at first but would steadily take on an unstoppable momentum, from a few spots of mild irritation through a steady drizzle of discontent to a shower of annoyance, culminating finally in a deluge of encumbrance and regret.

He dreaded the moment of reckoning and wanted to delay it until he was absolutely sure, but he knew the moment would come sooner rather than later. Consequently, he was aware that every date could be the one when he told her. One day he'd arranged to meet Carrie for lunch, but he had grown increasingly nervous as to whether a public restaurant was the right place to be if things became awkward. So he rang Carrie in the morning and told her he couldn't meet for lunch, as they'd agreed.

"I'm sorry Carrie, something's come up at short notice."

"Oh, I see. You always seem to have things crop up at the last minute. Anthony, is everything all right with us?" She sounded both terse and worried.

"Yes, of course. I am really sorry I have to cancel. I'll see you tonight though."

She seemed relieved. "That's more important, see you tonight."

That evening Anthony met Carrie after work and they took a stroll along the Embankment before an early evening drink. They held hands under the table in the pub and Carrie told him how much she loved him and couldn't wait to be alone with him. He was warm towards her and tried to reciprocate her sentiments. But he knew he was right; the tide of his infatuation had turned and there was nothing he could do to stop it. So it was with Carrie; his love for her, just a few weeks ago total and unequivocal, had begun to fade. He wasn't giving up without a fight, because his fickleness and lack of constancy was a source of anger and distress to himself, let alone the consequences it would have for Carrie. He tried to understand what was happening more than he'd done on previous occasions because this *had* been different. It had lasted a long time and become important to both of them, so it was more than just a flight of fancy. Perhaps it wasn't just that he'd changed; had she changed too, in a way that had affected his feelings for her? He had no answer to that; everything was moving so fast. All he knew for sure was that she was just as loving towards him as she had ever been and how did that provide the answer? He doubted anything would stop what was happening.

But this day wasn't to be the one where matters came to a head. Instead, in a last effort to cling on to the way it had been, he resolved to try to see her as much as before and make love as frequently, though he was unable to maintain the level of tenderness of the past. But it was becoming hopeless and he knew it, particularly as the fever of love was being replaced in his mind by the cold sweat of guilt and panic as he tried to calculate a way of extricating himself from his predicament.

Over the next few weeks Anthony spent more time planning a way of ending the relationship than he spent with Carrie. He told himself he was doing her a favour, as there was no future for them and things would only get worse the longer he delayed. He thought she must be aware of a change in his demeanour even if he tried to hide it and though she didn't say anything. The saddest aspect of all was that the more affectionate she tried to be, the more unwillingly resentful he became of her presence in his life. So he was in turn sulky or silent or picky about the things she said or did and he couldn't stop this sullenness, even though he despised himself for it. Finally, one Saturday morning, when Ruth was out with a friend and the children, Anthony and Carrie went for a drive into the country and a pub lunch. As they were walking along a lane from the pub back to their parked car, Carrie turned to him and asked, "What is the matter? Something has changed between us and I don't know why."

"How do you mean?" asked Anthony, knowing exactly what she meant and realising the time had come but trying to give himself a moment to prepare for what he knew would be distressing for both of them.

"You are more distant and colder somehow. It's not any one thing but everything seems different." She stared at him, her lovely face creased in anxiety and sorrow.

They stopped by a duck pond and leaned on the railings. Anthony took her hand. "I'm sorry," he said, "but I have to stop seeing you." He looked away at the water to avoid her shocked expression.

"But why?" she said, snatching her hand from his grasp. "We were so happy. I've not made any demands; I haven't tried to break up your marriage. I don't understand." Her eyes were filled with tears, but some sort of surface tension prevented them spilling over.

He couldn't face telling her the unvarnished truth, that he wanted it to end because one day soon he would have had enough of her. So he softened the brutality of it by telling her a partial truth. "I can't help it. I've come to feel more and more guilty about Ruth and gradually the shame of my treatment of her has come to overwhelm the love I feel for you. I am truly sorry to hurt you like this, but I have to give you up."

Carrie held out her hands in supplication, the tears falling now. "Please don't let this happen to us, Tony. We weren't doing any terrible harm – Ruth need never know. Can't we go on? You can see me less if it helps, but don't stop seeing me. I love you."

He hadn't planned to end it today, now, but since things were out in the open, he just wanted it over; he didn't want to keep seeing the harm he'd done to her etched in the expression on her face. "I can't. It's better to make a clean break of it."

He thought this sounded harsh enough and was prepared for Carrie to start sobbing but she didn't. She just looked at him for what seemed an age then spoke quietly and calmly, "I chose you. I could have had anyone, but I chose you. I didn't expect you to leave your wife and I never gave any indication that I was jealous of her or the children. I was happy to have a bit of you and I thought you were happy with that too. But now you have decided to indulge your guilt and shame about your treatment of Ruth when presumably she doesn't even know what you've done. You really are a self-centred, self-pitying bastard."

Anthony looked down at the water and was distracted by a long twig which, caught by some eddy in the water, sailed majestically beneath him. He figured that he deserved the opprobrium she poured on him and he counted himself fortunate, and probably undeserving, to have at least been spared her dissolving into tears or some other scene in a public place. "You have every right to be upset. I know I've behaved badly," he said, hoping that by heaping a few burning coals of shame on his own head he might obviate the need for any further wrath from Carrie. In this, he was proved right.

"It's such a terrible way to end, Tony," said Carrie, sounding more conciliatory. "It's not as if we were always quarrelling or couldn't stand the sight of each other any longer. We had something so special. Won't you just give it one more chance?" she pleaded.

"I don't think it will work to try to struggle on; I've made up my mind, I'm sorry."

"What, here and now? Is that it?" she asked, her voice calmer now.

Having come this far, Anthony was determined not to weaken or to backtrack, otherwise they would have to go through it again later. He nodded. "I think it's for the best."

"For your best," she replied. "I remember you said once that you thought eighteen months was the right time to hold a job: six months to learn the ropes, six to enjoy being competent and six to get bored. I suppose for you it's like that with a woman too, only it takes just nine months: three to win her heart, three to enjoy the conquest and then three to get bored." She was spent.

They stood looking at each other for perhaps a minute, then Anthony did start to weaken; he wanted to show he still cared. "May I drive you back to town?"

"No, thank you, I shall ask the landlord to get me a taxi." She turned to walk away and Anthony held out his hand, but she shook her head and carried on walking back to the pub. Anthony stood and watched her go, but she strode off and did not look back.

On the following Tuesday, there were two letters waiting for Anthony when he returned home from work. The first was a hefty electricity bill. The other was in the beautiful handwriting of Carrie and was brief and to the point:

Dear Tony,

I suppose that it is a forlorn hope, but I wanted to make sure that you meant what you said on Saturday and didn't feel trapped into saying something you didn't really mean by my catching you off guard.

If you still want to see me, I will be very happy to carry on as before and I promise never to make any demands on you. If I don't hear from you before next Wednesday, I shall know that you are sure that you want us to end and I will not trouble you further but wish you well for the future.

All my love,
Carrie

Anthony read the letter with a mixture of sadness and remorse and there was a part of him that wanted to reach out to her again, but it was driven by sympathy and not a desire to be how they were. He sat back in his chair, relieved that Carrie appeared ready to accept the situation without a messy ending. Thankfully, he had come through another of his infatuations, in fact the greatest one of all, without too much damage to himself and, he hoped, to Carrie. But he was resolved not to take anything this far ever again. He felt a strange kind of liberation, both from Carrie and from himself. He didn't reply to the letter, but he kept it in the bottom of one of his shoe boxes for a few weeks before he finally threw it away.

XVI

It was in the middle of May that Anthony heard from Cavalir again. He rarely recognised the handwriting when an envelope arrived because sometimes the address was typed and, when handwritten, the writing was not always the same. This time the message was different to previous ones, possibly written by someone not used to Latin script. Instead of advising him that another visa application was forthcoming, it was an invitation for Mr C Phillipson to meet Mr Sikora for dinner. He assumed that this meant it would be Cavalir. He was just asked to confirm that he would be available to meet at a quarter to seven the following Thursday. Anthony was suspicious but also curious. He was sure that Cavalir wasn't inviting him to dinner purely as a social gesture and guessed that this time it was for something other than the issue of a visa. Of course, he wanted to know, but there were two matters that gave him cause for concern. First, for the sake of his own safety, could he dare go to see Cavalir without anyone else knowing where he'd gone? Second, what would he be getting himself into? There was not much he could do about either question; who could he tell where he was going and what would happen if he turned down the offer?

Eventually, he telephoned Cavalir's answering service from a public telephone and left a message that he would be able to come. The following day, another postcard told him to wait outside Strand tube station at six-thirty on Thursday evening and to be reading a copy of the *Financial Times*. Having told Ruth that he was having dinner with Malcolm, he went to the tube station just before a quarter past six. At exactly six-thirty the man who had escorted him to his first meeting with Cavalir came out of the station and showed him a piece of paper.

"Could you direct me to this address, please?" he asked.

Anthony looked at the paper. Written on it was 'Wait a few minutes, then go to the Savoy Hotel and ask for Mr Czartoryski. Just point up the road to this man.'

Anthony smiled and pointed towards Fleet Street and the man thanked him and set off. Anthony went back to the *FT* and read a short article before he turned the other way and began walking slowly towards the Savoy Hotel. He stopped to look in a shop window and glanced back the way he'd come. A man in a trilby hat twenty yards away also stopped. Anthony could see it was his shadow from the day he'd walked down Hatton Garden. He found this strangely comforting.

As Anthony turned off the Strand and walked towards the hotel entrance, he saw that the Savoy Theatre was staging the play *Trap for a Lonely Man* and smiled grimly. When he arrived at reception, he said he had an appointment to see Mr Czartoryski. The porter asked his name, which Anthony unhesitatingly said was Phillipson, checked his guest list and made a phone call. After a few moments Anthony was invited to go to Mr Czatoryski's room. He took the lift, walked along the silent, wide corridor to the room and knocked on the door.

The door was opened by a man Anthony had never seen before, a shortish young man of slight build with a cheerful smile. He beckoned Anthony in without speaking.

As Anthony had expected, there was Cavalir. He was sitting on a sofa, looking through some papers, and he rose to greet him.

"So glad you could join me for dinner, Mr Fernard," he said, shaking Anthony's hand warmly and grinning broadly at him.

Anthony smiled back. Despite his suspicion and fear of the situation, he found himself warming a little to Cavalir. To his own irritation and disbelief, he could not help but acknowledge the man's charm. Warning himself not to be conned by this blackmailer and manipulator, he accepted the offer of a seat.

"May I introduce you to my colleague, Pawel Baran, he will make sure that we are not disturbed."

The young man smiled and bowed slightly and Anthony nodded.

"What can I get you to drink, Mr Fernard?" asked Cavalir.

"I'll have a Scotch on the rocks, please. May I ask what the purpose of this meeting is?"

Cavalir smiled. "Nothing sinister, I assure you. I merely want to thank you for your help and to cement our friendship a little."

"I'm not sure 'friendship' is quite the right word when our relationship is based on blackmail and exploitation," snapped Anthony.

Cavalir smiled again. "I'm sorry if that's how you regard it. As far as I am concerned, we have a partnership where you are rewarded for doing the odd service for me, with no harm to anyone."

Anthony took a large swig of his drink. "I hope you'll understand if I don't see it quite like that."

Cavalir shrugged and looked regretful. "Whatever you think of me, please let me at least give you an enjoyable evening."

Anthony nodded. His tetchy tone notwithstanding, he was still curious as to what this meeting was really about and if he would have any ability to control what happened. "Where are we eating? The Grill?" he asked.

"I thought dinner in this room would give us greater privacy and be more comfortable," said Cavalir. "I have taken the liberty of ordering for us. It will be arriving at seven o'clock."

Anthony looked round the room, which was in reality a suite. They were sitting in a lounge decorated in the Art Deco style typical of the hotel with dove grey and teal as the dominant colours. It was furnished with a sofa and two armchairs, a writing desk and chair and a small dining table and chairs. Off this room was a large bedroom and a bathroom. He felt less concerned for his vulnerability and allowed himself to relax a little. He accepted Cavalir's offer of another drink.

Cavalir brought the drinks over and they sat opposite each other in the two grey armchairs.

"Are you really Polish?" Anthony asked.

Cavalir laughed. "Well, I was born in that part of Poland which was in the Russian Empire, so I was born a Russian. After the war, the Great War, I became Polish, because my birthplace was then in Poland. After the last war, the borders were changed again and my birthplace is now, once again, in Russia. So what do you think I am, Mr Fernard?"

Anthony smiled. "It's what you feel you are, I suppose."

"I feel I am an internationalist. I look forward to the day when all countries cease to be the first call on their citizens' loyalty and affection."

Anthony gave a half-hearted smile. "That's a clever answer but doesn't really answer the question."

"Well then, cannot I be both a Pole and a Russian? What nationality do you consider yourself?" asked Cavalir.

"British, of course."

"Not English?"

"That too."

"There you have it," said Cavalir.

Anthony smiled. "Why do you describe yourself as Polish in your dealings with me, out of interest?" he asked, taking another sip of whisky.

"It's a matter of sentiment, not on my part, but for the British."

Anthony frowned and looked questioningly at Cavalir.

"You see, the British have a soft spot for the Poles. Our troops fought bravely, if sometimes a little quixotically, against the Germans in 1939, with our cavalry taking on the tanks and so on. Then they went from Poland across Europe to join the British army and fought with distinction in Italy and elsewhere. So your country likes Poland and its people, whereas you are suspicious of Russia and the Russians. If I wish to befriend an Englishman, it's better that I am a Pole." Cavalir took a Balkan Sobranie cigarette from a gold case and offered one to Anthony.

"Nonetheless, shouldn't you be smoking a 'Black Russian'?" asked Anthony, as he inhaled from the smooth, Turkish-blended cigarette.

Cavalir snapped the cigarette case shut and laughed again. "That would be a cliché and also a step too far for my republican beliefs."

A moment or two later there was a knock on the door. Anthony, who was feeling a little peckish, looked at his watch in case it was time for dinner; it was only ten-to seven.

The young man, Baran, went to the door and opened it, first a fraction, then wide open to reveal a young woman.

"Ah, Anna, perfect timing," said Cavalir. "Do please come and join us." He rose from his chair and walked over to greet the newcomer, kissing her on both cheeks.

Anthony's eyes followed Cavalir and he found himself staring at one of the most beautiful women he'd ever seen. She was probably in her late twenties with dark brown hair in a Vidal Sassoon geometric cut, and she was wearing a nut brown belted and part pleated dress in the latest fashion. In her high heels, she was slightly taller than Cavalir and only a couple of inches shorter than Anthony. He was hopeless at guessing perfumes, but whatever she was wearing, he liked it.

"Mr Fernard, may I present my personal assistant, Anna. She'll be joining us for dinner and will make sure that all goes smoothly."

Anna held out her hand to Anthony and smiled. "I am very pleased to meet you, Mr Fernard."

"And I you, Miss…?"

"Please call me Anna. My surname is unpronounceable."

Unlike Cavalir who, despite his perfect command of English, had a slight accent, Anna spoke English without a trace of one. Whatever Cavalir's assertion that she was his personal assistant, he poured her a drink as well as topping up his own and that of Anthony. The latter thought he shouldn't have any more until he'd eaten something, but he was being driven along by this tide of the unexpected. They sat down again for a couple of minutes and then there was another knock at the door which ushered in the arrival of dinner. Baran checked who it was and then opened the door to two waiters with a loaded trolley, an ice bucket and a food warmer.

The waiters laid the table for three while Baran took a seat by the door. They opened the wine and served the first course, leaving the main course on the food warmer under a cover. Cavalir declined the offer to taste the wine, so they filled three glasses with a white wine, replaced the bottle in the ice bucket and took their leave with a tip from Cavalir.

"I thought communists didn't believe in tipping," observed Anthony, conscious that he was becoming a little too relaxed.

"When in Rome," replied Cavalir, smiling. "Good health to us all," he said, raising his glass.

Anthony followed the gesture and Anna chinked his glass with hers. "Cheers," she said.

As they commenced the first course of scallops with a very fine bottle of Pouilly-Fumé, Cavalir continued the small talk, asking after Anthony's family and if all was well at work. Anthony was happy with this trivial line of conversation. Although the purpose of this meeting was continually on his mind, he was in no hurry to leave the comfort of the present convivial atmosphere. In addition, he found Anna quite charming. She didn't give much information about herself but asked him about his interests. He mentioned his fascination for medieval history and that he enjoyed reading.

"Do you like Russian literature?" she asked.

"Well, I don't know much about it. I've enjoyed what little I've read: a couple of novels by Dostoevsky, a few of Gogol's short stories and, of course, *War and Peace*."

"The Russians and the English seem always to enjoy each other's literature," she said. "We love Shakespeare and Dickens in Russia, and there always seems to be a play by Chekhov or Turgenev on the London stage."

"Why do you think that is?" asked Anthony.

Anna shrugged. "Perhaps we both appreciate great literature."

"It goes much deeper than that, Anna," said Cavalir. "I think we share the same virtues of stoicism, endurance and a dark sense of humour. We have a lot in common since both countries are on the edge of Europe and mistrusted by those in the heartland. That is why de Gaulle vetoed your application to join the European Economic Community; he knows you would not fit in and would both disappoint and be disappointed."

Anna merely smiled and Anthony thought he might get out of his depth if he tried to pursue the subject of European geopolitics with two people who had probably studied it professionally. In addition, he was just beginning to flag a bit with the unasked request still ever-present in his mind. However, he did not wish to provoke the issue in case it deterred him from enjoying the noisettes of lamb which Anna now served, together with another fine wine, a Crozes-Hermitage. He continued with the pleasant conversation by asking about the arts in Russia, the theatre, ballet and so on, while they ate.

It was over the dessert that Cavalir said, "Mr Fernard, or may I call you Anthony?"

Anthony, faced with a choice between feeling uncomfortable or pompous, chose the former and nodded.

"Please call me Wicus. Anthony, I have a favour to ask you."

"Oh, what's that?" Anthony tried to appear nonchalant, despite the alarm clutching at his insides.

"I believe you have a friend at the Foreign Office, Mr Malcolm Vinton?"

Anthony thought the conversation was now sure to become much darker, but it was pointless to prevaricate; they probably knew everything about him. "Er, yes; what of it?"

"I would very much like you to arrange an introduction to him for us."

Instantaneously, Anthony felt quite sick. At least he knew now what all this was about. He took a sip of wine to give himself time to think.

"I don't think I can. He is a friend of mine and I can't drag him into this." He'd lost his appetite. He put his spoon down.

"You won't be dragging him into anything," said Cavalir. "We should like to make his acquaintance, that is all."

"Because he could be of use to you, presumably."

"Possibly, but it would be entirely up to him."

"Like it's been with me; entirely my choice, but I had no choice."

"I have no intention of blackmailing him, or forcing him to do anything," said Cavalir, speaking now rather like a doctor or counsellor.

"Then what do you want from him?"

"We know he works in a section that processes information concerning our strategies and activities in foreign policy. It would be beneficial to both our countries to ensure that there is no misunderstanding by your country of what we are trying to achieve. Nobody would gain from it; consider the near-catastrophe over Cuba."

Anna looked at him with a sweet smile on her face. "He will not be under any pressure to do something wrong."

"I don't know how I can believe that; surely if that were the case, you could contact him direct via the Foreign Office."

"It's a question of distrust. Secrecy does not necessarily imply that one is doing anything wrong."

Anthony reflected for a moment. "That may be true. Then why can't you contact him yourself? Why do you need me, as a go-between or something?"

Anna smiled. "Not as a go-between, just to facilitate the first meeting."

Anthony shook his head. "I am not a spy and I can't get Malcolm caught up with spies."

Cavalir refused to become impatient. "Anna, let's have some coffee and a brandy, shall we?"

He turned back to Anthony. "Why are you in the West so mistrustful of Russia? Our foreign policy has been consistent for at least four hundred years. We are a big country; we are not interested in expansionism. Our principle is always to protect ourselves from expansionism by others and thereby maintain our national independence. In so doing we have served the interests of Europe as a whole. For example, in the eighteenth century we stopped that mad Swedish king..."

"Charles XII?" interrupted Anthony.

"Yes, Charles XII. He would have taken over much of northern Germany and Poland, but we stopped him. Then it was Napoleon, who was stopped by Russia and then, of course, Hitler. We lost forty million people in the Second World War. Yet, somehow we are the enemy. Do you not find it strange that the Soviet Union and China were allies of the Western powers in the last war but are now the enemies, whereas Germany, Italy and Japan are now your allies? George Orwell made a similar point, I believe, in *1984*."

Anthony smiled. "Orwell didn't have much time for the Soviet Union once he'd seen Stalinism in action during the Spanish civil war."

"Ah, yes; I've read *Animal Farm*, a very amusing book. If you go to Russia now, you will see that what you refer to as Stalinism is dead and Russia has escaped from the authoritarian repression done in his name. Your country has not been as successful in getting rid of its system of self-protecting, immovable elites."

"Immovable elites?"

"The ruling classes which stop change happening in the circles of power and protect their own position through privilege, the education system and so on."

"That's rather an over-simplification of our social structure, if you don't mind me saying so."

"Perhaps, but have you noticed how many of those who have defected to the Soviet Union from Britain are from the upper middle-class? They were appalled by the corruption and decay of the privileged economic and political system, even though they benefitted from it. They could recognise the innate moral superiority of true socialism."

"I haven't got much time for any of these political '-isms,'" said Anthony.

"Why is that?" asked Anna, smiling at him benevolently.

"Well, if I believe in anything, it's fairness. But none of them are concerned with fairness; socialism prefers equality to fairness, conservatism prefers inequality to fairness and liberalism prefers freedom to fairness."

Cavalir smiled at him. "The world will never be fair, Anthony, we have to do what we think is for the best. Anyway, isn't 'fairness' a subjective term?"

"I think every human has an innate capacity to know objectively whether something is just or not, that's why we have the jury system."

"Ah, natural justice, you have Plato on your side." Cavalir seemed to be enjoying the conversation.

Anthony was quite enjoying this discussion too and hearing the arguments for communism expressed without the anger and personalisation of some of its domestic protagonists. He thought of asking, but decided not to, about Kim Philby. He looked at Anna, who had sat quietly through this discourse. "I suppose you agree with everything Wicus says?" he asked.

Anna shrugged. "It is irrefutable. Where else in a democracy would the aristocracy have the right to a seat in the legislature purely because of their birthright? Would you like another drink, Anthony?" she said, holding the brandy bottle over his glass.

He found himself pleased that she had used his first name. She was smiling pleasantly and her blue eyes pierced him with their gaze. "Yes, please," he said, and watched her pour a rather generous large brandy into the balloon glass. He made a mental note to nurse this drink for the rest of the evening.

"Isn't that the point of all this?" he said, resuming the debate. "You believe that our system is corrupt and you aim to encourage such systems to be overthrown, to be replaced by something similar to your own. Look what you've done across Eastern Europe. So the espionage is a part of the policy of destabilisation of our state; it's not purely defensive."

Cavalir shook his head. "Perhaps there are some idealists who think like that, but the Warsaw Pact countries are our buffer against expansion from the West. Introducing them to socialism was necessary to that strategy; it was a means to an end. We have no need to annex any other territory. Unfortunately, the Western Allies don't seem to understand that. This is why we must continue to protect ourselves." He offered a cigarette to Anthony, who politely refused.

"So, you are telling me that Russia has no aggressive intent against the West and all this espionage in America and Britain is purely for self-defence."

Cavalir nodded and exhaled a steady stream of smoke from his nostrils.

"The British and Americans would say the same about their activities," said Anthony.

"Of course; the balance in espionage must be maintained, just like the balance in armed forces and nuclear weapons. In a way, it's all a game. Secret services have agents and double agents to tell each side what the other side is doing and security services to prevent this information getting through and to feed misinformation to the other side."

He sat up and tapped the flat of his hand on the table. "I have enjoyed our discussion. Not quite up to the standards of the Greeks, but we have shown the same degree of humour and willingness to listen to the other. Now, I must bring us back to the point."

Anthony had been thinking about the arms race and suddenly he was jolted back to the here and now and Cavalir's proposal. He said nothing.

"Will you provide us with an introduction to Mr Vinton?"

"I told you, I can't drag him into any kind of espionage."

"It's not about espionage, Anthony," said Anna.

Anthony knew she was adopting this soothing tone to win him over, but it still had an effect. "What is it then?"

"As we said, perhaps he could provide us with the answers to questions which would enable us to avoid misunderstanding. There would be no requests for secret documents or anything of that kind. He would not be required to violate his integrity."

"I'm still not comfortable with it."

"Just enable us to meet him. It will be his decision whether to help or not and, as I said before, no blackmail." She looked at him with an expression of innocent invocation.

"And if I don't help you?"

Cavalir answered this question. "I hope we can achieve this outcome pleasantly, but I must insist, Anthony."

Anthony looked at Anna and felt it would be better if it were settled pleasantly too. "What would I have to do?"

"Do you like cricket?"

That was definitely the last question Anthony had expected and he smiled involuntarily. "Cricket? Yes, I do, actually."

"That's all you need do. Go to a cricket match. The Second Test at Lord's; will you be attending?"

"I hadn't thought about it yet."

"Well, whether or not you do go on any other day, I should like you to attend on the last day, Tuesday 25th June, in the company of Mr Vinton."

"Why the last day?"

"The seats in most of the stands are not booked in advance and people can sit where they wish. It makes it easier for people to move around and perhaps make the acquaintance of strangers."

"But sometimes the matches don't go on to the last day."

"That's true, in which case I shall have to think again."

"It's comforting to know that you aren't able to influence the results of Test matches," said Anthony, intending to take a drink of brandy but finding his glass empty. Anna offered to pour him another, but he held his hand over the glass. "So let me get this straight," he said, "you want me to take Malcolm Vinton to the Test match and you will have one of your people there who will somehow make contact with us and introduce himself to Malcolm."

"*Herself*, actually, but otherwise correct."

"Could I have another cup of coffee, please?" asked Anthony, glancing over at Anna, who immediately took his cup and refilled it.

"What am I expected to do?"

"We know Mr Vinton is a shy man, so you may have to smooth the way a little, otherwise you need only behave naturally."

Anthony lit one of his own cigarettes and drank some of the freshly poured coffee. "How do you know so much about Malcolm Vinton?" he asked.

"I don't, just a little of his background and a few assumptions based on his private life."

"What do you know about his private life?"

"He has none."

"And you will give him one?"

"If he wants it."

Anthony looked again at Anna. *If this were the woman Malcolm met, he would be a very lucky man,* thought Anthony and he rather hoped it wouldn't be her. She smiled at him and he hoped even more.

"I need a couple of minutes," said Anthony and rose from the chair in which he'd been seated for over two hours. As he began the walk to the bathroom he thought he was definitely a little drunk. He closed the bathroom door and leant over the large cream basin, splashing his face with water and staring at himself in the mirror. He was being asked to betray Malcolm and knew he would do it. He came out of the bathroom to rejoin the others. Baran was still seated at the door, eating a sandwich. Cavalir and Anna were exchanging a humorous comment of some sort and Anna was laughing. They stopped talking when he came into the room and watched his passage back to the table.

"Very well," said Anthony. "I'll get in touch with Malcolm and fix the trip up."

"Excellent, Anthony, let us know via Mr Sikora when you have made the arrangements. It will be quite straightforward on the day. Anna and a friend will look out for you in the Mound Stand," said Cavalir. He clasped his hands together. "Enough of these business matters; let's enjoy ourselves now."

"I think I ought to go," said Anthony.

"Please stay for one more drink," said Cavalir.

Anna brought over some shot glasses and a bottle of vodka and poured four drinks. She offered three to Baran, Cavalir and Anthony, and kept one for herself. Anthony wanted to refuse, to make some stand of non-complicity in their celebration of his betrayal, but what was the point of an empty gesture? He took the glass and, as he hesitated to drink, Cavalir gave him a let-out.

"To the health of us all," he said, raising his glass. "*Za zdaróvye*."

"*Za zdaróvye*," said Baran and Anna.

Anthony raised his glass and drank the whole glass in one gulp. Then he stood up. "I really must be going now," he said.

Cavalir shook his hand and Anna said, "I hope to see you again," as she took his hand. Baran smiled and said nothing as he opened the door for him.

As Anthony left the Savoy a chilly wind hit him, but he decided to walk a while to try to sober up a little. He went back along the Strand then turned down Savoy Street to the Embankment. Passing up the opportunity to go to the Temple station underground, he first strolled and then marched along to Blackfriars station, by which point he'd had enough and took the Circle line to Liverpool Street.

The walk gave him a chance to clear his thoughts about what he'd just agreed to. On the face of it, he had done nothing less than set up one of his friends to potential compromise by a Russian agent. Yet it was true what Cavalir had said; Malcolm was a free man. He was not married and would not be open to blackmail unless he agreed to break the Official Secrets Act. He would be guilty of putting Malcolm at risk, but the final choice was still Malcolm's. It wasn't a very good analysis, but it was one Anthony thought he could live with. In any case, the prospect of meeting Anna again made it, despite his forebodings, something to look forward to.

The following morning Anthony gave Malcolm a ring.

"Hello, Tony, how are you?"

"Fine, thanks. Do you remember over lunch with Ronnie the other week, we talked about the Test series this summer? I wondered if you had any plans to see the Test match at Lord's."

"Well no, I haven't been to a Test match for years. The last one was against New Zealand at the Oval in 1958. It was the one when John Reid and Bert Sutcliffe batted out the final day."

"Yes, I remember it; they managed to avoid a 5-0 whitewash. I was there too, funnily enough. Look, I haven't got tickets for Lord's and I'm not sure if there are any left for the first few days. I was thinking of going on the last day if the match is still live; perhaps you'd like to come? We don't need to book; we can see how we feel nearer the time."

Malcolm demurred. "Yes, I would, but I'd better check my diary. Hang on a minute." He paused and Anthony heard a rustle of pages. "Yes, I can do it. Shall we pencil it in and definitely go if there will be play?"

"That's great, Malcolm. I'll confirm with you the day before."

"Do you fancy a drink before then?"

"I'd love to Malcolm, but I'm a bit tied up next week; I'll ring you at the end of the week to see if we can do something."

"OK, bye."

Anthony then left a message with Mr Sikora's office that he would be attending Lord's on Tuesday 25th June.

The following week Anthony did arrange to have a drink with Malcolm on 6th June. They met after work at the King Lud and they had rather more to talk about than they'd expected. On the previous day it had been announced that John Profumo had resigned, after admitting that he'd lied to Parliament.

"It was only a matter of time," said Anthony. "All these court cases concerning people connected with Christine Keeler were bound to uncover things about Profumo. You can imagine what Freddie Pilling was like at work; going on about it and how he'd told us so and now he'd been proved right."

Malcolm shook his head. "I'm quite appalled, though; all these cover-ups of people with connections in high places. It makes you wonder what else is waiting round the corner. Quite frankly, I'm shocked how much corruption there is connected to the establishment; they've forfeited the right to be the ruling class."

Personally, Anthony felt sorry for Profumo and his wife, Valerie Hobson, who had promised to stand by him, as politicians' wives nearly always say they will. The fact was, Profumo had been reckless and had lost his career, without actually doing anything to endanger the security of the country. This was reflected in the view generally held by the newspapers, as well as the government, that the only reason he'd had to resign was that he'd lied to the House of Commons. So Anthony was surprised by the vehemence of Malcolm's remarks and guessed Cavalir would have been pleased to hear of his growing cynicism. He thought he ought to change the subject. "Still, on to more pleasant matters. I'm glad we could arrange that day out at Lord's, I'm really looking forward to it."

Malcolm smiled. "So am I. I wasn't much of a player myself, but I always enjoyed playing at school. You were quite a decent batsman Tony, if I remember. You played for the school, didn't you?"

"Just a few times; I was a bit headstrong, always going for too many shots. I did enjoy it though."

"Do you still play?"

Anthony smiled. "No, never liked fielding very much so got fed up with giving up a whole day to it. Now, as for Lord's, I suggest we sit in the Mound Stand on the 25th. It's big enough, there's a good view and we're not far from the Tavern if we fancy propping up the bar for a bit."

They reminisced about some of the great matches they'd seen and told each other stories about the wonderful cricketers of the past, even if they'd never actually seen them. For a while this delightful distraction enabled Anthony to forget why he was really going to the cricket and what this might mean for Malcolm.

XVII

The day of his visit to Lord's arrived and Anthony was on tenterhooks. Having agreed to go to the match with Malcolm and booked a day's leave he learned on the radio that play was likely to be delayed due to rain but was still probable at some point. He phoned Malcolm and they agreed to turn up at the ground at twelve o'clock and have lunch at a nearby pub once they knew when play was likely to start. He assumed that Cavalir would arrange things as far as Anna was concerned.

After lunch, they purchased tickets for the Mound Stand at the gate and, having surveyed the rows of empty seats for a minute or two, chose a pair that suited them. When play finally started at half-past two, much of the ground was only sparsely populated. Traditional lack of enthusiasm for the last day of a Test and the poor weather had deterred many from attending what promised to be an exciting day. As Ken Barrington and Brian Close came to the wicket to resume their overnight innings, the Mound Stand was still pretty empty, though there was a steady trickle of people coming in. Malcolm said how much he was looking forward to watching a run chase and thought England could do it.

Anthony smiled and agreed but really his thoughts were elsewhere. As they had arrived in the stand, he'd scanned the seats looking for two women seated together without male company, but there were none, except for two middle-aged ladies knitting furiously a few rows away from where they were sitting. He had chosen seats with plenty of space around them, conscious that he must keep two free seats next to theirs or at least one either side. However, it was soon clear that he needn't have worried as the stand remained resolutely thinly populated. After each ball was bowled, he would look round again for signs of Anna and her friend, but they failed to appear.

Then, at a quarter past three he saw the figures of two women standing at the back of the stand and looking at the rows. He thought he could make out Anna, though she was some way away and he had to stop himself from waving. At the end of the over, he stood up and as the steward allowed the newcomers to take their places, Anna saw him and she and her companion came down the steps to join them. A few seconds later Anna was saying to Malcolm, "Are these seats taken?" pointing to those next to Anthony, and Malcolm was replying that they were free. The two women squeezed past the standing men and Anna took the seat next to Anthony while the other woman sat next to her.

"Good afternoon," said Anthony.

"Good afternoon, said Anna, giving him a subdued version of the smile she had greeted him with when they first met. "This is the first cricket match we have ever been to. They said this morning on the radio that it could be very exciting, so Maria suggested that we both skip off work to give it a try."

"Do you know much about cricket?" asked Anthony, keeping one eye on the match.

"Not really, probably nothing, only that the team which scores the most runs wins."

"Exactly, and England need to get to 234 to win the match, so less than a hundred to go."

Anna nodded. It was a cool day and she was wearing a cream mac over her summer dress. As on the previous time he'd met her, she was impeccably dressed and looked lovely. He glanced over at her companion and smiled at her. She was blonde and probably just as attractive as Anna, though perhaps not so much Anthony's type. She smiled and waved, and Anthony wondered which of these two was destined to become somebody in Malcolm's life.

"Well, if you have any questions about the play and what's happening, I'll be only too pleased to help if I can," said Anthony.

Trying to be as natural as he could, Anthony turned to Malcolm and chatted to him about the way the match was going. Now that the women had arrived, he felt his job was just to be himself and to assist, if necessary, events unfold the right way. In fact, he was already becoming enthralled by what was going on in the middle as Barrington hit two elegant, almost effortless sixes in one over and the fearless, bare-headed Close came down the wicket to the West Indian fast bowlers to try to push the score along.

"Excuse me," said Maria, repeating the request when Anthony didn't respond the first time. "What are the 'Extras' on the scoreboard?"

Anthony leaned over a little, trying not to press against Anna. "They're runs scored without the ball touching the bat. It's a bit complicated so I'll point it out to you when it happens."

Maria nodded.

During the next over a ball was bowled, which took an odd bounce and could not be stopped cleanly by the wicketkeeper.

The batsmen took a run and the umpire signalled a bye. Anthony explained this run had not been scored off the bat so was a bye, an example of an extra. Maria nodded, satisfied with the answer. Then Anna asked how many overs would usually be bowled in a day and Maria asked about fielding positions. Both interruptions Anthony enjoyed dealing with.

Anna said, "If it's not too much trouble, perhaps one of us could sit next to your friend and he could answer her questions rather than us keep interrupting you."

"Did you hear that Malcolm, you wouldn't mind, would you?"

"No, of course not," said Malcolm, without looking away from the play. "If I can be of help."

So at the end of the over, Maria moved into the empty space next to Malcolm. As Anthony watched out of the corner of his eye, he saw Maria soon engage him in conversation about the match and Malcolm, comfortable with the subject matter, seemed not in the least tongue-tied or diffident. As well as answering her questions enthusiastically, he actually took the initiative in pointing things out to Maria and soon they were talking about things other than cricket. All seemed to be going well.

The match was a very close one, with England whittling away at the target but wickets falling every time they appeared to be on top. The tension and excitement mounted with every over and Ted Dexter, the England captain, said later that it may well have been the finest Test ever played at Lord's. So, despite the distraction surrounding the day, Anthony soon became increasingly caught up in the events on the pitch.

At a quarter past four the players walked off and Anna asked what was happening. "Is it finished?"

"It's the tea break," said Anthony. "Would you like a cup of tea?"

"Oh, yes, please," said Anna.

"I'll get them," said Malcolm, jumping up.

"I'll help you," said Maria, and she followed Malcolm to the tea bar under the stand.

Anna turned to Anthony. "It's nice to see you again," she said.

"Glad to see you too," he replied.

"I'm pleased. No hard feelings about this?"

Anthony shook his head. "Not really, you're just doing your job; but I don't think I could do it." He paused. "Come to think of it, I am doing it by tricking Malcolm. Who am I kidding?"

"Maria will be kind to him. The happier he is, the more useful he will be."

Anthony found her reply chilling, even if it were meant to put his mind at rest.

A couple of minutes later Malcolm and Maria arrived with two trays carrying four teas and four cream buns.

"Perhaps we should introduce ourselves," said Anna. "My name is Anna and this is my friend Maria."

"That's Anthony and I'm Malcolm," said Malcolm. "That's funny; our initials match, A and M."

"Is it a coincidence or is it symmetry?" said Maria, laughing and revealing her perfect, white teeth.

Anthony smiled but wondered if it was even true; was that her real name and was this other one really Anna? He could see his job was done and all he would have to do was go with the flow. For now, his attention was focused on the match and he tried to impart his interest to Anna. With one over left, England still needed six runs to win and had two wickets left, but one batsman, Colin Cowdrey, was injured and unable to bat.

"Who do you think will win?" asked Anna.

"It's hard to say. Without wishing to bore you, there are four possible results. If England get six runs, they win. If they get five runs but lose their wickets on that score, it's a tie. If the West Indies get two wickets while England are still behind, they win and if none of the above happen, it's a draw."

Anna laughed. "I think I understand that," she said, not very convincingly. "The crowd is getting quite excited."

It was true, there was a loud murmur around the ground as Anthony's explanation was repeated by hundreds of similar observers. Wes Hall came charging into bowl and, after a couple of singles, Derek Shackleton was run out on the fourth ball of the over. To avoid defeat, Colin Cowdrey had to come in with a heavily plastered, broken wrist, received when he'd been batting earlier. The two batsmen chatted for a moment in the middle then David Allen wisely played out the last two balls and the match was drawn.

"It was a draw?" asked Anna.

"Yes, after all that excitement, it's a draw," said Anthony. "You know, cricket is an allegory for life: it starts with a clean slate with lots of hope and potential, always involves elements of chance with some people being luckier than others, has moments of excitement and pleasure interspersed with long periods of tedium, is often interrupted by the vagaries of climate or physical misfortune and, despite all the promise, often ends with a draw."

Anna smiled. "But this was a very exciting draw, looking around I could see everyone thought so." She took out a cigarette and Anthony lit it for her.

As the crowd began to disperse, Anthony noted that the two young women stayed in their seats. He wondered whether this was a moment when he ought to push things along; perhaps this was what he was supposed to do. "Did you enjoy the match?" he asked Maria.

"Yes, very much," she replied, leaning across Malcolm, her bosom pressed against his arm.

"If you're not in a hurry, we could have a drink and discuss the match. We might be able clear up any thoughts or questions you might have; after all, it's the duty of all cricket lovers to help others to appreciate the game."

Malcolm laughed. "Or bore them to death trying. But yes, please do join us for a drink."

Anna and Maria looked at each other and Maria responded with an expression of shy pleasure. "Yes thank you, we would like to have a drink; we'd like that very much."

"Let's go to the Tavern," said Anthony. "We can go straight in without leaving the ground. It'll be emptying a bit and you can take in some of the tradition of Lord's."

They walked over to the Tavern, where they found a table for four and Malcolm went to the bar to buy the drinks, Maria offering to help with them. While waiting to be served he pointed out a picture of Albert Trott, the only batsman ever to hit a six over the top of the pavilion at Lord's.

"Well done," said Anna. She sat facing Anthony. "Everything will be fine." She nodded towards the bar, where Malcolm and Maria were talking and laughing together.

Anthony was less sure, but when he looked over at Malcolm, chatting to Maria, he had never seen him look so happy.

The men had beers, while the women had vodka and tonic. The conversation flowed, covering a range of topics without once touching on the subject of cricket.

"So, what do you do, Anthony?" asked Maria.

"I'm a civil servant, in the Home Office."

"Sounds interesting."

"But it's not really, I'm dealing with routine matters most of the time."

"What about you, Malcolm?" asked Maria.

"I work in the diplomatic corps. That's also not as interesting as it sounds."

"Malcolm gets invited to a lot more posh parties than I do," said Anthony, "so it's more interesting in that way."

The two young women smiled and Anthony took the opportunity to look at Maria more deliberately than he had before. She was probably, like Anna, in her late twenties. Blonde, blue-eyed and more Slav in her features than Anna, with high cheekbones and a petite nose. She was probably a little heavier than Anna and possessed a fuller figure than her friend. Anthony certainly found her very attractive and was sure whichever of these young women deigned to bestow their favours on Malcolm, he would be powerless to resist and unlikely to try.

The two women painted a picture of themselves for the benefit of Malcolm. They revealed that they both worked as secretaries, Maria with a wool warehousing company and Anna for a commodity broker. They were very convincing, describing the work they did and talking about the perils of being an attractive young woman in an organisation with its fair share of predatory males. Maria said she liked her boss because he kept his hands to himself, and she and Anna laughed. They talked about living in London and its social advantages in terms of amenities and the range of entertainments. Anna also revealed that each of them had a flat in London to make the best of what was available in the capital. The young women were friendly and flattering, and this was obviously adding to the enjoyment for Malcolm. He was clearly having a good time.

Anthony tried to appear interested and contributed occasionally to the animated conversation of the other three. But he was mostly a quiet observer of what he considered a strange charade conducted by himself and the two women, while Malcolm, an unwitting dupe, was being dragged into whatever scheme Cavalir had lined up for him. Yet he could not but help be consoled by the fact that Malcolm appeared happy and that Anna had assured him that things would go well.

"Are you hungry?" asked Malcolm, as they came to the end of their first round of drinks.

The women looked at each other, as if trying to assess what the other thought.

"Well, I am getting a little hungry," said Maria.

"Me too," added Anna.

Anthony went over to the bar and came back with some menus. He glanced down it. "It's typical pub fare, if you can face a pie or something like that."

"Oh, I like pies," said Maria. "We grew up on them where I come from."

"And where's that?" asked Anthony.

"Yorkshire."

"Oh, whereabouts?" asked Malcolm.

"North Riding, Easingwold."

Anthony was very impressed. He was unable to test Maria as he had not the slightest idea where Easingwold was or what happened there. Then he felt a frisson of excitement when Malcolm spoke.

"Ah, Easingwold, lovely part of the country. I had a couple of holidays there when I was a boy. You must know The George, we stayed there."

"Yes, I do. My uncle worked there when he was young."

Malcolm shook his head. "Isn't that odd, what a coincidence? I'm afraid I can't remember the staff. Enjoyed staying there though; lovely situation at the foot of the Howardian Hills and lots to see and do."

Maria smiled. "I probably didn't make as much use of the area as you did; you know what it's like when there's somewhere beautiful or famous on your doorstep. I remember the first time I saw Castle Howard, though, what a wonderful place."

Anthony was impressed that Maria was not in the least fazed and could only watch in admiration as the interchange of views took place. "So what would you all like to eat?" he said.

Maria waited to see what Malcolm chose and then asked for the same. Anna and Anthony went their own ways on the menu.

During the course of the meal Maria explained how, after working in the woollen trade in Yorkshire, she had eventually been transferred to the company's London office. Anna had always lived in Hertfordshire until she came to work in London and had then met Maria. Since then they'd been firm friends.

Anthony was amused by the panache with which the two young women spun their web of lies to establish their personalities for the equally admiring, though ingenuous Malcolm. Almost semi-detached from the conversation, he waited to see what would happen when the meals came to an end.

"Oh, it's after eight o'clock," said Anna. "I suppose we ought to be going soon."

Anthony wasn't sure if he was supposed to say or do anything at this point but decided to leave it to the experts. Fortunately, they were on the ball.

"We've so enjoyed ourselves, thank you; it's a pity to break up the party," said Maria.

"Must you go?" asked Malcolm. "The evening is so young and it's still quite sunny. Perhaps we could have another drink somewhere else. Or we could all go back to my place if you like."

Once again Anna and Maria looked at each other. "Well, only if you let us go Dutch on the meal; we like to pay our way," said Anna.

Malcolm raised his hand to object. "No, we wouldn't dream of letting you pay. It was our idea." He called out to a waiter for the bill.

"I'm a married man," said Anthony, thinking he ought to play a cautious role. "Much as I'd like to..."

Anna interrupted him. "Don't worry, we'll all be each other's chaperone," she said. "Do come."

If he didn't know she was acting a part, Anthony would have believed it mattered more to her than anything that he should come with them.

Once again, the young women offered to pay their way for the meal but finally accepted Malcolm's generosity and the foursome headed to Malcolm's flat in Bentinck Street. This was a new experience for Anthony too as he had never been in the flat himself.

The second-floor apartment was spacious, with two bedrooms, a large lounge-cum-dining room, kitchen and bathroom. Anthony was impressed. It was the room of a man with conservative, refined taste and reminded him of a gentlemen's club. The furniture was substantial but comfortable, and the heavy curtains were offset by light wallpaper and a pale green carpet. The walls were adorned with a painting of an Indian palace, a reproduction of Turner's *Rain, Steam and Speed* and some impressionist-style paintings which Anthony did not recognise.

"Have you lived here long, Malcolm?" asked Maria, sitting on a Chesterfield, kicking off her sandals and putting her feet on a pouffe.

"I bought it five years ago with some money left to me by my father. Some of the things are from my family. I haven't spent half the time here since I moved in as I've been abroad quite a lot."

Maria nodded. "Do you like working abroad?"

"I do, but it can be unsettling so far as your connections at home are concerned. Can I get you a drink?" He looked round at all of them. Then he put on some light background music while he served the drinks.

The conversation flowed over a range of topics, but the subject of work was skirted over and nobody mentioned politics or current affairs. Rather, they talked about art and music, the pressures of modern life, travel and their holiday plans for the summer. The two women were lively and sociable and fully engaged in the conversation, but Anthony noticed that they drank more slowly than he and Malcolm. He was aware of this, because he'd been watching them as an apprentice watches a master at work. He admired the skill with which they built rapport and developed a social intimacy with their host. They were charming, witty and amusing, mildly flirtatious, and good listeners. They used the whole range of positive speech and body language gambits to ensure that Malcolm would like them and want to spend more time with them. And Anthony knew it was working, because it was working on him too. But he was waiting for the endgame and it came at about a quarter to ten.

Malcolm had just put on some more music and the conversation had gone into a bit of a lull when Maria, sandals back on, pulled him away from the radiogram and began a slow dance with him.

After a couple of minutes, Anna looked at her watch and said, "I have so enjoyed meeting you both, but I really must be going as I have an early start tomorrow morning. Are you coming, Maria?"

Maria looked a little disappointed and held onto Malcolm. "Oh, what a shame. We're having such a nice time and it's still light; it's not exactly late."

"Perhaps one last drink?" suggested Malcolm.

"Not for me, I have to go," said Anna. "But you stay if you like, Maria, you're a big girl now." She smiled and looked fleetingly at Anthony.

Anthony took that as a cue and rose from his wing chair. "I must be going too. Sorry to break up the party."

Malcolm looked hopefully at Maria and she smiled. "I'd like to stay for a little while, if you like, Malcolm. I'll ring you tomorrow, Anna."

They all said their goodbyes and a few minutes later, Anna and Anthony were in Bentinck Street.

"Thank you, Anthony, you were very helpful today and this evening," she said as they walked along the road towards Bond Street tube station.

"What'll happen now?" asked Anthony.

"They'll become close and Maria will make him very happy. You need not worry."

"I could do with another drink," he said, "how about you?"

She smiled. "OK, I'm off duty now. I know a discreet little place and it will not get busy until much later."

Anthony was pleasantly surprised by her agreeing to his suggestion. Perhaps they could have a less business-like relationship after all. They changed direction and she took him to a small club in Soho which had booths where people could not be overheard against the loud, but not too intrusive, background music. They ordered some overpriced drinks, which Anna paid for. At first, they talked about general, unimportant matters – how the day had gone, what a pleasant evening they'd spent – but Anthony wanted to know more about her.

"How did you get into this job?" he asked.

"How do you think?"

Anthony sipped the expensive, not very good, whisky. "I suppose it's because you believe in whatever it is you're working for, in good versus evil or something like that."

She nodded. "You could put it that way."

"I guess you have contempt for people like me who do it because I have to and then accept payment for my squalid services."

"Not really, I'm only interested in the bigger picture. If what you do helps what we're trying to achieve, you're an asset and that's the only way I look at it."

"So you would do what Maria is presumably doing with Malcolm now without any qualms?"

"You mean gain the confidence of someone for our purposes? Of course, it's what we do."

"Including seduction?"

Anna smiled. "If that's what it takes, why not? It's only sex."

"Is there nothing that could be asked of you that would make you feel uncomfortable?"

"If there was, I wouldn't tell you because then you would know my weakness. But there's nothing that I can think of; the ends justify the means."

Anthony nodded. "Is that supposed to make me feel better?"

Anna shrugged. "Not necessarily; your motives and principles are not mine and therefore I could never completely trust you. That's why I brought you here rather than to my apartment."

Anthony had never considered the possibility that she might take him to her apartment, yet now he felt slightly disappointed. He had to remind himself that everything, the wonderful smile, the mild flirtations, the kind words, were all part of the job. She probably wasn't interested in him as a person at all.

"So your motives are on a higher plane than mine. Is Cavalir like that too?" He thought that he might have overstepped the mark with that question, but she answered it.

"Not exactly. Cavalir is a pragmatist; he does his duty and is an honourable, loyal man, but he believes in his country, not the political philosophy which it has embraced. I am different."

"You are more principled?"

"I have come to believe that the socio-political system I support is the only right way forward for the world. I work towards that end."

"And that's why you would have done what Maria is doing today?"

"Of course; he's not attractive to either of us, and I might have preferred that it were you, but that's irrelevant."

Anthony smiled. "It's really that straightforward for you?"

"Yes. Have you read *Darkness at Noon* by Arthur Koestler?"

"No."

"Read it; then you will understand." She finished her drink.

"Would you like another?"

"No thanks, I have some work to do." She stood up.

Anthony got up too and they walked up the stairs and out into the fresh night air.

"Thanks again for today," she said, shaking his hand. "I liked working with you."

"Will I see you again?" he asked.

"Perhaps."

Then she walked off, leaving him standing, staring after her, troubled and conscious of being alone in his world.

XVIII

A FEW DAYS LATER, ANTHONY WAS AT HOME, watching television. The phone rang and it was answered by Ruth. After she had spoken to the caller for a few minutes she came into the sitting room. "It's for you, Tony; it's Malcolm."

Since their day together at Lord's, Anthony had spoken to Malcolm only once when, a week later, they'd both had lunch with Ronnie. The government had finally admitted that Kim Philby had defected and much of the conversation had been spent discussing the state of the security services. While Ronnie could see the black humour in yet another failure at the centre of the system, Malcolm was disparaging about the state of British Intelligence and its apparent inability to avoid lurching from one embarrassment to another. He was especially scathing about the initial recruitment of a suspected reprobate like Philby.

Anthony was surprised to get a call at home, since Malcolm always rang him at work. He hoped there wasn't a problem, but that worry was immediately dispelled by Malcolm's upbeat exchange of pleasantries and they agreed to meet for lunch a couple of days later at Anthony's regular pub venue.

Anthony was early for his lunch appointment and he'd just ordered a drink when Malcolm came bounding into the room with a broad grin on his face.

"Hello, Tony, it's good to see you," he said. "I asked you to meet me because I couldn't wait to tell you how well things have gone for me since that visit to the Test match. I would've done sooner, but I wanted to make sure."

"Good to see you too, Malcolm, you seem in very good spirits."

"I am; I'll tell you why after we've ordered."

"So what's the big news?" asked Anthony, once their food and drink were on the way.

Malcolm beamed. "Well, it's about Maria," he said. "After you and Anna left the other week, Maria stayed on, as you know. She didn't leave until about eleven and agreed to go out with me again. So the following week, we went out for dinner at a nice little restaurant that she knew and it went on from there. We've been out for dinner two more times since and I took her to the pictures on Monday. I'm seeing her again at the weekend. We seem to get on so well and we've only known each other just over a month. It's fantastic and all because of the chance encounter at Lord's. I suppose it was meant to be."

Anthony smiled. "I'm glad you get on so well. Why do you think that is? Shared interests, or maybe it's the chemistry between you?"

Malcolm scratched his chin, searching for an answer. "I don't know, really. She seems to be happy with whatever ideas I come up with. I've suggested lots of things: theatre, ballet, a boat trip, a day at the coast, and she can tell me later what she likes best. I've been given a couple of tickets for Glyndebourne to see *The Marriage of Figaro* and she's already agreed to come with me to that. So whatever the reason, we just seem to be happy spending our time together."

Malcolm continued talking, extolling the virtues of Maria and how glad he was to have met her, but Anthony wasn't listening. He was hoping that Maria really did like Malcolm but knew that, even if she did, he was watching, even participating in, a con trick in which his friend was the fall guy. From an objective viewpoint, he wondered what Maria's game plan was. He was drawn back into the conversation by Malcolm's next sentence.

"Maria doesn't want to neglect her other social relationships, of course, and she suggested we might be able to go out as a foursome, you know, with her friend Anna. I said I'd ask, but I suppose it would be awkward for you, even if it was just as friends?"

Anthony nodded. "It might be tricky," he said, playing for time. He was thinking, *Whose idea was this? Probably Maria's, but why? Was Anna keen, and if so, what was behind it? After their last conversation, was it likely she had any personal interest in him?* "I don't mind going out as a foursome; as you say I don't have to be other than a makeweight. Obviously I'd rather not mention it to Ruth; it might be difficult to explain."

Malcolm looked quite elated. "No, of course not, just a little socialising. That's really good of you, Tony. I think Maria wants to get involved in all aspects of my life."

"What did you have in mind for this foursome, not dancing I hope?"

Malcolm laughed. "Certainly not. We thought perhaps a meal or a few drinks."

"That sounds OK to me, perhaps drinks would be best. Just let me know when. The main thing is that you're having a nice time with Maria. I'm very pleased for you."

"Yes," said Malcolm. He paused for a moment and his expression became more serious. "Tony, when I rang you the other evening, Ruth said something that I thought rather strange."

"Oh, what's that?" said Anthony.

"Well, she said she was pleased to speak to me and was glad that you'd renewed your friendship with an old school friend. Then she mentioned something about us meeting up regularly, once a week or something like that. I made some sort of non-committal grunt, but what on earth did she mean?"

"She must have meant every month, slip of the tongue, perhaps." Anthony was floundering and he knew it.

"No, it was definitely to the effect that you'd seen me a lot and even that you'd stayed over at the flat a couple of times."

Anthony looked down for a moment. "I'm sorry Malcolm, I owe you an apology."

Malcolm frowned. "Why? What's going on?"

"The fact is, Malcolm, that I have been having a bit of a thing with a girl and, I confess, I have sometimes told Ruth I was seeing you whereas I was spending time with her."

"Including nights when you didn't come home, I suppose."

"Yes."

Malcolm pursed his lips then took a drink of his beer. After a few moments he broke what was for Anthony an awkward silence. "I wish you'd told me, Tony; we're friends, you could've trusted me. Instead, I feel you've treated me like a mug, a convenience."

Anthony shifted in his seat. "You're right, I'm sorry. I didn't want to get you involved in case it put you on the spot. I should've asked your permission."

Malcolm wasn't totally mollified, but he seemed to accept the apology. "All right, just tell me if it happens in the future so that I won't be put in an embarrassing situation."

"Thanks Malcolm, that's very decent of you. I doubt it'll happen again as I don't see the young lady in question anymore."

Malcolm nodded. "Still, at least I don't have to worry about your scruples regarding a foursome with the girls."

Anthony thought he was about to be chastised but then Malcolm smiled. "Really, I am glad you can come. I'm really looking forward to it."

"I'm sure we'll have a great time."

"It was the first time I'd spoken to Ruth; she sounds very nice."

"She *is* very nice, but you know how it is."

"Not really. I'm just grateful to have one woman interested in me."

"It's a good way to be," said Anthony.

Anthony didn't expect to hear from Malcolm for another week but then he called the next day and they agreed to meet after work the following Thursday for their foursome. They arranged to have a light meal at a restaurant in Marylebone and then go on to meet Anna and Maria at one of the bars at the Hilton at eight o'clock. Anthony, with no idea how the evening would pan out but unable to resist contemplating all possibilities, told Ruth he would be late and might stay at Malcolm's. At dinner, Malcolm was in a good mood, looking forward to the date with Maria and Anna. Any mild annoyance he'd had over Anthony using him as an excuse to see Carrie seemed to have disappeared. He said he was perfectly happy to put Anthony up for the night if the situation arose.

They arrived early for their date with Anna and Maria, but they weren't kept waiting long. After about five minutes their dates pushed through the swing doors and waved as they saw them. The weather had hardly been very warm for most of the month, but they were both dressed for the calendar rather than the weather in pretty, scoop-necked summer dresses with abstract patterns. They wore light cardigans over their shoulders.

Maria kissed Malcolm on the lips and then shook hands with Anthony, giving him a peck on the cheek. "Very happy to see you again, Tony," she said, sitting on the banquette next to Malcolm.

Anna shook hands with both the men and sat on a chair next to Anthony. She smiled at him. "So we did meet again after all."

"I'm glad," said Anthony. "What would you like to drink?"

When a waiter had served them with drinks and mixed nuts, Maria lifted her glass to Anthony. "Thanks for coming this evening, Tony," she said. "I want to get to know Malcolm's friends better and hopefully, later, his family." She placed her hand on Malcolm's knee and looked at him affectionately.

Anthony smiled, but inside he felt repelled by Maria's actions. He hated her for leading Malcolm on and filling his head and his heart with feelings that were encouraged by deceit and falsehood, and he hated himself for his part in it. But also a small part of him was repulsed by the thought that this beautiful, vivacious woman was willing to give herself to this unattractive, certainly stolid and perhaps tiresome, man. Not out of love, which could cloud her perception and clothe his image in a gentler light, but in all its stark reality purely for a cause she may not even fully believe in. He thought what a wretched couple they were.

Then he looked at Anna, who was also smiling, and thought it would be the same for her; any relationship with someone like him would be based on falsehoods and ulterior motives. Yet his ego still urged him to believe it might not be so, especially when she whispered to him, "I'm glad we had the chance to meet again; I wasn't very nice to you the last time we met."

He smiled. "I was probably expecting too much."

"Not necessarily," she said.

Before Anthony could respond, Malcolm interrupted, "Hey, what are you two whispering about?"

Anthony turned his head and grinned at Malcolm, who looked flushed and happy, like a small boy who'd got what he wanted for his birthday.

"We were just saying what a good couple you make," said Anna.

Malcolm flushed a little more and looked even happier while Maria squeezed his knee and kissed him on the lips.

Much to Anthony's relief, the conversation then settled along less sugary lines with a brief reference to their afternoon at Lord's then on to a humorous discussion about British weather and how awful it had often been when on holiday as a child. Anthony thought it amazing that both Anna and Maria could trot out their own examples of sitting on the beach in their macs at Scarborough or Hastings and traipsing around shops or amusement arcades when the weather was awful. Even more impressively, they could also recall their favourite McGill postcards and Anna said that her mother was always vetoing her father from sending a really risqué one to her own parents. He began to wonder if there was any subject on which they couldn't hold their own or whether they manoeuvred the conversation to areas they had mugged up on. He was tempted to try them on something else.

"Talking about childhood experiences, what were your favourite books when you were small?" he asked.

There was a brief exchange of looks between Anna and Maria and they were both silent. Anthony thought he'd hit on their weak spot. They could hardly start talking about Gogol or Pasternak or Tolstoy, nor whoever the Russian equivalent of Lewis Carroll or Beatrix Potter was.

But then Malcolm spoke up. "I remember mine very well, the Just William and Billy Bunter books at first and then later

Conan Doyle and Kipling and all those books about boys at public school, even though I never went near a public school myself."

Anthony nodded and thought how peculiar it was he'd read books like *Tom Brown's School Days* or, even more weirdly, *The Fifth Form at St Dominic's,* written by someone who'd never been to public school for boys who would never go to public school. "What about you girls?" he asked, determined not to let them off the hook.

"I liked Enid Blyton," said Anna. "*Malory Towers,* that kind of thing."

"Louisa May Alcott and Edith Nesbit," said Maria. "I think I preferred the earlier writers more; I don't know why."

Anthony smiled. Malcolm had given them time to think but they were good, very good. He looked at Anna and she smiled, and he knew that she knew. He wasn't going to try to catch them out again.

They had three or four drinks and became more relaxed. Maria and Malcolm held hands much of the time, but there was little other physical contact between them. Anthony's arm was only an inch from Anna's, and he was aware of her physical nearness but that was all. She and Maria went to the ladies' room to 'freshen up', though Anthony regarded that as a cover for planning what they were going to do later. When they came back, he could smell Anna's perfume more than before and he idly fantasised what her plans might hold in store for him. He looked at his watch and it was a quarter to eleven. If he didn't leave soon, he would have to stay up in London.

"I don't like to break things up, but I'm afraid I shall have to go soon," he said, reaching over to finish his drink.

"Shall we have one last drink, Anthony?" asked Malcolm. "You could stay at the flat if you like."

"No Malcolm, the poor man has a long journey, and he wants to go home," said Maria, pretending to scold him. "I'll have another drink with you back at your flat."

Malcolm looked very pleased by Maria's intervention. "What about you, Anna?"

"No, thanks, I'll be on my way soon."

After one last half-hearted attempt to delay Anna's departure, Maria and Malcolm stood up and, within a couple of minutes, they'd promised to be in touch, made their goodbyes and were gone.

Anthony looked at Anna. "I wanted to have a little time with you alone," he said.

She smiled. "Why?"

"Several reasons; let's just say you fascinate me." He took out a packet of cigarettes.

Anna laughed and accepted a cigarette. "That's a very good line," she said. "Which film did you take that from?" She took a light from him and blew the smoke out of the side of her mouth in a stream towards the ceiling.

Anthony smiled. He didn't answer.

"Shall we have another drink," said Anna, "or must you really be on your way?"

Anthony waved to the waiter and ordered fresh drinks for them.

"Are you satisfied with the way things are going between Malcolm and Maria?" he asked.

"Really, Anthony, that's not the sort of question you should ask, but yes, they're getting on well. Malcolm likes her very much, I think."

"Maria is extremely attractive, and she plays her part well; most men would find her company very desirable. Malcolm certainly looks extremely happy. If things are going so well, what was the point of this foursome?"

"Maria wanted Malcolm to know how seriously she was taking their relationship, so she suggested meeting his friends from time to time and things like that. I was happy to go along with it."

Analysing the situation like this was, for Anthony, intriguing but also rather gruesome. "So, this is purely a professional occasion for you?"

"Not purely."

"What then?"

"I didn't like the way our last drink together ended, and I wanted to make it right." She smiled and took a sip from her drink.

"No ulterior motive then?" Anthony gave her a suspicious look.

"No, I'm not on duty now, if that's what you mean."

"That's good," he said. "About that other evening; I didn't think afterwards that you'd said anything particularly unkind. It was more the hints about what might have been that I thought about afterwards."

Anna nodded. "I know, I thought about them too; they were true but perhaps I shouldn't have said them."

Anthony smiled. "I'm glad you did." He looked at his watch again; it was after eleven. "Look, I'm sorry; I'll have to go, otherwise I shall be searching for a room for the night."

"There's no need, I have one."

Anthony stared at her for a moment, not sure he'd heard her correctly. "What room?"

She seemed amused by his bewilderment. "Here, at the hotel. I thought we might need more time to talk things over in private. Of course, if you need to go home tonight, I'll understand."

Anthony shook his head. "No, I can stay over."

"Good," she said. "It's terrible to be always in a rush." She sipped her drink and stubbed out her cigarette.

Anthony did consider the possibility of some trick or subterfuge on Anna's part, but what was the point or the need of that? He was already hooked into this mad world of hers and Cavalir's, so she had no need to entrap him again. Now that the room had been mentioned, it was hard to think of anything else other than what she might have in mind. He emptied his glass.

After Anna had finished her drink, she suggested they go upstairs and continue the conversation there. She already had the key in her bag and led the way to the lifts and her room on the eighth floor. When she unlocked the door, it opened to reveal a generous double room. The hotel had only been open three months and it still radiated that feeling of newness, with its pristine plain sage green carpet and its unmarked furniture and bed headboard. The furniture was in the modern style, but the wood was dark to add a classic feel. Anna sat on a low, button-backed leather sofa and Anthony took one of the small, elegant occasional chairs.

"It's a lovely room," he said.

Anna nodded. "It's the first time I've stayed here; I like it very much. The bar was nice too."

She stood up and put one of the tall table lamps on before taking her cardigan off and flinging it on the bed. Then she went over to the console table and picked up the room service menu. "What would you like me to order?" she asked. "I must say I'm feeling a little hungry myself."

So was Anthony, he realised. "Just a snack and a glass of something, please."

Anna rang room service and ordered a couple of steak sandwiches, a bottle of Côtes du Rhône Villages and some coffee.

The room felt a touch too warm and Anthony opened the door out onto the balcony a little before taking his jacket off.

Then he returned to his chair. "Does Maria know that you have booked a room here?" he said, finding himself trying to figure out motives again.

"Of course."

"Will she tell Malcolm too?"

"Probably."

"But why?"

"He might be worried that you won't get home all right. Also it might be helpful later."

"Later?"

"Yes. Later on, there may be things that Malcolm says or does to help us that make him feel guilty. Most men assume that their friends are morally superior to them, because they don't know what goes on in their friends' innermost thoughts nor do they usually know of their most shameful actions. Guilty feelings are always relative, so Malcolm will be even more ashamed when he compares himself to you, an apparent paragon of virtue. But if he were to know that you are willing to have illicit sex, he will compare himself less unfavourably to you and therefore feel not so bad about what he does for us. It does not help us for him to suffer remorse."

"But who says I am going to have illicit sex tonight?"

"Nobody, but it doesn't matter; he has only to suspect it. Anyway, I'm sure it's crossed your mind."

"So this *is* a set up. I thought so."

She shook her head. "No, it's not a set up. I genuinely wanted us to have some time together, but you're free to go home and to tell Malcolm whatever you like. It just so happens that the circumstances might lead Malcolm to think you're not as morally superior as he does at the moment. And you're not, are you, unless you've told him you have a mistress?"

"Actually, I have told him about Carrie, so there's no need for this charade to convince him that I'm not a paragon of virtue; he already knows."

Anna shrugged. "OK, you have the room; I can get home tonight." She collected her cardigan from the bed and started to put it on.

Anthony felt simultaneously indignant and reproved. He wished he'd not raised the subject of why they were here, as they seemed to be back in that same slightly fractious atmosphere which this time together was supposed to dissolve. Except this time, it was ending disastrously.

Anna looked at him for a moment then she burst out laughing. "I was only joking," she said. "I'm not going anywhere."

She walked over to him and put her hand on his shoulder. "Let's not quarrel," she said and kissed him briefly on the lips. Before he could respond, she had gone over to her handbag and taken out her cigarettes, lighting one for each of them.

"Are you in a relationship yourself?" asked Anthony, sitting back and inhaling deeply on his cigarette.

Anna smiled. "Would it matter to you if I were?" she asked.

"I don't think so."

"Well, I'm not at the moment. It's easier, probably best, not to have one in my job."

There was a knock on the door and a waiter entered with a trolley and their food and drink. He laid the small table for them, opened the wine and left, accepting the tip from Anthony graciously.

They found the food excellent, especially because they were so hungry. The wine too was superb and helped fuel a rising tide of wantonness in Anthony. After they'd eaten, Anna poured them coffee, spilling some in the saucers to the amusement of them both, and they smoked more cigarettes while the talking slowly petered out.

"God, I'm tired, it's been a long day. I'm going to bed," said Anna suddenly, kicking off her shoes.

Anthony looked at the slightly fuzzy face of his watch; it was half-past twelve. There was nowhere else for him to go now, but fortunately, Anna didn't seem to want to get rid of him.

She walked over to him and bent down with her back to him, silently gesturing for him to unzip her dress. Then she stepped out of it, sat on the bed to undo her stockings and peel them off, pulled off the rest of her clothes and rolled over into bed.

Anthony took off his tie, shoes and socks and, a little unsteadily, his trousers. Then he turned off the lights, removed his shirt and underpants, and climbed gingerly into the bed. It was very dark and he could only just make out the shape of her back. He ran his hand down her back and then round the front, cupping a breast in his hand and moving his body over to press against hers.

She turned round and kissed him but then went back to her former position under the covers. "Go to sleep now," came a muffled command.

Anthony released his hand and turned away; he felt very sleepy and not entirely disappointed that she had rebuffed his advances.

He awoke with a headache; neither a splitting one nor a thumping one, rather it was a grinding pain somewhere behind his eyes. He looked at his watch and saw it was half-past seven. He had to be at work in less than an hour and a half, and this would usually be a signal to jump up, as he hated rushing in the morning. But, not today; he needed time to prepare himself and the sheets felt so good. He turned his eyes and looked at Anna, her position unchanged from when he'd switched the light out. He sat up, leaning on his elbow, and stared at her admiringly: the fine dark hair, the elegant neck beneath it, the pale peach skin of her back which had barely a blemish. His eyes followed the line of her spine to the tailbone and the gentle rise of her bottom. He held back from touching her with some difficulty.

Perhaps subconsciously aware of his gaze, she turned over on her back, opened her eyes and smiled at him. Her make-up had been badly disturbed in the night, the lipstick gone, there was mascara under her eyes and the eyeshadow had spread outside its intended limits. She looked a little crazy and he felt tender towards her. His eyes flicked down at her body and then back to her face.

He smiled at her. "Good morning," he said.

She smiled back at him. "Good morning," she replied and, putting her hand round his neck, she pulled him over her and they kissed in a long embrace.

Her hand ran over his back and backside and by the time she brought her hand round to stroke his chest he had forgotten his headache and urgently wanted her. There was some token foreplay, but she didn't want to wait and they both came quickly. Anthony waited until the last of her aftershocks, then he rolled off her and fell back, hot and breathing hard. They lay there silently for a few minutes. Anthony felt his headache return.

"How are you this morning?" he asked, eventually.

"Fine, a bit of a headache; it was the wine, I think. And you?"

"The same."

She laughed and went into the bathroom and came back a few minutes later in a courtesy bathrobe. She had removed the remnants of her make-up. "Would you like some breakfast?" she asked, walking towards the telephone.

"Yes please, egg and bacon, or something like that, and tea."

She smiled. "Ah, the British cure for a hangover: a hearty breakfast." She phoned room service and ordered for Anthony and some kedgeree for herself, also with tea.

"Are you going to work today?" she asked.

Anthony looked at his watch, it was a quarter past eight and he could still go into work late. He couldn't be bothered to find an excuse. "No," he said. "How about you?"

"I have the morning off because I worked last night." She shrugged. "Perhaps I should say I was theoretically on duty and available for work."

"Nice work, if you can get it."

"And you can get it if you try." She went over to the door and looked at the room details. "We have to be out by eleven," she said. "Are you in any hurry?"

"No, I have all day," said Anthony. He went into the bathroom and thought about a bath but decided on a shower. There was a complimentary razor in the bathroom and he was about to shave when he heard a knock on the door signifying breakfast had arrived. He left the shave for later.

"I think I'd better phone in while I think of it," he said and telephoned Frank Hodgkin to give his apologies due to a gastric bug of some sort which had kept him in the bathroom much of the night. Then he sat down and started on his bacon and eggs.

"Do you feel guilty if you take a day off when you're not ill?" asked Anna, tucking into her kedgeree.

"Not particularly, why do you ask?"

"I suppose it's because *I* would. Not that I ever do."

Anthony raised his eyebrows. The breakfast was greatly accelerating the process of clearing his head and he was just about up for this little debate about principles. "I assume you can claim expenses for last night. Don't you feel bad about claiming for what was pretty much just an evening out with bed and breakfast thrown in?"

She smiled. "And you, that was the best bit. No, I don't feel guilty because it's a legitimate claim within the rules. I won't claim for any money I didn't spend while at the Hilton. I stick to the rules."

Anthony nodded. "Well, I generally follow the rules, but you can't obey them blindly; you must use discernment. I'm with Douglas Bader – I think it was him – who said 'Rules are for the guidance of wise men and the obedience of fools'. There are too many issues that really matter to waste your conscience fretting over piddling little things like the occasional day off work, or white lies, or petty infringements of the rules. Anyway, blind obedience to the rules can bog things down and stop anything being done."

"Who's Douglas Bader?" asked Anna, nibbling on a piece of toast.

"He's a former RAF fighter ace; he flew in the war despite having lost his legs in an accident."

"Ah, I remember him now, very brave but perhaps a little crazy? The kind of hero that appeals to the English."

Anthony smiled. It was one of the few times that she had said something that, though perfectly pronounced, sounded slightly un-English in the turn of phrase. "Your English is so good and the pronunciation is perfect, Maria's too. How did you both master the language so well?

"*Yu vood razer I speeek lark zis?*" she said.

Anthony laughed. "Excellent."

"I went to a very good language school at home and since then it's been lots and lots of practice. I'm still trying to get better."

After they'd finished their breakfast, Anthony went into the bathroom and had his shave. When he came out, Anna was lying on the bed, her legs exposed above the knees where the dressing gown had fallen open. She was writing something in pencil in a little notebook. He looked at his watch, it was ten-past nine. "Are we going back to bed?" he asked.

Anna looked up from her notebook. "No, we are not lovers. This is not the beginning of anything; it's the end." She got off the bed, picked up her clothes and make-up bag and walked into the bathroom, closing the door behind her.

A deflated Anthony got dressed and poured himself another, now stewed, cup of tea while he reflected on how badly he'd judged the situation.

When she came out, she was the Anna he'd first met. She looked beautiful and alluring but professional and slightly distant, definitely out of reach.

"I'm sorry if I was abrupt with you," she said. "But I doubt I will see you again. I can't and I don't want to get involved. Besides, I think you have enough complications in your life."

"Well, it's not as complicated as it was; I'm not seeing Carrie anymore. I suppose you're right, but it's hard not to think about what might have been."

"You're too romantic for your own good," she replied. "I suppose there's a vacancy for your mistress now, but I shan't be applying for the job."

"I didn't mean it like that."

She smiled. "I know. I think we ought to go now."

Anthony followed her out of the room and they walked in silence to the lift. When the doors opened, they joined an elderly couple who said 'Good morning' in an American accent and all four rode in silence to the foyer.

As they approached the reception desk, Anna stopped and turned to Anthony. "You go now and I'll give you a couple of minutes before I leave. I enjoyed the time we spent together, but I have already stretched the lines I should not cross. Goodbye, Anthony, I wish you happiness." She kissed him on the lips and turned back to the counter to surrender the key and pay the bill.

Looking back at Anna once more, Anthony walked out of the hotel and onto Park Lane. It was not even ten o'clock, so he could hardly make the journey home yet. He considered whether he ought to go into work and receive a hero's welcome for rising from his sick bed but, then again, he was just as likely to be seen playing the martyr by those who would never dream of coming to work once they'd secured a day off sick.

So he decided to have a day to himself. It was a lovely, warm day and he wanted to get out of a stuffy London but in a leisurely fashion rather than taking a train. He took a Central line tube as far as he could to the end of the line at Ongar station. He sat idly watching the changing scenery once the tube came out of the tunnel at Stratford and progressed through north-east London out to Wanstead, Woodford and Epping, before changing onto the single-track connection to Ongar.

Emerging from the station into the small market town of Chipping Ongar, he began with a cup of coffee in a small, rather twee, tearoom, then walked round the town for a while before taking the two mile walk out to St Andrew's Church in Greensted. He didn't have a particular interest in old churches, but ever since he'd lived in Woodford he'd meant to visit this church because of its extreme antiquity; the oldest wooden church in the world and probably the oldest extant wooden building in Europe. When it came into view, he was not disappointed and found himself in awe of the pitch black Saxon oak walls, thought to date from the mid-ninth century during England's murky transition to one country. The church was empty and he picked up a leaflet and wandered round, feeling almost embraced by the walls and ceiling of great, once living trees. Ancient though they were, these walls were not in need of protective coverings and he ran his fingers over their grain as others had done for a thousand years. He took his time viewing the main points of interest, mostly, like a stained glass window, tributes to King Edmund the Martyr, the king of East Anglia. His body lay in the church in 1013 on its way to reburial in Bury St Edmunds. Anthony was not a religious man, but he found the atmosphere conducive to reflection and he sat in one of the pews, outwardly staring ahead but inwardly looking at himself.

He mulled over Anna's comment about his life being too complicated. He knew she had a point, even if he was no longer seeing Carrie. But he wasn't sure he was yet ready to unravel all the complications to go back to his former unvarying life where nothing ever changed and the past stretched into the future, unalterable and totally predictable. He had sometimes found the stresses of his new life a bit too much, but the thrill of uncertainty, the frisson of the unexpected, the fear of detection, all made him feel more alive. How could it be better to live life as if there were only the mundane, where fears would be based on hypochondria or loss of face, tragedy on running out of sugar or the train being late, ambition on the weekly football pools and excitement found in a fairground or horror film? He remembered back to the worst day of the Cuban crisis and how such pointless things were occupying most people even when oblivion stared them in the face. That had been him once, but not now. If anything, he felt he had space for a little more uncertainty and he knew that if Anna had wanted to see him again he would have jumped at the chance. Then he thought about Carrie and had a twinge of regret, but it was only a fleeting moment.

He left the church and walked back to the town where he had lunch and a pint in a large old pub where he got into conversation about nothing in particular with an elderly man looking for some company to help fill his day. Afterwards he meandered his way back to Woodford, stopping off at Epping for another walk and a cup of tea before going home. On the way, he remembered he had again been notified of a package to collect from the newsagent's and that reminded him of Shirley.

XIX

Returning home from work the following Tuesday, he stopped off at Leytonstone to pick up his latest package. It was the same day of the week he'd collected his last envelope, and he hoped that following a pattern would give him the best chance of seeing Shirley again. Sure enough, as he approached the shop door, he could see her leaning on the counter. The door was open today, presumably because of the weather, and he walked straight in. Shirley looked up from the *Evening News* she was reading and smiled. She looked very pretty in her sleeveless summer top and bright pink skirt. She was holding a freshly unwrapped Cadbury's Flake in her hand.

"Hello, Mr Phillipson, I was beginning to think you'd forgotten your package or that something had happened to you."

"Hello, Shirley. You noticed I hadn't been in?"

"Of course, when a package hangs around for more than a few days I wonder."

"I hadn't forgotten, but I've been very busy lately. Still, here I am now. It's very warm today, isn't it?" he said, pulling his shirt collar away from his neck a fraction.

"Yes, still, it's great to have some sun; the weather's been horrible this month. You must be boiling in that suit. Would you like a cold drink? We do iced Jubblies, or perhaps you'd like a glass of squash?"

"Oh, yes, please."

Shirley went in the back and came back with a glass of diluted lemon barley water. She handed it to him and watched him drink it while she put the Flake in her mouth and, after a moment or two, eventually took a bite from it.

A middle-aged man walked in the shop. "Hello, Shirley, twenty Weights, please. I see you're doing a drinks service now, mine's a pint of bitter."

Shirley grinned. "Come off it, Stan, he's come a long way, you've only walked ten yards."

Stan smiled and settled for the cigarettes.

After Stan had gone, Shirley said, "I'll get your package."

"No rush." Anthony finished off the drink and handed the glass back to her.

Before she could answer, another two customers came in and Shirley was tied up with them for a few minutes. As the second of them went out another customer came in and Shirley looked over at Anthony and rolled her eyes.

When this last customer had departed with her quarter of boiled sweets and a copy of the *Star*, Shirley's attention went back to Anthony. "Busy time, don't get a moment to myself, let alone a chance to talk."

"Perhaps we could talk later," said Anthony, on the spur of the moment.

Shirley did not appear in the least surprised by the suggestion. She smiled. "OK, I finish at half-past six." She looked at her watch. "Only another twenty minutes; I'll meet you at the bus stop, that one over there. I'd better get your package, after all, that's what you came for." She went into the back room and came back with a large envelope and the receipt book. "Won't keep you a minute," she said to the new customer standing behind Anthony.

"A big one for you this time, Mr Phillipson," she said, as he signed the book.

"Thanks," said Anthony, then he nodded at her and walked out of the shop.

It was too hot for a long walk, so he made his way to the local department store along the high street and browsed around the men's department for a few minutes, politely declining assistance from the staff. He realised he was walking around with the large envelope in his hand and, unable to get it into any of his pockets, he went to the gents' room and locked himself in one of the cubicles. When he had quietly opened the envelope, he found himself staring at a thick wodge of banknotes of mixed denominations. A quick count revealed a total of £300. He put some of the notes in his wallet, some in the back pocket of his trousers, some in the small safe pocket under the waistband which he always had inserted in the front of his trousers and the rest he put in the remaining inside pocket of his jacket. Thinking he'd killed enough time, he walked back towards the shop and took his place a couple of yards from the bus stop just before half-past six. He could see over the road that there was a man behind the counter now and Shirley had disappeared. A second later she came out from the back room, said a few words to the man, lifted the counter flap and left the shop. She looked over at Anthony and then started walking up the road on her side. Anthony mirrored her action on his pavement and, when the road was clear, he bounded over to join her.

She smiled and stopped. "I thought we'd get away from the shop before we met up; don't want everyone knowing our business. Where would you like to go?"

"How about the 'Green Man'? It's not far."

"Sure."

"Is that man in the shop your father?" asked Anthony as they walked along.

Shirley laughed. "Who, Mr Grainger? No, he owns the shop. I just work there. He always opens it in the morning at half-past six and takes over when I finish. I work from eleven till my finish time."

They went up the High Road a few hundred yards and walked into the grand, curved building which was the current manifestation of the great old pub. It wasn't too busy, the after-work drinkers having moved on and the evening crowd yet to arrive.

"What would you like to drink, Shirley?" asked Anthony, taking a pound note from his wallet.

"I'll have a gin and bitter lemon, please."

Anthony ordered a pint for himself and they took a seat in the window. "Well, here's to you," said Anthony, raising his glass.

"Cheers," replied Shirley, reciprocating the gesture. "It's ni— Sorry." She stopped in mid-sentence as Anthony had started to speak at the same time.

"Sorry, I was just going to ask if you'd worked at Grainger's long."

"Three years. When I left school, I began working in a greengrocer's, but I felt like a change so that's when I started at Grainger's. I thought my hands wouldn't get as dirty but now they get covered in newsprint instead of earth."

"You prefer this job?"

She nodded vigorously. "Definitely. I started off as a junior, but now Mr Grainger lets me run the shop; I don't start till late and that suits me. I don't like getting up early."

Anthony smiled and looked at Shirley as she sipped her drink. She was very pretty, but he thought she looked even younger than the last time he'd seen her, despite the best efforts of her make-up.

"What about you?" she asked. "I suppose you have some kind of business?"

"Why do you say that?"

"Well, you know, you have to call in for these packages. I thought they might be deliveries of some kind for whatever you do."

Anthony smiled again, this time he felt a little uncomfortable. "I don't exactly run a business, I just do the occasional freelance job for someone and the packages are part of that."

Now Shirley smiled and regarded him sceptically. "I think some of the people who use our letter holding service must be up to no good. After all, if everything is above board why would you need to use a private collection service, what's wrong with the Post Office? You're not one of them, are you?" She realised that she had just used a double entendre without meaning to and giggled.

Anthony suddenly reviewed his opinion of Shirley. She was much smarter than he'd assumed, and he began to have second thoughts about his decision to ask her out. He laughed and hoped he sounded convincing. "I use your service because I travel around a lot and can't always be contactable. I also assumed it was confidential and the shop could be trusted to be discreet."

Shirley coloured a little. "Oh, of course, I was only teasing. You can trust me, Mr Phillipson, I didn't mean anything by it."

Anthony smiled. His suspicions about her intelligence were confirmed, but he felt he had the situation more under control. She had gone too far and now she regretted it. "Call me Craig," he said. "Are there any good restaurants near here?"

"Well, they serve meals in here and it's quite good and not too expensive. I don't know of anywhere within walking distance that's posh; not that I usually get the chance to go to one. Have you got a car?"

"Not with me."

She shrugged. "Then your choice is a bit limited."

Anthony was more than a little disappointed. Flushed with all the money he had on him, he wanted to do something a bit special. He couldn't celebrate with Ruth because she would wonder where the money came from. So, he had planned to push the boat out this evening in the company of this attractive young woman. Now there was nowhere to go to push the boat out and, after her nosing around about his business activities, he wasn't quite so keen on spending the evening with Shirley. His enthusiasm was deflating like a football with a burst inner bladder. Not ready to give it all up, he downgraded his expectations and settled for the Green Man and for playing it by ear as to how long he spent with her. "Would you like to have dinner with me or do you have other plans?"

Shirley, who had looked subdued since being corrected a few minutes earlier, cheered up. "Well, thank you; I'd like to very much, and no, I don't have anything else lined up."

They took their drinks to the lounge bar and a young waitress took their order. Anthony encouraged Shirley to have whatever she wanted and offered her the chance to share a decent bottle of wine, but she preferred to stick to gin and bitter lemon. He ordered the bottle anyway.

"So you weren't expected home for dinner this evening?" asked Anthony, as they waited for their fillet steak and chips.

"No, my mum and dad run a fish and chip shop in Wanstead; they won't be home till eleven."

"What about the rest of your family?"

"I've got a younger brother, Lenny, he goes straight to the shop from school. They bring me home fish and chips if I want it, but sometimes I go out and anyway, I don't want fish and chips every day of the week, I'd put on stones."

"No, I suppose not."

Shirley didn't ask him any more questions about himself and Anthony reciprocated; he had only the slightest interest in Shirley as a person. Rather she could satisfy his need to spend money on someone without having to reveal where it came from. He gathered from their conversation that she was not 'going steady' with anyone and that she would never 'two-time' a serious boyfriend. He felt she imparted this information to him to show that she had scruples and standards of behaviour.

Shirley revealed that her interests were going to the pictures, socialising with her friends in coffee bars or at each other's homes, listening to music and Saturday night trips to Hammersmith Palais or a similar rendezvous. Dates with young men could result from most of these activities.

Over her third gin and bitter lemon, Shirley intimated that her interest in Anthony was partly due to the fact that there was something mysterious and therefore interesting about the people who used the poste restante service and also to the fact that she had never been out with an 'older man' before. Anthony, being at the mid-point of three score years and ten, realised he could justifiably be considered to be on the downward slope of life. Much of their conversation took the form of Shirley talking about herself and her interests and hopes for the future, while Anthony aimed to reveal as little about himself as possible. The enthusiasm with which Shirley dominated the conversation enabled him to come to his own conclusions about what she thought of him based on the hints and vague suggestions she made. Rather than his relative silence being seen as irritating or empty-headed, she seemed to think it added to his attractiveness and a desire to get to know him better, something which became more apparent as the evening wore on and the drinks flowed.

Over dinner, while Shirley did most of the talking, Anthony spent much of the time refilling his glass, listening and not listening. Afterwards he had a brandy while Shirley stuck to her regular drink. He looked at the clock; it was half-past eight and he was wondering what next when Shirley answered for him.

"Would you like to come back to my place?" she asked.

"What about your parents?"

"Oh, as I said, they won't be home till eleven."

He settled the bill and they came out into a beautiful sunny evening which still retained the heat of the day. Anthony took off his jacket and Shirley loosened his tie. "It's too hot to be trussed up like a turkey," she said, removing his tie and putting it in her bag.

They walked back down the High Road for a few hundred yards, before turning off the main road. Then they turned again onto a long road lined with substantial late Victorian houses with bay windows on both floors. They stopped at a house with a dark green door and white painted sills and pillars round the windows. Shirley found her key after a great deal of slightly wobbly searching in her bag and they went into the hall and then into the bay-windowed front reception room.

"Do you want a drink?" she asked. "I think my dad's got a bottle of whisky somewhere, and port."

"I think I've probably had enough," said Anthony, sitting heavily onto a light coloured buttoned-back sofa.

"So have I," said Shirley, giggling and sitting close to him.

He put his arm round her and she moved her pretty, smiling face towards his. Though he was definitely attracted to her, he felt impelled to kiss her more because it was expected of him rather than through an overwhelming desire. So they kissed for a few minutes, first gently and then more passionately, as desire overhauled other considerations.

"We could go upstairs if you like," said Shirley, using that time-honoured phrase guaranteed to raise a man's hopes and expectations, even if they were not always delivered.

He followed her up to her bedroom, a quite large room at the back of the house, decorated in a subdued, but modern, geometric patterned wallpaper. Though the furniture was adorned with feminine things, the overall effect was not something that only a woman could live with; its theme was essentially modern and assertive. Posters of James Dean and Steve McQueen adorned the walls and a framed, signed photograph of Roy Orbison was on a chest of drawers.

"You like Roy Orbison?" asked Anthony as he sat on the double bed.

"I think he's the greatest, I've got most of his records." She walked over to a cabinet with a large number of records and, after searching through some singles, she took one to the record player on the chest of drawers. After a few seconds, the dramatic tempo of 'Running Scared' filled the room.

"I don't fancy him, though, even if he is younger than you," she said, smirking and sitting on the bed next to Anthony to kiss him. She started undoing his shirt and put her hand inside, running her fingers through the hair on his chest. "Don't expect too much tonight, first date," she added, kicking off her shoes. She was not wearing any stockings and her legs felt cool to his hands. There was some discarding of clothes and some exploration of each other. He was surprised to enjoy once again the embrace of such a young woman. She was surprised that a man whom a few years ago she'd have regarded as middle-aged seemed quite youthful and not in the least 'falling apart'.

"You're lovely," said Anthony, embracing her near-naked body and kissing her on the neck."

"You're not so bad yourself," she said, stroking his chest. "You look so young; not that any man's bits and pieces ever look particularly young," she said, laughing as she undid his trousers.

Both were drowsy from a long day and rather a lot of drinking together. Coupled with the need to restrain their urges, this led to sleep eventually conquering desire.

"Shirley, we're home." A distant voice half-penetrated Anthony's dormant consciousness but then he was awake as Shirley sat up with a jolt.

She jumped off the bed, wearing only her underpants. "Quick, get up, my dad will bleeding well kill you if he finds you in my room." She quickly put on a dressing gown hanging on the back of the door and called out, "Down in a minute."

Anthony sat up. Luckily he was half-dressed, but his appearance was not one in which he would like to receive visitors. He adjusted his underpants and did up his trousers, then undid his trousers as he struggled to find his shirt.

"Stay here and don't make a noise," said Shirley. "I'll make sure the coast is clear and then you'd better go."

She left the bedroom and Anthony, now mentally alert but physically still moving in slow motion, did as he was told and found his shirt, shoes and jacket, and put all these on. He couldn't remember what had happened to his tie, but he felt less vulnerable and more respectable once he'd made a slapdash use of Shirley's hairbrush. Bothered by the possible appearance of Shirley's father, he tried to think up possible excuses to explain his presence in this room, but soon realised that the mere fact of his hiding made any acceptable explanations unlikely to hold water. So he waited, standing behind the door and half-considering whether he should go for the traditional secret lover's hiding place of the wardrobe.

After only five minutes, though in this silent suspended animation it seemed an eternity, he heard soft footsteps on the stairs and Shirley appeared in the doorway, her finger to her lips. She beckoned to him to follow her and they walked in unison down the stairs. As they approached the bottom, he could hear conversation coming from a room at the end of the hall and down a couple of stairs. Shirley sprinted on tiptoe silently along to this room and grabbed hold of the handle, then turned and waved at Anthony to go. He had less than ten feet to the front door, which she'd left ajar for him, and he made his escape in a second or two, not even daring to look back.

Anthony walked back to the station totally dispirited. An evening that had promised so much had ended like something out of a Brian Rix farce. By the time he got to the station it was nearly half-past eleven, but there would be trains running for a while yet. The first one in was going to Newbury Park, but the next one would take him home. He sat in a nearly empty smoking carriage, the only other passengers a middle-aged man who appeared to be asleep, despite holding a half-lit cigarette in one hand, two workers who'd just finished a shift and were talking rather loudly and a young woman repairing her make-up. Anthony sat back in his seat and lit a cigarette. He had a slight headache, presumably the consequence of his polishing off a bottle of claret, plus a few other drinks. But the point had arrived when he could start to see the funny side of things. He smiled as he thought of the excesses of the evening and the consequent failure to consummate his relationship with Shirley, followed by his undignified exit. It reminded him of a scene from *Tom Jones*, a film he'd taken Ruth to see just a couple of weeks ago, before it had descended into farce with his hiding and then escape. And, anyway, the day had been a success in one way, because he still had the money. He felt the folded notes in each of his pockets.

When he arrived home, it was well after twelve and the house was in darkness. He crept up the stairs and went into the bathroom. He could smell Shirley's perfume on himself and, when he looked in the mirror, he saw her lipstick was on his shirt. He scrubbed the collar of the shirt and left it on the towel rail; it would be dry in the morning. Then he had a strip wash and put on some of his aftershave to dampen any remaining scents. When he finally got to bed, he inadvertently woke Ruth.

"You're late," she mumbled, then rolled over and went back to sleep.

XX

On the 10th August, Anthony took his family for their annual two-week break to Sidmouth in Devon. They used the main trunk roads, but the journey was often slow with a crawl in heavy traffic on the A30. Eventually they had to make an unscheduled stop because the car was overheating after being stuck in a jam. They pulled over to a roadside café for tea and cakes, but when they returned to the car, it wouldn't start. Anthony gingerly eased off the radiator cap to reduce the pent-up pressure and left it to cool off for a while longer. But, after a top-up with water, it still wouldn't start and now the battery was almost flat. Anthony tried again, using the starting handle, but even then the car refused to oblige. The children sat glumly in the car and Ruth stared at the engine, willing it to start.

Perhaps it was seeing Ruth's forlorn look or just a willingness to help; either way two young men came over and asked if they could be of assistance. Each of them tried with the starting handle but without success, a disappointment lightened for Anthony by a slight boost to his bruised ego. After some discussion, one of them noted the slight incline in the road and, as the traffic was moving fairly slowly, they were able to push Anthony's car out onto the road, ably helped by the driver who'd stopped to let them out. The young men then drove their own car up behind Anthony's before giving it a bumper to bumper push start once a sufficient distance had opened up in the road ahead. Away they went, Ruth and Anthony waving out of the window and their rescuers flashing their lights in response.

Elated emotionally, though exhausted physically and mentally by their travails, they finally arrived at the hotel in the early evening. They were welcomed at reception by an elderly porter who asked after their journey and took them up to their room, a spacious corner room which had a view of the sea, even though the hotel was not on the seafront.

"I hope you enjoy your stay," he said, as he handed Anthony the keys to the room. "You may not be aware that we've had a number of famous visitors over the years and, as a baby, Queen Victoria stayed here with her parents in 1819."

"Really?" said Anthony.

"Yes, it was a sad story actually. It was in the winter and her father, the Duke of Kent, caught a cold and died from pneumonia in the January, while they were still here. His own father, King George III, died six days later, so the Duke's funeral was put off for a month; very sad for the widow. To top it all, someone discharged a firearm near the building while the family were here and the bullet entered Victoria's room. Had she been shot who knows what would have happened?" He recounted the tale with a relish honed by years of practice.

The two boys, earlier hardly interested in the adult conversation, were now listening intently to this tale involving shooting and a firearm.

"They didn't stay in this room?" asked Ruth, hoping to see a bullet hole.

The porter smiled. "No, madam. Well, if there's anything else you need just ring '0' on the telephone." He tousled the hair of Jonathan as he smiled at the two boys on the way out.

"Gosh, this makes a change from the usual bed and breakfast," said Ruth, bouncing on the bed and looking out of the window at the rain. "At least we'll have a nice room to come back to if the weather stays like this."

Anthony smiled. The scale of their holiday accommodation had gone downhill once Ruth had given up work to have a family and they hadn't holidayed in a hotel for several years. It wasn't so much that all the bed and breakfasts they'd stayed in were bad; some were very good. It was just the awareness of being in someone else's house with no right to come and go as you pleased. So there were the very wet days when the beach or sightseeing was out of the question and they spent their time wandering round the town looking for something for the children to do. Thanks to the money he'd received from Cavalir, those days were gone, at least for this year.

The same could not be said for the weather, which was unsettled for most of the holiday. The family didn't mind because there were some mostly dry days for playing or just sitting on the beach, days for walking and exploring, and days for keeping out of the rain by going for drives and visiting tourist attractions. They could also go back to the hotel and make use of the lounge if the weather was bad or if they just felt like a quiet afternoon. They had booked half board, so they dined at the hotel, which was able to cater for the dietary demands of two small boys.

One day on the beach, Anthony and Ruth were sitting in deckchairs reading their books while the two boys were hard at work creating a castle. Anthony looked up from his book. He was reading a new novel, *The Collector* by John Fowles, and he paused to reflect on the nature of the disturbed protagonist. But his concentration was broken as he found himself interested in the boys' groundworks and construction. They had erected a large mound of sand, flattened at the top and bearing a central keep and corner turrets made from sand pies using their smallest bucket. Each tower bore a small flag from the packet Anthony had bought from a shop that morning: the Lion Rampant of Scotland, the Welsh Dragon, the Irish Harp and the Three Lions of England. The Union Flag fluttered – or rather, stood out stiffly – over the central keep. Anthony admired the symmetry of their structure and had been impressed by the willing attention the boys had paid to his explanation of the significance of each flag before they commenced construction. Around the mound, the boys were now busily digging a moat with a channel leading out to the advancing waves of the sea. Their initiative and hard work had now attracted a volunteer in the form of another boy of Laurence's age, who was digging where instructed by Anthony's elder son.

As his two sons basked in the sunshine and were blessed by the unspoken admiration of their father, Anthony reflected what a blissful existence he could have had; a good wife and a happy home life which made no burdensome demands on him, two fine sons, a secure job which was not onerous and gave him a reasonable income and time to pursue his outside interests. He didn't regret his affair with Carrie, but as time passed, he was increasingly glad it was over. Any residual guilt he had about his treatment of her was countered by the thought that she was bound to meet someone else. Nor was he interested in revisiting his brief dalliance with Shirley, which had nonetheless given him pleasantly amusing memories. Then his mood turned darker as he thought of the business with Cavalir, a permanent feature somewhere in the background of his life which would recur from time to time when he least expected it. *If only*, he thought, *if only*. Reluctantly his mind turned to the entrapment of Malcolm, the unknown consequences of which continued to trouble him.

He deliberately pushed that last thought away and looked over at Ruth, who was deeply immersed in a magazine. While Anthony was dressed quite neutrally in a pale blue short-sleeved shirt and cream linen trousers, Ruth had adopted a beachwear outfit of a navy and white halter neck top with matching shorts below her bare midriff. He stared for a moment or two at her full breasts and her cleavage glistening slightly in the sun and then regarded her as a whole, from her naturally wavy, dark blonde hair and the fine features of her face down to her full figure and well-shaped legs. He thought what a very desirable woman she still was. Being on holiday with the family had magnified his awareness of his sentiment towards them all and, as he looked at Ruth, a wave of warm affection swept over him.

Aware that he was staring at her, Ruth turned to him. "Everything all right?" she asked, lifting her sunglasses from her eyes.

"Yes, I was just thinking how lovely you look in that outfit."

She smiled and ran her hand down her clothes. "Glad you like it."

"It's you I am admiring," he said and, reaching over, he lay his hand on her very warm knee.

She laughed and squeezed his hand before returning to her magazine.

Over the course of the holiday, he had frequently found himself revisiting his relationships with Ruth and his sons. Now that his affair with Carrie was over, he had finally found the time to face up to the fact that he had neglected Ruth. She had too often, perhaps always, been at the bottom of his list of priorities when it came to personal relationships and he did regret that. He also realised how little he had seen of the boys over recent months, often getting home as they were about to go to bed or too pre-occupied at weekends to give them anything other than the odd moment of casual interest in what they were doing. He resolved to use what was left of the holidays to get into the habit of spending more time with them and carry that on when they returned home. Naturally he also spent a lot more time with Ruth and in the evenings, once the children were in bed, Ruth was reluctant to spend long in the lounge or bars of the hotel in case the children needed her, so they went to bed quite early too.

Early nights enabled them to put Shaw's dictum of maximum temptation and maximum opportunity into practice. This was by no means unusual on their holidays, but this time Anthony was more adventurous than he had been in the past, introducing Ruth to some of the things he had learned and tried with Carrie. To his surprise, Ruth not only didn't balk at anything he did but seemed quite enthusiastic.

"Where did you suddenly get these new ideas of love-making from?" she asked one morning. They had been interrupted during one fairly gymnastic exercise by a knock on the door signalling the arrival of a chambermaid with morning tea. They managed to disengage and appear relatively normal, exposing only their heads from under the covers when the young woman came in. She in turn adopted a sphinx-like expression and laid her tray on the chest of drawers with a polite 'Good morning'.

Anthony looked thoughtful as he nibbled at a rich tea biscuit and then took a sip of tea. "Someone showed me a sort of manual which had some interesting ideas, but I wasn't sure how you would feel about it. It's always harder to talk about sexual matters than actually doing it, isn't it?"

Ruth nodded and sipped her own very hot cup of tea. "It's more interesting doing than talking about it too," she said. "Tea's too hot, where were we?"

Anthony returned home from his holiday in good spirits. He knew himself too well to be absolutely sure that he would never again kick over the traces, but the holiday had rekindled in him the joys to be had in living a more settled lifestyle.

On their first evening back, after a long and tiring return journey, they were sitting in the living room with cups of coffee. Anthony was looking round the room and reliving that strange sensation whereby even a well-remembered home acquires a new interest and charm after an absence of a couple of weeks.

"I've been thinking," said Ruth.

"Oh?" said Anthony, stirring from his reverie.

"There are several things, but they all sort of connect. The first one is that I wanted to say thank you for a lovely holiday; the boys and I really enjoyed it despite the bloody awful weather and Laurence said it's the best holiday he's ever had. It was a lot to do with you, because you've seemed a bit semi-detached from us lately, I don't know why, but you were more like your old self these past two weeks. We don't need to discuss it, I'm just glad about it.

"The second thing is that I think one of the reasons you spend more time with the family now is that as Malcolm has a girlfriend, you don't see as much of him as you used to. I wouldn't want you to lose contact with him again, though, so I thought it might be nice if we had them both round for dinner one evening."

Anthony smiled. "I'm pleased you enjoyed the holiday, I did too. As to inviting Malcolm and Maria round, I think that's a great idea, especially as you haven't met Malcolm yet, let alone Maria. What's the third thing?"

Ruth paused and seemed to brace herself. "Since Jonathan started school, I've got a lot more time on my hands and I don't want to spend all my time around the house; I thought I might go back to work. It would make things easier in some ways." She looked at him as if she were asking a question rather than making a statement of intent.

Anthony noticed her hesitation. He could guess what his father's response would have been to such a suggestion by his mother. He was more equable about the idea. "I don't want you to feel you have to go out to earn any money; we can manage all right and things are a little better financially now," he said, not sure of her motive.

"I know middle-class men don't like their wives going out to work in case they're seen as failing in their role as breadwinner, but it's not about the money."

Anthony nodded. "What *is* it about then?"

"I told you, I don't want all day, every day, to be centred round domestic chores."

"What did you have in mind?"

"I thought I could go back to the library, that's what I know best and I used to love it. Before we went away Janice mentioned that there would be a vacancy coming up soon and I've been thinking about it a lot."

"I really don't mind at all in principle, but isn't it a bit soon for that? The children are still so young."

"I have thought about that, but it won't be a problem," said Ruth, smiling and sounding less defensive now that Anthony seemed not averse to the idea. "It's a part-time job, half-past nine till one o'clock, three days a week and possibly the odd evening. I'll take the boys to school in the morning and pick them up in the afternoon; nothing will change as far as they're concerned."

Anthony nodded his approval. He knew she had loved being a librarian and so returning to it would not be a decision based on financial considerations. She would be happy and he wasn't bothered if others saw it differently; he certainly didn't feel it would reflect badly on him.

"So you don't mind?" said Ruth, checking.

"No, I think it's a good idea and you can always do more if you wish when the boys are older."

"That's great; I'll ring Janice tomorrow to see when it's likely that I'll be wanted. Would you like another cup of coffee?" She walked over and picked up his cup.

"Yes, please," said Anthony, wondering if a second cup of coffee signified more items on Ruth's agenda.

Sure enough, when Ruth returned with the coffee she said, "Another thing, Tony, we haven't been to the theatre for such a long time; would you take me to see *Oh, What A Lovely War!*, I think it's at Wyndham's Theatre? Audrey says it's very good. She's seen it twice, once at the Theatre Royal Stratford and once in the West End." Her friend Audrey was a regular theatregoer.

Anthony was not a great lover of musicals in general but was more interested in this one because of its serious subject and satirical approach. Anyway, he was pleased to oblige Ruth. "Of course," he said. "I'll check for tickets in the morning."

Ruth smiled and yawned into her hand. "I think I'll go up. I hope you're not going to ignore me in bed now that the holiday is over," she said, a coquettish smile belying the reproachful tone.

XXI

Anthony phoned Malcolm a couple of days after they returned from holiday. Malcolm was enthusiastic about accepting the dinner invitation for the following Saturday, saying that Maria was sure to want to meet Ruth.

Saturday evening arrived and Ruth had prepared a three-course dinner of poached salmon, boeuf bourguignon and Pear Belle Helene. The men wore suits and the women cocktail dresses, Ruth having to breathe in while Anthony did up the zip. Malcolm brought a very good bottle of Nuits-St-Georges and some flowers for his hostess. All seemed set fair for a good evening. Maria was excellent company, interested in Ruth's conversation, inquiring about the children and mildly flirtatious towards Anthony. Malcolm was quieter and seemed a little subdued when he arrived but slowly began to relax and engage with the conversation. Ruth was enjoying the evening as everything had gone well with the food and she found the company pleasant and interesting. Anthony was a little nervous about Malcolm inadvertently revealing something that Anthony would rather he didn't, so there were moments when he was on edge. The first of these came when Ruth referred to Malcolm's friendship with Anthony.

"It's so good to meet you at last, Malcolm," she said. "I've heard so much about you from Anthony. You must be his closest friend from school now."

"Oh, what makes you say that?"

"Well, he sees Ronnie from time to time, but he has spent many evenings with you and you've been kind enough to put him up when he's stayed over in London."

"Ah, yes," said Malcolm. "Always happy to oblige. I've got a spare room at the flat, so it's no trouble."

"You haven't had to do it for a while," said Ruth. "Not since before we went away… when was the last time? I can't remember."

Malcolm stared at Ruth with a vacant expression and Anthony realised he'd never told him what happened with Anna the night they went out in a foursome. He was about to interject when Maria beat him to it.

"It was that night we had drinks with Anthony after you had a meal together. We left it too late for the tube, so Anthony stayed."

"Yes, that's right. It was back in July," said Malcolm robotically.

Anthony nodded and Ruth smiled.

The second incident was perhaps less serious but troubled Anthony more, even if he wasn't sure why.

They were talking about work and the overlaps between the Home Office and the Foreign Office and how Anthony sometimes had dealings with the Foreign Office, though not with Malcolm's section.

"My company has dealings with the ECGD and their work obviously has links with the Foreign Office," said Maria.

"ECGD?" said Ruth.

"Export Credits Guarantee Department," said Maria. "They provide support for British companies who export abroad. I'm glad I know about it because I feel I'm a little more in the picture about Malcolm's work."

"It's good for a woman to take some interest in her man's work, after all it takes up the greater part of his day," said Ruth, pouring some more wine into everyone's glass.

"Maria certainly takes an interest in my work," said Malcolm. "Perhaps too much interest."

Anthony looked at Maria and the smile, there all evening, had gone from her face. But only for a second or two, then she laughed.

"Malcolm's right; I'm too nosy. The trouble is, when you're a girl from a working-class background in Yorkshire, the Foreign Office seems so glamorous and you want to know more about it, especially if someone you're close to works there."

"It's really not as glamorous as people think," said Malcolm. He was smiling, but Anthony thought he still looked troubled.

After dinner, Maria helped Ruth clear away while the two men had another drink. Malcolm was quiet and gave single word replies to Anthony's attempts to get a conversation going.

"Everything all right?" said Anthony. "You seem a bit pensive."

"Yes, I'm fine." He sat up straight and smiled.

"Still going well with Maria?"

"Yes, it's great in every way; I think it's becoming quite serious for both of us. I've taken her to see my mother and they get on well." He looked at his watch. "It's after ten so we ought to be going soon."

"Time for a coffee, surely?"

Malcolm nodded and a couple of moments later Maria and Ruth came in with a tray, laden with coffee and mints.

Maria sat next to Malcolm and held his hand.

Anthony found himself watching their behaviour together and trying to determine whether any of Maria's closeness was genuine. Not that it mattered; she was probably having sex with him anyway, whatever her feelings for him. As Anna had pointed out, in their job they saw it as 'only sex'.

Soon after coffee, Maria suggested they go home and they exchanged farewells at the door with their hosts before walking off briskly to get the last tube.

As the door closed, Ruth asked Anthony to unzip her then she stepped out of her dress and went into the kitchen to finish clearing away. Anthony followed her to give a hand.

"I think it went all right tonight," said Ruth.

"Yes, the conversation flowed and the food was great. It was all down to you, you did very well."

Ruth smiled. "Thanks, such a lot of work for four people, though. Still, it was nice for me to meet them both. Maria is lovely, isn't she?"

"What, you mean looks?"

"Looks and personality; she's lively and good company. From what she told me in the kitchen, they see each other a lot and she thinks Malcolm would like to marry her, but she's not sure about it herself."

Anthony smiled. "He's taken her to see his mother; you never know if that's a good idea or not."

Anthony's life continued in its newly established pattern. It was now late September and he hadn't heard from Cavalir since the arrangements for the cricket match. The matter of Malcolm and Maria was dealt with as far as he was concerned and he assumed that it would continue to its destination, whatever that might be. He'd pushed the whole issue to the back of his mind. He saw Ronnie as usual but he hadn't heard from Malcolm for a month. Then one evening, he received a phone call at about ten o'clock.

"Who can that be at this time?" exclaimed Ruth, who felt that nine-thirty should be the cut off for a phone call, unless it was a matter of life and death.

"I'll get it," said Anthony. He went out into the hall and picked up the receiver, giving his number.

"Mr Fernard?" said the voice of a well-spoken woman.

"Yes," said Anthony.

"This is Mrs Muriel Vinton, Malcolm's mother. You won't remember me, but I believe I saw you at one of the school parents' days."

"Good evening, Mrs Vinton. No, I'm sorry, but I don't remember, it was a long time ago. How are you?"

"I'm fine, thank you. I'm ringing about Malcolm; he's had an accident."

"An accident! Is he all right?"

"Well, he has a broken leg, but apart from that he seems to be uninjured."

"What happened?"

"I don't know exactly. He is staying with me for a couple of days and he went out for a walk this evening, with the intention of stopping off for a drink at the local pub. It seems he was hit by a car. The police are investigating the matter, but the driver of the car apparently claimed that Malcolm walked right out in front of him. I don't think that's very likely."

"Is there anything I can do?"

"Not at the moment. He's mentioned you to me as a friend of his, so I thought you'd like to know. He's in the main hospital in Sevenoaks if you wanted to find out more."

"I'll certainly do that. I'm very sorry to hear about this. Does Maria know?"

"I haven't been able to get in touch. I don't seem to have the right number for her."

"Perhaps I could sort that out. I'll come and see Malcolm tomorrow."

"Thank you, Mr Fernard, I'm sure he'll appreciate that, as do I. Visiting time is seven o'clock until eight o'clock." She then gave Anthony her address and telephone number if he had any queries or had to change his plans.

"Well, thanks very much and please call me Anthony. I'll see you tomorrow. Goodbye."

The next day, Anthony telephoned Ronnie to keep him up with events, had a snack after work and then went down to Sevenoaks. Rather early for visiting time, he sat in a waiting area, flicking through a selection of ancient magazines, until it was time to go to the ward. Standing at the ward doors before they opened, he cast his eyes round at the waiting huddle of people, trying to guess if any of them might be Mrs Vinton. But when the doors opened, it was only Anthony who made for Malcolm's bed.

Malcolm was sitting up in bed, one pyjama trouser leg cut off to the hip to accommodate his broken leg, which lay on the bed, plastered from his foot to above the knee. He was reading a book but put it away as soon as he saw Anthony approaching him.

"Hello, Tony, what a nice surprise," he said, holding out his hand and smiling broadly.

"Hello, Malcolm, how are you? Not in much pain, I hope." He handed his friend a box of chocolates he'd picked up from a shop near the station.

"I'm fine, actually, the leg doesn't hurt much. They say it was a clean break. I'll be going home in a couple of days."

"What happened, exactly?"

"Well, I was taking a stroll on the main road near where my mother lives and my mind must have been on other things because I went to cross the road and didn't see the car. Very stupid of me, all my own fault. I've given a statement to the police to that effect. I don't want to get the poor bloke in trouble. He was as white as a sheet afterwards."

"Does Maria know about the accident?"

Malcolm shook his head. "No, there's no point. I'm not seeing Maria anymore."

"What? You're not seeing Maria anymore?" repeated Anthony, shocked by the news.

"Yes, I don't know what happened really. I thought things were getting better all the time, but then Maria told me at the weekend that she couldn't carry on with our relationship. She said something about not being ready to settle down and she didn't want to feel trapped. It's a bloody thing." He'd started the sentence fairly nonchalantly but then his voice began to waver towards the end.

"Oh, I'm really sorry; you got on so well," Anthony said, genuinely sympathetic but equally concerned with trying to figure out what exactly was going on. Things were happening too quickly. "She might change her mind when she thinks it over," he said, attempting to sound upbeat.

"I know it sounds ridiculous, but I don't have her address so I can't write to her. I have her telephone number, but it seems to be disconnected or something like that, so I can't get in touch with her at all. I still don't quite believe it."

Anthony nodded his agreement. "It's such a shame. How are you bearing up?"

"Oh, all right, it's not as if we were in a long-term relationship. Life goes on, and I'll start bouncing back soon enough." He smiled faintly. "Did you see Anna again?" he asked.

"No, just the two times, at the cricket and then at the Hilton. Why do you ask?"

"Oh, no reason."

They were both silent for a moment.

"We'll have a get-together as soon as you're up and about, Malcolm."

Malcolm smiled. "Yes, that'll be great."

"How long do you think you'll be off work with this?"

Malcolm shook his head. "I'm not sure. The plaster will be on for ages and it'll be hard for me to get into work. I suppose I could use taxis and crutches; I'll see what the doctors say. It's a bugger, really, because I'd only just been transferred to a new job."

"New job?" said Anthony.

"Yes, I was only told last week. Due to transfers of staff and likely future postings of those involved, I've been moved to the Scandinavian section. I was supposed to move officially next week so that's all gone for a Burton."

"How do you feel about the move?"

Malcolm shrugged. "I don't mind. I think it would involve Sweden and Finland, so not NATO and not Warsaw Pact for a change."

Anthony was about to ask another question when Malcolm's mother arrived at the bed. He guessed she was in her early sixties but had worn well with a slim figure and a face that was barely lined. She was smartly dressed in a finely cut grey suit with burgundy accessories and Anthony couldn't help but remark inwardly that she was nothing at all like Malcolm, not to look at nor in her demeanour.

"Hello, darling," she said, kissing Malcolm and giving him a hug. "Hello, Anthony, I'm so pleased to meet you at last," she continued, shaking hands with him. "How's our patient today?"

Anthony smiled. "In good spirits, I think."

"How are you feeling?" she said, turning back to Malcolm and placing her hand on his shoulder.

"I'm fine, thanks, Mother, no pain, just bored; until Anthony came, of course."

The three of them talked light-heartedly about life as a hospital patient; the strange daily timetable, the efforts to combat boredom and the difficulties of ever establishing how well or unwell one is or when one is likely to be better. Then the conversation moved onto trivial housekeeping matters and, after five minutes or so, Anthony thought he would take a break and give them some time on their own.

"I'll pop out for a cigarette and see if I can get a coffee, back in a quarter of an hour," he said, and walked off before either of them could protest. He wandered from the ward, asked a porter who told him how to get to the tearoom, then went down the stairs to find a small refreshment area run by 'Friends of the Hospital'.

A cup of tea was served by a friendly woman in her late seventies from a large two-handled teapot into one of thirty cups paraded on a tray. After some coaxing, he was seduced into buying a large rock cake by the tea lady's companion, a younger woman with an attractive smile.

He took his tea and cake to an empty table and cut slowly and steadfastly into the rock cake against a background of rattling crockery and the cheerful chatter of visitors, fresh from doing their duty and now able to speak above the quiet semi-whisper expected in the wards. At last he could ponder in relative silence the extraordinary conversation he'd just had with Malcolm. He concluded that Malcolm had outlived his usefulness and had been unceremoniously dumped by Maria. It was so callous yet so perfectly logical. He could only imagine how Malcolm was taking the loss of Maria behind the unreal, cheery facade he had presented to him and to his mother. He abandoned the cake halfway through and lit a cigarette, trying to rehearse the conversation he would have with Malcolm's mother when visiting was over.

A few minutes later, Anthony rejoined Malcolm and his mother. He watched them from the end of the ward, hoping to pick up a sign as to Malcolm's real feelings from their behaviour, but they both seemed quite relaxed and talking about inconsequential matters. They smiled at him as he approached the bed.

"Did you manage to get a drink, Tony?" asked Malcolm.

"Yes, thanks, I had a cup of tea and a cake. Have you had a chance to tell your mother about Maria?" asked Anthony.

"Yes, he has," interjected Muriel. "Some of these young women nowadays, they seem to blow hot and cold in their relationships. I suppose they feel more free to choose than my generation. Never mind, there are plenty of others who will recognise Malcolm's fine qualities and attractions, don't you agree, Anthony?" she said, her expression turning from one of dismissal to encouragement.

"Oh, really, Mother," said Malcolm.

Anthony smiled. "I've said all along that Malcolm undersells himself and would be a good catch for any woman."

Malcolm looked pleasantly embarrassed with that assessment.

They continued chatting until the bell went for the end of visiting. "I'll come and see you again next week, whether you're still in hospital or at home," said Anthony. He shook Malcolm's hand and patted him on the shoulder.

"Thanks for coming, Tony, it was good to see you again," said Malcolm.

Anthony stood back from the bed while Malcolm and Muriel made their goodbyes, then he walked with her out of the ward, both turning to wave as they neared the door.

"Malcolm seems in good spirits," said Muriel. "Although I'm sure he's disappointed with Maria not wanting to see him anymore."

"Yes, considering all that's happened to him, I thought he was quite upbeat about things."

"He'll be fine. I hope he'll stay with me until he's fully fit; work can wait. You'd be most welcome to come home with me for a drink, Anthony, or perhaps you'd like a lift somewhere?"

Anthony refused both offers, citing the time and the closeness of the station and he went straight home.

He telephoned Muriel the next day and arranged to see Malcolm early the following week. At Tuesday lunchtime, he rang Muriel to check whether or not Malcolm was home yet. A woman's voice he didn't recognise answered.

"Hello, is it possible to speak to Mrs Vinton, please?" asked Anthony.

"Who is it calling?"

"My name is Anthony Fernard. I'm a friend of Malcolm's."

"It's not possible to speak to Mrs Vinton at the moment. Can I ask when you last saw Malcolm Vinton?"

"That's a strange question. Who am I speaking to?" said Anthony.

"This is WPC King of the Kent Constabulary. Would you mind answering my question, sir?"

"Well, it was last Friday, when he was in hospital. Look, what's all this about?"

"Please hold on for a moment, sir."

"All right," said Anthony, a sense of unease rising in him as he was kept waiting for what seemed an age, a feeling exacerbated by someone waiting to use the phone looking at him appealingly.

"Sorry to keep you waiting, sir," said the policewoman. "I take it you don't know that Mr Vinton had an accident last night?"

"What, another one?" Anthony could hardly believe his ears.

"Yes, I'm afraid so."

"Is he all right?"

"Unfortunately Mr Vinton is dead."

"My God! What happened?"

"We're not sure exactly, but he appears to have drowned in the bath."

"That's terrible, is someone looking after Mrs Vinton?"

"We are presently giving support to Mrs Vinton and her sister will be here this afternoon."

Anthony put the telephone down and put his hands over his eyes. The person waiting to use the phone tapped on the glass and Anthony came out, forgetting to hold the door as he wandered away from the box. He didn't know yet what had occurred, but he had a sense of foreboding that what was playing out now was a horrible reckoning for events he had initiated. He walked into the nearest pub and had a large Scotch, then went back to the office where he spent the entire afternoon working through all that happened since that day at Lord's over and over again. Perhaps if he'd taken a different course, the result might not have been the same. But though the chain of events could have followed a myriad of patterns, none of it counted for anything. That one day when he set Malcolm up was all that mattered, because it had led directly to where Malcolm was now, on a slab in a mortuary.

He telephoned Ruth and told her what had happened and that he would be going to Sevenoaks straight from work. She was too stunned to ask for details and he was glad. He couldn't face talking to anyone until he had ascertained the gruesome facts about this tragedy for which he undoubtedly bore some responsibility. He then phoned Ronnie Benson to give him the news. Ronnie was shocked but not distraught;

his renewed friendship with Malcolm had never really developed beyond a lunch or two with Malcolm and Anthony. Ronnie took down the address of Muriel Vinton so he could send a sympathy card and asked Anthony to let him know of the funeral arrangements. Anthony was grateful for Ronnie's support, aware that, as far as Ronnie was concerned, Malcolm had been a charitable duty rather than a friendship.

He forced a cheese roll down his throat while having a beer in the station buffet at London Bridge, then set off once again for Sevenoaks. At the station he took a taxi to Muriel's house on the outskirts of the town.

Knowing that Malcolm's family were fairly well-off, he was expecting Muriel's house to be impressive and he was not disappointed. It was situated on a leafy lane well back from the road with a drive laid out in an arc with two entrances. The taxi driver pulled up outside the front door and, as it was still light, Anthony could see the house in all its fine Edwardian grandeur: resplendent with gables, balustraded balconies and stained glass windows, especially to the front door. He rang the bell and, after a minute or so, the door was opened by a woman who resembled a younger version of Muriel.

She smiled faintly. "Yes?" she said.

Anthony mirrored her expression. "Good evening, my name is Anthony Fernard, I'm a friend of Malcolm's. I hope it's not inconvenient, but I called to give my condolences and to offer any help to Muriel that I can."

The woman nodded. "Please come in, Muriel is in the sitting room. She mentioned your name when she was talking about people that need to be contacted."

"Perhaps I could help with that?" said Anthony, as they stood in a large square carpeted hall.

The woman nodded again and held out her hand. "I'm Muriel's sister, Joanna. It's very good of you to come. Muriel is in a state of shock, as you can imagine. I'm sure you have lots of questions; let's go into the drawing room," she said, opening the door for him.

Anthony found himself in a large room which ran the length of the house with French doors looking out on the garden. It was furnished in good quality but heavy furniture, the threat of an oppressive atmosphere dispelled by light wallpaper and a pale carpet with a subtle rose pattern. It reminded him a little of Malcolm's flat. He took the offer of a seat and chose a firm but comfortable wing chair.

Joanna poured them both a drink, brought them over to the low coffee table and sat opposite him.

Anthony looked at her, waiting for her to speak but not wanting to rush her. She appeared calm and again he thought how much she looked like her sister, just younger by perhaps seven years and with dark hair in contrast to her sister's grey. She was equally elegant, wearing a black dress with pearls.

"It's a ghastly business," she said. "Poor Malcolm; I never thought he had much luck in life, but this…" She stopped and took a sip of her drink.

"Exactly what happened?" asked Anthony.

"Well, as I believe you know, Malcolm had his leg in plaster beyond his knee after that accident and he could only get about on crutches. He came home yesterday in an ambulance and last night said he'd like a bath. Muriel wanted him to wait until there was a man here who could help him, perhaps yourself or another friend, but he was insistent. So they somehow managed. Using a crutch to support himself, he was able to get his good leg in the bath and then ease himself down to a sitting position, while keeping the leg in plaster on the edge of the bath so it didn't get wet. Muriel offered to help him, but he'd have none of it. She insisted that he leave the door open, or at least unlocked, in case he got into trouble.

"Anyhow, Muriel listened out for him and he seemed to be all right, but after he'd been in the bath for over twenty minutes, she became concerned. She went to the bathroom door, but it was locked and she couldn't get an answer from Malcolm. She called the police and they were there within minutes. They got the door open, but he was lying there on his back, with his face under the water."

Her voice had remained firm while she spoke, but when she finished, she took a handkerchief from her sleeve and wiped under her eyes.

Anthony took a large gulp of his drink. "What do you think happened?" he asked.

She shook her head. "I suppose he slipped under and couldn't get up. With the door closed, his mother probably wouldn't have heard if he'd called out. The police will want to investigate it and there's sure to be an inquest. Muriel is devastated, as you would expect, and blames herself. Would you like to see her?"

How Anthony dreaded situations like this when one fears being inadequate to the task of giving comfort to the bereaved, this time made worse by the nature of Malcolm's death. He overcame his apprehension. "Yes, if she's up to it. I shan't mind if she'd rather not," he said.

Joanna smiled. "I'm sure she'd like to see you." She rose and went out of the drawing room, crossed the hall to the room opposite and closed the door behind her.

Anthony finished his drink and looked round the room, idling the time away until, a couple of minutes later, Joanna returned to take him to the sitting room.

Muriel was sitting in an armchair with a shawl round her shoulders, though it was not a cold day and she was fully dressed. She smiled weakly at him and held her hand out to him.

"I'm so sorry, Muriel," he said, taking her cold hand in his.

She nodded. "I still can't quite believe it," she said, looking at him with staring and swollen eyes.

"No," he replied, completely lost for words, even those of the clichéd variety.

"I wanted to stay with him in the bathroom, but he wouldn't have it. I think he was embarrassed; but I'm – was – his mother, he was my flesh and blood, there was nothing to be embarrassed about. I should have insisted; it shouldn't have happened." Her face was screwed up as she fought off the tears, but they still came and she sobbed.

Anthony bowed his head and Joanna walked over to Muriel and put her arm round her shoulder. All three sat in silence in the gathering darkness and none of them could break the sepulchral spell, to move, to speak or to put on the lights. Eventually, acknowledging that in the midst of death we are in life, Joanna stood up, drew the curtains and switched on the table lamps.

"Do you think you could eat something, Muriel?" asked Joanna.

Muriel shook her head.

"What about you, Anthony? You must be famished."

"I had a snack before I left London."

"Let me get you an omelette or something and then you can help me with one or two things."

They walked quietly, almost tiptoeing, out of the sitting room and went to the large kitchen that lay at the back of the house. She soon found what she wanted from the refrigerator and the cupboards, and in ten minutes or so had produced a cheese and tomato omelette which they shared with some bread and a cup of coffee.

"I suppose Muriel will depend on you a lot over the next week or so; will you have any help?" asked Anthony.

Joanna smiled. "Well, Pamela, Malcolm's sister, will be flying over from Rhodesia tomorrow and she'll be a great help, and then there's you."

"I don't suppose I'll be much help. I didn't know Malcolm's circle of friends and acquaintances well and I've only met Muriel since Malcolm had the accident when he was run over."

"You don't know what a great help you are just being here," she said, pouring him another cup of coffee. "People whom Muriel can turn to are rather thin on the ground because both our parents were the only child. Her late husband had a brother and a sister so I guess she has nephews by marriage, but I don't think she has kept up with them very much. Pamela is now our last close relative." She looked wistful as she drank some coffee and added, "I had rather hoped Malcolm would be around when I am in my dotage, but it wasn't to be. That does sound very selfish of me, doesn't it?"

"How many of us can resist the urge to consider whether a tragedy that has befallen someone else has consequences for ourselves? Not many, I think."

"You're very kind, but I've spent my life doing exactly what I wanted. I didn't like the idea of anyone depending on me, so I really shouldn't expect to be able to depend on someone else later in life."

"What have you spent your life doing?"

She gave a brief summary of a career spent in the travel industry, working for Henry Lunn, Thomas Cook and the Orient Express Company. During the war she had been attached to Army Intelligence, but she glossed over that period in her life. She resisted Anthony's promptings to relate some of her interesting assignments during her travels.

"I'd like to talk more," she said. "But for now I think I ought to take up your offer of contacting people who need to know about Malcolm."

Anthony was disappointed. He was enjoying talking to this interesting woman, but perhaps she was bored by him. "Yes, of course," he said. He looked at his watch, it was a quarter past eight. "We should be able to get through a lot this evening."

"Fortunately, Malcolm brought his address book with him when he came to stay," said Joanna. She went over to the dresser and picked up a small leather address book. "I've put a tick by all the people I know, so I'll do those. If the entry has two ticks, it means they know, one way or another. Perhaps you could make a start ringing round the others. If they ask about the funeral, tell them it will be after the inquest and I'll write to let them know in due course. Use the telephone in the drawing room and do help yourself to a drink. I'd better go and see how Muriel is."

Anthony took the book and went to the drawing room, where he helped himself to a drink. He looked through the book and was struck first of all by how few names were in it for someone of Malcolm's status and background. His own entry was in capital letters, as were those of Ronnie and Maria, this last entry showing merely a question mark for the address and a crossed-out telephone number with an exclamation mark beside it. He thought what an efficient woman Joanna was; each page having a tick in red by one or two entries. There were two ticks by Pamela's number, by Malcolm's superior at the Foreign Office, the local vicar and one or two other names. Ronnie's name was not ticked, but he remedied that. Then he started the melancholy process of telephoning strangers to advise them of the death of someone whose relationship with them he didn't actually know.

The first person was listed as Ed Adams and Anthony noted the address was in Brentwood, Essex. It did not yet have an STD exchange, so he asked the operator to connect him. The phone rang and a male voice answered.

"Hello," said Anthony. "Is that Mr Edward Adams?"

"Edgar Adams, speaking."

"Sorry," said Anthony. "My name is Anthony Fernard and I'm a friend of Malcolm Vinton, who I believe you know."

"Yes I do, although I haven't been in contact with him for years," said Adams. He sounded wary.

"I'm afraid I have some bad news. Malcolm died last night."

"Are you sure? I can hardly believe it. Was he ill?"

"It was an accident. He'd broken his leg in a car accident and took a bath; he must have slipped under the water and drowned."

"Poor old Malcolm, that's just awful. I used to work with him in the FO. We were both on the staff in Copenhagen for a time. I'm afraid we lost touch afterwards, haven't seen him for four years or so. Well, I am sorry. Were you a close friend?"

"We were at school together and got in touch again over the past year. I knew him quite well."

"I'm sorry to hear about it. I'd like to come to the funeral if I can; would you let me have the details when you have them?"

Anthony assured him he would and soon after ended the conversation. He ticked the name and put an asterisk as well to indicate an interest in having the funeral details.

Most of the calls followed a similar pattern. A succession of men, the occasional woman, who had worked with or had a vague social connection with Malcolm, all expressing surprise and commiserations with Anthony but only marginally affected by Malcolm's death. Some, like Edgar Adams, wished to be kept informed of funeral details but most asked only for him to pass on their sympathies to the family.

There were two exceptions. The first was a man named Ian Scoresby, who had known Malcolm for seven years since they first met at a local astronomical society. Although Malcolm had attended meetings only rarely, they had maintained contact through correspondence and Malcolm had visited the man's house a few times to spend the evening in his small observatory. Scoresby seemed genuinely saddened by the loss of someone he called a friend and expressed his regret that he hadn't kept in touch more. The other call that didn't fit the pattern was to a woman, Marjorie Trane. By the time he rang her it was after nine o'clock and she sounded suspicious, slow to answer his initial inquiry as to whether it was her. When he gave her the bad news, she didn't answer for a minute or two and he realised she was crying.

"I'm sorry to be the bearer of such a shock for you," said Anthony, painfully aware of the inadequacies of the telephone in showing sympathy or giving comfort.

"Oh, Mr Fernard, it's just so tragic. I think he had such a sad life and now it's ended in the most desolate way."

"Did you know him well?"

"Not as well as I wanted to. He was just so shy. I think he liked me and I gave him plenty of encouragement, but we never got past the stage of being friendly work colleagues."

Anthony thought, *If only it had been you and not Maria, but it's no use playing the 'What If' game.* "Would you like to know about the funeral arrangements?" he asked.

"Yes, please, it's the least I can do. I had better go now, thank you for calling. Goodbye." And she put the phone down.

Anthony replaced the receiver and looked through the remainder of the names in the book. There were two that he had to contact and it was only just nine-thirty. He decided to finish the job and they didn't take long; one of the people wasn't even sure who Malcolm was, until she'd been given more information. The other was a friend from university who hadn't seen Malcolm since the early 1950s.

Having finished, he poured himself another drink and sat in the armchair reflecting on his conversations with Malcolm's friends and acquaintances, mostly acquaintances. A glance at his watch was enough to convince him he ought to make a move for the long journey home.

He knocked on the sitting room door and went in. Muriel seemed a little better; she had discarded the shawl and was reading from a book.

Joanna smiled when he came in. "How did you get on?" she asked, offering him a cigarette from a box on the coffee table.

"I got through all the unticked names in the book, so I guess it's done. I put an asterisk by the name of anyone who expressed a wish to be informed of the 'arrangements.'"

"Oh, that's a good idea, well done," she replied. "Can I get you a drink?"

"No thanks, I'll have to be getting back to London, I've got a bit of a journey to get home."

"Where do you live?" asked Joanna.

"Woodford Green in Essex."

"Central line," said Joanna. "Would you like a lift to the station?"

"Well, if it's not too much trouble. I could always get a taxi."

"We wouldn't dream of it, Anthony," said Muriel. "It was so good of you to come down this evening. You were such a good friend to Malcolm; he would have done anything for you." She stopped speaking abruptly as she held back the tears.

Anthony nodded but he was unable to speak, as Muriel's compliment cut deep into him. He could only stand silently while he waited for Joanna to bring the car round to the front of the house.

At last, Joanna broke the awkward silence when she came in to say the car was ready. Anthony patted Muriel's hand and followed Joanna out to the car, a two-tone Rover 90. On the way to the station, Joanna asked about Anthony's friendship with Malcolm and about his wife and family, small talk to fill the empty space as they drove along. When they arrived at the station, Joanna thanked him once again for being such a help to her and Muriel, and Anthony asked her to keep him informed of the date of the inquest as he wished to be present. Then they shook hands and Anthony started his long journey home.

The inquest took place early the following week at eleven o'clock in a small courtroom in Sevenoaks. Anthony gave the impression to Frank Hodgkin that he was likely to be called as a witness and was given the day off to attend.

The courtroom was dark with heavy mahogany furniture, a suitable backdrop to the harrowing proceedings. On the bench sat the coroner, a small man with a large bald, dome-shaped head, dressed formally in a black jacket and grey-striped trousers. He wore half-moon glasses, over which he watched the people taking their seats. The nameplate on his desk indicated that the coroner was a doctor by profession, which was presumably an advantage in assessing the medical evidence. Beneath and to the side of the bench sat a police sergeant who was acting as clerk. There was no jury present as foul play was not suspected. A solitary journalist, notebook at the ready, occupied a bench on the other side of the courtroom. The public area was almost empty: just Muriel, Joanna and half a dozen other people, including a policeman, some of whom Anthony assumed were witnesses. He sat with the two sisters and they exchanged mournful smiles.

The case proceeded quite quickly. The coroner began by reading a statement from the pathologist who'd performed the post-mortem. This confirmed that, without doubt, Malcolm had died from drowning. He then clasped his hands together and looked over his glasses.

"This court is not convened primarily to determine the cause of death, which this statement makes clear was death by drowning. We are here to clarify and come to a conclusion as to the circumstances which conspired to bring this death about."

Muriel was not asked to take the stand. Instead the first witness was the policeman, who read from his notes a statement he had taken down from Muriel as part of his own testimony.

The policeman gave an account of going to Muriel's house with a colleague, in response to an emergency call by Muriel. He said that he'd been forced to kick in the bathroom door as it was locked from the inside. He found Malcolm lying in the bath with his face underwater and one leg, the broken one, balanced on the edge of the bath. He had tried to revive Malcolm, but it was clear he was dead. While waiting for the ambulance, he had briefly interviewed Muriel Vinton and she'd stated that she had asked Malcolm not to lock the bathroom door in case he had difficulty in the bath.

"Did Mrs Vinton suggest that she was concerned about her son's mental state prior to taking the bath?" asked the coroner.

"No, sir," replied the policeman.

The police sergeant then read a summary of the police report concerning Malcolm's road traffic accident in which he'd broken his leg. It found that Malcolm had appeared to step out into the road in front of the car. No blame was attached to the driver of the vehicle involved.

The only other witness to be called was a doctor who had attended Malcolm after he was taken to hospital following the accident. He said that Malcolm had been very distressed when he was first admitted.

"Was this because he was in pain and discomfort?" asked the coroner.

"No, the leg was not giving him too much pain; it was a simple fracture and the ambulance staff had made him comfortable at the scene of the accident."

"What was the source of the distress, in your opinion?"

"It's hard to say exactly. He said something to me about having 'failed again', but when I asked him what that meant he wouldn't elaborate. I did question him about the accident and how he'd come to walk into the road in front of a car. He said that he'd been distracted by thinking about big changes in his life. Apparently, he was about to be moved from his post at work and he'd broken up with his girlfriend. So I assume worries about these matters were the primary sources of his distress."

"In your opinion, was Mr Vinton's mental state sufficiently equable for him to be released from hospital so soon after the accident?"

The doctor didn't answer for a while, perhaps half a minute, "At the time I didn't see any compelling reason, physically or mentally, why I shouldn't grant his request to be discharged."

The coroner made a few notes and looked at all the evidence he had before him and then proceeded to sum up.

"This is a very unfortunate case. Mr Vinton was a man with undoubted abilities and talents who had everything to live for. In her interview with the police constable, his mother said that she had not known him so happy and contented for many years. Perhaps a sudden reversal of fortune in his private life and uncertainties over his career disturbed his frame of mind.

"Doctor Hughes was unable to be precise concerning Mr Vinton's state of mind while he was in hospital. However, it is singularly remarkable that someone should be the victim of two very unusual accidents in the space of a week. We have no satisfactory explanation as to why Mr Vinton should walk out into the road in front of a car with no apparent concern for his safety. With regard to the incident that cost Mr Vinton his life, it is surely rather odd to lock oneself into the bathroom when any rational person would be aware that taking a bath in his condition presented fairly obviously a degree of risk. It is also strange that Mrs Vinton heard no cries for help even though, because of her own concerns, she had remained within earshot while her son took his bath. On the other hand, it may well be that Mr Vinton's locking of the bathroom door was due to nothing more sinister than force of habit or absent-mindedness. It is a matter of weighing up the evidence as to the state of mind of Mr Vinton."

Anthony looked at Muriel and saw she was listening intently to the coroner. He thought he could guess what was coming in the coroner's summation and surmised it might be too much for her. He stood up and strode the twenty feet towards the bench, stopping at the desk of the surprised, slightly alarmed, police sergeant.

"I'd like to make a statement," he said.

The sergeant looked at the coroner, who had stopped speaking when he saw Anthony approach him. The coroner nodded and the sergeant took down Anthony's name and address before asking him to take the oath and go into the witness box.

"Please give your name," said the sergeant.

"My name is Anthony Fernard and I was one of Mr Vinton's closest friends."

"Please proceed with your statement, Mr Fernard," said the coroner.

"Thank you, sir. I spent a considerable amount of time with Mr Vinton while he was in hospital after the car accident. Whatever his frame of mind when he was first admitted to hospital, he seemed in a very positive and optimistic mood when I spoke to him. He gave the impression that he had come to terms with the loss of his girlfriend and was looking forward to moving on with his life and taking up his new post at the Foreign Office. He certainly did not seem distressed or upset in any way, either regarding his present circumstances or for the future."

The coroner nodded. "Thank you, Mr Fernard."

Anthony went back to his seat and the coroner resumed his summation.

"I am most grateful to Mr Fernard for his intervention, which has helped me get a more balanced view of Mr Vinton's state of mind at the time of his death. In view of all the evidence now placed before me, I find for an open verdict."

A few minutes later, Anthony was standing outside the court with the two sisters. Muriel looked much better than she had a week before, but he thought she had lost weight and seemed rather fragile. She placed her hand on his arm. "Thank you for coming today, Anthony, I can't thank you enough."

"I think we could all do with a drink," said Joanna. "Will you come back with us for a little while, Anthony?"

Anthony agreed and they went back to Muriel's house. After their first drink, Joanna offered to refill the glasses, but Muriel declined. "I'm feeling rather tired, dear, I think I'll have a lie down. Why don't you buy Anthony lunch? He's got a rather long journey back."

Anthony smiled in the affirmative to Joanna, and he took Muriel's hand and kissed her on the cheek.

"Thank you again, Anthony, you've been such a good friend to us all."

Joanna and Anthony drove into town and went to a Trust House hotel for lunch.

They sat in the bar, looking at the menus.

"Thank you for today, Anthony," said Joanna. "I don't know what we'd have done without you. The coroner was heading for a suicide verdict until you interrupted him. You knew that too, didn't you?"

"Yes," said Anthony.

"Was it true, what you said about Malcolm?"

"Pretty much it was what he said to me."

"We'll never know what he meant, but it doesn't matter; an open verdict is fine. The other option would have broken Muriel's heart. She has enough to bear as it is."

"Yes, coping with bereavement and loss is so hard."

"Not just that. She hasn't been well for some time and is quite poorly; she couldn't face telling him."

"I'm sorry to hear that. Is it serious?"

"We're not sure yet, more tests next week. I am quite worried about her."

"Is Muriel's daughter here; wasn't she coming over?"

"Pamela? Yes, she did come over but couldn't stay here indefinitely. Her husband's farm is a family affair, so it's all hands to the pump. She'll be back for the funeral. But I don't know after that."

Anthony looked at Joanna and felt sorry for her. She had chosen a life without responsibilities and had accepted the reciprocal consequence that she might face a lonely old age. Now, circumstances were imposing on her the sole guardianship of her sister.

They had a very pleasant lunch. Joanna was vivacious, charming and humorous, and Anthony enjoyed her company. This time, she was more open about her career as a travel representative and regaled him with stories of some of the more exotic places she'd visited as part of her job. She had particularly enjoyed her time with the Orient Express, visiting the Balkans frequently and her favourite city, Istanbul. She had stayed at the Pera Palace Hotel several times, met many famous film stars and once was invited to a reception with Kemal Atatürk, who had his own suite at the hotel. Once again, she barely mentioned her work with Army Intelligence. Then she asked Anthony about his life and he thought how mundane and boring his career must seem to her, especially as he couldn't mention the one thing she would find of interest. They had a half-bottle of Chianti between them but Joanna, conscious that she was driving, stopped drinking after one glass.

Over coffee and cigarettes, Anthony asked Joanna how much time she would be able to take off work to help Muriel with the funeral and so on.

She shook her head. "I don't know. I'm resigned to taking annual leave if necessary, but I can't be absent for too long. I'm just hoping that Muriel will be all right and be able to carry on at that house. I suppose she could come to stay with me if all else fails."

"Where do you live?"

"I've got a flat in Chiswick."

"Well, let me know if there's anything I can do to help. I'll be more than happy to."

She smiled. "That's very sweet of you; I'm sure I'll manage, but thanks for the offer."

After coffee, they set off for the station, Joanna driving very carefully, sedately even. They reviewed the inquest again and Joanna repeated her thanks for his quick action in swaying the verdict. At the station, Joanna walked with him to the platform, Anthony's train not due for a few minutes.

"Thanks again for all you've done for us, Anthony," she said. "Your wife is very lucky to have you and if I wasn't old enough to be your mother, I'd make a play for you myself." She laughed and kissed him on the cheek as his train arrived.

"I'll see you at the funeral," he said, leaning out of the window as the train began to pull out of the station. "Bye."

She waved. "Bye."

As she had said she would, Joanna arranged the funeral and related matters herself. It was a simple funeral at Muriel's local parish church and Malcolm was interred in the family plot next to his father. The organist was very good and the congregation of over forty were in strong voice as they sang the hymns, 'Immortal, Invisible, God Only Wise' and 'How Great Thou Art'. As the coffin was taken from the church, the music played was the Sibelius piece used as the theme music of *The Sky at Night*.

Anthony was surprised by the number who came to the funeral and he was pleased for Malcolm and Muriel. The Foreign Office was well represented by colleagues past and present, as well as several senior staff, including the Deputy Permanent Under-Secretary and a junior minister whom Anthony remembered from the reception at Lancaster House.

As they stood outside the church, Ronnie came over to him.

"A bad business, poor old Malcolm," he said. "Just as things seemed to be going well for him too, he seemed so happy the last time I saw him. Is his lady friend here?"

"Er, no Ronnie; they'd split up before the accident."

"Oh dear, that's a pity. So perhaps things weren't going quite so well. I saw the inquest recorded an open verdict, I thought it would have been death by misadventure." He rubbed his chin. "There wasn't a question over his state of mind, was there?"

Anthony shrugged his shoulders. Though he tried to appear neutral about it, he was sure his eyes betrayed his true feelings.

Ronnie patted him on the arm. "Oh well, it doesn't matter now. You've got nothing to reproach yourself for, Tony; Malcolm was always telling me what a good friend you were to him. I'll see you for lunch in a couple of weeks, I'll give you a ring."

Anthony nodded and Ronnie smiled and went over to talk to one of the Foreign Office people.

At the reception afterwards, held at a local hotel, Joanna introduced Anthony to a few fairly distant relatives as well as Pamela and her husband. Pamela was a couple of years younger than Malcolm, very pretty and well-dressed in an elegant black dress and jacket. Anthony had noticed that she had been calm and impassive throughout the church service and at the graveside. She told Anthony that she felt quite detached from England now; having lived in Rhodesia for eight years she now thought of that country as her home. Her husband was a very large man who spoke with that Rhodesian accent that sounded English most of the time, with just occasionally the hint of a Southern African clipped vowel, not that he spoke that much. While Anthony and Pamela were in conversation, he stood quietly in the background looking round the room or at his watch. As the couple moved on with their circulation of the room, Anthony thought Pamela was very like her mother, or at least like Muriel as she had been when he first met her. Muriel now looked even frailer than the last time he'd seen her.

Apart from Muriel and Joanna, the only tears shed at the funeral were from a tall, not unattractive woman of about thirty, who Anthony guessed was Marjorie Trane. She stood alone at the reception, nursing a glass of wine, and Anthony introduced himself to her.

"Oh, hello," she said. "It was you who rang me with the news."

"That's right."

"It was a lovely funeral, the vicar spoke well, and movingly I thought."

"Yes," said Anthony. "He was very good. I don't think he knew Malcolm that well."

"Who did?" said Marjorie. "Malcolm wouldn't have thought he had this many friends. So often people leave it until someone dies before they show they care; I suppose that goes for me too." This thought prompted Marjorie to reach for a handkerchief from her handbag.

"Yes," said Anthony.

"I wish I'd told him how much I cared," she said, the tears coming more freely.

"You mustn't reproach yourself," said Anthony.

"At least he had a good friend like you; he was fortunate in that respect."

"I let him down as much as anyone," said Anthony.

"Thank you for trying to make me feel better," she said. "I think I'll go now. It was nice to meet you." She put her handkerchief away and closed the handbag with a decisive click of the clasp. Then she shook hands with Anthony before going over to make her farewell to Muriel.

Apart from Ronnie and Anthony, the only other friend at the funeral not connected with the Foreign Office was Ian Scoresby, Malcolm's astronomer friend. Anthony had a brief conversation with him. Then he spotted the doctor from the inquest and told him that he thought it was a kind gesture for him to come to the funeral. They maintained a conspiratorial silence on their own views as to the underlying cause of Malcolm's two accidents.

By now Anthony thought he'd worked the room enough and decided it was time to leave. Seeing that Joanna and Muriel were together, he seized the chance to say goodbye to both of them and make his exit. It did cross his mind that

Ronnie might like to go back to London with him, but Ronnie was nowhere to be seen and he guessed that he hadn't come back to the reception. In any case, Anthony was in no mood for conversation.

"Anthony, thank so much for all you have done," said Muriel. "Please keep in touch, won't you?" she said, her cold cheek brushing his, as they embraced.

Anthony nodded and said something vague about 'later in the year'.

Joanna smiled and kissed him. "Thanks," she said. "It's been nice knowing you."

Then he left.

XXII

It was the day after the funeral that Anthony succumbed to guilt, or perhaps it was shame. In life, there was always something to be guilty about. There were the minor little failings, like forgetting to carry out a task he had promised to do or being irritable with the children or harsh with Ruth. At a deeper level were the flaws in his character, a source of frustration brought on by perpetual weaknesses for which he had no answer, despite repeated attempts at personal self-improvement. At the very least, these failings flirted with most of the seven deadly sins on a regular basis and sometimes embraced them. Particularly noteworthy was a tendency to idleness in all its forms, which ticked 'sloth' on the list; an inability to resist the charms of pretty well any attractive woman that offered herself to him, tick 'lust'; and the occasional desire to drink more than was sensible, tick 'gluttony'. Of the others, he thought 'envy' and 'avarice' not too serious, and 'wrath' he was almost free of, but it was always possible that the relative absence of these was a by-product of his large capacity for 'sloth'. Then there was 'pride' and who alive can escape 'pride'? A double tick for 'pride'.

However, while they remained tendencies with the occasional lapse, these flaws were the undercurrent of the flowing waters of his moral life, which marked him when they rose temporarily to the surface, without defining who he was. At the summit of his guilt were actions which caused him periods of remorse and internal struggle and these were relatively rare; the affair with Carrie and the accepting of payments for his work for Cavalir were prime examples. But, once he stopped committing the wrong, the end of the affair with Carrie or the completion of each task for Cavalir, the guilt faded and his great capacity for self-forgiveness, if not self-justification, would re-assert itself.

But this morning he rose filled with a different kind of guilt. It had begun in the night when he woke at about three o'clock and found himself thinking about the funeral and the reception afterwards. The mere thought of it led to him becoming hot and breaking into a sweat. He knew he would always remember what he had done to Malcolm; the betrayal by which he had helped create the events in Malcolm's life culminating in his suicide. But he believed, certainly hoped, that like all his other sources of guilt, this too would eventually fade. He would come to regard the weight of his responsibility as being moderated by the difficulty of his situation and the extenuating circumstances that forced him to betray Malcolm. The real culprits were those who sought to use Malcolm for their own purposes.

No, that was not what dominated his mind as he tossed and turned in the bed. It was the shame he felt when he remembered what Muriel and Joanna, Ronnie and Marjorie Trane, and perhaps others had said: that he had been a good friend to Malcolm. This was not just a feeling of guilt for something he'd done; it was the guilt of what he'd done magnified by the praise heaped upon him for being the opposite of what he really was. He was lauded as the stalwart life supporter of someone whose death he'd contributed to. It is perhaps too easy to forgive ourselves when others condemn our actions but how hard it is to forgive ourselves when there is no one else to accuse us.

In the morning, things didn't seem so bad; they never do. After all, Malcolm may genuinely have had an accident in the bath and even if it was suicide, it was his choice; Anthony had neither assisted in it nor encouraged it. Anyway, he'd turned things round at the inquest, so he'd done what he could. Over breakfast he was quite cheery, joking with the boys and discussing Ruth's work at the library, which she was really enjoying.

Then he got on the train and tried to read the paper and he found himself thinking about it all over again: poor Malcolm being duped at the Test match while he stood by, watching Maria trap him; the distraught face of Muriel and the tears of Marjorie while they and others praised him at the funeral. All of it whirring round in his head and filling him with self-loathing. He tried to start reading his newspaper again, telling himself this feeling would fade; guilt always fades.

But as the days went on, the guilt didn't fade. It was always there, parked in a special part of his psyche where it lay dormant so that he could deal with the rest of the demands on his mind. Every now and then it would pop into his head when some word or event triggered it, like a dog in a kennel which barks automatically whenever anyone walks near, and then he had to go through it all over again. He tried ways of dampening it. He spent much of his free time with the children when he got home from work and in the evenings, he was as engaging with Ruth as much as he'd ever been, concentrating on her every word so that his mind would not wander to the memory of his guilt. When left to his own resources, he filled his mind with plans for projects he might undertake around the home or garden. Occasionally he threw himself into his collection of stamps, buying the latest catalogue from Stanley Gibbons and poring over information he'd rarely troubled with before like watermarks, perforations, margins and varieties. He spent more time with crosswords and other puzzles to give his mind plenty to do, searching through the cerebral filing cabinets of knowledge, whether worthwhile or trivial, and blocking the pathways of reflection and self-examination. He even tried the old cliché of drinking to forget, but when he drank a lot he didn't forget; he just woke with a hangover which made him think why he'd drunk too much and the dog would bark again. So he just left his guilt and shame where it was and day after day he would wait apprehensively for that time when his defences, smokescreens and distractions would be exhausted and he would go through it all again and loathe himself a little more, never a little less.

Ruth never asked why he often seemed morose or distant. He assumed that she put it down to Malcolm's strange death and the questions that had raised in his mind. Sometimes he half-hoped that her patience with him would wear thin and she would ask him what was wrong, and he would be able to tell of this horror that was driving him mad. But this was not a case of 'a problem shared is a problem halved'. Telling Ruth, telling anyone, would not halve the guilt.

It was while he was shaving one morning that the possibility of atonement came to him. Surely the way to assuage shame or guilt was to do something positive to level the balance sheet of good and evil in some way. It happened all the time: people repaying money they'd stolen years before or writing a letter of apology for some long-ago quarrel or estrangement. When he thought about it, he had made some attempt at atonement after the affair with Carrie ended. He'd tried to be more engaged in his marriage to Ruth, showing her more love and support than he'd done for years. But how does one atone for playing a part in someone's death? There was nothing to be done for the victim, only justice for society: sometimes hanging, otherwise imprisonment. He could hardly try to confess to being involved in Malcolm's death, he'd be regarded as insane. He finished his shave, none the wiser as to what he could do to atone for his betrayal of Malcolm.

He went down to breakfast and there, in the post, was another missive from Cavalir. It informed him that a Doctor Agnieszka Arciszewska would require a visa for her placement with a scientific laboratory in Cambridge. Was there no end to it? Then he knew what atonement would be; he would put an end to it.

The day came for his lunchtime meeting with Ronnie and they met at their usual place. At first the conversation revolved around the impending demise of Macmillan's premiership and the shenanigans in the Conservative Party over a replacement. Anthony was enjoying the distraction of this spectacle of Ronnie leaning back in his chair with the two front legs off the ground and his thumbs in his waistcoat pockets, while he pontificated about the 'magic circle' which controlled the Conservative leadership selection. Then, out of the blue, Ronnie mentioned Malcolm, and Anthony's as yet unformed plan of atonement bobbed to the surface of his thoughts.

"Pity about old Malcolm, he'd have loved all this palaver about the Tory leadership. I miss him more than I thought I would, even though he was a rum old bugger. I suppose we'll never know for sure whether or not he took his own life."

"Well, if he did, it was my fault," Anthony blurted out. There, he'd said it, and he felt a peculiar mixture of relief and horror as the words tumbled from his mouth.

Ronnie was rocked back in his chair by this revelation and the movement was enough to disturb the equilibrium of his chair's balance on two legs. For a fraction of a second, he maintained his equipoise then gravity triumphed over acrobatics. The chair went over with him, thumbs stuck in his waistcoat, still in it. A waiter, his expression of faux concern just about holding in check the smile in the corners of his mouth, rushed over and helped him up. Ronnie straightened his tie, took a swig from his drink and stretched his back gingerly.

"What on earth do you mean?" he said.

Anthony had had time to compose himself and he nearly lost his nerve, making a half-hearted attempt to retract his confession. "Well, I was the one who encouraged him to get involved with a woman. Perhaps he couldn't cope with the rejection and I should have thought of that."

"For God's sake, Tony, you can't take responsibility for someone else's actions. It's not as if you were the cause of his relationship with Maria coming to nothing."

That second comment of Ronnie's reinvigorated Anthony's determination to tell him the truth. "I was not the cause, but I put him in a situation where this outcome was likely."

"I wish you'd stop talking in riddles, Tony."

"Look, I can't talk here. Perhaps we could go for a walk?"

Ronnie looked at his watch. "Well, I haven't got long."

"How about us meeting somewhere very quiet after work? It's really important."

Ronnie shrugged. "Well, all right. Let's meet in Soho Square Gardens at five-thirty, by the Charles II statue. What's all this about anyway?"

"I'll tell you then."

Anthony spent much of the afternoon vacillating between a determination to tell Ronnie everything and a desire to draw back from what might be the beginning of his ruination. Atonement didn't seem quite so attractive when he thought through the ramifications. He still didn't know which side of him had won when he left work for the day. He arrived first and stood by Cibber's eroded and weather-beaten statue of the Merry Monarch until Ronnie appeared a few minutes later. It had been a dry, fairly pleasant day and they had no hesitation in sitting on a bench for their discussion.

"Thanks for sparing the time Ronnie," said Anthony.

"Pleased to be of help," said Ronnie.

"Not to beat about the bush, I've been involved in giving assistance to a Russian spy ring."

Ronnie stared at him for a moment, his mouth open. Then his expression changed to a grin. "Oh, come on, Tony, stop mucking about; what do you really want to see me about?"

"I'm afraid it's true. I was the victim of an entrapment and they used me to get things done for them at the Home Office."

Ronnie look sceptical. "How could they entrap you? They must have had something on you."

"I accepted a gift and didn't declare it."

"You silly sod," said Ronnie. "You know the score on gifts. I can't believe you could be so stupid."

"It was the week of the Cuban Missile Crisis when I met you for lunch. The news was bad and I thought it was all up. I arrived back from lunch and there was an envelope waiting for me; I'd had a few drinks and I thought 'what the hell' and kept the money. I know it was stupid, but I wasn't thinking straight."

"But once they started putting the pressure on, you could still have got off the hook if you'd reported it. It would be a disciplinary matter, naturally, but no likelihood of you going to jail."

"They also knew that I was having an affair."

"Bloody hell," said Ronnie, rubbing his hand over his forehead. "Do you remember what they called you at school?"

"I think it was 'Scraper' or something like that; nobody said it to my face."

Ronnie nodded. "It was 'Scrapes' actually. You were always getting into scrapes of one sort or another: dodging off early to meet a girl, missing classes to play table football or records at the local café, using a crib for Latin translation, and on and on and always getting caught. Well, you've really got yourself into a scrape this time. So what did you do for these people exactly?"

"I issued visas to people who did not have a definitive right to come to the UK for the work they were going to do, without proper clearance."

"How many?"

"Possibly three, definitely two, but there's another one pending from this morning."

Ronnie puffed out his cheeks. "It's not that bad then. I still don't see what this has to do with Malcolm."

"I also had to help arrange for Malcolm to meet Maria."

"You mean that Maria was part of the ring?"

"Yes."

"And Maria was detailed to get information out of him?"

"Yes."

"So you think that Malcolm didn't play ball or had outlasted his usefulness and he was just dumped."

"Something like that."

For the first time in the conversation, Ronnie's expression was one of disappointment, perhaps even contempt. "What a mess! Why did you have to tell me, Tony? It's stretching our friendship to ask me to share the burden of it with you when I don't feel very sympathetic at the moment."

"I'm not asking you to share the burden. I want you to arrange for them to take me in."

"What, are you mad? You'll be ruined. Think of the effect on your family."

"It'll never end unless I break my contacts with these people and if I try to stop, they'll pull the trigger with my job and Ruth. So I'll still end up where we are now. At least this way I'll have some say in what happens."

Ronnie's tone softened. "Are you sure you want to turn yourself in?"

"Yes, I realise it's going to be tough on Ruth and everyone who cares about me, especially my parents. But I'm doing it for Malcolm. I used his friendship then I abused the trust he placed in me; I owe it to him."

"Or his memory, it's too late to do him any good. I think we need a drink; I definitely do," said Ronnie.

They walked in silence to the first pub they found and ordered two large Scotches then sat in a quiet corner.

"Well, here's to you, Sydney Carton," said Ronnie, raising his glass.

Anthony smiled weakly, raised his glass and took a mouthful of his drink.

Ronnie leaned over and spoke quietly. "The only good thing is that you'll still be able to turn Queen's evidence as it were, rather than being picked up like the Portland spies or Vassall. That should count in your favour. So what do you want me to do exactly?"

"Can I just say that I do appreciate your lending a hand. It can't be easy for you, but I need your friendship now more than ever before."

Ronnie nodded.

"Well, I thought that you might be able to arrange a meeting with somebody from MI5 or Special Branch, or whoever it is. Or do I have to give myself up to the police?"

"The police will refer it to Special Branch, who will liaise with MI5. I do know people, so I can sort something out. Look, I realise that you feel you deserve some kind of retribution, but don't indulge your remorse too much; think of your family. You made a stupid mistake and that led you into wrongdoing, but you're not totally responsible for all that happened. Would you be satisfied with a confession of guilt and an attempt to make amends in some way?"

"Yes, I think so."

"I think the best approach is to play it 'softly, softly'. I'll tell them that you'd like to talk to someone about a possible entrapment. Then you can say you were lured into this and once in, were too scared to find a way out."

"It's not that far from the truth, in a way."

"Are you going to tell Ruth?"

"Not yet. I would rather find out what will happen to me before I break it to her."

"Leave it with me and I'll set up a meeting." Ronnie took the glasses over to the bar and asked for two more of the same.

When he returned, he chinked his glass to Anthony's. "We'll sort it out, don't worry."

Anthony nodded. "Thanks Ronnie, I feel better about things already."

A few days later, Ronnie rang Anthony at home to say that he'd arranged an introductory meeting for him with a Major Brasscott and a colleague, to be held in an anonymous office in Whitehall. Ronnie told him to take with him all the details he had about this network he'd become associated with. The meeting was set for two-thirty on the following Monday and Anthony arranged to have the afternoon off so he wouldn't have to explain anything to Frank.

At the appointed time and place, Anthony arrived with his briefcase. This in itself made the day seem odd, as Anthony never took a briefcase or any other case to work. It was a standing joke among his colleagues and many other office workers that most people who carried a briefcase used it solely to carry their sandwiches for lunch and a book or newspaper. Inside Anthony's case was a sheaf of papers detailing all he could remember about his dealings with Cavalir. That morning he had obtained from registry the files relating to Cavalir's brother and the people he'd granted a visa to under Cavalir's direction, and he'd copied out the salient details of each case. He also made a list of all the people he'd come across through the Cavalir connection, with addresses where he knew them.

He was taken by a woman at reception up a flight of stairs. She knocked on the door and in response to the answer 'Enter', ushered Anthony into a large office with high windows and a thick, traditionally patterned Axminster carpet. Behind a desk sat a man in his late forties with dark hair and a matching moustache. He was wearing a tweed suit with a light checked shirt and knitted green tie. He looked as if he'd popped into the office, having arrived back late from a weekend in the country. He rose from his chair, smiled and extended a hand to give Anthony a warm, firm handshake.

"Mr Fernard? I'm Roland Brasscott, how do you do? This is Mr Lacer." His strong voice and clipped accent did nothing to dispel his appearance of an English country gentleman.

Anthony looked over at Mr Lacer, who was seated by the window and made no attempt either to stand or to acknowledge Anthony. Lacer presented a persona which was almost the antithesis of Brasscott. He was dressed in a dark business suit with a white shirt and silver grey tie. Yet this frame of calm solemnity contained a more florid portrait. His body mass was well-developed to the point of being generous, his complexion was that of an embarrassed lobster, his expression was one of silent rage and menace. He gave the impression that he could explode at any moment. Anthony smiled and nodded anyway.

Brasscott invited Anthony to take a seat facing him and Anthony sat down in a chair that was lower than Brasscott's and not very comfortable.

"Cigarette?" said Brasscott, opening a silver box and then producing a lighter.

Anthony noticed that his hand shook a little as he held the cigarette to the flame, and he wondered if all these gestures of welcome and hospitality were being used to assess him.

"I gather that you would like to talk to us about some difficulties you're having which might involve national security. Something to do with people who have links with the espionage operations of a foreign power?"

"Yes, that's right."

Brascott nodded, the smile now fading from his face. "Start wherever you like and explain what happened." He picked up a pen and opened a notebook.

"It began the week of the Cuban Missile Crisis. I was feeling pretty despondent about the threat to the world if war broke out and when I got back from lunch, there was a letter for me with a gift in it."

"What was the gift?"

"A cheque for £100."

"What did the letter say?"

"That the cheque was a token of the giver's appreciation for processing his brother's visa application."

"Had you processed this particular application?"

"Yes."

"You knew that you should have immediately reported this to the relevant officer in your department?"

"Yes, but I was a bit short of money at the time and, in a moment of weakness—"

"You could still have rectified the mistake at any time."

"I know."

Brasscott made some notes, a practice he continued in response to every answer given by Anthony. Anthony looked at Lacer, whose expression of coiled anger was unchanged.

"Then what happened?"

"Nothing for over two months and then I was asked…"

"What form did this next approach take?"

"Initially a letter, asking me to arrange a visa for someone to come to Britain for work."

"From whom?"

"The same man who'd sent the letter of thanks and the cheque."

"His name?"

"Cavalir, Lieutenant Colonel Cavalir. It wasn't his real name, as I checked, and the Colonel Cavalir who'd come to Britain after the war died several years ago."

"Then what happened?"

"I refused to comply with his request by letter. Then he rang me at home. When I refused again, he blackmailed me into going to see him. He then put pressure on me to do what he asked. Eventually I agreed to do it."

"You still have details of this person that you gave the visa for?"

"Yes." Anthony took the papers out of his briefcase and handed the relevant note to Brasscott.

"What were the grounds for the blackmail?"

"The fact that I'd accepted the cheque and also they threatened to tell my wife about an affair."

"With a woman, presumably."

"Yes."

"Were you paid for doing what they wanted done?"

"Yes."

"This is a far more serious matter than the first cheque," said Brasscott.

"You're a bloody mercenary," barked Lacer in a gruff voice. "No principles at all."

Anthony squirmed in his seat. Once again, he thought back to his many interviews in the headmaster's office. "I'm not proud of any of this," he muttered.

They went through the rest of the evidence: the subsequent requests for more visas, the meeting at the Savoy, and finally the visit to the Test match and the meetings with Maria and Anna. Anthony handed over each sheet of paper as it became relevant to their discussion: the people he'd granted visas to and the reasons for the visa applications, the address of the newsagent in Leytonstone, the details of the office arrangement in the name of Mr Sikora. He mentioned Anna and Maria by name but said he had no further details about them. Brasscott took notes in a shorthand system of his own and Lacer interjected occasionally to tell Anthony what he thought of him.

"Why did you decide to come clean? Were you afraid you might be caught?" asked Brasscott.

"No, I felt guilty about what I'd done, especially because I drew Malcolm Vinton into it and the chain of events that followed may have led Malcolm to kill himself."

"What makes you think he killed himself?"

"I thought it unlikely that he would have been stupid enough to lock himself in the bathroom when it was possible he could get into difficulties. Also he didn't call out, as he would presumably have done if he'd been in trouble in the bath."

"Why do you think he committed suicide?"

"I assume it was partly because Maria threw him over and perhaps because she'd extracted information from him. I suppose he put two and two together and it was all too much for him. Obviously, it's all just speculation without a note."

"There was a note, rather it was a letter."

"But, at the inquest…?"

"It was posted to MI5 on the day he died."

"So he did intend to kill himself?"

"He doesn't say that was his intention in the letter, but that appears to be the case. He had put two and two together, as you suspected, and realised that Maria's only interest in him was the information she hoped to get from him. I gather that he asked for the posting to a less high security area himself to check his suspicions, and that's when Maria called it a day. In his letter, he claims never to have given her any information at all. If so his behaviour was entirely above reproach."

"So why?"

"Why kill himself? Reading between the lines, lots of things were playing on his mind. He was disappointed with the conduct of the security services, particularly over the Philby affair. He had known Philby in Beirut and was surprised that nothing had been done about him earlier. Then of course there was the business with Maria. Perhaps he gives a clue in his letter when he ends with the line 'I can't be bothered anymore'. But you knew him far better than I did and are more likely to understand why the balance of his mind was temporarily disturbed."

Anthony reflected for a moment on this answer, but he had nothing to add. "What will happen to me?" he said.

Brasscott put down his pen and scratched his right ear. "Ah, so you are not entirely consumed by guilt; you are concerned also with your own skin. Perhaps this is a case of active remorse; by confessing and co-operating with us, you hope for leniency?"

"I wasn't conscious of that."

"It just comes naturally to you," observed Lacer with a sneer.

"It's of no consequence," said Brasscott. "We're not swayed by sentiment either way. Let me summarise the situation. It is debatable whether you have definitely broken the Official Secrets Act 1911 or the extra clauses in the 1920 Act. A court of law would have to decide that. Other than that, you have taken money for gain in return for services rendered against the provisions in the Civil Service code of conduct, so you are certainly liable for disciplinary action on that count. As to the matter of Malcolm Vinton, you introduced him to a woman whom he suspected might be a spy, but he behaved impeccably. I suppose you might be guilty of some kind of pimping and, of course, you betrayed your friend. Your actions certainly created a situation that may well have contributed to his death. As far as I know, betraying your friend is not, per se, a criminal offence."

"You're a useless bloody toerag," said Lancer.

"So what are you going to do?" asked Anthony.

"Nothing as far as a prosecution is concerned. I realise that Vinton's death sits heavy on your conscience, but that is entirely a matter for you. Don't expect us to give you some kind of penance to help complete your act of contrition. As to the information you have given us, we will use it to monitor Cavalir and his operations, so you have been useful in that respect. With regard to your own position, you will resign your office with immediate effect and not return to the Home Office after this meeting. Furthermore, you will be blacklisted from working in any post in any Civil Service department or other government agency. I have a letter here for you to sign."

He passed a letter, with the date and Anthony's address at the header, across the desk.

"The outcome of the meeting seems to have been decided even before it began," said Anthony. After a cursory glance at the simple letter of resignation, he signed it and passed it back to Brasscott. "Won't it look weird if I just disappear from the Home Office overnight?"

Brasscott smiled. "Not at all. Your section head will be informed confidentially that you have accepted the offer of immediate resignation to avoid disciplinary action over your breach of your terms of employment. He'll know how to convey the news to his staff; you'll be forgotten soon enough.

"One last matter; you will have to contact Cavalir and tell him that you will be unable to do anything else for him as you have been transferred from the Home Office. I appreciate that your mind will be preoccupied with other matters in the days ahead, so I have prepared a letter for you to copy out and send to him. It is not to be posted for seven days. Do not add anything else to the letter and refuse to have any further links with Cavalir or his associates. If you receive anything else from him, send it to me at the address on this card. Above all, don't tell him you have given evidence to us. If we get even a hint that they've got wind of your confession, or you reveal the contents of this conversation outside this room, we will throw the book at you. This is not an idle threat." He handed a business card to Anthony.

"This all seems very reasonable of you," said Anthony, putting the business card and the draft letter in his inside jacket pocket.

Brasscott shook his head. "This is not about being reasonable, merely expedient. We take the view that the new government will not wish to pick up where the last one left off with yet another spy story for somebody like Chapman Pincher to get his teeth into. There's certainly no stomach in Whitehall for any more bad publicity arising from yet another dodgy civil servant, not after Vassall and the Portland brigade. Nor do we want the furore over Kim Philby or the embarrassment of Profumo being stirred up again. You would just be a small fish causing a big splash. In other words, you're more trouble than you're worth."

"If it was left to me, I'd hang you up with piano wire round your balls, you putrid scumbag," said Lacer, his large face now the colour puce.

Brasscott smiled again. "You must excuse Mr Lacer's language, but he is a patriot and finds your behaviour quite impossible to comprehend, let alone countenance. I'm sure you understand that many other people would find your actions reprehensible and will conclude that you have an unsavoury character. After all, in a position of trust, you put your own personal and selfish interests ahead of those of your country and your fellow citizens."

Anthony nodded. "I do understand it; I agree with that opinion. Thank you for your time." He rose from his seat and offered his hand to Brasscott.

The latter looked away, and Anthony picked up his empty briefcase and walked out of the office, quietly closing the door behind him. He held onto the wooden rail as he slowly descended the shallow steps to the foyer. As he reached the bottom, he saw Ronnie Benson waiting for him.

"Hello, Ronnie, what are you doing here?" he said, a grim smile on his face.

"I thought you might need to see a friendly face," said Ronnie. "By your expression, I can see you could do with a drink."

They took a brisk walk away from Whitehall down Great Scotland Yard and eventually found a quiet bar.

The bar was almost empty, even those able to stretch their lunch hour to three o'clock having departed. Ronnie bought them both large Scotches and they sat in a corner of the bar.

"How did it go?" asked Ronnie.

"What did you tell them?"

"Only that you were worried you might have compromised yourself in some way and had been approached by agents of a Warsaw Bloc power."

"They seemed to know everything. They even had a suicide note from Malcolm. He hadn't given any secrets away or anything like that."

Ronnie shook his head. "Poor old Malcolm, what a waste. So why did he do it?"

"They didn't show me the letter, but he closed it with 'I can't be bothered anymore'. I don't think he knew I betrayed him."

"I hope not," said Ronnie. "Although would it have made things any worse for him? Look what he did."

They sat in silence for a minute or two, Anthony staring down at his drink, unable to look his friend in the eye.

"What happened at the meeting?" said Ronnie eventually.

"I've been dismissed from the Home Office as of now and I won't be employed again in any public service."

Ronnie nodded, appearing as if he was going to say something but didn't.

"I have to write a letter to my contact, saying that I have been transferred and won't be in a position to work for them anymore."

"What a mess," said Ronnie. "What will you tell Ruth?"

Anthony shook his head. "I don't know yet. A version of the truth, I suppose."

Ronnie finished his drink. "I'm sorry, but I've got to get back to the office. Will you be all right?"

"Yes, I think so. Thanks for coming over and for everything you did; I don't know what I would have done. I do appreciate you standing by me."

Ronnie smiled. "Let he who is without sin cast the first stone and all that," he said.

"Will we still be able to meet up for lunch and the occasional drink?"

Ronnie shook his head. "I wish you well, but it can't be the same; I don't know how you could've done what you did, especially to Malcolm. Do you know that comment by EM Forster: 'If I had to choose between betraying my country and betraying my friend, I hope I should have the guts to betray my country'? I think I understand that, but you have betrayed both and that is beyond me. It wasn't as if you had some kind of political belief; it was just for the money and to save your skin. It's all pretty despicable. In any case, it wouldn't do my career any good to be seen in your company, that's if my connection to you hasn't already buggered it up." He stood up and offered his hand. "Perhaps in the future," he said.

Anthony shook his hand. "I'm sorry, Ronnie."

He watched Ronnie leave the bar and then got himself another drink, a beer this time. He took the letter he had to copy for Brasscott out of his pocket. He read it three times and wondered how long it would be before Cavalir figured out that he'd been sacked. He asked the barman for a sheet of writing paper and an envelope, a request which nonplussed the barman at first, though he was able to supply them after going to the manager's office. Then Anthony copied out the letter and addressed it to Mr Sikora, affixing a threepenny stamp he found in his wallet. He put the letter in his inside jacket pocket, ready to post in seven days, as instructed. He guessed Brasscott and his team would use this time to investigate the various addresses Anthony had given him.

He felt he ought to go home but wasn't ready to face Ruth quite yet, so he had another pint and glanced through an early edition of the *Evening News* that someone had left on a table. He could find nothing that interested him.

Reluctantly, he began to consider what to say to Ruth. He would have to tell her about leaving his job at the Home Office and why he'd done so. But should he tell her about being blackmailed and, if he did, would he confess to her about Carrie or his mercenary activities, or both? How much could she take at once? How would she react? Everything seemed to be falling apart.

The more he tried to plan his meeting with Ruth, the more daunting it seemed. He even toyed with the idea of delaying things and pretending to go to work every day for a while until he could figure out what to do, but that was a hackneyed old ruse and he couldn't see himself doing that without going mad. Eventually, after another large Scotch and several cigarettes he headed for the tube and home, not sure what he would do but hoping for the courage to be able to face Ruth with something approaching the truth.

XXIII

Anthony turned the key in the lock and stepped into the house. Jonathan came running out of the kitchen to greet him.

"Hello, Dad," he said, in the new style of address he'd adopted in recent weeks. He had assumed a more grown-up persona in line with his new status as a schoolboy.

"Hello, Jonathan, have a good day?"

Jonathan was playing, not very adeptly, with a yo-yo. "Yes. Dad, when are we going to get the fireworks for Guy Fawkes Night?"

God, Guy Fawkes Night, thought Anthony. *How different it had been this time last year, when everything had been going so well.* "Soon," he said, patting his son on the shoulder.

Before Jonathan could press the matter, Ruth came out of the kitchen, smiling at him. Today was one of her library workdays and she always seemed just that little bit more full of life. Anthony knew she really enjoyed being back at work, if only part-time, and he was pleased for her.

She walked over to him, put her arms round him and kissed him. "Mm. You've been drinking, what have you been up to?" she said, standing back with an amused, quizzical expression on her face.

Anthony smiled wearily. Where to begin when the enormity of what he had to tell her confronted him like a mile-high mountain with no way round it and no finger or footholds less than a hundred feet above the ground? He needed time to think.

"I had a drink with Ronnie. I'll tell you about it later."

"OK," she said. "Come on, Jonathan, time to get washed for tea."

Over tea, the boys quizzed Anthony again about Guy Fawkes Night. Laurence said that, with his guy, a larger and more sophisticated version than the previous year, he'd already raised over three shillings and would be buying some bangers and sparklers the next day.

"Don't you light any fireworks," said Ruth. "You shouldn't be buying any at your age," she added.

"Mr Perkins always tells us to be careful with them," said Laurence, his frustration at not being trusted evident on his face.

Ruth looked at Anthony for support, but none was forthcoming. He remembered when he was Laurence's age, he'd bought fireworks with his friends and they had taken considerable care, born of fear and the threat of parental chastisement, when lighting them. If his memory served him right, it was the older, teenage boys who behaved more recklessly when playing around with fireworks. In any case, his mind was concentrated on finding a strategy for his conversation with Ruth.

The evening proceeded on its well-worn path. After their meal, the boys played while Anthony looked at the newspaper, on this particular evening a fruitless exercise, as he could not apply his attention to any of the stories or articles. While Ruth finished off in the kitchen, Anthony spent some time playing a board game with the boys; this evening they had chosen Snakes and Ladders. Then the boys went upstairs to get ready for bed followed by his reading them both a story. Finally he rejoined Ruth for a cup of coffee while they talked over their respective days before switching on the television.

Tonight, Anthony poured himself a large drink when he sat down with his coffee.

"Are you all right, Tony? Is something wrong?" Ruth asked, as they sat in the sitting room.

"I've got something to tell you," he began, "and I'm afraid it will come as a shock."

Ruth went pale. "What is it?"

"I've been sacked."

"What! Why?"

"I took a bribe. It's a very serious matter and I was asked to resign with immediate effect."

"Oh, Tony, I can't believe it. Why did you do such a thing?"

"It's rather complicated. It started when I accepted a gift and it turned out to be an entrapment by a spy ring. Then they forced me to grant visas to people who should not be over here."

Ruth's expression was one of sheer bewilderment. "It's like a made-up story about someone else. I can't understand how you could've been so stupid. Why didn't you go to your superiors and explain what had happened?"

"I can hardly believe it myself. It wasn't easy to tell anybody once I'd taken the first payment and there were other factors."

"What other factors?"

"Well, the money did come in handy; it was a temptation."

"So that's why you have been so generous since around this time last year; I should have pushed you as to where the money was coming from. I think I need a drink too."

She walked over to the drinks cabinet, poured herself a gin and tonic and brought the Scotch over to top up Anthony's drink. "You said factors, what else?"

Anthony considered for a few moments and thought, *No more lies.* "They also threatened to tell you I was having an affair unless I co-operated."

A smile of disdain briefly crossed her lips as Ruth shook her head. "You are a bloody fool, Tony. You should have come to me, I already knew."

"You knew?"

"Well, I had a pretty good idea anyway, you left plenty of clues about. There was the time you stayed up in London when we went to Rottingdean during the Cuban crisis. You have never volunteered for extra duties at work ever since I've known you, let alone staying up in town and working on a Saturday. But that could have been nothing, so I ignored it. Then, an old friend, Malcolm, appeared from nowhere and you saw him every week, sometimes staying at his flat. That was so suspicious, especially as you were conveniently unable to give me his telephone number. When he phoned up that time and I finally got to speak to him, it was obvious that he hadn't seen you as often as you'd implied. That confirmed it, but I think by then the affair was over. Honestly, Tony, just because you're a fool, don't ever again take me for one as well." She sat back in her chair and took a drink from her glass.

"Why didn't you raise it with me? Didn't you want to know what sort of relationship it was?" asked Anthony, lighting a cigarette.

"Oh, you can be sure I thought about it, but while I didn't ask, I could still believe I might be wrong. It enabled me to be more objective and to treat the situation as an academic exercise. I had to work out what I wanted the outcome to be and I decided that, on balance, I wished to keep you as my husband; as much for the boys as for me.

"There was always the danger that if I did confront you with it, you might feel boxed in and ashamed and think you had no alternative but to leave. So I played the longer game. I know some women would take a different view, and that would be right for them, but I set myself the task of helping this affair to blow over. If that didn't work within a month or two, I would still be able to dump you if I chose to. Unlike lots of other women, I didn't have to stay with you for financial reasons, so I didn't feel trapped. I'm lucky in that respect. I suppose you could take that as a compliment."

Anthony nodded and finished off his drink, rising to refill their glasses. With what he'd had already that day he was beginning to feel a bit drunk but *in vino veritas* and this was a time for being honest.

"When you talked about helping the affair blow over, what did you mean exactly?" he said.

"Well, I thought I'd remind you how interesting I am and what you'd be missing if you lost me, in lots of different ways. So I made a bigger effort. Valentine's Day was when I knew things were moving in my direction because you stayed with me rather than spend it with her."

"That was quite an evening," Anthony said, suddenly aware that he hadn't been pulling all the strings in the way his relationship with Carrie came to an end.

"When did it finish?" asked Ruth. "May?"

"Yes."

"It lasted longer than I thought it would. My patience was being stretched, but you know what life's like; I stuck to my plan for one more week and then another week and then I guessed it was over. After that, I chose to forget about it, especially as things got better between us. Now that I know all that you were up to, perhaps I shouldn't have bothered."

Anthony looked down at the floor. "I'm sorry; I've messed up everything."

"Yes, I thought I knew you and now I don't. The affair was one thing, but now everything seems so sordid. I've got to get over it all over again and at this moment I'm not sure that I can."

"I understand, but I hope you will be able to, because I do love you and I have been trying to make it work."

A tear ran down Ruth's face. "I know." She took the bottles from the drinks cabinet and topped up their glasses again.

"There was that one night in July when you didn't come home, but I suppose that was a genuine stay with Malcolm?" asked Ruth, after a long silence.

Although he had promised himself not to lie again, he thought it could only hurt Ruth unnecessarily to know about Anna, so he didn't disabuse her of her misunderstanding. "Yes," he said.

"Did you love her? Was there a time when you thought of going off with her?"

"I thought I loved her for a while, but I never considered leaving you."

Ruth nodded. "I don't want to hear any more details about the affair or this other woman. That matter is finished, but if you ever do something like that again, we're finished too."

Anthony nodded but said nothing.

"Anyway, back to your run-in with MI5; I assume they caught up with you in some way?"

"No, I owned up."

Ruth raised her eyebrows. "Why?"

"I felt bad about what I'd done." He had intended to go on and talk about Malcolm, but he stopped himself. He desperately didn't want to lose Ruth and the boys, and he wasn't sure if she could take even more awful truths about him at this moment. She already knew he could betray her and had still to come to terms with it, but how could she also accept that he'd betrayed a friend who'd then killed himself? He decided to leave that for another time, perhaps never.

Her tone softened a little. "Well, I'm glad you've come clean with the authorities and got out of it. Presumably you won't hear from your operator, or whatever you called him, again?"

"I shouldn't think so. I only did three or so jobs for them; I was hardly central to their operation."

"Talking about jobs, what will you do about work after this?"

"I don't know. There are plenty of jobs around so I should be able to get something. References will be a problem, so I may have to take a lower level position and work my way up again."

"Well, I'm working now, so that's a help, and I don't want to hear ever again from you that my parents shouldn't do things for us. They may well have to if you don't get a job quickly; unless of course I go back to work full-time and you look after the home." She smiled at the look of horror which spread over his face.

And that was how the conversation ended and, at Ruth's insistence, neither ever spoke of Anthony's affair or his career in espionage again.

Anthony sent his letter to Cavalir, c/o Mr Sikora, seven days later and when, a few days after that, he phoned the number, they said Mr Sikora was no longer using the service. He didn't hear from Cavalir again.

Believing that the pain for them would be too great, Anthony and Ruth felt it better to lie to both sets of parents about what had happened. Ruth said it was a white lie and that the true horror of life made us all hypocrites. They told their parents that Anthony had decided on a change of career and left it at that.

The children were told nothing and the fact their father was at home for several weeks on an 'extended holiday' was a source of pleasure and excitement rather than of concern. After initially being unable to contemplate Guy Fawkes Night, Anthony threw himself into the preparations and had no trouble finding the money to make it as spectacularly successful as the previous year. The warmth generated by the obvious pleasure and excitement of their sons seemed to melt some of the ice that surrounded his relationship with Ruth, as for one evening at least they could celebrate together as a family.

He never heard from Ronnie again nor from any of Malcolm's family. It was almost as if that passage of his life and all the people in it were being excised from his past, and therefore his consciousness. He missed Ronnie at first but gradually got over it, proving the adage that most friends serve their purpose at particular times in one's life. He met his old friend, Jim Stanton, more often now. Over time, he thought about what he'd done less frequently and the shame, if not the guilt, slowly sank into the shadows of his mind. The dog had stopped barking. However, for a time he had very bad dreams which disturbed his sleep, and whenever the phone rang and he didn't recognise the voice, especially if it was a foreign accent, a pang of terror momentarily had him in its grasp. But after a while, even that faded. From her attitude towards him, Ruth appeared to forgive him, and their relationship slowly returned, on the surface at least, to something approaching the way it had been before his confession to her. What she really thought about him he did not know and dared not seek to know.

Anthony managed to use a tenuous friendship with one of his former colleagues, now a manager at the insurance company he'd once worked in, to get him a job. So he started with the company again, near the bottom of the ladder, a few weeks after he resigned from the Home Office. Life resumed the smooth, calm, unhurried and impecunious course Anthony had known before. The work he did was routine and he soon mastered it. He could see himself working his way up the ladder of promotion in due course. In the meantime, he enjoyed working with a new assistant, a very pretty girl named Madeleine. She claimed to be impressed by the rapidity with which he grasped new rules and procedures, and the way he could quickly spot flaws in the system which might be exploited by those less honest than themselves. Maybe he would look forward to the office Christmas party this year.